The Weather Gods

SUSAN LOUINEAU

DEDICATION

For Anaïs

By the same author

THE CHAPEL IN THE WOODS

ACKNOWLEDGMENTS

The characters and events in this work are fictitious, any resemblance to individuals living or dead is entirely coincidental. There are, however, some real people to whom I owe a great debt of gratitude for their time and advice. I would like to thank Philip Digges and Catherine Rosell for their painstaking checking and rereading, and their endless encouragement that got me through to the end.

I am also grateful to Margaux Laspeyres, Suzi Pheby, Derek Thompson, Susan Buchanan, Flick Merauld and Judith Smalley for their discerning feedback.

Susan Louineau
Oxford

ONE

Porth Taran, 11th August 1990

Every storm brings with it a sense of foreboding.

The streets of Porth Taran were thronging with holiday makers enjoying the last few weeks of summer. The cottages that sheltered beyond the harbour wall shone blue and pink and cream in the midday sun. Couples walked hand in hand and chaotic families wielded pushchairs and beach paraphernalia as their children clamoured plaintively for ice cream. Parents clung fearfully to their offspring as they scrambled to the top of the harbour wall to walk along it and look down into the swirling waters far below. Babies were crying in the uncomfortable heat. Older children were sitting on the quay with crab lines loaded with bacon and soggy bread, watching eagerly for a tug on their line. Teenagers in wetsuits gathered at the seaward end of the harbour, waiting for the tide to rise high enough for them to leap off the quay and plummet into the depths beneath. Seagulls wheeled and swooped as they scanned the throng for an unguarded pasty or a vulnerable cornet. At the head of the harbour, like a sentinel guarding the village, stood

1

the church with its famous clock tower that kept time as well as the day it was built, over a hundred years before.

A rumble of thunder roared across the village. A momentary calm fell on the crowds as they stopped and looked skyward. The seagulls skittered nervously from the slate ridges of the cottages along the harbour to clumsily flutter a few feet in the air before returning to their perches, their heads darting left and right, alert for danger.

A breeze began to dance through the rigging of the boats, setting their halyards jangling. The Helford Maid, a Cornish fishing Lugger, started to bob on its moorings; its newly painted hull glowed blue against the darkening sea.

Jack Jewell came out on deck and looked at his watch, high tide was due in two hours. The heat had forced him into a sleeveless tee shirt but now he shivered; the temperature had dropped sharply. He reached for his cagoule that hung just inside the wheelhouse and, pulling it on, he looked out across the little port to the open sea. A couple of merchant ships were just visible on the horizon, en route for Felixstowe or Tilbury or perhaps further afield to Scandinavia or Holland. It was when the ships were in close to the shore that you had to worry. Besides, the shipping forecast had been good that morning. He turned and behind him, up above the moor that sheltered Porth Taran, a dark lone cloud hung still and threatening. He zipped up his cagoule and leant against the wheelhouse. He watched as the cloud lengthened and stretched, changing from dark purple to a rich green its edges gilded by the sun. It cast a long finger of shadow along the surface of the rushing stream that tumbled down from the moors and cut the small village in two. He frowned as the shadow slowly crept further towards the harbour, painting the sparkling green water to a dark slate.

Down on the beach, to the east of the church, Johnny Treglown, atop the lifeguard chair, rubbed his head and vowed he wouldn't touch a drop that evening. He cursed himself for seeing closing time at the Ship Inn yet again on a work night. Feeling the chill breeze, he wished he hadn't left his sweatshirt up in the hut. He climbed down from the chair to move it further up the beach and out of the path of the rising tide. Then he picked his way between the windbreaks and sandcastles to the shore to move the flags and the rescue board. It was spitting. He looked up in surprise for the sky was clear and bright. Then he saw it. Just over the village hung a single cloud darker than he had seen in a long time. He frowned, and then shrugged, it would blow over. The beach was at its busiest, every square metre was planted with a wind break or a beach tent. He headed for the steps up to the lookout hut. His sister's café at the back of the beach was overrun with customers. A queue of visitors stretched from its terrace and down the concrete steps, along the peat shelf and onto the beach. He was glad his days of helping Demelza were long past. The café's windows were steamed up. It would be hot and noisy in there with babies crying and parents yelling at their children, not to mention the customers complaining about the quality of the bread, the prices, or the time it took to be served or actually anything else they could think of.

Demelza stood at the fryer and shook the chip basket.

'Cheesy chips for three!' she yelled as she plonked a large basket on the counter. As she turned back to the fryer her belly suddenly tightened. She gasped and closed her eyes. 'Not now,' she whispered. She wasn't due for another three weeks. It must be one of those Braxton Hicks contractions the midwife had told her about. Nothing to worry about. She plunged another basket of frozen chips into the oil.

'Cheese sandwich on brown!' Spike yelled as he slammed yet another order onto the counter.

'Coming up!' She wiped sweat from her forehead and reached for a glass of water. She put the cool liquid to her lips and drained the glass. Just four hours to go and she could put her feet up. She could feel her ankles swelling in the heat. By rights she should have stopped working a week ago. She sighed and tore open yet another loaf and began to butter the slices as fast as she could. Then came another. Demelza's stomach tensed again. This one was stronger. 'Piran!' she called under her breath. He'd promised her. He'd said that was all she would have to do. Just say his name and he would be there. She stared at the sizzling oil. But it wasn't true; he wasn't here. He was dead, somewhere beneath the waves where she couldn't see him or talk to him. He had let her down. Her father had been right. He'd said it hadn't he?

'That one's a wrong 'un. For all his family money and power, he's a wrong 'un, you mark my words!' he'd said as he waved a finger at her.

But what could she have done? He was the love of her life - no one gets to choose. She buttered another slice, waiting for her anger to subside. She hacked a slice of cheddar from the consumer sized hunk and set it between the buttered slices. She stared down into the sizzling fat. Demelza Treglown of Nancewartha. Then Demelza Jewell of Tregarron, wife of Piran Jewell. Then one day, on the happiest day of her life thus far, she became his widow. He hadn't wanted to move out of there, she knew that, but she thought she'd suffocate in the belly of the Jewells. She did love them. All of them, even Di. Poor Di. And now she was a widow, just like her.

'Cheese sandwich on brown!' she yelled. As she slid the plate onto the counter her stomach tensed again, stronger than before. 'Spike!'

'Only got one pair of 'ands!'

Demelza set the chip baskets on their props out of the boiling oil and flicked off the fryers. She sank to the floor on all fours and breathed the way the midwife had told her. 'Piran, where are you, boy?' she whispered.

The breeze had grown into a wind and was whipping up the waves out in the bay. It was more than choppy now and Jack tidied his tools and his workbench into the wheelhouse. The cloud had widened and was casting its darkness across the whole village. The swell was coming in with the tide and the Lugger began to pitch back and forth. Jack lengthened the mooring rope and added another at the bow. The water had risen quite a distance already. As he secured the bow rope, he glanced across the harbour at the other vessels in the bay and wondered if he should send an alert. He'd seen these conditions before. The Lugger rose on her moorings. It had got so dark that the cars in Main Street had switched their headlights on, in the middle of a summer's afternoon. He went into the wheelhouse and grabbed the radio.

As drops of rain spotted the sand in great spoonfuls, the queue outside the café began to fall away. People pushed and jostled inside to escape the downpour. Above the noise of the chattering customers, Demelza could hear raindrops hammering on the roof slates.

'Melza?'

'Down here!'

Spike peered over the fryers. 'Oh my giddy aunt! Stay there.' He turned around and faced the customers. 'That's it folks, we're closing early. Come on, chop, chop!' He clapped his hands then grabbed a booklet of raffle tickets from the cupboard beneath the till. 'Anyone still eating gets a free voucher to come back another time.'

Demelza groaned; that was going to cost a fortune. But still, he was right. How else could they kick out a café full of customers into the pouring rain? Her stomach tightened again. She braced herself and focused on Spike's voice as he herded the customers out onto the beach.

'Come on! It can't be helped. Off you go. Don't forget your voucher.'

The customers glared and moaned as they trickled out into the rain.

Spike picked up the phone. 'Spike here, at the café. Can you tell Johnny, it's on the way? Demelza! You know, the baby! Quick!'

Johnny raced back down the wooden steps from the lifeguard hut, taking them two at a time. The rain, by this time, was sheeting down. He had to push past a swarm of disgruntled holiday makers who were streaming out of the café. Pushchairs were blocking the entrance to the café, so he skirted round along the beach to the front of the building. A torrent of water was pouring down the side of the café and across the beach cutting a deep channel in the sand. He waded through it up to his knees and clambered up onto the terrace and vaulted over the railings. He stuck his head through the serving hatch from the terrace to see his sister on all fours panting behind the chip fryer.

'Melza! I'm here. You hold still. How many have you 'ad?'

'Six, I think it is now. They're coming dead fast about three minutes apart. Can you call the midwife? The number's on the board.'

Then came the noise. It was an almighty roar. Not thunder, but like the deep bellow that echoes around the bay when another bit of cliff falls into the sea. Jack looked upstream towards the moors. The stream had swollen rapidly, it was now the size of a small river; it was spilling over into the children's play park. Then movement in the landscape caught his eye. A shelf of water carrying debris and branches was heading downstream towards the harbour and doming as it went.

He glanced over at the visitors' centre; the windows were steamed up, it must be jammed with people. The other side of the harbour was clear except for a few parked cars and the pub which was set high enough to keep its patrons safe and out of the way. He yelled into his radio again then leapt from the deck onto the quayside and ran as fast as he could to the visitors' centre. By the time he'd reached the doors, the lifeboat station's siren was sounding.

'Carrie, there's a river surge, we've got to get everyone upstairs.' Jack scrambled through the pushchairs and beach bags to the back of the centre and flung open the fire doors. In the courtyard behind was an iron fire escape which led up to a flat roof somewhere beneath the centre's attic storeroom. 'Follow me! Everyone, this way! Quickly, up the steps.' He stood waving his arms and bellowing. 'Leave your belongings; hold on to your children!' he shouted. There must have been thirty people in there. He wasn't sure the floors upstairs could take it.

Carrie was the last to put her foot on the bottom step. Satisfied that all were out of harm's way, Jack ran to the front window to check on the river just in time to see the surge hit the supermarket car park with a crash. The water came down on the cars like an anvil, crumpling them like tin foil; a deafening wrenching sound filled the air. A lamp post bent sideways and was left hanging over the road, wavering precariously in the force of the water as it continued to flow through the village and out to sea. A blue hatchback car that had been parked in the harbour road was picked up and swept down the street and lodged against the ice cream kiosk. Then another, and another. The church bells began to toll. As the kiosk gave way from its foundations, its structure too temporary to withstand such a torrent, it was lifted and carried off in amongst the sea of cars bobbing like tin cans on a pond.

The surge pushed on towards the harbour, as it swamped the slipway it took down a telegraph pole which pitched and dove beneath the waters. Jack held his breath as it was launched into the air just feet from the Lugger. The huge wooden caber was tossed like a matchstick against the harbour wall; it flicked upright and over the wall and cartwheeled towards the visitors' centre. Jack ran for the fire escape scooping up a small girl whose curiosity had got the better of her and was coming back down the steps. He crouched with her between his knees as the telegraph pole smashed through the doors of the visitors' centre sending shards of glass flying through the air until it wedged itself across the reception desk. The water rushed in, filling the centre like a rock pool. It reached up to the fourth step of the fire escape and was rushing into the courtyard behind.

'Breathe, Demelza,' said Spike as calmly as he could.

Demelza could do nothing else. 'God, Spike, it's coming.'

Spike was ashen faced. 'Johnny, you got hold of them yet?'

'Ages ago, mate. I can hear them.'

Overhead, the sound of helicopter rotors slicing through the air added to the roar of the water.

'They're landing on the beach. I'm gonna guide them in.'

Water was streaming under the doors and across the lino as the surge reached the steps to the beach.

'What the hell is going on out there?' cried Demelza desperately.

'It's just a storm, my lovely, don't you worry about it. You're safe with us. Come on, let's get you up on a table.'

She closed her eyes and clenched her fists as she braced herself for another contraction.

Spike gently but forcefully led her through the rising waters and heaved her onto the largest table in the café.

A paramedic appeared at the door and waded over to her. He slipped a blood pressure band onto her arm. 'I'll need some towels or blankets if you've got 'em.'

'Aprons and tablecloths?'

'That'll do. Come on, now, Demelza is it?'

Demelza nodded.

'Let's have a look at you. Now you need to listen to me because your baby is going to be born very soon. If you can lie on your back now.' He looked up at Spike. 'Mr er …'

'Spike. Just call me Spike.'

'Right, Spike. You stand here just next to me with that bundle of tea towels. Any good at rugby?' The paramedic was grinning.

A second paramedic ran in to the café.

'The baby's crowning, there's no time,' said the first. 'Now breathe slowly, Demelza. Don't push, not just yet.'

Demelza whimpered with the pain. She could feel her belly tensing again.

'Now, with this next contraction, push as hard as you can. Squeeze my hand and push.'

Demelza groaned as she strained one last time.

Merryn Jewell was born into a bundle of tea towels in Spike's arms.

'It's a girl, Melza!' he cried, a tear rolling down his face.

TWO

Porth Taran, 11th August 2010

Sunshine flooded Merryn Jewell's bedroom. She never closed the curtains; it was always better to fall asleep looking at the stars. Outside, the streets were silent. The boats were motionless on a mirrored sea, and a gentle veil of mist swathed the harbour with the promise of a warm day.

As she lay in the remnants of luxurious slumber, she remembered that today was her birthday. Merryn Jewell was twenty. Twenty sounded better than nineteen. Nineteen was frivolous and naive. Twenty was mature, serious, more professional. She pulled the duvet cover up to her nose, turned on her belly and stretched. She lay still for a few minutes, fighting off the urge to sink back into a deep and delicious sleep.

The whooshing of the coffee machine and the clatter of plates rose from downstairs; the bed and breakfast was fully booked and her mother and Spike would be preparing breakfast for the guests. At last, she pushed herself to sitting and swung her legs over the side of the bed and stood up. She showered quickly. She pulled on a long white linen dress and slipped on a pair of flip flops. She brushed her hair smooth then shook out her titian curls so that they lay evenly across her nut-brown shoulders.

'Twenty,' she said out loud as she looked in the mirror. 'Merryn is twenty.' She sucked in her cheeks and pouted at her reflection, then laughed. She went downstairs and gathered up a bag of broken crockery that her mother had left for her in the hall and stepped out into the clear morning air and set off for the harbour. She always breakfasted at the gallery when the bed and breakfast was full. She liked peace and quiet in the morning and Spike and Mum had enough to do without her getting in the way.

She walked down the harbour road in bright sunshine. With each step closer to the gallery, her excitement and pride grew. When she thought of the stifling years she'd spent at school learning physics and maths, she shuddered. Even the art had been limiting. Now she could do what she loved best, in the most beautiful part of the world that she was fortunate enough to call home.

Only fishermen were stirring this early in Porth Taran. Some were tinkering with their boats; some were lining up lobster and crab pots on the quay, untangling their tail ropes and laying them out carefully in sequence ready to be loaded onto their boats. She wandered past Uncle Johnny's surf shop, its shutters still closed. She passed Sunbeams; its racks of linen smocks and beach clothing were shrouded in darkness within. Nearly all the businesses in Porth Taran were named after the weather, there was: The Sunshine Creek Café, Clouds Ice Cream Counter, The Pot of Gold chocolate shop. She'd named her gallery Rainbow Mosaics because on the rare occasion it rained there was always a ray of sun vying with the drops, casting bright luminous arcs across the sky. Indeed, Porth Taran was an enigma in the world of meteorology;

over the past two decades it had enjoyed a microclimate that had baffled meteorologists across the world.

The gallery was in the harbour, right opposite the Ship Inn that stood on the other side of the little port. From the window she could see the boats and watch the fishermen setting sail, and up above the pub was the moor that stretched across the headland, blanketed with heather and gorse, and the odd tree bent double by the relentless Atlantic winds. High on the ridge, at the tip of the headland, stood a single granite house perched on the seaward most point, silhouetted against the sky.

She reached the door of the gallery. Elwood Curnow was already sitting on the bench opposite, just as he was every morning. A raven hopped and picked at the ground near him. As usual Elwood's eyes were closed and a gentle hum issued from his mouth. He looked to be in quite a good state, Merryn thought; he must have behaved himself at The Ship the night before. His eyes flicked open as she turned the key in the lock.

'Good morning, Elwood.'

'Mornin'' Ambis.' He heaved himself to his feet, leaning heavily on his staff and painfully took a bow.

Merryn curtseyed in reply and Elwood beamed.

She unlocked the gallery and swung the door open, setting the wind chimes jingling in their mismatched tones. She put the bag of broken crockery on the side, picked up the kettle and set it to heat. She stood for a moment and looked around her. She sighed with satisfaction. She'd come a long way since her studio shed at the back of the B&B. The walls were hung with mosaics of local bays and creeks, while others were simply of the sky on dramatic weather days, these were her favourites.

She loved Porth Taran and she loved Cornwall, but more than both of those, she loved the sky. Infinite and open, yet constant and always near, it symbolised freedom with an exciting transience. The sky had the power to change the colour of the sea. It served as a projector for the sun's rays to dry out the land and parch it until it cracked. It was the backdrop that held the clouds aloft to soak the land and fill its ravines with rushing torrents, to water the crops to feed the people and give life. The perfect cycle; the sea evaporated into the atmosphere until the water gathered into clouds; dark clouds, jagged clouds, soft clouds, clouds of every hue. Then like magic it would return to the land in sheeting rain, spotting rain, torrential rain, horizontal rain or incessant mizzle.

She glanced out at the harbour; the veil of mist had risen to cloak the headland, its edges dissipating into the blue like evaporating steam.

Elwood was struggling to his feet again.

Merryn glanced at her watch; it was early – he'd be off to the pasty shop to order his lunch. The kettle clicked off and Merryn filled the coffee pot with hot water.

Today she would start a new mosaic. She thought a tree. A tall bold tree that had been growing for a hundred years. On a beach, with great roots that sunk deep beneath the sand to draw moisture from the water table, and behind it, an endless sky. She pushed down the plunger on the coffee pot and poured the dark liquid into a mug. She fetched a fresh board and laid it on her workbench. The chimes buffeted together in the doorway and she cursed herself for forgetting to bolt the door behind her.

'We're closed!' she called out. 'Open at nine!' She waited for a response but she was met with silence. She stuck her head around the corner.

A dark haired, young man was standing looking at her mosaics.

'Didn't you hear? We're closed, we open at nine.' She tried to keep the irritation from her voice.

The man swung round. 'G 'day,' he was grinning.

Merryn pursed her lips sternly.

'Aw, yeah, sorry, I couldn't help but come in and have a look. This stuff is amazing!'

She stepped out into the shop. 'That's very kind of you but I'm afraid we're closed for another couple of hours.'

He didn't answer, still gazing at the art on the wall. 'Oh! Sorry, yes. Did you do these?'

Merryn nodded. 'Do you like them?'

'They're beaut.' He turned around and stepped towards her holding out a hand. 'Sorry, I should introduce myself as we'll be neighbours. Matt Bunda.' He held out his hand. 'I've just arrived to start work at Porth Taran Weather Centre.'

Merryn shook his hand. 'Merryn Jewell, pleased to meet you. Aren't you a little early?'

'Yeah, I know, I landed in London late last night and managed to hitch a lift with a fella I met on the plane. I just got here.' He gestured to a rucksack leaning against the shop front on the pavement outside. 'Lucky he was coming all the way down here, eh!'

'You've come from Australia?'

'Yeah, I guess the accent gives it away.'

'Well, not many people say 'G'day' around here.' She suddenly felt embarrassed. 'I'm sorry, I'm forgetting my manners, you must be worn out. Seeing as we're going to be work neighbours, can I get you a coffee?'

'Aw, thought you'd never ask. Coffee would be ripper.'

Merryn disappeared out to the kitchen in the back of the shop to fetch another mug. 'You were lucky to get just one lift all the way here to sleepy Porth Taran, it's at least a six-hour drive from London.'

'I think we did it in about four and a half.'

'Who gave you a ride?'

'Finn, I think he said his name was.'

'Finn McGann?'

'Tall fella, middle aged, really nice car.'

'Yep, that's him. He lives just up there.' Merryn pointed to the square stone house perched on the ridge.

'Wow, that's quite a location!'

'I've always thought it must be amazing to live there. You're kind of in the weather all the time.' She poured some coffee into the second mug. 'So, tell me. What are you going to be doing at the weather centre?'

'Ah, I'm researching for my PhD. I'm studying microclimates.'

'A meteorologist, then?'

'Yeah, I guess I am. Seems strange; not long finished my degree.'

'This is a long way to come. Aren't there any places in Australia where you could do it?'

'Well, yeah but none with the weird weather patterns you get here. Besides I've always wanted to come to England.'

'Where are you staying?'

'Ah, no idea! I haven't sorted that out yet. They said to talk to a lady called Carrie? She works at the visitors' centre?'

'That's right, I know Carrie, but I'm not sure she's got much room, single mum and all.'

'Ah well, something'll come up.' He sipped his coffee.

'My mum runs a bed and breakfast, Little Rosewarne. It's at the top of the hill. It's fully booked this week though, I'm afraid, what with the school holidays...'

The chimes jingled again and Bea appeared in the doorway brandishing a present. 'Happy Birthday, to you!' she sang and threw her arms around Merryn. Here, and you have to open it now because I want to see your face when you do.'

Matt shuffled. 'It's your birthday? Many happy returns!'

Beatrice looked sideways at Matt and then raised her eyebrows at Merryn. 'I'm sorry, I'm intruding.'

'No, no, not at all. Erm, Beatrice this is ...'

'Matt. Pleased to meet you.' He held out his hand.

'Pleased to meet you too!' Beatrice was beaming a little too much.

Matt picked up his mug and knocked back the coffee. 'Listen, girls, I shall leave you to chat. Thanks for the coffee, Merryn. See you around.' He winked at them both and headed for the door.

They watched as he slung his rucksack over his shoulder and headed towards the visitors' centre.

'Who's he?' said Bea, swooning.

Merryn shrugged her shoulders, 'Just another scientist come to study the weather.'

'Honestly, Merryn, you seem to be immune to even the best-looking men, though I'm not complaining. Leaves more for me!'

'I don't have time for all of that, I've got this place to run.'

Beatrice helped herself to a coffee and gazed around the gallery. 'It's looking really nice in here now. I love the chimes, very esoteric. Where did you get them?'

'A guy from Praa Sands. He makes them out of bits and bobs he finds on the beach. Really clever, and I like that he's making something brought in by the wind to blow in the wind.' She paused gazing through the window at the sky. She sighed. 'To flirt with the wind.' She jingled a chime absent-mindedly.

'Aah, Merryn Jewell, always your head in the clouds! Come on open your present.'

Merryn sat down at the workbench and set the parcel in front of her. 'Now I wonder. Is it a book? Or jewellery? Or a ticket to take me far away from here on a wonderful adventure?'

'Well, you won't know until you open it.'

Merryn pulled away the paper to reveal a light-coloured wooden box. It looked old and a little worn. 'Beatrice it's beautiful.'

'Open it, silly.'

Merryn slid up the tiny brass latch and opened the lid on soundless hinges. Inside, the box was lined with blue crushed velvet. And nestled in its soft finery was a gleaming brass wind gauge. 'Bea, this is gorgeous. Thank you! Where did you get it?'

'In that antiques shop in Penzance. You know, about halfway up Causeway Head on the left.'

'Does it work?'

'The man in the shop reckoned so. Now, I must get off to work. You have a lovely day, it's going to be a busy one! We will all be waiting for you at The Ship at seven o'clock sharp, your mum said.'

A steady stream of customers came and went. The wind chimes were her bestsellers and they'd almost been cleared out; she'd need to order some more. Porth Taran was getting busier with the approach of the bank holiday and the little village would be full to busting point by the following week.

Merryn emptied the till, washed up the cups and pulled down the blinds. She set off for home along the harbour road.

Uncle Johnny was outside his shop. He'd taken off his top and was hosing down wetsuits.

She smiled to herself as she watched him admiring his reflection in the window; and why not, he was in good shape for his forty-two years. She skipped to one side as a torrent of water gushed along the pavement from his hose pipe.

'Hey birthday girl!' He twisted the tip of the hose until it ran dry and hung it over a deckchair to drip. 'All set for tonight?'

'Can't wait.'

'Think your mum's already gone over the pub. Best get a move on.' He grinned and tapped his watchless wrist playfully.

'Well, you're not ready!'

'Not ready? What d'ya mean not ready? The best-looking man in Porth Taran? No need to prepare this body.' He flexed his biceps like a Victorian boxer.

Merryn laughed. 'Well I definitely need to, so see you later.'

The church on the headland chimed seven as Merryn stepped through the front door of The Ship. A cheer went up and she curtseyed theatrically. Every seat was taken, and the bar was jammed. She recognised almost everyone. Even Philip Tresize, chair of the Parish Council was there, he must have buried the hatchet over her fighting him for the change of use of the gallery. The optics were festooned with balloons and Steve and Jane had hung a banner right across the bar with *Happy 20th Merryn!* painted on it.

Her mother pushed through the crowd and put her arms around her. 'A very, very happy birthday to you, my love.' She kissed her on both cheeks. 'Come and sit by me and Jack.'

'Happy Birthday, Merry!' yelled Spike. He planted a noisy kiss on her cheek.

Beatrice gave her a hug and Rowan was ready with a pint of her favourite cider.

Uncle Jack leant over and kissed her hand. 'Happy Birthday, my buttercup.'

It looked like a few had been there a while already for she could detect slurring and some were already swaying a little. Porth Taran rarely missed an opportunity for a party, no matter what their differences; they always came together to laugh and talk and celebrate.

Demelza Jewell stood up and tapped a knife on a glass. 'Quieten down now, folks!'

A hush fell over the gathering.

She coughed and cleared her throat. 'As you all know we are here to celebrate my Merryn's birthday. My beautiful daughter is twenty years old today!' She held her arms out to Merryn. 'Now how old does that make me?'

'Over the hill!' someone shouted from the back.

'Trust you, Samuel Laity!' she chided smiling. 'As you all well know, my daughter Merryn never does anything by halves and the day she was born was no different.'

The guests shuffled to get comfortable. It was a story they heard every year, yet they never tired of it.

'Twenty years ago today, Porth Taran was devastated by floods. The moment that river surge hit the back of my café was the moment my Merryn decided to come into this world. Thanks to the air ambulance and Spike here ...'

Spike blushed, then stood up and took a bow. Another cheer went up.

'And my brother, Johnny ...'

Johnny followed suit.

'We were whisked off to hospital in a helicopter, safe and sound. Every year since that day, I know we have all conjured those events in our mind's eye and we remain thankful that there were no casualties or loss of life.'

A murmur swept the pub and heads nodded solemnly.

'Get on with it, Demmy!' .yelled Samuel Laity.

'And now, ladies and gentlemen it's time to party, so, take it away Taran singers!'

From the back door of the pub gentle tones of male voices singing *Happy Birthday* came drifting through the bar, in perfect a cappella harmony.

Merryn clapped her hands in delight. She hugged Demelza with a tear in her eye.

The drink flowed and everyone joined in with the singing. A great roar of laughter went up at one point, when poor old Elwood who had been propping up the bar fell off his stool with a great thud.

A couple of the lads helped him to his feet. 'Come on Elwood we'll see you home,' said one of them supporting his arm.

But Elwood snatched it away from him and staggered over to Merryn's table. 'Happy Birthday, Ambis. It is a great day but,' he solemnly waved a finger at her, 'Danger is afoot. You must keep your wits about you,' he slurred. 'Look after her Melza.'

Demelza shook her head disapprovingly.

'Think you've definitely had enough Elwood, you'll be better off in bed,' said Uncle Jack.

Elwood eyed him and opened his mouth to say something, then thought better of it.

'Come on Elwood, best be off,' said one of the lads.

Elwood allowed himself to be guided towards the door.

Merryn giggled shaking her head. 'Ah Elwood, he's an odd one.'

'He was dropped on his head as a baby. It's known for a fact, isn't it Melza?' said Jack, turning to his sister-in-law.

'So they say, but you know what this village is like. If there's any rubbish to be gossiped, they'll do it better than anywhere else.'

'I'm not sure I'd trust him with my life but he's harmless; not an evil bone in his body,' said Jack, swilling down the last drops of his ale.

After Elwood had been helped out of the door and down the steps, the party goers began to fall away. Merryn was getting a headache, she knew she'd drunk too much.

Spike stood up. 'Come on, Merry. You look like you could do with your bed.'

Merryn glanced out at the harbour, the lights were swathed in sea mist and a layer of tiny droplets coated the window pane. 'Don't fancy walking up the hill in that,' she said, screwing up her face.

'Well, we'll have to my dear. No choice. Uncle Jack has had a fair few so he can't drive us - it's our feet or sleep here!' said her mother, laughing. She took Merryn's hand and squeezed it affectionately. 'It's tomorrow morning I'm dreading. Fourteen full Englishes and that couple from London who've complained about everything from the moment they stepped inside – don't fancy that with a hangover.'

'Mum, I almost forgot. An Australian came to the gallery today looking for somewhere to stay. He's here for a while, I think, studying meteorology.'

'He's called Matt, isn't he?'

'Yes, that's it, you met him?'

'He came up to see me earlier. I can't put him up for a fortnight, not 'til the bank holiday's gone over. Jack has offered him the Lugger to sleep on. He seemed like a nice sort. Don't you think, Jack?'

'He's alright, he is, I reckon. P'r'aps you'll keep an eye since you're just in the harbour, Merryn?'

'Of course. Now let's get off.'

THREE

Elwood was slumped on the bench outside in the harbour, as Merryn arrived at the gallery. His worn black overcoat was even more crumpled than usual. A flash of sunlight glinted from the collection of gold and silver chains that hung about his neck.

She got close enough to be sure that he was still breathing but was beaten back by the smell of beer fumes. She hastily took a gulp of fresh salty air. Satisfied that he was simply asleep she retreated to open up the gallery.

Elwood woke with a start at the jingling of the wind chimes. 'Ambis! Where are you?' He sounded panicked.

'Good morning, Elwood. I'm here.'

'You're safe?'

'Of course, I'm safe. I think you must have been dreaming.'

'Dreaming?'

'That's right. You'd dropped off.'

'Dropped off?'

Merryn signed. 'Well, I'd better get on.'

He started to get up, leaning hard on his staff, he winced as he got to his feet. 'That was no dream, it was a vision! I'm telling you, Ambis.' His voice was shrill, almost angry.

'A vision? Elwood, are you sure you're quite alright?'

A frown spread across his face.

'I think you've got a hangover. It was a big night last night. Go home and sleep it off.'

He stared back at her, his eyes were wide and terror dressed his face. He shook his head, took the longest pendant that hung around his neck between his fingers and kissed it solemnly. He waved a finger at her. 'There's danger come to Porth Taran, I tell you.' His eyes rounded with gravity. 'You go careful, Ambis.' Then he turned and began to hobble up the harbour road towards Main Street.

Merryn watched him limp away. A chill breeze wafted down from the moor making her shiver. She pulled her cardigan tightly round her and went inside to make coffee.

In her workroom, the board she had laid out to start her new mosaic lay untouched. A thrill went through her. Each new work was another adventure, a fresh discovery. She took her pad and began to sketch. First, a tiny thumbnail, for she liked the mosaics to have meaning even from a distance. Then as you got closer, more and more of the picture would be revealed; pictures within pictures, releasing their secrets, drawing the observer into their magical powers.

A thick dark charcoal trunk with splayed, sinuous roots and above, thicker branches reaching wide, like a candelabra. The root system would need to be almost as big as the canopy and certainly as broad to support its great spreading branches.

She glanced up at the trees on the headland. Like us, we are born of a simple tiny spark between two people. Untouched and pure, we wait for life to shape us into what we are today. The sturdier our foundations, the more successful and fulfilling our lives will become. She sipped her coffee. A tree blossoms and sets seed. The seeds are then blown from the branches, sometimes caught in thermal currents and carried off some distance before floating to the ground. A seed that falls on soft fertile earth will grow healthy and tall, branching up into the sky, to bloom and set seed all over again. A seed that falls on rocky ground may struggle to survive, soaking up every drop of water before it drains through the harsh arid earth beneath. A tough seed with a hard, outer shell can survive to germinate and grow. It may be weak and spindly, it may be downtrodden and never bloom or it may beat the odds to rise higher and stronger than the others. If the seed germinates and grows there is one certainty; it will be an oak or an ash, a sycamore or a cedar; of its parents' species.

She gazed out of the window and her eyes fell upon Finn's house perched high on the headland. Gnarled rowans were scattered round and about, outside its garden walls. They grew slanted, leaning inland. They were fighters; they had survived. Just inside the garden was one tree that stood tall, dark against the glowing azure sky, its branches angular and jagged, a warrior tree, reaching higher than the rowans, its infantry. She stretched a sheet of paper over the board and traced an outline of the trunk and branches. Sliding the charcoal on its side and pushing it abruptly to leave sharp edged strokes jutting in all directions.

A siren broke her peace. She dropped her charcoal and rushed outside to look. A fire engine screamed round the head of the harbour and sped up the hill to the top of the village. Just beyond where the ambulance had disappeared, a column of smoke rose into the sky, apparently defying the wind, as if it was being funnelled by an invisible force. Holiday makers stopped to look, then continued on their way, more used to the hustle and bustle of city emergencies.

Carrie, from the visitors' centre appeared at her side. 'What's all that about then?'

Merryn shrugged. 'Just a barbecue gone wrong, I expect.'

Behind them, Matt staggered out of the visitors' centre. He was gasping and clawing at his throat. His tanned face had turned a deep red and his eyes were watering.

'Matt! What's the matter?'

He coughed and spluttered, staring at her helplessly.

'Paper bag!' shrieked Carrie.

Merryn ran into the gallery and grabbed one from the string by the till and ran over to him. She held the bag over his nose and mouth. 'Slow, even breaths,' she said in a calming tone.

His breath was rasping and rapid but as he relaxed his breathing evened out.

Carrie fetched a chair from the visitors' centre and sat him on it, on the pavement.

Merryn let him hold the bag himself and stood up straight.

He lowered the bag, and stared up at her. He looked worn out.

'I'll get you a cup of tea. Lots of sugar.'

Merryn went back to the gallery and boiled the kettle. She was just pouring hot water into the teapot when Matt appeared at the door, red-faced but looking distinctly better.

'Sorry about that.'

'Are you OK?'

'Think I'm right now, thanks. Don't know what happened there.'

'Are you asthmatic?'

'I used to be when I was a nipper. But I haven't had an attack in ten years.'

'What could have brought that on?'

He shrugged his shoulders and shook his head. 'Search me.'

'You scared the living daylights out of us.'

'And me! Sorry mate.'

Merryn passed him his tea. 'Just glad you're still with us.'

He took a gulp of tea and swallowed hard. 'I think you ought to get checked out by the doctor though.'

'Yeah, I will. Perhaps there's something in the atmosphere that's causing it.'

'Well, there's that fire up the hill, but that's too far away.'

Matt shook his head. 'It can't be that. Smoke has never been a problem.' He took a sip of tea. 'I'm very lucky that I am so well looked after.' He looked up at her smiling.

'Oh, don't be daft, I was just here. Anyone would have done the same.' She found herself blushing.

'I've embarrassed you, I'm sorry.'

'What, me? Embarrassed? Not at all.' She flicked her hair nervously. 'Now you drink up your tea. I can't stand round here chatting all day.'

He took another gulp eyeing her sideways. 'You know your family are really kind and they sure know how to party!'

'You were there, last night?'

'Of course, what else is a lonely bloke to do?'

'I didn't see you.'

'I was lurking at the back. Jack, he's your uncle?'

'Yeah, Uncle Jack is my dad's brother. He's a lovely man but some folk think he's a bit stiff. That's just his way. An old softie, really; he doesn't suffer fools though, be warned.'

'I'll try not to slip into that category. Anyway, I'm chuffed he let me stay on his boat. What an apartment to land, eh?'

'Well appointed, I think the estate agents would say.'

They both laughed.

Matt gazed around the gallery walls. 'You know I wasn't just saying it, I really do like your stuff.'

'Thanks.'

He pointed at a mosaic above the till. 'That one's amazing!'

It was one of Merryn's earliest works. A grey windy day over the ocean, the waves whipped up in grey-blue glossy porcelain and the sky swirling above it in shades of white, and pale purple.

'You've managed to show the force of the wind without a single tree or flag to blow in it.' He stared at it thoughtfully. 'You can't see the wind, but you can sense it.'

Merryn looked at him hard, not even Beatrice had picked up on that. She'd thought it was because she hadn't done it very well. 'You are the first person to admire that mosaic.'

'Really? I'm surprised.' He looked around at the others. 'I reckon that, at first dibs, would be my favourite.'

'It's mine too,' she said quietly.

'If I had my own place, I'd buy it off you.'

'It's not for sale,' she said a little too gruffly.

'Aah, it really is your favourite!' he laughed.

Merryn nodded apologetically.

'Well, I'd better be off. Thanks for the tea.'

Another siren swung round the harbour. 'Jeez, something's kicking off up there, it's the police now.'

Merryn stuck her head out into the street. The column of smoke had dissipated into a fine trail. 'Looks like the fire's out though.'

'Yeah. Well, see you around.'

Merryn went inside and picked up the phone.

'It's Elwood's place,' said Demelza. 'Apparently he had a fire in the garden and it got out of hand. They've taken him up to the hospital in Truro. Johnny's gone with him.'

'Is he badly hurt? I just saw a police car going up there.'

'Did you? I don't know; I'm waiting for Johnny to call.'

Merryn turned back to her work, with fire in mind. A fire tree. Contrasting dark and light foliage with flecks of amber, set with scarlet blossom. Her mind kept flitting back to Matt. His tanned neck above his sweatshirt as she'd held the paper bag to his face. His smile that enveloped his face and quite literally shone. She could see Bea's point, but there was something else. He wasn't just good looking, there was something special about Matt. Something special about the way he looked at her.

A family approached the gallery and pushed open the door. She shook herself and quickly scrawled 'firebuds' on the edge of the sheet and went to serve them.

The gallery was busy all morning and Merryn hadn't managed to go near her new work. She was beginning to feel hungry and locked up the gallery and headed out into Porth Taran.

Rowan was on the forecourt outside the surf shop, waxing a longboard. His hair had bleached blonde through the summer and his skin was as brown as cinnamon.

As she approached, she could hear giggling coming from an upstairs window opposite. Two girls on a balcony were and leaning over the railings looking out over the bay, though their furtive glances in Rowan's direction were unmistakeable. Their presence clearly wasn't lost on Rowan either, for he threw a coy glance up at the balcony then continued to wax his board.

'Hi Rowan.'

He jumped and turned around at the sound of her voice.

'Going for a surf?' she teased; for the bay was as smooth as a mill pond.

'Naah, there's no swell, I thought I'd just go for a paddle after work, it's a beautiful day.' He put down the wax and washed his hands in the oil drum filled with soapy water to soak wetsuits. 'Anyway, what can I do for you? Johnny's up at the hospital.'

'Yeah, mum said. I was just passing. Fancy a pasty?'

Rowan glanced up at the balcony opposite, the girls had gone. 'Good plan, I'm a bit peckish myself.'

'I'll go and pick a couple up. Back in ten.'

'Sure thing.'

FOUR

Rowan was good company. Merryn enjoyed his easy manner and uncomplicated vision of things. It was two o'clock, the village was quiet, the sun had beckoned the holidaymakers to the beach and the harbour waters lay still. Merryn wandered back to the gallery and back to her workbench.

She pulled the drape off the mosaic board. 'Firebuds,' she read. She rummaged through her crockery bags for just the right flame red but couldn't find what she was looking for. Under her workbench in the stack of unbroken crockery she found a crimson plate. It would be just big enough. She took it out and set it next to the sketched leaf clusters on the mosaic board in full light. With her hammer she tapped it gently until it fissured and fell apart. Then with her cutters she set about splitting the pieces into roughly shaped buds trimming down any sharp edges as she went. She closed her eyes to see the tree she was creating. She would need more than one shade on her fire buds for fire itself was not even but streaked with many hues. She retrieved her precious collection of cadmium enamels and tipped one of the buds with yellow and another with orange and blew on them to dry them.

She placed them carefully, angling the painted tips as if the sun was reflecting off them.

A steady trickle of holiday makers came and went as she worked. Some bought postcards or a wind chime, others just browsed. Nearly all of them stopped at least for a moment and admired her mosaics hanging on the wall.

Merryn felt suddenly restless, she looked at her watch, it was nearly five. Outside, the tide was rising and the water in the port had become a little choppy and the rigging on the boats was beginning to rattle in the breeze. The harbour was busier with visitors returning from the beach.

In the distance, she could see Matt walking up the harbour road towards the jetty to the Lugger. She watched him stop and turn towards the gallery. Merryn quickly looked down, lest he catch her looking at him. Realising it was unlikely that he could see her in the back of the shop from there, she risked peeping up again. He'd changed direction and was walking towards the gallery.

She could feel a light sense of panic welling up in her, she started to rearrange the mosaic pieces on her board nervously She didn't dare look up until he pushed the door open making the chimes dance.

'G 'day!'

'G 'day!' replied Merryn awkwardly, trying to sound as if she was mocking him.

The door slammed shut behind him, sucked to by the wind.

'Struth! The weather changes fast round here.'

'That will be our maritime climate so typical of this part of the northern hemisphere you know.'

'You seem to know a lot about it?'

'Oh, I just listened at school.'

'Well, I'd be interested to find out what else you know. What time to do you finish for example?'

She looked at her watch. 'About now, actually.'

'In that case, I'd like to offer you coffee at my humble abode on the water.'

She didn't answer straight away.

'If that's OK, I mean,' he went on, 'If it doesn't get too windy we could sit on deck.'

Merryn broke into a smile. 'Why not?'

'Great, then see you as soon as you're ready?'

'Sure thing.'

She watched as he turned and stepped back through the door into the street and set off for the Lugger. The more she watched him, the more attractive he became. He had dark skin, darker than just olive skin and his features were quite fine, save for quite a large forehead below a head of curly black hair. His face lent itself well to smiling, almost as if it had been set up for that sole purpose.

She tidied up her workbench, trying to suppress the flutter rising in her stomach. She checked herself in the mirror and brushed her hair, pulled down the blinds, locked the front door and headed over to the boat, her tummy flipping curiously as she went.

Matt had set a couple of old folding wooden chairs of Uncle Jack's on deck; they were splattered with paint and varnish.

'We should be alright on this side of the wheelhouse, the wind is coming from behind. I'm afraid I only have two mugs.'

Merryn made a show of looking around her for more people. 'And I think that'll be fine for just us two, don't you?'

'Well, yes I guess so,' he laughed. 'I won't be a tick.' He disappeared down below.

Merryn settled herself on one of the chairs and lent back looking out over the harbour. She remembered playing here when she was small while Uncle Jack worked sanding and revarnishing the deck.

Matt reappeared and handed her a chipped enamel mug of thick black coffee. 'Oh, I don't have any milk.'

'That's fine, I can cope.' She took a sip. 'So, how do you like Porth Taran so far?'

'Well, I've been here precisely thirty-six hours and I already have a lido-side residence and an attractive talented artist for a friend; I think I'm on to a winner.'

'Well, thank you,' Merryn laughed.

'How do you find Porth Taran?' he asked.

She shrugged. 'I've lived here all my life; it's home and obviously, I love it.'

'And you've never travelled?'

'Well, I have seen lots of places far away from here but no, I've not travelled.'

He looked at her quizzically.

'Oh, ignore me, it's all in my mind. No, I've not travelled, not yet. I suppose I haven't really felt the need. I have everything I need right here. Now, Australia, that's an amazing place. Tell me, which part are you from?'

'I was born on a tiny island just off the coast of Townsville in Queensland, up in the north east. You won't have heard of it. Hang on, I'll show you on the map. There's an atlas down below.' He disappeared below deck reappearing with an old hardback. He flicked through the pages then laid it open on his lap. 'I grew up just here in Townsville.'

Merryn followed his finger to a dot right on the east coast of Queensland.

'And, here, you see that blob just there? Out in the ocean?'

Merryn nodded.

'That's it, that's Palm Island. That's where I was born right there in the Pacific Ocean. My grandfather still lives there.'

'Right on the Great Barrier Reef? I can't imagine what that's like.'

'Well, in a nutshell, it has a tropical savannah climate with a mean rainfall of about a thousand millimetres per annum and a tendency for tropical cyclones.'

'Thank you, mister meteorologist.'

'You're welcome!' His smile radiated like a flame in a darkened room.

Merryn felt a rush of warmth and hastily looked down at the atlas. 'And you've come all that way to work at our weather centre?'

'Yep. Palm Island's weather has common characteristics with Porth Taran's in that its weather can be markedly different to the land mass not so far away from it. I want to find out why. It's the subject of my doctorate to examine the factors that create microclimates.'

'But we don't have cyclones here. In fact, we don't have any extremes of weather, well not for years anyway.'

'Not since August 1990, I believe?'

She looked at him sideways.

'It's famous in the world of meteorology you know. I was in the pub that evening. The evening of your birthday. You were born during one of the most famous weather events in Porth Taran. Everyone was talking about it; quite a way to come into the world!'

'Oh that. I think it's the only thing that drives me mad about this place. Every year, on my birthday, the villagers make a big fuss. It was terrible, some people lost their businesses and their possessions were ruined in the flooding but thankfully no one died, we were very lucky.'

'And you have clearly brought a ray of sunshine to the place ever since, that's what your folks say anyway.'

'Don't you start!' Suddenly thirsty she knocked back the mug and drained the coffee. 'What about your family?'

'Well, there's only my grandfather in Palm Island, as I said, and my mum lives in Townsville. That's it.'

'I always imagined Australians to be blond.'

'And with a surfboard surgically attached to their armpits?'

'Sorry,' she giggled.

'There are lots of different nationality origins in Australia, you know; lots of Greeks and Italians.'

'So, which one are you?'

'Well, it's a bit more complicated than that but that's a conversation for another time.' He looked at his watch. 'Jeez, I'm sorry but I've got to fly. Finn McGann's invited me on a tour of the coast on his dive boat.'

'Oh, that will be quite something. It's stunning round these waters.'

'Yeah, I'm looking forward to it. Finn seems like a good sort?'

'I think he is, he's quite a private person, I don't really know him.'

'Listen, I'm sorry to cut you short; it's really rude of me …' he gulped down the rest of his coffee. 'I'd like to do this again.' He shut the atlas looking away, then glanced up at her shyly. 'If you would?'

Merryn could feel her face heating up. 'No worries,' she blustered. 'Isn't that how you say it?'

'Bonzer!' he said, laughing.

Demelza Jewell was in the kitchen at Little Rosewarne wiping down the oven. She stopped and straightened herself, rubbing her back. She was tired. Every August was the same. By the middle of the month the exhaustion would begin to overwhelm her. Every day was an endless round of cleaning, washing, cooking and making beds. She had started to count down to the bank holiday weekend. It was always the busiest of the year, it was unfair that it sat at the tail end of the season when everyone in the tourist industry was past their best. The last blast of summer that packed out every B&B, rental property, holiday park and hotel in the region. The streets would be teeming, the roads rammed. Just another couple of weeks and then the golden season would come. The beaches would be returned to them. The great swathes of damp sand shimmering the reflection of the sky, unblemished by countless picnic blankets of August, car parks laid bare. On sunny days the local families would make their way down after school and work and congregate with wine and barbecues to chat and pass the time of day with their neighbours. It was funny, in the winter everyone would hunker down by their wood burners keeping out of the way of the wind and horizontal rain and the supermarket became the social hub. When she lived all those years out at Tregarron she remembered how lonely she would get, away from the village, through the long winter evenings. Spring and autumn were the best; bluebells would blanket the woodland and shady lanes in April and May, and in the autumn, wood smoke scented the air. She liked to walk out across the heather magenta clad moors and along the empty beaches to watch the waves.

'A penny for them.' Spike appeared by her side, a soapy sponge in his hand.

'Ah, just thinking about the end of the season.'

'It won't be long, love. We'll make it through.' He leant down and kissed her on the forehead and then turned to wipe down the tiled wall.

She watched him as he sprayed and scrubbed the porcelain behind the cooker. His body was still impressively muscular for his age, but Spike was getting on. He was younger than her but perhaps his wild youth was beginning to take its toll. She'd noticed he was becoming forgetful. She'd had to set up a big blackboard next to the cooker to write the orders on; it was harder to miss than bits of paper.

She glanced through the window at the street. Rowan was wandering up the pavement. She looked at her watch; he would have finished work. Merryn wouldn't be long either. In fact, she was a little late. She was such a hard worker that one. Still no sign of a boyfriend. Demelza sighed. It was strange, she was such a pretty girl. Perhaps growing up without a dad made her different somehow. She rinsed out her cloth and hung it on the tap to dry.

Spike put his head around the corner from the prep area. 'I'm done cleaning down the tiles. I'll get on to the fridge.'

'It's already been done, love.' She omitted to mention that he had done it himself that morning, straight after serving breakfast.

'Well, in that case, let's have a cup of tea, you go and sit yourself down, I'll bring it in.'

She kissed him on the cheek and did as she was told. This was her favourite part of the day. The moment when the work was done, and she would sit down for a chat with lovely Spike and sometimes Merryn, if she got home on time.

Spike came in from the kitchen carrying two steaming mugs and set them on the dining table. 'Any news on Elwood?'

'Johnny called earlier, they're letting him out of hospital tonight.'

'He's a crackpot that Elwood.' He pulled out a copy of The Cornishman from the magazine rack and spread it in front of him, while he sipped his tea.

Demelza looked at his worn wrinkled face. He'd abandoned his nose ring of old but the tell-tale mark remained on his nostril. He'd shaved off his Mohican when he'd started to lose his hair. Only his tattoos on his neck gave away his old self. It was twenty years since he'd pitched up for the interview, with his strong London accent and his outlandish appearance. At first she was worried he'd scare the customers away, but it was his smile that had reached her; his demeanour was so cheerful and jolly that she couldn't help warming to him.

When he'd first arrived in the village, Piran had never thought much of him. 'Coming down here and nicking our jobs,' he'd said. 'And what does he think he looks like?'

But Piran was wrong; he'd been Demelza's rock. Since that day, when she'd agreed to take him on in the kitchen where he couldn't frighten the customers, he'd been by her side. He'd taken only one sick day in two decades and that was when he broke his arm surfing. Even in plaster he'd come in and pushed a broom around. For his outrageous exterior, behind it was a man of integrity and substance who kept his word.

FIVE

Merryn unlocked the gallery door. Elwood's bench was empty. She was surprised how disorientated she felt by his absence. He'd been there every single morning since she'd opened the gallery just over a year ago.

A chill but gentle breeze mottled the surface of the water in the harbour. She glanced over at the Lugger. Matt was standing on deck looking out to sea, his back to her. He wasn't tall, not like Uncle Johnny or Rowan but he was broad. He began to turn around. Merryn quickly pushed open the gallery door and hurried inside.

She flicked on the kettle and uncovered her mosaic. The firebuds glinted back at her, their cadmium tips gleamed in contrast with the crimson china. The colours danced together in time with her nerves. She took a deep breath to quell the curious jittery feeling that was building within her. Trying to anchor herself, she tipped some grout into a pot and added water. This was the magical part; the emergence of the unknown, the evolution of her vision. She was just the tool by which images came into existence. Sometimes the process was as she'd imagined from the start and then others would take on a life of their own, like this one. Plotting itself while she merely evaluated and adjusted her technique to the feeling that it gave her. She coated the underside of each bud with grouting using a fine paintbrush and then positioned them, nudging them into place with a pair of tweezers.

She sipped her steaming tea as she watched a jittery wind dance across the little port, keeping the tourists from the beach and the gallery busy.

At last Merryn laid down the final vibrant bud of fire in the traced branches of the tree and she blew the china dust from between them. The sun flooded through the gallery window, catching the cadmium and making the colours glow.

She sneaked a look at the Lugger through the window but the deck was empty, Matt must be have left for work.

A screeching of brakes heralded the arrival of Uncle Johnny's van. Elwood was in the passenger seat. Johnny helped him out onto the pavement and held an arm for him to lean on as he heaved himself onto the bench and leant his staff in the crook of his arm.

Merryn reluctantly went to greet them.

'Can you keep an eye on him?'

'Should he be out and about already?' She loathed her own unwillingness but taking responsibility for an old injured man was not what she had hoped for today.

'He's fine now, back to his usual self. He's just a bit confused. He needs to get out, Merryn. He's been stuck in that hospital; a bit of air is what he needs.' Uncle Johnny kissed her on the cheek. 'Thanks darlin', I'll be back later to pick him up. If there are any problems give me a bell at the shop. You're an angel.' And he was gone.

Elwood was sitting bolt upright, his hands bound in two bandaged globes, held out straight in front of him like an Egyptian mummy. Poor Elwood. She overcame her irritation and waved at him kindly, he bowed his head reverently in response. The trill of the gallery phone took her back inside.

Matt's Australian brogue came over the handset. 'Thought you might like to witness first-hand my discovery of a Cornish pasty.'

'Aha, did you now?' She stalled.

'Yeah, well, maybe a bit presumptuous but we've all got to eat, right? I could pick some up for us to share?'

'Come to think of it I am quite hungry,' she said, salvaging her composure.

'I'll be over.' The line went dead.

Merryn hung up and found herself looking in the mirror again. She flicked at her hair and realised that she was actually quite brown, despite spending so much time indoors. She'd been blessed with honey coloured skin that tanned easily and had escaped the sensitive translucence of the typical redhead. The powerful Cornish sun, reflecting off the sea had streaked her copper hair with blonde.

Half an hour later the chimes jingled, and Matt appeared in the doorway carrying a bundle of paper bags and a large bottle of sparkling water.

'It's a blaster today! Shame to sit in here and eat them, do you reckon you could close up and we could eat them on the beach?'

Merryn was about to accept when she remembered Elwood. 'Oh.' Her face fell. 'I've got to keep an eye on Elwood for my uncle.'

Matt glanced over towards the bench at Elwood in his bandaged glory. 'That's OK, here is good.'

Elwood pushed himself to his feet, leaning on the bench with one elbow. He began to wave the swathed globes frantically. His staff fell to the ground and he looked as if he would topple over. He let out a piercing, high-pitched wail.

Merryn rushed outside. 'Elwood, whatever is the matter?'

'Get away!' he whispered in an urgent croak.

Merryn took a step back.

'Get away from him!' He thrust one of his bound arms violently in the direction of the gallery, wincing in pain as he did so.

'From who, Elwood?'

'Bunjil!'

'Bunjil?! What are you talking about?'

'Stay with me, Ambis. I will guard you with my life!' His voice deepened as he gestured painfully for her to get behind him, then he began to wail again.

Merryn clapped her hands over her ears to shut out the dreadful sound. 'Stop, Elwood, for pity's sake!'

Matt came out of the gallery.

Elwood's screams got louder until his voice cracked and his face froze in an agonised grimace but no sound came out. Then in a gruff eerie voice that didn't sound like him, he said, 'Keep away from Ambis! Go away from here! You will not have her. You will not take her from us, Bunjil.'

'Bunjil?' Matt was frowning.

'I know who you are! You are not welcome in these parts,' and then he resumed his howl.

'Matt, go back inside and call Uncle Johnny at the surf shop, the number's on the noticeboard above the till.'

Holiday makers on their way back from the beach were hanging back, reluctant to approach the scene.

Merryn sat on the other end of Elwood's bench and spoke to him in calming tones. 'It's alright, Elwood. Johnny is coming, it's alright.' But the wailing continued.

Johnny's van came into view. Johnny jumped out. 'Come on old boy, let's get you home and settle you down with a nice cup of tea.'

'He's in there. Get him out!' Elwood wailed.

'He's talking about Matt,' said Merryn.

Johnny looked puzzled. 'Come on, me old mate. Matt is allowed to be in there, let's get you home.' He managed to bundle Elwood into his van and drove him away still making an awful sound.

Merryn went back to the gallery feeling shaken. 'I'm so sorry. I've no idea what all that was about!'

'He's a bit of a case, isn't he?' Matt looked worried.

'You could say that. We have a few in Porth Taran,' she laughed, attempting to shrug off her own concern.

'I guess it's normal that strangers aren't welcome in such a small community.'

'Please don't think that. We are overrun with visitors every year, and without them we wouldn't have a livelihood. We like visitors in Porth Taran. Elwood is just old, and he gets crankier as the years go by.'

'He was in the pub the day I arrived, at your birthday bash.'

'He got rather drunk that night.'

'It was weird; he didn't take his eyes off me the whole time. Think I'd better steer clear.' He paused, 'Do you know if he's ever been to Australia?'

'I shouldn't think so. 'I think the furthest Elwood has ever been is Truro. Why do you ask?'

'He mentioned Bunjil.'

'Yes, what is that? Have you heard of it?'

'Bunjil is the Aboriginal God of creation. My Grandfather told me the stories when I was small.'

'That's strange. I think Elwood just has a vivid imagination, he must know that you're Australian. He must have looked it up. He's simply embroidered the whole thing. I know he reads a lot. They say the walls of his house are lined from top to bottom with bookshelves, though I've never been there.' She sighed shaking her head. 'Come on. At least we can go to the beach now. Let's grab those pasties and hope they haven't gone too cold!'

Jack Jewell looked out over the ocean from the clifftop at Tregarron and breathed deeply. This was what he lived for, this landscape that he had known all his life. This landscape that changed every time he laid eyes on it. Some days it was dark and threatening, its turbulence enveloping your soul, and on others its frivolous blues and vibrant yellows teased you to good humour; that's how his father had described it. He'd said this was a land for all feelings with the power to change those that entered there. Today, the landscape was joyful with an azure sea ruffled playfully by a teasing breeze. At his feet the dogs circled and sniffed, scrabbling here and there when they picked up the scent of a rabbit or a fox. This spot was Jack's favourite. He visited every day as he checked the perimeter wall of the farm. Just beyond the wall the land also belonged to Tregarron but it fell away steeply to the granite cliffs and the Atlantic Ocean below. The walls, built more than a hundred years before, stopped the dairy cattle that were bred and raised here, from venturing too near the cliffs and falling to the sea below. From here, he could see Port Taran in the distance, nestled in a crease of the rocky coastline. Fishing boats were skirting around the Lizard peninsula, some heading in and out of Porth Taran's tiny harbour. Further out, ships sailed steadily towards Penzance and Lands' End, and on to Ireland, or the West Coast of France.

As a child he had spent many hours sitting on this wall watching them. He would imagine the Mayflower departing from Plymouth and travelling past Porth Taran and past Tregarron on its way to the Americas. This wall wouldn't have been there then but Tregarron Farm was. It had survived almost four centuries. Centuries of farming families just like his with their joys and disappointments, their tragedies and their celebrations.

He turned to return to the farmhouse but realised he was still clutching the posy of wild flowers that he had gathered on his walk. He bent over and picked up the wilted posy of the day before from the base of the wall and replaced it with the fresh one. He held the wilting stems high and released them into the wind. He watched as they were quickly whisked along the cliff and then disappeared from view.

Merryn stayed rather longer on the beach than she should have done and by the time she got back to the gallery there were quite a few customers waiting for her to open up. The till rang all afternoon. Just as business died down, the man from Praa Sands arrived with a delivery of wind chimes.

It was late when she had finished unpacking the chimes and hanging them on display. At last she could get back to work on her fire tree. She could feel a lightness and an excitement about her new friendship. She admired the buds nestling in the sketched branches like flaming eggs of shiny scarlet and amber. Jewels suspended ready to burst forth and give life. A continual cycle of reproduction and regeneration. Now for some open flowers, blossoming radiantly, in the prime of their life before they would wither and set seed. She rummaged in her tile fragments and retrieved as many pieces of crimson china as she could find. Some were already the right shape and others needed to be chipped and sanded to the shape of teardrops, sometimes narrow and widening at the tip or symmetrical ellipses with pointed ends. Then she found some bright yellow porcelain and through a process of trial and error she managed to fashion a number of stamens. It took at least an hour to amass enough parts for just four or five blooms. Just a handful of blossoms would be enough to bring a natural joy to the canopy.

Outside, in the harbour, the air was still and warm. On the opposite headland The Ship's tables were thronging with visitors who'd piled in for an early evening drink on its sun-drenched terraces. Couples were walking arm in arm along the port towards the sea. She watched them feeling an uncharacteristic envy. Matt Bunda was quite something; he was intelligent and funny. She couldn't help feeling a familiarity with him that she knew was impossible. He was so different from the awkward or brash boys she'd known at school or even Rowan. Dear, sweet Rowan with his aloof but kindly manner. Matt Bunda was thoughtful and curious and, Bea was right, he was good looking too.

Her thoughts were interrupted when Johnny pushed open the gallery door.

'Buy you a drink?'

'You owe me a large one,' she said sternly.

'I need to talk to you,' said Johnny frowning.

'Do you?' said Merryn a little taken aback, for Johnny was rarely serious. 'Is Elwood alright?'

'See you at The Ship in, say twenty minutes?'

Merryn nodded.

She sighed and covered her mosaic with the drape; it would have to wait until tomorrow. She emptied the till of cash and stowed the money sack in her handbag.

When she reached the pub, Rowan was at the bar ordering drinks. 'Merryn! What can I get you?'

'Just a scrumpy for me, please.'

Rowan beamed; this was turning out to be a good week.

'You seen Uncle Johnny?'

'He's outside on the south deck.'

Johnny was sitting at one of the wooden tables, leaning against the whitewashed wall of the pub. His mood appeared restored for his eyes lit up when he saw her. 'Ah, my favourite niece,' he chirruped.

'And your only niece!' she laughed.

He stood up and took his wallet out of the back pocket of his jeans.

'It's OK Rowan is getting me a drink.' She sat down on the opposite side of the table. 'Now, what's up?'

Johnny's face resumed its solemnity. 'Look, I'm sorry about all this stuff with Elwood, I don't know what's got into him.'

'I just don't understand why you're taking so much notice of him. Is he having some kind of breakdown?'

'He's OK. I mean, his body's OK, his arms are pretty badly burnt. There's something wrong though.'

'How do you mean?'

'He keeps going on about you and asking if you're safe.'

'Me?'

'He's asking for Ambis.' Johnny avoided her gaze and glanced down nervously into his beer.

Her reflex reaction was to say it was all nonsense but she knew Uncle Johnny cared deeply about Elwood. 'I don't really understand any of it. Do you know why he calls me Ambis?'

Johnny shook his head. 'I want to ask, but I don't want to encourage him.' He took a sip of beer. 'He kept on and on saying you were in some kind of danger.'

'He's getting on a bit, our Elwood. Perhaps he's just losing it.'

Johnny ran his finger up the side of his pint glass, tracing the path the bubbles were taking to the surface. 'He was shouting another strange name too.'

'Yes, he did that outside the gallery as well. What was it?' She tried to remember. 'Bunjil, he said. That was it, Bunjil.'

'That's right. The thing is, I'm not sure it's his usual mumbo jumbo. He was so frightened.'

'Matt said Bunjil is the name of the aboriginal god of creation.'

'Eh?'

'Yes, I know. I am not called Ambis and I am certainly not in any danger. I think you're right to be worried about him but please don't start worrying about me. I promise you, Uncle Johnny, I am just fine.'

Johnny lent back on the bench and took a long drink. 'You're right, he is getting on, poor Elwood. And, for all his madness, he's alright is Elwood.' Johnny took a breath in and in a small awkward voice he said, 'You know, I trust him.'

'But why do you care so much?'

He looked out to sea and pursed his lips and sighed. 'We just go back a long way, that's all.'

Rowan appeared looking hot and flustered with a tray of drinks. 'It's packed in there and I'm parched!'

'Thanks Rowan, but I've got a hot date.' Johnny picked up the fresh pint from the tray and glugged it down in one go. He looked up at Merryn and Rowan's startled expressions. 'Well it's Friday isn't it?' and he strode down the steps taking them two at a time.

Merryn was shaking her head and smiling. 'I swear, that man will never quite grow up.'

'I hope I don't either,' said Rowan with a mischievous twinkle.

'Do you know why he takes so much care of Elwood?'

He shrugged. 'Ah, I think he's just a good guy - you know he'd do pretty much anything for anyone.'

'Hey you guys!' Beatrice appeared at the top of the steps. 'They told me at the bar you were up here. I've got an idea!'

Rowan and Merryn exchanged glances and smiled; Beatrice was always having ideas and some of them had been quite mad.

'What this time?' they said in unison.

'Well, I was thinking. It's not often someone new comes to the village, and certainly not our age. How about we give that Matt a warm Cornish welcome?'

'I think that's a great idea, but what do you have in mind?' asked Merryn.

'How about a barbie on the beach? Say tomorrow? We could get a few of the guys together with the guitars and that way he'd know a few more people. I was going to suggest it anyway, I mean autumn won't be long and we usually do our annual bash about now.'

'Alright, I'm up for that. Great idea I'll borrow the big barbecue from the surf school and duck into Helston for some meat.' Rowan's face fell.

'What's the matter?'

'I don't get paid until the end of the month.'

Merryn made a face and took the cash sack from her handbag. She pulled out two twenty-pound notes. 'That should cover a bit of meat and stuff, everyone will bring some booze and food anyway, and we always end up with too much.'

'I'll make the salads then,' said Bea.

SIX

Elwood was in his sitting room. He stared at the Eightfold wheel of the year that was pinned to the wall above the fireplace. He loved the names of the druidic festivals; Samhain, Alban Arthan, Imbolc, Alban Eilir, Beltane, Alban Hefin, Lughnasadh. He liked to chant them; it felt calming. Alban Elfed was approaching, and he must seize his chance. He must be ready. He looked down at his bandaged hands and sighed. He could not even carry out a ritual for a speedy recovery without help. He knew he couldn't fight Bunjil alone. A mere pagan in the face of the God of creation; he stood little chance. He must see the High Priestess if he was to protect Porth Taran and Ambis. He must see her in good time. If only Johnny had the spirits like Ambis, then he would understand the danger. He would realise Ambis must be venerated and protected and that Bunjil's powers may be greater even than hers. They could fight Bunjil together.

The clock struck seven and Elwood heaved himself to his feet. Ambis would be heading for the gallery soon and he must go for his daily stroll before she arrived. He slipped his feet uncomfortably into his boots. Johnny had fastened the laces so that they were tight enough for the boots to stay on his feet and loose enough to slip them on and off without having to use his hands. He pulled on his trench coat and tucked the staff in the crook of his elbow and set off out of the front door and down Main Street towards the harbour.

The sky was clear, and the harbour was swathed in a thin yellow mist. Halfway down the hill he turned off Main Street to cut through the back streets to the beach. He stood on the green right on the cliff edge and breathed in the salty air. He could never fathom how people could live in Truro, suffocated by the traffic and buildings when all this was just a drive away. The sea was glassy and the air unusually warm for the early hour. The temperature had been steadily rising for a few days now. He let his staff drop into the marram grass at his feet and stared out at the ocean. He fixed his gaze on the curvature of the horizon. He held his arms out to his sides and then closed his eyes. He visualised himself standing upright, his arms asunder on the spinning globe, leaning towards the moon, then away from it. The sun flickering its orbit around the Earth with him, Elwood Curnow, on its prow. Blessed to be invited, blessed to know it and blessed to feel it. He stayed like that for a few minutes. Unable to hold his staff in his hands, he could not offer his usual morning exaltation, so instead he murmured it under his breath.

'Under the power of the sun and of the sky, of the speed of lightning and the force of the wind, I go forth today from this rock, that is my foundation, to protect this village and all those who take shelter here.' He closed his eyes for a moment then took a bow towards the east.

When he opened them again he felt nourished and renewed. He looked around him. Only the oyster catchers were stirring, digging and prodding at the sand, their bright orange beaks illuminated in the morning light. The sand was swept smooth by the last tide but for the tracks of sea birds looking for a meal. The beach cafe wouldn't be open for hours and the holiday makers were still entrenched in slumber.

He bent down, awkwardly hooked his staff over his arm and headed towards the lifeguard hut. He crossed the green towards the harbour road. As he neared the church, he turned in along the lane that ran behind the shops but as he stepped into it he saw there was a barricade. A digger stood abandoned by a gaping hole that stretched across the full width of the road. Just a few days he had been out of action and already something had changed. He stopped and looked to see if there was a way past, but his only way around would be by the church. The great edifice stood at the entrance to the little port, on an outcrop of rock. There was only one pavement running right alongside it. Elwood shuddered, he crossed the street to walk down the road on the opposite side, as near to the great harbour wall as he could without scraping himself on its rough stone. He quickened his step and as he came level with the church, his head began to swim, his ears heated up and he swallowed and held his breath until he was well clear. Then he breathed deeply again once the danger was passed. He reached the bench outside the gallery and sat down heavily and waited for his head to still. The sun was already making its way from the east, and it wouldn't be long before Ambis arrived. He sat there on the bench and waited.

Merryn stepped out of the front door of Little Rosewarne into the sunshine. A sense of excitement had been with her since Bea had suggested the party. It felt like an age since they had arranged one altogether. This one felt more special than the others. She would drop in on Matt later to invite him and hoped that Bea hadn't got there first. The weather was really warming up and the feeling of the crisp fresh morning sunshine swirling around her bare legs was luxuriating. From a distance she could see that Elwood was already on his bench. She swallowed and consciously deflected a twinge of alarm.

'Morning Elwood, feeling better?'

'Good morning, Ambis.' He stood up pushing on his elbows to propel him upright and took a bow. 'I am on my way to recovery,' he said importantly.

'Glad to hear it, Elwood.'

He looked more like himself. He'd shed his coat, revealing his thin wizened arms still swathed in bandages from just below the elbows. She'd never noticed just how thin he was. She wondered if his lunchtime pasty was his only meal, she began to understand Johnny's concern. This man was alone in the world.

She unlocked the gallery and as she closed the door behind her she looked through it to the harbour beyond. Uncle Jack's Lugger was rocking a little on the rising tide, the deck was empty. She must wait for Elwood to leave before she could visit Matt; there was no point provoking a repeat of yesterday. The sooner she got into the gallery, the sooner Elwood would be on his way.

She pulled back the drape from her mosaic. The firebuds had dried nicely and the stamens she had cut were where she'd left them. She laid them out angled in varying directions some in full bloom and others semi-open. She set them amongst the charcoal sketched branches and adjusted them until she was happy with their positions before dabbing them in to place with the glue.

The air in the little shop was becoming heavy. She pushed the kitchen window ajar and then propped the front door open to allow a light, flowing breeze to dance amongst the chimes. The bench in the street was empty. She'd been so concentrated that she hadn't noticed Elwood leave. She glanced over at the Lugger but it was closed up; Matt would have gone to work by now. Her stomach fluttered both with excitement and anticipation. Merryn had never felt anything like this before. She'd always thought 'love', well, the romantic kind, was vapid and an illusion, but now she was beginning to understand. Whenever she came near him she could sense a powerful draw, was this chemistry? She smiled and turned to her mosaic pieces, carefully gluing them fragment by fragment in just the right place.

She worked until lunchtime uninterrupted. The heat had driven the holidaymakers to the beach and Porth Taran was quiet. When she looked up the clock showed half past twelve. The harbour road was beginning to bustle with tourists looking for somewhere to eat. She turned the sign on the gallery door to closed, locked up and set out for the visitors' centre.

Upstairs in the weather station, Matt was sitting in front of a bank of computer screens.

'Hello, I wasn't sure if you'd be working on a Saturday,' said Merryn.

'Well, you are, so I figured I may as well too.' He winked.

Merryn managed to suppress a blush. 'There is more to Porth Taran than just hanging out with me.'

'I don't believe you.'

'I was just wondering if you would like to come to a barbecue on the beach tonight. If you're not busy, of course.'

'Hmm, let me consult my diary. He leant back in his chair and looked at the ceiling screwing up his eyes. He snapped back quickly. 'Definitely free. Yes please, sounds good.' He broke into a broad smile and held her gaze. 'What's the occasion?'

'Oh, we do it every year. You know the old gang from school and anyone else who wants to join in. It's fun!'

'Well, then, how can I refuse?!'

'It can get quite chilly after the sun goes down and the breeze off the Atlantic kicks in, so we like to start early, say five o'clock? I'll drop by and we can walk down together.'

'Excellent, though I can't see it being chilly tonight. The heat is rising and it's going to be a scorcher. I'm keeping an eye on it. We could be heading for a record for Porth Taran.'

'Really?'

He clicked on one of the screens in front of him.

'Check this out.' A graph flashed up with a number of abbreviations along the bottom of it. 'We could be about to smash the UK record and set a new highest temperature.'

'Well, that'll be perfect for the barbecue then.'

Matt frowned. 'It's rather strange. The last record was set in Faversham in Kent in 2003. Cornwall has never come near breaking the record before. I shall have to keep an eye on it this afternoon.'

'Oh, that is a shame. I was hoping you might like a break and go for a walk on the beach.'

'When I say keep an eye on it, it doesn't mean I have to stay here. You see all the data is fed to these computers and I can look at it later. The only thing I have to check manually is rainwater and that's irrelevant at the moment because there hasn't been a drop since I arrived, well apart from the drizzle on my first night.'

'So, is that a yes to a walk on the beach?'

'Sure is, let's go.'

The beach was seething with holidaymakers. There was barely a space to swim between the lifeguard's flags. Families had set up their parasols for shade as the heat was really beginning to beat down. The light was reflecting off the sea, adding to the glare.

'I think there'll be a rush on the docs on Monday, I can see this lot turning red in minutes,' laughed Merryn.

'You know, it's not fashionable to be brown in Australia.'

'Isn't it? Here, we go to any lengths for brown skin. Fake tan and sunbeds are all the rage. Then they'd have to be because we don't get much really sunny weather. Well, not in the rest of the UK, just Porth Taran.'

'Australian girls like to keep out of the sun, they think white skin is better.'

'You're nice and brown though.'

'He looked down at his arm. 'Yeah, I guess, but it's not a tan you're looking at, it's my natural colour. We are dark in our family.'

'I was wondering about that. I did ask the other day, are you Greek or Italian?'

He shook his head and looked away.

'What's the matter? Have I said something wrong?'

'No, no, you haven't.' He breathed in. 'It's just, my heritage is entirely Australian. I don't mean fifth or sixth generation, I mean since forever.'

'You mean...'

He nodded. 'I'm a native Australian, aboriginal. Well at least half. I don't know who my father was, but I'm pretty sure he was white, or I would be a lot darker.'

'I see.'

'Does that shock you?'

'No. I mean it shocks me that you don't know who your father is. I mean it must be awful not knowing.'

Matt shrugged. 'I dunno, some facts you live with all your life, I guess. It's not shocking to me, just old hat.'

'Yes, I know what you mean, actually. 'I can see your aboriginal features now. You don't seem very proud of your heritage.'

'Oh, on the contrary, I am! I am very proud. You see I was born on Palm Island, I showed you on the atlas? It's an aboriginal mission. Actually, it was a penal colony in the old days. My people have not been well treated and Aboriginals struggle with alcohol. They drink too much, break the law and often wind up in jail. It's given them a bad reputation.'

'That's so sad.'

'It is sad. Western ways just don't suit my people. In Australia, I hide my origins, if I can. My features give me away to some. I wait until I know people well, at least better than just an acquaintance. You see there are still plenty to judge us. On the one hand, the state goes to extreme lengths to embrace our culture by supporting our artists and musicians, but on the other, the stigma is still very much alive and kicking.'

'What, you mean racists?'

'That's right. I wasn't sure about coming here. You know being badly received because of it, for being different.'

'Well, that would surprise me. As you may have noticed there are very few ethnic minorities in this area, but that's because there is so little work, not because they wouldn't be accepted.'

'Yeah? Good to know.' He glanced up at the cliff. 'You see that bird?'

'Where?'

'Up there, above the cliff. It's floating on the therms.'

Merryn looked up, there was a large black bird hovering with its wing tips splayed like fingers.

'What type is it?'

'Probably a buzzard, they often hover there.'

'A jet-black buzzard? That's cool.'

Merryn looked again. It was hovering over Rinsey Head. It was crow-like, and its beak a bright red-orange. 'Actually, I don't think that is a buzzard.' She screwed up her eyes. 'It could be a chough.' She looked closer and then stood up. 'I've only ever seen them at the bird sanctuary. They're native to here but they almost died out, they've been trying to reintroduce them.'

'Back home, if we see a man o' war flying, the elders say that there is bad weather on the way.'

'A man o' war?'

'Yeah, it's a huge black seabird. Bigger than that. Every time I saw one, sure enough, right behind it, was a storm.'

'And look at us basking in the sunshine!' Merryn sat down again and stretched out on her back, on the sand, feeling its heat on the back of her neck.

Matt went quiet.

Merryn opened an eye. 'What's wrong?'

'This is a pattern I have seen before. The weather heating and heating until it bursts. We could be in for a huge storm.'

'Not in Porth Taran. We don't have storms here.'

'Listen, there's something I need to check, I think I have to get back. You coming?'

'I'll lie here for a bit. I'll come and fetch you later, for the party.'

He leaned over to her, kissed her quickly on the cheek, stood up and was gone.

Merryn lay in the sand feeling a little startled. She touched her cheek. She closed her eyes to feel the place where his lips had touched her.

SEVEN

Merryn lay in the sun until she could feel herself cooking. She clambered to her feet, dusted the sand from her clothing and wandered back through Porth Taran's sleepy sun-drenched streets. There was no one around. While the holidaymakers were on the beach, the locals must have been driven into the cool of their houses. Beads of perspiration formed on her brow, she couldn't remember a time it had ever been as hot as this.

She unlocked the gallery and turned the sign back to open. As she stepped inside, she realised that she had forgotten to cover her mosaic and as the sunlight flashed off the glass of the opening door, the firebuds and open blossoms glowed against the brown backdrop of the board. Set amongst emerald leaves and a cerulean sky, the effect would be magical. Now, for the leaves, the receptacles of life that spread open to the light, to soak up the energy. They should be strong and armoured, yet elegant. They must be always able to feed and nurture with whatever the elements provided to ensure the foundations, the flowers and the fruit could continue to generate year after year.

She pulled out her crockery drawer and rummaged for a rich dark green, she would need a lot of it. Finding nothing suitable she went to her kitchen and glanced through the cupboards. There was a tall, earthenware jug glazed dark green. She didn't think she'd ever used it; a discarded receptacle to be transformed into a giver of life. She took it from the cupboard and wrapped it in a cloth and began to hammer it into large chunks. Should they be spiky or smooth? Large or small? It would depend on the conditions the tree would have to survive. Conifers have needles to protect them from excessive evaporation in strong summer heat, and from the cold in sub-zero temperatures. She looked up to the trees on the headland by Finn McGann's. Those leaves were thick and jagged, almost macabre. Then, behind the supermarket, she could see the tops of the horse chestnuts, poorly suited to the coastal winds, their leaves stained with salt burn. Yet they still grew prolifically all over the village; they were fighters.

Darkest chromite cobalt green and olive and then cadmium green for the newest leaves. She sifted through her box of broken greens and laid every piece out on her board. She set about cutting them to size, fashioning them into sharp triangles, and softer ovals, and long thin needles. She positioned them in clusters of differing hues within the canopy sketch line. She stood back and then rearranged the lighter shades to point in the same direction as if the sun was shining on them from the top right-hand corner. Like hands splayed to catch the sun, caressing the wind and washed by the rain.

She touched her cheek and closed her eyes and felt her stomach swoop with anticipation. Love, like the sun, the rain and the wind, is powerful and today, for the first time, she knew it.

The chimes on the door jangled and Rowan appeared carrying a stack of cardboard boxes. 'Here, give us a hand.'

'What's all that?' she asked absently, still in the thrall of her work.

'The meat.'

'Oh, of course, sorry. How much did you get? This looks like it could feed an army!'

Rowan was looking especially pleased with himself. 'Loads and loads, I've had to store it all in the surf shop fridge and at your mum's, but I've run out of space. Have you got any room in yours?'

'How on earth did you manage that with just forty pounds?'

'I went to that wholesale meat place this morning in Helston and their fridges have given out with the heat. They can't get anyone to mend them until Monday, so they had to get rid of everything.'

'Wow, I hope we'll have enough people to eat it all.'

'Aw, no worries there, not with Bea on the case! I've got The Celtic Crackers to come down and play and Johnny's ordered a barrel of Spingo from the Blue Anchor. It's gonna be the party of the year!'

'Wow, that's brilliant! Beatrice will be so pleased.'

Rowan glanced down at the mosaic. 'Is that your new one?'

Merryn quickly covered it over with the drape. 'It's not ready yet!' She could never bear to share her unfinished work lest the opinions of others coloured its development and took it away from its natural path.

His face fell.

'Oh, Rowan, I'm sorry. It doesn't matter, honestly. Don't take me too seriously.'

He leaned over and took her hand.

She flinched and started to pull away but he tightened his grip.

'Merry, I do take you seriously. I take you very seriously indeed.' His voice faded to a whisper.

She snatched her hand away to push an imaginary strand of hair out of her face.

'I came to ask you... if you would come with me to the party tonight.'

'To the party?' Merryn stalled. Dear, sweet Rowan who she'd been friends with all her life stood in front of her like a nervous child.

'Yeah, to the party.'

'Well, of course I'm coming to the party. You know I am.' She began to fiddle with the drape.

'Yes, but what I want to know is. Will you come with me?' He was looking at her directly now. His expression was serious.

'Come with you? Has Uncle Johnny put you up to this?'

'No, of course not! Look, I've always liked you, Merryn.'

'And I've always liked you and that's why we're friends.'

'Merryn, it's more than just like, it always has been.'

Merryn wanted him to stop. 'Thank you for asking me, it's really very sweet of you. But, you see, I've already agreed to collect Matt to take him to the barbecue.'

Rowan's face darkened. 'I see.'

'But we'll all be there, we can party like we always do,' she said brightly. 'Do you remember all those beach parties we used to have, even when it was freezing cold? And having to run away from PC Fenton who was desperate to catch us drinking underage.'

'Yeah, fun wasn't it?' He was trying to sound upbeat, but a look of dejection cloaked his face. 'Well, never mind, perhaps another time.'

Merryn didn't answer.

'Don't forget to bring the meat, will you?' He turned and left the gallery, his shoulders hunched.

Merryn sat back down at her workbench. Rowan, her dearest, oldest friend had feelings for her. Where had that come from? They were friends. That was all they were. Had she missed the signs? Had she led him on?

She'd known him as long as she could remember. Right, from that first day at primary school in reception they'd been friends. She remembered the jumper, his mum had knitted for him. It was a grey V-neck, trimmed with a red stripe. He was always bringing things to school that he'd found on the weekend, a bird's nest fallen out of a hedge, a fossil and once he brought a slow worm in a cardboard box and all together, as a class, they had rereleased it into the undergrowth at the edge of the school playing field.

It was always the three of them that hung out in the playground, Merryn, Rowan and Bea. Then they went on to secondary school together. Bea became more distant then. She made new friends and widened her circle. For Rowan and Merryn nothing really changed. They stuck together and carried on as before. He'd never let slip about his feelings for her, if they were, in fact, long harboured. Maybe this had come about because Matt had arrived. It was true, she had never been interested in anyone, not anyone who had paid her any attention. Merryn hoped that this wouldn't mean the end of their friendship, it mattered too much to her. She sipped at a bottle of water and gazed out of the window at the harbour where the air was as thick as treacle and there was no movement in the halyards. The tide was ebbing and the majority of the boats were perched inert on the sandy harbour floor drained of sea water. She sighed and began to glue the leaves in place.

Elwood got off the bus at Penzance Bus Station. Three tramps were sitting on the pavement, leaning against the tourist office, they were surrounded by an array of carrier bags stuffed with what looked like jumble. One of them had fallen asleep with a plastic litre bottle of beer resting on his chest. Another was sat up, blankly staring straight ahead and the third was lying face down on the pavement. He stepped over him carefully. It wouldn't be long before the police turned up to move them on. Poor buggers! He would've tossed them a couple of coins to buy meths but his hands were too sore.

His mother had told him he'd end up like that if he didn't pull his finger out. He'd thought he would too. 'Tainted' she'd called him. After all that business at the church, if he couldn't find God she'd said, he couldn't find anything. But she was wrong. Her God had almost finished him off. His gods had saved him. It was the heritage of the old ways that had given him his deep sense of belonging. Druidry and Wiccan had been his rock for many years. They had given him the power to control his life.

And then Ambis was born and he knew that Porth Taran was blessed and its people would be safe so long as she watched over them. He remembered when he'd first seen those magical eyes. Demelza Jewell was wheeling her around Porth Taran and she'd just learned to sit up and look out at the world around her. Those eyes had seared his soul. Straight away he'd known that Ambis wasn't like her father. She was much more special. She hadn't inherited his quick temper and impulsiveness. She looked at things long and hard, always thinking and absorbing. Even the weather had changed, it was as if the climate smiled when Ambis arrived.

When she'd taken her first steps she was immediately steady on her feet. He remembered how, when she was a little older, and she used to walk up the hill holding onto her mother's hand, she would stop outside his house and peer through the agapanthus at him while he sat in his deck chair. He would wave, and she would giggle and wave back. Then on the very first day of Ambis's twenty-first year, evil had come to the village. He should have planned for this, he should have prepared rituals well in advance.

He crossed the bridge over the dry dock to walk along the prom. It was cooler here for there was a wind blowing from the south. He felt a chill and pulled his coat on. He glanced back in the direction of Rinsey Head and Porth Taran. The headland was clearly visible even ten miles away. The difference in temperature between Penzance and Porth Taran was always stark, though he had never known it so warm over there yet here it was cold enough to wear a coat.

He watched the orange sails of the sailing club dinghies darting round the bay veering towards St Michael's Mount then disappearing behind it to reappear tacking through the white crested waves. Penzance was teeming with people. Cars lined the streets outside Jubilee Pool and the tables outside the Bosun's Locker were already filling up for lunch.

He pushed on along the seafront. Should he have been more vigilant? What could he have done to divert this threat of evil? Only Trevina could guide him now. He turned away from the sea to climb the hill past Penlee Park, the library and into town. His joints were aching by the time he reached the bottom of Causeway Head. He glanced up at the steepest street in Penzance and groaned. He tried to relieve the pain by leaning on a wall and stretching his legs out behind him. He sighed and trudged painfully up the hill until he reached *Mind's Eye,* Trevina's shop. He rested outside to catch his breath and recited a little chant to be sure there would be no other customers within.

He stepped inside and as he'd hoped, the shop was deserted. There was no sign of Trevina either, but he could hear her voice, even and rhythmic coming from somewhere within. He waited patiently for her to sense his presence; it was never good to interrupt someone at their work, it could have devastating consequences. He didn't have to wait long for the distant chanting quieted and she appeared silently in front of him. She was not much older than Ambis. Her hair was the colour of mahogany and reaching to her waist it swung like silk.

'Elwood.' Her voice was soft. She frowned when she saw his hands. 'Come, you are troubled. Come and sit with me awhile.'

He followed her into the back room. He bent down painfully to sit on the cushions strewn around the wooden floor. When he was settled he looked up into her feline eyes that shone emerald in the half light of the back room. He marvelled at the wisdom and serenity that emanated from such a young woman.

She listened carefully as he told her of Bunjil, and of Ambis and the threat to the village. When he had finished she remained silent for a time, her frown deepening. Then she raised a finger and shook it, admonishingly at him.

'You should know better than to trifle with fire spells, Elwood. It is not for the uninitiated.'

Elwood could feel heat rising from his neck.

'Evil spirits approach us in many forms,' said Trevina solemnly, 'But the most common of all come from within ourselves.'

Elwood held his tongue as he struggled with the outrage that was welling up inside. Had he not already undergone the humiliation of counting the doctor's fingers and answering what year it was? And now, in his own area of expertise, was he to be questioned?

'You believe that this Australian is Bunjil?'

He nodded.

'Tell me why you think this.'

'I can sense it. One night in The Ship. I saw him staring at Ambis. Then, later, during the night, I woke with this name in my head. I had never heard it before but when I discovered that Bunjil is the Aboriginal god of creation, you know, in Dreamtime culture. I looked it up. Well, it all came clear. He's Australian,' he said with conviction.

'As much as I know that Bunjil is all powerful, he is not evil. It may simply be that this young man has fallen for your Ambis. She is beautiful, is she not?'

Elwood nodded. 'Very.'

'Then, you may be mistaken. I must consult the High Priest before I can give you advice. In the meantime, I advise you to carry out a simple ritual to keep this Australian at a distance, if indeed he does pose a threat to Ambis and Porth Taran. But, you must not harm him. Do you understand?' She waved a finger at him again.

'I will not harm him.' Elwood tried to slough off the intense feeling of disappointment that was besieging him.

'A standard hex of isolation should be enough and as soon as I have heard back from the High Priest I will be in touch.'

Elwood, recovering his composure, nodded reluctantly. Still, at least he had been right to consult. Trevina would only call on the High Priest for serious matters. He, himself had only ever seen him from a distance at ceremonies. His face was always obscured from view in his great hooded cloak. He wondered if this might be his chance to actually speak with him.

Merryn covered over the board carefully with a layer of cling film to guard from the heat drying the glue too quickly, and pulled the drape over the top. She packed up the fragments of broken crockery and stowed them away in a tub

Her nerves for the party were rising, she took some deep breaths. She wanted nothing to spoil this evening. She wondered what it would be like to be part of a couple. She had watched Beatrice with her boyfriends and thought it must be rather claustrophobic always having to think of someone else. But then Beatrice liked that. She liked the constant attention and to be in charge, to organise everything and tell everyone what to do. It was one of the reasons Merryn liked her too. With Beatrice you never really had to think; she would organise all the entertainment, the food and even decide how everyone would get there and you could just sit back and enjoy.

Even at primary school she'd arranged elaborate hopscotch tournaments and once she had even persuaded Rowan to stand in one end of the French elastic while his friends laughed at him.

Dear, sweet Rowan with his unkempt brown hair streaked with blonde from the sun. There was no doubt that he was a very handsome young man, yet he had never had a girlfriend. Her heart leapt a beat. Could it be that …? No, that was ridiculous, he'd just had a silly idea. The heat must be getting to him. She stood in the doorway of the gallery and fanned herself with a small mosaic board.

The heat really was becoming oppressive. She'd brought her clothes for the party down to the shop that morning but with the rising temperature she would have to go home and have a shower before she went to call for Matt. She smiled to herself. This must be the first time she had ever consciously planned what she would wear to something more than an hour beforehand. She'd even brought make-up with her. She almost never wore it. Perhaps she was becoming a grown up at last, she giggled to herself.

Elwood arrived back in the heat of Porth Taran. He could see Ambis standing in the doorway of the gallery. The little port was crowded with holidaymakers and locals filled the tables outside The Ship. An ice cream van was parked at the head of the harbour, the queues were winding right up the street into the supermarket car park.

His hands were sweating beneath the bandages and he felt uncomfortable. He couldn't remember a time when it was ever as hot as this. Even those seemingly endless days of his childhood when the summer holidays were spent jumping into the sea from the harbour wall. He glanced over to the spot just outside The Ship where he'd tried out more and more inventive acrobatics as he leapt off the quayside into the cool water. Youngsters who'd discarded their wetsuits in favour of board shorts were congregating on the harbour wall watching for the tide to come in far enough to resume their antics. He envied them. He looked back over at the gallery and he could see Ambis moving around inside now. Satisfied that she was safe, he shed his jacket and walked around the head of the harbour and past the surf shop. The heat was making him tired.

Johnny and Rowan were sitting on upturned buckets outside. Both had their tops off and they were chatting animatedly.

'You coming tonight, Elwood?' called Johnny.

'Coming? To what?'

'Bea has organised a beach barbecue. The Celtic Crackers'll be there and a barrel of Spingo, I'll call for you if you like?'

Elwood hesitated. 'You're alright, I'll make my own way.'

Johnny shrugged. 'Proper job.' And he stuck his thumbs up.

He scurried on up the hill. This was his chance. Everyone would be there; it would be the perfect opportunity to carry out his ritual. Then he glanced down at his hands. It wasn't going to be easy with the bandages. He got back to his house and glanced up at the moon chart on the sitting room wall. It was going to be full, there was no time to lose. He would need something belonging to Bunjil, if his hex was going to be effective. He took a deep breath, it could be dangerous if Bunjil retaliated.

Merryn, showered and changed at home. She pulled on a blue mini dress from her wardrobe for the temperatures didn't look as if they were going to cool. She slipped on her best leather flip flops. She carefully applied eyeliner, mascara and lipstick. She looked back at herself in the mirror and was pleased.

She had never chased after anyone in her life but there was something about Matt Bunda that she could not ignore. He wasn't brash or arrogant like so many of the surfer dudes she went to school with. His smile, his laugh and his innate gentleness were captivating.

She set off, stopping by the gallery to collect the meat before calling for Matt. She could see that the Lugger was closed up. He must still be at the weather station.

Carrie was tidying up the office at the back of the visitors' centre.

'Looking forward to the party tonight, Merryn?'

'Should be a good one! Are you coming?'

'Wouldn't miss it. Alright if I bring the kids?'

'Of course, the more the merrier.'

Carrie looked her up and down. 'You look rather nice.' She raised one eyebrow. 'You got a hot date?'

Merryn blushed to her roots. 'What in Porth Taran? I should be so lucky.' And she quickly climbed the stairs to the weather station.

Matt was sitting in front of the bank of screens. All the windows were open yet the air was still and heavy. 'Jeez no one told me it could get this hot over here.'

'To be honest, that's because it doesn't. Well, not normally. I can't remember a summer this hot, ever.'

Matt frowned as he stared at one of the screens.

'What's the matter?'

'It's probably nothing ...'

'But?'

'Well, if I had this collection of data in Townsville I would say that there was to be a real dramatic storm. You see this heat is building and building, but all around there,' he pointed at the map around Penzance. 'The air is cooler and it's set to get colder with the arrival of a front from this direction.' He gestured at the Irish Sea. 'When the two fronts meet we're in for some trouble.'

'What kind of trouble?'

'If we were in Australia I would say tornadoes.'

'Tornadoes, here in Porth Taran?'

'I've been on to Culdrose weather station but they've told me to stick to learning about our weather before I go trying to predict disasters.' He rolled his eyes.

'Charming!'

'Yeah, well. Maybe they're right, I am a rookie, after all. There's nothing else I can do; I've told them. I've done my duty even though I may have been ridiculed in the process.' He tore himself away from the screen and beamed at Merryn. 'Still, enough of the weather! We've got a party to get to!'

Outside, Elwood skulked in the alley that ran along the side of the visitors' centre. He'd watched as Ambis had carried her heavy bag inside. He leant inside the recess of a boarded-up doorway, a good way back from the entrance, where he would not easily be spotted and waited. He prayed that Ambis and Bunjil would leave in good time for him to slip inside before Carrie locked up.

He could hear voices and then footsteps echoing on the spiral staircase inside. He froze as he heard the deceivingly dulcet tones of Bunjil as he responded to Ambis's tinkling laughter. His courage rose as he thought of the good he would be doing for Porth Taran in protecting his realm from the evil spirits that assailed it.

Bunjil's dark head emerged from the entrance and Elwood's pulse quickened. He pressed himself flat against the boarding in the recess. She was clearly under his spell for they were lost in each other. He could see they were not likely to glance up towards him hiding in the alleyway. They turned and walked away from him, their voices fading in the distance.

Elwood sidled further up the alley and peeped through the main entrance. The clock on the wall said five, he had plenty of time; Carrie wouldn't lock up until half past. He couldn't see her behind the counter, but there were still a few tourists browsing the pamphlets and display boards. He would need to pick his moment. He slipped inside the entrance and pretended to read the posters displaying the boat trip timetables, keeping his ears carefully trained on what was happening behind him.

It wasn't long before he heard the tourists walking across to the information desk. He glanced back quickly.

Carrie appeared from the office at the back. 'Can I help you?'

'We're looking for a list of good restaurants in the area,' said the tourists.

Carrie disappeared back into the office and Elwood took his chance. He almost ran past the tourists and then tiptoed as fast as he could up the spiral staircase praying that the echo of his boots on metal did not reach Carrie's ears.

He'd never been upstairs to the Weather Station before. The room was lined with computer screens flickering. Elwood noted that they hadn't been turned off which could mean that Bunjil was planning to come back.

He must work fast. He glanced around the room until his eyes fell on a desk strewn with paper and the remains of a sandwich. As he approached it, he could feel Bunjil's energy. He braced himself and stepped bravely towards it. Over the back of the chair was a hooded jacket slung carelessly. That would be too big to carry for the hex, he needed something smaller. There was a bulge in one of the pockets. Glad of the bandages to shield his skin from the energy, he took the jacket clumsily between his bound hands and shook it upside down. A cloth pouch fell to the floor with a light thud. He bent down to look closer, it was a pair of binoculars. He clumsily scooped them up into his knapsack and headed back to the top of the stairs. He listened but there was silence. The tourists must have gone. He thought quickly. There was nothing for it, he would have to boldly walk down the stairs and face Carrie.

'Elwood! What are you doing up there?'

'Carrie! Err, I was looking for Ambis. I saw her come in here.'

'Merryn? She's already gone, Elwood. You really shouldn't be up there.'

'Oh yeah sorry, well,' he said quickly. 'I shall catch up with her at the party.'

Carrie nodded. 'I shall be there later too.'

'Right you are then. Catch you later.' And he slunk out of the door as quickly as he could.

EIGHT

As Merryn and Matt approached the beach, the screech of feedback from amplifiers echoed along the cliffs. Vans and shabby estate cars, some with boards piled on the roofs, obscured the double yellow lines all along the beach road.

'I see Bea has been on the jungle drums, it's packed!' said Merryn.

'Everywhere is packed here.'

'Only in the summer. In a couple of weeks, it'll be a ghost town. They'll all go back to their busy up-country lives and we will get to enjoy the September weather in peace. Is Australia very different to here?'

'The temperatures are, for one thing, though not today. I hear you guys surf all winter too?'

'Yeah, well the die-hards do. If you stay long enough, I am sure you will too.'

'Not a chance. Not without a titanium wetsuit.'

'Ah you softy, not as tough as us Cornish!'

'You calling me a lightweight?' Matt was smirking.

Merryn laughed. 'I'd love to go to Australia and see it all for myself.'

'Would you?' He turned and took the bag of meat from her and held her hand in his. 'Perhaps, I will get to show you one day.' He smiled and gently tugged her towards the rocky path down to the beach.

Merryn stumbled behind him, savouring the delicious feeling of his hand in hers.

The air was heavy and still. Even the sea barely made a sound as it lapped gently onto the sand. The Celtic Crackers had set up under the awning on the terrace of the café. They were doing their sound check. Rowan was standing importantly by the sound desk as they tuned up and tested the settings.

'This is a great place,' said Matt. 'A café right on the beach away from all the houses – quite a spot for a party, it's almost like home.'

'I was born here.'

'Yes, I know you were.'

'No, I mean I was born right there, in that café.'

'Really? That's where you and your mum were airlifted from?'

'That's right, I was in quite a hurry to get out, so I was born on a table in there.'

'Jeez, that must have been quite a day what with the storm and everything.'

'I think that's why everyone makes such a fuss each year.'

Merryn realised that she hadn't been to the café for a long while. The place gave her a sense of comfort each time she came. She was reminded of the summers she'd spent playing amongst the tables and chairs while Mum and Spike worked. A little way along the beach, she could see the sand dunes where, with Bea and Rowan, she used to leap from the edge of the green into a pit of sand formed between the dunes. When they'd tired of jumping they would go and pester Spike for ice-creams. Later, as they got older, they would sit there for hours, late into the evening, playing guitars and drinking beer. This evening there was a group of teenagers doing just that. She felt a pang of nostalgia sweep her. No place is truly owned, we are just the guardians of our environment until we pass it on to the next, after we have tired of it or left this world. She glanced up at the far end of the beach, oyster catchers were fishing in the low tide, picking at the mussel beds, their scarlet beaks illuminated in the evening sun.

Matt and Merryn trudged up the beach towards the party in companionable silence. It was as busy as a Saturday afternoon and it was almost six o'clock. Tiny columns of white smoke towered at intervals from disposable barbecues. A few holidaymakers, in bathing costumes lounged on picnic blankets under parasols shading themselves from the still searing sun.

'Hey, you guys!' Johnny was striding towards them. 'Let me take that meat it looks heavy.'

'You're alright, where shall I dump it?'

'Over there past the band. Rowan's got a load of iceboxes.'

'Sure.' Matt went off to find Rowan.

'You're looking lovely, Merry.'

'Thanks, Uncle Johnny.'

'He's a lucky boy, that Matt. And don't you forget it.'

'Uncle Johnny, stop! Don't interfere. Anyway, we're just friends.'

'Interfere? Course not, Merry.'

She looked at him searchingly. 'You already did. Didn't you?'

'What? Interfere?'

'Rowan came to see me.'

'Yeah, he said.'

'He wanted me to come to this party with him.' She glared at Johnny.

'Yeah?' Johnny was frowning, 'So?'

'You know,' said Merryn indignantly, 'He wanted me to 'come' with him, as his date.'

'Ah, he finally got around to asking you then. Well good for him!'

'What do you mean finally?'

'Merryn, for an intelligent woman you can be pretty unobservant. You must be the only person in Porth Taran who doesn't realise that Rowan has burnt a candle for you since the year dot.'

Merryn stared at him, dumbfounded.

'Oh, come on, you must have realised. He's been hanging around you since primary school.'

'Johnny, we're friends! Just friends, that's all.'

'Yep, just friends with Matt, just friends with Rowan. Do you really not see, sweetheart?'

Merryn didn't answer straight away. 'But why now?'

'I would say your reason's over there, carrying a bag of meat.'

'Uncle Johnny, promise me that you will not interfere.'

'Of course not, I have much better things to be doing, and there's one of them now.' He strode off towards a well-endowed blonde who was tottering down the cliff steps in inappropriately high heels.

Elwood was in his sitting room in full preparation. With difficulty, he stuffed a length of string into his pocket wincing as he knocked his wounds. Next, he tipped the binoculars still in their pouch onto the carpet. The pouch was fastened with a zip. He sighed, looking at his tightly bound hands. He would have to undo the bandages if he was going to manage the zip. Anyway, he knew he wouldn't be able to tie the knots in the string without undoing them later on.

He pulled away the tape that secured the edges of the bandage with his teeth and carefully unwound it, preparing himself for the sight of the wound. As the bandage fell to the floor, a large patch of yellow stained gauze remained on his palm. He could see that the skin beneath had bubbled and popped. It was oozing pus, soaking the gauze pad and keeping it firmly stuck. He flexed his finger and flinched at the pain as the movement pulled on the wound.

He set to work on the other hand, more easily now that his fingers were free. At last both hands were released from their wrappings. He took a roll of gauze and carefully wrapped it around each of his fingers leaving the ends hanging. Then he wrapped his palm catching in the ends, and then his wrists and lower arms almost to his elbows. He held his hands out and moved his fingers, it was painful but possible. He was ready.

He sat down on the carpet in front of the coffee table and crossed his legs with difficulty. He set a candle on the table and lit it. He stared deep into its flickering light and recited slowly.

'A spell of safety, here I cast,
A word of strength to hold me to the last,
For me no danger shall I befall,
Nor harm nor threat until my mission has been met,
A shield around me, above and below,
By power of three my magic will save me.'

Then he unzipped the pouch with his fingertips and upended the binoculars onto the carpet. He slipped the pouch into his pocket with the string. He slowly wrote out an incantation onto a scrap of paper, his fingers ached as he gripped the pencil. He added it to the pouch and the string. He leant back and straightened out his legs, wincing as his joints released. He rolled onto his side and gently pushed himself up, cursing the pain. Age was a ghastly affliction.

He fetched a trowel from the garage and wedged it in his belt. He took his thinnest trench coat, for the heat was still oppressive, and pulled it on ensuring that the trowel was concealed at his waist.

Merryn glanced around for Beatrice and spotted her walking towards the terrace where Matt seemed to be deep in conversation with Rowan. She was dressed to kill in a sleek black mini dress showing off her tanned legs, on her feet a pair of leather roman sandals showing off flashes of scarlet painted toenails. She wondered who the target was this evening. She watched as Bea reached the terrace, flicking her hair and tossing her head back like a playful pony. Merryn could hear her laughter dancing across the sand. She wouldn't, would she? She'd said she thought he was hot when she'd seen him that first time at the gallery and she'd gone to all this trouble to organise a party to welcome him to Porth Taran.

Merryn flicked off her flip flops and set off for the terrace. The sand was burning the soles of her feet making her break into a run. By the time she reached the café Beatrice had slipped her arm through Matt's and had steered him away to meet the band.

Rowan was waving at her. She jerked to a stop.

'Merryn, are you alright. You look like you're in a rush?'

'What? Err, no, the sand was hot, that's all.'

'Thanks for bringing the meat.'

Merryn ignored him and glanced nervously in Beatrice and Matt's direction. She could feel her heart pounding in her chest.

'Earth to Merryn! Are you alright? You've gone a little pale. Here.' He pulled out a chair. 'Sit down a second.'

She plumped herself down, wishing Rowan would leave her alone. 'I feel a bit funny.'

'I'll get you a glass of water.'

The heat was suddenly stifling, there was no air, not even here by the sea. Rowan returned with the glass and Merryn drank it in one long draught. 'I think it's this heat, thanks Rowan.'

He beamed at her, stroking her shoulder.

Merryn could feel herself cringing from his touch. She held her breath. What was happening to her? She was jealous of Beatrice and now appalled by her dear friend Rowan.

A cheer went up from the partygoers and Rowan and Merryn swung round to see the man from the Blue Anchor awkwardly wheeling a barrel down the steps from the green, desperately trying to stop it slipping out of his grasp and rolling all the way to the bottom.

'There's the Spingo!' Rowan tore off to help.

Merryn got up and went into the café to top up her glass of water. When she came out Beatrice and Matt had completely disappeared.

Johnny was entertaining his date who was fixed on him and giggling at his every word.

Rowan was setting up the barrel just inside the café. He expertly poured a finger of beer into a plastic cup and then made a show of holding it up to the sun as if to check the beer's quality. He took a large swig and washed it around his mouth as if it was a fine wine. Gathered eagerly around him, a group of young men watched him intently. He swallowed and then held the empty cup high shouting, 'Let there be beer!'

A whoop went up and the men jostled to get their plastic pint glasses filled.

Merryn took her glass of water and went to find her flip flops where she'd left them on the beach.

'Jeez, I thought I'd lost you!' Matt was sitting on the sand in the shade of the café steps, leaning against the terrace wall.

'Hey,' said Merryn, as calmly as she could manage.

Elwood waited until the sun began to sink lower in the sky. There was no point in going down to the beach before the moon was clearly visible and he didn't trust himself not to be led astray by the Spingo. He needed all of his wits about him.

As soon as he felt it was time, he straightened his back, held his head high and solemnly stepped out of his front door and walked gravely down the hill towards the harbour.

The little port was thronging with holiday makers laughing and drinking at the Ship and the Harbour Inn. The atmosphere was light and full of celebration. Elwood remained focussed on his task. He took even steps in rhythm with the chant he recited in his head. He could see the moon low in the sky, pale in the light of the sun that still flooded the planet. He cut down the side streets, carefully avoiding the church now that the road works had been completed. He reached the cliff road. The twang of electric guitars and the beating of drums echoed around the beach. Quite a crowd had gathered around the café, heaving and pulsating in time with the drumbeat.

Elwood went to the cliff edge, just a little way along from the lifeguard hut. He took the trowel from his belt and laid it down next to him as he settled himself on the grass. He patted his pocket to be sure the binoculars were still in place. He hunkered down as low as was comfortable and waited.

Matt and Merryn were dancing to the Celtic Crackers' cover of Echo Beach and Merryn felt dizzy with happiness. The sun was slipping to the west and the heat was beginning to subside with it. She was hot and suspected she was turning a rather unflatteringly bright pink and was considering a swim to cool herself down.

Beatrice joined them, dancing in her usual hippy way, holding her arms in the air and pirouetting, showing off her slender figure and her brown legs. As the number came to an end Merryn fanned her face.

'You look hot, Merryn, why don't you sit down a bit and cool off? There's someone I want Matt to meet,' said Beatrice. She grabbed his hand and whisked him off into the café. Merryn was left standing on the sand, whilst Matt looked back at her frowning as Bea pulled him away. Bea could be so rude and Merryn tried to quell her annoyance.

She took herself off towards the shore to dip her toes. She scooped some sea water into her hands and doused the nape of her neck sending a refreshing shiver through her body. As she looked out at the reflection of the moon dancing on the surface of the sea, Uncle Johnny appeared behind her holding two glasses of beer.

'Pint of Spingo?'

'Thanks Johnny.' And she took one from him, drinking a long, cool gulp. 'Where's your date?'

'Ah, she had to go. Something about babysitters.'

Merryn's back was aching so she sunk to the sand crossing her legs.

Johnny joined her. 'Where's yours?'

'Beatrice commandeered him.'

'Ah, I see.'

'Johnny?'

'Yes, my darlin'.'

'Why didn't you ever get married and, you know, have kids and all?'

'Nah, that's not for me, my lovely. Marrying and bringing up a family's alright for some, but me, I need my freedom. I like to do what I like, I'm too selfish for all that compromise and sacrifice stuff.'

'You make it sound dreadful.'

'No, I'm sure it's not. Look at your mum she was so happy with your dad.' He sighed and looked out to sea. 'I didn't envy her pain after he… you know.'

Merryn swallowed. She had often wondered how it must have felt for Mum when she heard the news. The uncertainty of not knowing what had happened or if he was coming back, going on for weeks, then months and then all hope fading as time went by. Merryn had felt the sadness every day since she was old enough to realise that you were supposed to have a father. 'What were they like together?'

'Your mum and dad?'

Merryn nodded.

'They were best friends. In love. You know, like properly in love. Joined at the hip.' Johnny picked up a mussel shell from the sand and began to scrape at the barnacles that had clamped themselves on to it. 'I used to want to be like them. Find a girl, the right one for me and know I always had a best friend.'

'And you didn't find one.'

'Ah, I don't need that. I have lots of friends and,' he smiled, 'And a fantastic niece.' He put his arm round her and kissed her cheek noisily.

'Johnny!' Merryn pushed him away laughing. She went quiet again. 'What do you think happened, Johnny?'

'To your dad? You must know all this?'

'I never really wanted to before.'

Johnny looked at her in surprise. 'You've never asked your mum?'

Merryn shook her head.

'I think you should probably be having this conversation with her, my darling.'

'I don't want to upset her or worry her. You tell me.'

'Well, let's start with what he was like. Piran Jewell was a special guy, Merry. He wasn't like most blokes. He liked a josh and a drink with the boys like any of us. He was guilty of getting home late from the pub every now and then too. But he knew stuff.'

'What do you mean?'

'Well, he always knew when the sea would be safe, when it wouldn't, and I never saw him checking a forecast. It's like he sort of knew naturally.'

'So, him disappearing in a freak storm that no one else saw is a bit unlikely.'

'No storm was recorded, not anywhere round these shores that day. Not that that means there wasn't one. It's just no one saw anything.' He hesitated. 'Except Elwood, of course.'

'Elwood?'

'Yeah, Elwood says he was on the shore down Rinsey way and he saw your dad's boat.' He stopped and breathed in deeply as he looked out to sea.

'Go on.'

'You know what folk say about Elwood, that he's got a screw loose, but I know differently. He seems to have a sixth sense about things. I know he drinks too much and comes out with some mumbo jumbo but don't write it all off. I suggest you talk to him yourself. He'll tell you what he saw, and you can make your own mind up.'

'Why didn't you ever tell me?'

'You never asked before, sweetheart. And it's not my place. Your mum might be furious with me if I interfered. Anyway, what's the point in dwelling on it, we're all here and we're all happy. Your dad is gone and that's sad, but life has gone on and it goes on.' He tipped up his glass and drained the last of the beer. 'Come on, let's get back to the party.'

NINE

Elwood's protection spell had worked. It was so efficient that he could pick up Bunjil's binoculars with no ill-effects at all. He could no longer feel the force of his energy, even when he put the binoculars to his eyes.

He was surprised just how far he could see with them. He could see people right close-up down on the beach, even in the darkness, though the moon was bright. He could see Ambis walking up from the water's edge with Johnny. He could see her solemn expression. Something was wrong? He quickly scanned the party and then relaxed, Bunjil was nowhere near her, at least. He looked into the crowd of dancers, but he couldn't see him there either. Maybe he'd given up and left. His spirits lifted. Perhaps his protection spell was enough to do the job. But he wanted to be sure.

He laid out the binoculars and the pouch next to the trowel. He took the string from his pocket and in the moonlight, he tied one end to the pouch's zip pull. As he threaded the string through it to make a knot, pus from his palm oozed over the string. Panicked he tried to clean it off with the edge of his shirt. Now something of his would be included in the hex. He didn't have another piece of string. He could feel beads of sweat forming on his brow. He could now become subject to the hex, but he knew he mustn't abandon, not now. The circumstances were too good to miss, and he couldn't be sure that the outcome would be changed. What did he have to lose?

He looked down at the crowd of dancers and at Ambis sipping her drink by the terrace café. She must be protected and Porth Taran with her. He fastened the string, took out the scrap of paper and as he tied the first knot in the series, he began his incantation.

'With this knot, I bond this hex; you will not tarry, nor will you rest,'

Merryn couldn't see Matt anywhere, or Beatrice for that matter. The Celtic Crackers were playing their closing number and a few couples were holding each other close as they danced.

'Knots of power, knots of strength; The gods of the sea will get thee hence.' Elwood tied the third knot.

There in the middle were Matt and Beatrice. She was leaning into Matt's shoulder and giggling and tossing her head back, revealing her long slender neck. She couldn't see Matt's expression from such a distance.

'Evil, peril and darkness reign; Of you nothing will remain.'

Then Beatrice leaned towards Matt's face and kissed him squarely on the mouth.

'Hex of anger, hex of hate; Bring him down, I will not wait!' Just as Elwood tied the very last knot the sky lit up with a giant crack of lightening. He jumped. The loudest rumble of thunder he'd ever heard followed straight behind.

Merryn's body stiffened. She felt as if her soul was being wrenched from deep within her. There was a buzzing and a crackle and the band's amplifiers went dead. She had to get away. She ran towards the beach steps and tore up them towards the cliff top.

Elwood sat stunned as he watched Ambis sprinting across the beach barefoot. She was heading up the steps towards the lifeguard hut and now she was running straight for him. What was she doing? Panic started to engulf him. He could feel is heart rate rising and his stomach swooped. She was going at quite a pace. She was getting closer. How did she know? Elwood cowered shielding his head with his arms and closed his eyes tight shut and held his breath.

Tears were running down Merryn's face. The wind had got up and was blowing fiercely onto the beach. Rain began to fall mingling with her tears and drenching her. As she reached the green, in the corner of her eye she could see a bundle on the edge of the cliff. It was big enough to be a figure huddled in the dark. She veered her course to avoid it.

Elwood released his breath as Ambis ran past him and away along the edge of the cliff. Why was she running like that? Had Bunjil done something? Anger began to rise inside him.

He looked down at the beach. People were running everywhere. Some were running for cover to the café, others were streaming up the steps to the lifeguard hut. Out at sea he could see flashes of white water in the darkness. The waves seemed to be breaking on the horizon.

He looked down at the knotted string and shook his head. Johnny had always said that he had it in him to change things. Hadn't he done that for the vicar? He'd tried. Of course he had.

The tide was creeping up the beach at an unusual pace. More and more partygoers from the beach reached the green at the top of the steps. The band was hurriedly dismantling their equipment and trying to get it inside the café before the water ruined it. The rain had stopped but the wind strengthened. Elwood tried to stand up but the wind knocked him off balance and he fell on his face with a thud. He scrabbled in the sandy marram grass and spat grains out of his mouth. The moon was obscured by thick dark clouds and it was hard to see. He looked down and could see water covering the entire beach. The waves were almost licking the cliff face. He knew he must bury the hex to complete the ritual. As he grabbed the trowel, the string slipped from his fingers. The wind picked it up and whisked it away. Elwood gasped, all would be lost.

The sea had reached the cliff and seemed to be climbing it. He knew he had to get out of its way. On his hands and knees, he began to crawl across the green towards the road. He winced as his hands pressed against the rough grass, but he could sense the sea advancing behind him. He made it halfway across the green but as he approached the road he knew he must stand up or he would be trampled by the partygoers. He was further away from the sea now and the wind wouldn't be so powerful here. He pushed himself to standing and braced himself against the gale and leant forwards planting his feet sturdily with every step so as not to be knocked off balance. At last he reached the edge of the green. He bent his body over the wall and threw himself down on the other side. He lay there for a minute catching his breath. It was sheltered behind the wall and he gathered himself. He peered over the top as the moon reappeared from the clouds. He could see a huge dark wave on the horizon. At first it seemed to be motionless, but he could just make out that the crest of it was growing higher and higher. A hollow rumble that seemed to roar from the belly of the earth grew with it.

Merryn stood on the cliff top, her eyes closed, she fought against the battering wind to remain upright. She wanted to feel the weather, to feel cold, uncomfortably cold. To feel another kind of pain, the sort she could deal with. The wind pulled at her clothing. But now it was warm and soothing, and it made her angry. She wanted to feel anything, anything but this.

She could sense people running past her. There was a long low hum coming from the sea that got louder by the second. It was as if the sea could feel her pain. Suddenly the wind dropped and for a moment there was silence. Then the air was filled with the sound of people shouting and screaming as they ran towards the village to take cover. She willed the wind to return, to scoop her up and throw her from this cliff. She took a step closer to the edge of the cliff. She could feel the peat beneath her feet, springy with the roots of marram grass that wove through it. She stood with her toes right up to the edge and looked out over the ocean.

Over the sea, the clouds cleared, and the moon shone lighting up a ridge of water which was swelling larger and larger as it approached the shore. Then she heard the hum which mounted in volume as she watched. She held her arms down by her side and closed her eyes.

From the darkness images of Matt and Bea rose in her mind. Bea was laughing and throwing flirting glances in Matt's direction. She leaned forwards, then Bea kissed Matt. Her stomach swung and she felt faint. The hum was louder now. Bea took Matt's hand and pulled him up the beach giggling as she went. In the pit of her stomach she could feel a knot of fury growing. Her head was spinning and she wanted to cry out loud, to sob and howl. The fury swelled until she could take it no more. She would not be beaten. She turned and began to run towards the village, joining the exodus from the beach.

The hum behind her became a roar and her legs worked faster and faster to take her away from its source. As she reached the church its bells had begun to ring. The lifeboat station's siren was sounding. People were pouring out of the Harbour Inn to see what was going on. The harbour road was a sea of people. People were standing on the terraces of The Ship opposite and calling to the crowd. The party goers colliding with the pub patrons as they rushed towards higher ground behind the harbour head.

Elwood joined the throng. The fear was infectious. The mountainous wave was just a little way offshore now, its summit visible behind the church steeple. As people poured from the restaurants and pubs and looked up, their faces were suddenly dressed in fear and they too turned on their heels and ran. As he reached the surf shop the crowd seemed to slow and people began to sink to the pavement puffing and blowing.

Elwood reached the supermarket and stopped and turned to look back at the harbour as the gigantic wave came up over the lifeguard hut curling high. Elwood watched as it headed for St Petroc's. It seemed to slow as it approached the steeple, then it all but stopped as it flicked backwards before smashing against the steeple with an almighty slap of seething frothy sea water.

The spray engulfed the harbour and reformed into a torrent as it fell and swept up the length of the harbour. It swallowed the boats and sucked them under. As they resurfaced they were tossed a little way above the water and landed hard back down again, some were missing masts, others had their hulls gouged as they had collided beneath the waters.

Jack Jewell's Lugger vanished under the wave and then re-emerged, caught on the crest of the swell and was swept so hard towards the head of the harbour that when it collided with the harbour wall it was lifted clean out of the water. Like a tin can it shot into the air and with a deafening crack and wrenching sound, it embedded itself on the ridge of the supermarket roof. Elwood sank to the pavement and shielded his head with his arms from the splintering wood that flew all around him.

Merryn held her breath as the water washed over her, knocking her to the pavement. In a moment the water rose and covered her face. She closed her eyes tight. Perhaps this was it. She held her breath as she listened to the shouts of the people and the roar of the sea deadening, getting fainter, then they were replaced with a rhythmic bubbling sound. The waters swirled pulling her downward. Her breath was running out and panic began to grip her. Something hard hit her. A searing pain blazed across her scalp. She could hold it no longer and released her breath. As she opened her lungs she thought of Demelza and Uncle Johnny, of Jack and Rowan and Bea. Then she thought of Matt. Of how he had come to Porth Taran and swept her off her feet, showing her a possibility that had never before tempted her. And as she thought, she realised she was still breathing. In and then out. No water entered her lungs but appeared to part just in front of her mouth. She could feel herself being carried by the current, completely submerged, yet she could breathe freely. Fear rose up in her. Someone was near her. A warm hand gently gripped her wrist and started to pull her along. The pain in her head was subsiding, she could feel herself floating, trailing behind the pull of the invisible hand, as if she was flying. The waters around her became calm. She opened her eyes and glanced downwards but all she could see was darkness. She touched her head and could feel a gash washed clean by the sea but there was no pain. She looked around her for the person who had held her but there was no one. Just the bubbling and swirling waters.

TEN

Demelza sat in darkness in the dining room at Little Rosewarne. A single candle burned in the centre of the table. Her head was pounding from lack of sleep. She fixed her gaze on the flame and concentrated on keeping her expression frozen lest she crumble. She'd spent the night making tea and toast for the guests, who had come downstairs, woken by the storm. Now, they were all safely in bed. Spike had gone out to look for Merryn. Beside her the telephone sat silent. She'd drawn back the curtains so that she could see the first glimmer of dawn when it came. Outside, the wind had died down and she could hear vehicles passing to and fro and distant sirens still filled the air. She listened intently for the sound of the front door opening and good news arriving. She closed her eyes, resisting the agony that was rising within her. The memories of the night Piran disappeared vied at the edges of her mind but she would be strong, she would not let them in. They had been through so much, her and her little family, they had had their quota, they could take no more.

The last great storm should have been the happiest day of her life. The day Merryn came into the world, the day just a little piece of Piran was returned to her. The day that she knew she was no longer without him.

That night in the hospital, Piran was there. He had held her hand through the labour, he was the first to cradle their baby daughter when she had drawn her first breath. He had smiled at her and stroked her forehead and in his deep gentle tone he had said, 'You done good, Melza. She's a cracker our little one.'

She'd opened her eyes to meet his, gazing down on her and their new-born. His smiling face was so full of pride and love.

Then he was gone. The chair next to her bed was empty. Only the drip stand hovered over her and little Merry was bundled tightly in the clear Perspex trolley cot sleeping deeply, her eyes tightly shut.

The clunk of the front door made her leap to her feet. Spike, Jack and Johnny appeared in the doorway of the dining room, their faces tense and drawn. Spike put his arms around her.

'No one has seen her, my love.'

Demelza's heart lurched.

'No news is good news,' said Johnny. 'She'll be holed up somewhere sleeping. You'll see.' He rubbed his sister's shoulder.

'And the gallery?' whispered Demelza.

Jack shook his head. 'The front window is smashed, it's a right mess in there.'

Demelza's face crumpled.

'But Merry wasn't there, Melza. There's no sign of her. Johnny is right, she will have taken shelter somewhere. We need to wait for daybreak, it's chaos out there, there's nothing we can do until then.'

'Did you go to Bea's?'

'Yes, she's safe. Matt was there too. They haven't seen her since the party. They said she took off suddenly.'

'She took off?'

'Yes, before the storm hit. Bea said she looked upset.'

Demelza's brow furrowed again.

'But if she took off before the storm then she'll have been safer than everyone else. Don't you worry Melza, she'll be just fine,' said Johnny.

Demelza said nothing.

'We'll find her,' said Jack.

'What if…?' whispered Demelza,

'No, Melza.' Jack's voice was firm. 'Listen to Johnny. No news is good news. If something had happened to her, I'm sure we would know by now. The fire brigade has evacuated every property around the harbour and so far, there are no serious casualties. She will have gone off with one of her friends and will be sleeping soundly somewhere on someone's floor.'

'Of course, she will,' said Demelza. 'Another hour and it will be light.' She glanced at the clock on the wall.

Merryn opened her eyes. She could feel a draught blowing over her. She shivered. She was wet through and her bones ached. Outside she could hear shouting and a helicopter whooshing overhead. Her head was pounding. She pushed herself up to sitting to find herself in a damp musty darkened room surrounded by lobster pots, buoys, and fishing nets. The walls were built of stone and on one side was a huge pair of wooden doors like a warehouse. The floor was cobbled with channels set in it running out beneath the doors. She realised she must be in one of the linneys along the harbour. High up was a small grilled opening that allowed just enough light into the room to see. She rubbed her head and pulled her hand away sharply when she felt the mess of congealed flesh and hair. It began to sting.

She gingerly hauled herself to her feet checking her limbs for breaks or sprains but only her head seemed to be the problem. She went to the door and grasped one of the iron ring handles and twisted it sideways. It turned easily but when she pushed it, it wouldn't open. It seemed to be jammed against something. She tried it again but still it wouldn't give. She started to feel faint and grabbed the handle in both hands and rattled it as hard as she could, but the effort was too great, and her vision became grainy and the thumping of her heart filled her ears. She blacked out.

Jago Penberthy wandered down to the harbour to check his fish shed. Boulders from the seabed were leaning against the door and it took him a little time to clear the debris. At last he wrenched open the door and there on the cobbles, just behind it lay Merryn Jewell. Her eyes were closed but Jago could just make out the rise and fall of her chest. He couldn't tell if she was asleep or unconscious so he touched her arm and tried to jog her awake. She didn't stir.

'Jack, over 'ere!'

Jack and Johnny looked round.

'It's Merry! She's 'ere!'

Jack and Johnny both ran towards him.

'She's alive but she's not moving. We need help!' shouted Jago.

Johnny took out his phone and called 999.

Jack knelt down beside his niece and gently stroked her forehead. 'Oh Merry, my buttercup. What has happened to you? She must have got caught in that wave. Look at this on her head, she must have banged it some hard. Looks like it's been washed clean, perhaps it was the seawater. Johnny get me some fresh water. We mustn't move her, but we do need to wake her up.'

'Ere, Johnny here's a bucket.' Jago had been rummaging in the back of the linney. 'I can't fill it here as the water's off. You stay there I'll go and see if I can fill it in the harbour.'

Johnny took out his phone. 'I'm gonna call Melza.'

'Hang on, Johnny. Let the ambulance get here and check her over first. It will only frighten her, there's nothing she can do.'

Johnny hesitated and looked at his phone, then slipped it back into his jeans.

Jack was patting Merryn's cheeks gently.

She began to blink and wriggle then she opened her eyes.

'Merry! Merry, you're OK. We're here now. Johnny and me.'

Merryn looked up blankly at the looming figures hunched over her.

'It's me, Uncle Jack. Johnny's here too. You're safe.'

At last recognition came. She smiled weakly at them, but her head hurt and she wanted to sleep. She closed her eyes again.

Jago arrived with a filled bucket just in time. Jack splashed a little water on her face and she coughed and spluttered to consciousness again.

'Stay with us Merry, no sleeping, not till the ambulance gets here.'

'Where's mum?' she asked in a small voice.

'She's just coming, my darling.' Jack looked at Johnny and nodded.

Johnny stepped away to call Demelza.

In his bedroom, Elwood was stirring from a deep sleep. He twitched as his brain ran through the final performance of a delicious dream. He let out a luxurious sigh, as he stood in the centre of the ring of the Grove whilst all around him cheered with respect. He opened his eyes and took in the long ago painted wall of his room, mottled with mildew.

The wind had died down and he could hear shouting out in the street. He heaved himself up on his elbows, mindful of his burns, and looked around him. Nothing had changed here, but inside himself and outside in Porth Taran he knew that nothing would ever be the same again. He swung his legs over the side of the bed and stood amongst the books and screwed up bits of paper that littered the carpet. He kicked them like autumn leaves as he padded to the landing. For that was all they were now. No longer would he have to turn to the writings of his mind to fend off the misery and doubt, ever trying to make sense of it all. Now, those pieces of paper had become the strippings of a dying soul before it is regenerated and reborn as a higher being. Elwood Curnow was approaching his zenith. He stood up straight and pulled his shoulders back and held his head high and descended the stairs.

He stood on his front step behind the agapanthus, now flattened by the wind. An electricity board van sped past, its light flashing on its roof. In the harbour he could see police cars and an ambulance parked up in the spot where his bench used to be. This is what he had done. A ritual that could cause such devastation was a responsibility indeed. Then he remembered Ambis. How could he have been so vain? Without locking his front door, he set off at a run, his joints suddenly as painless as a young man's. An ambulance was parked at the mouth of the harbour. He dodged the debris, leaping piles of planks and rubbish as he went. As he reached it, its engine started and it pulled away. He tried to peer inside, but the windows were blacked out. Jago, Johnny and Jack were standing outside Jago's lock up.

'What's going on?' he asked urgently.

'It's our Merry, Elwood,' said Johnny.

His face went white.

'She's gonna be OK. She's bashed her head but she's conscious – they'll sort her out at Treliske, you'll see.'

'What happened?'

'She's hit her head.'

'How'd she do that?'

The men shook their heads and shrugged.

'The thing is, I don't understand how she could have ended up in my linney, 'said Jago, frowning. 'The door's always padlocked. I checked it yesterday.'

'There's no padlock there now, perhaps you got it wrong, Jago,' said Jack.

'Nah, that was definitely padlocked. I jiggled it an' everything. And it was bolted shut from the outside. How on earth did she get in there? Someone must have shut her in.'

'Who would have done that?' said Johnny.

The men fell silent.

'Jack if you get word of Merry first, call me and I'll do the same. I need to make a start on the mess at the surf shop.'

Elwood carefully stepped through the debris to head for home. If Ambis was safe, then his ritual had been effective, the real proof would be in Bunjil's whereabouts. He changed direction and made for the visitors' centre. The top floor was devastated. The roof was caved in and the windows missing. Elwood cheered up, he could well have hit his target. He began to stroll back slowly up the hill feeling quietly pleased with himself. With the weather station destroyed this could be enough to send Bunjil back to where he came from and Porth Taran could continue its sleepy journey to the end of time.

A TV Broadcasting van was parked at the head of the harbour. A young smartly dressed woman with bright red lipstick was talking into a microphone in front of a camera.

'Porth Taran was devastated by a freak wave in the early hours of this morning. Just one casualty has been taken to hospital, their condition is not yet known. Over a hundred homes are without electricity and the clean-up operation is underway. Villagers have reported that there was a party on the beach when...'

Elwood stepped round her and tried to continue his journey. The young woman stopped him and held the microphone to his chin.

'Sir tell us about your experience of the storm.'

'What me?'

'Were you here in Porth Taran last night?'

'Err, yes I was at the party on the beach.'

'Can you tell us what the atmosphere was like?'

Elwood raised his eyebrows and thought for a moment. 'Well, it was electric. There was a kind of tension, you know. Everyone was enjoying themselves, and the band was playing and then this wind started.' As Elwood got going his tongue loosened.

Matt and Beatrice were drinking coffee in her parents' kitchen. As soon as the electricity came back on Beatrice turned on the television to watch the news. Elwood appeared on the screen.

'Weather forecasters are saying that this was a freak storm,' said a smart young female journalist.

'This is no freak storm, it was a full moon,' replied Elwood.

'That man really is the limit!' Beatrice rolled her eyes.

'Full moon?' said the journalist frowning.

'Yeah, you see that is the best night to perform rituals to protect ourselves from evil spirits,' continued Elwood. 'I was up on the cliff when the storm started. I was performing a hex ...' The television cut to the studio.

'What is he like? Does he really think he caused that storm?' said Bea.

Matt was lost in thought.

'Matt?'

'Listen, Bea. What happened last night,'

Bea's face fell.

'I like you,'

'Yeah, yeah, but not like that?'

Matt shook his head. 'I'm sorry, but no. I'm sorry if I gave you a different impression, but…'

'It's Merryn, isn't it?'

Matt didn't answer. He fiddled with his coffee cup. 'I really appreciate you putting me up, your sofa is almost as comfortable as the bed in Jack's boat.'

Bea said nothing.

'Thanks for coffee and all but I need to go and find Merryn. She looked real upset when she took off like that.'

The setting sun cast a golden filter over the thick sea mist that veiled Porth Taran. Merryn stood at the head of the harbour, leaning against her mother. Her head was still throbbing despite the painkillers, but she needed to come and see. She stared at the boats coated in fine silt, some lay on their sides and others were upended and jutting from the muddy sand of the harbour floor like eerie sculptures looming in the fog. The pavements were strewn with debris. There were dumper trucks parked, one on each side of the harbour, already piled high with planks of wood and sections of mast and litter bins that had been torn from their fixings. Gulls thronged to pick at the dead fish, crabs and jellyfish that were scattered across the tarmac. They were beginning to release a fishy stench.

She looked around for Jack's boat but couldn't be sure if it was one of the muddy craft before her.

'The Lugger. Where is it Mum?'

'Look behind you.'

Merryn turned and there on the roof of the supermarket, with half its hull missing was the Helford Maid.

'Is…, is everyone alright?' Merryn whispered not trusting her voice.

'Yes, my darling, everyone is safe.' Demelza rubbed her daughter's arm, gratefully. 'And so are you.' She kissed her daughter on the forehead.

'So, no one was hurt?'

'No one, except you. It's a miracle when you look at this damage. Come on, my lovely why don't we go home? You need to get some rest. Concussion will leave you feeling tired for a long time.'

Merryn shook her head. 'I need to see the gallery.'

Demelza knew there was little point in arguing. 'Then I will come with you.'

As Merryn began to walk along the harbour, she remembered running up the steps to the cliff edge and then lying on the ground and sobbing as the wind and rain pummelled her. Then there'd been that terrible noise. That deep hollow rumble. She remembered running with the others, and then, nothing.

As they reached the gallery, she could see that the front door was missing, its hinges wrenched off its frame. Plastic sheeting had been stapled over it. The shop window was cracked in a spider's web formation and had been taped over to stop it collapsing. Merryn pulled the plastic over the doorway aside. Muddy boulders from the sea bed were strewn across the floor, the sopping carpet was rucked up beneath them. Most of the mosaics had been stripped from the wall and others hung at an angle. Some of their frames were splintered and split but their images were intact. She was thankful she'd taken the time to seal them with boat varnish.

She stepped inside and picked her way through the gloom and across the debris to the kitchen. She flicked on the light switch, but nothing happened. She tried the kettle but again nothing.

'Come on Merry. You can't do much here until the electricity's back on. And until you feel better. Let Uncle Jack deal with it.'

'Mum, you get back. I'll be home soon. I promise. I just need to go through things a little.'

Demelza frowned.

'Honestly, I'll be alright.'

Demelza gave in. She hugged her daughter and left reluctantly.

At last alone, Merryn found some candles in one of the kitchen cupboards. They were wrapped in plastic so had been saved from the damp. She found a lighter and flicked the flint until it sparked. She lit the candles and set them around the little gallery casting an eerie glow through the fog filtered light.

As the gallery lit up she saw her treasured wind mosaic lying on the floor, its frame damaged and hanging off on one side. She picked it up and pulled away the broken frame. With her hand she wiped the tiny splinters and silt from the surface of the tiles; it was perfectly intact. She dried it with a tea towel and leant it carefully against the wall.

Then she remembered the firebuds. Her workbench was empty. The board must have been swept off by the water. She looked behind the bench. On the floor the board lay on its edge, its cling film wrapping gone. The grain of the plywood was water stained but the surface and edges had resisted swelling, the marine ply had done its job, though the firebuds had come unstuck. The scarlet fragments lay strewn across the floor. Only the leaves had remained. She retrieved the board and laid it on the workbench. Leaves that soak up the sun and feed the plant, bringing the goodness from the sun to nourish its roots, these had not fallen. They had survived the storm. But the blossoms that would procreate, give new life had been dashed, and scattered.

Her mind wandered to Matt. He obviously hadn't gone back to the boat. He must have gone to Bea's. Well, they were welcome to each other. Anger swept her; she should never have allowed herself to get pulled into such a charade. Of course, he would go for Beatrice; leggy, educated, dynamic Beatrice. How stupid could she have been? Love was an illusion, a device to maintain hope. Her head began to pound again.

ELEVEN

Rowan took a break from mopping out the surf shop and stepped outside onto the pavement. The fog still hadn't lifted and Porth Taran remained swathed in its woolly mantel, deadening the sound of the tractors and dumper truck engines. He glanced down the harbour at the mess that lay everywhere. Jack's boat on the supermarket roof had become the focus of every headline. No one would forget this in a hurry.

He'd made it home safely, not long after the lifeboat station warning had sounded, though he'd lain awake most of the night worrying about Merryn and listening to the wind and the sirens of the emergency services. In the pandemonium he had lost track of her, and of Bea.

Knowing that Merry was safe was a relief. He wandered down the harbour and sat on the wall near the gallery. He could see her silhouette through the fog as she moved around behind the sheeted up window. He longed to go in and help her, but he'd made a fool of himself and his pride wouldn't let him. He shouldn't have listened to Johnny. Of course she'd turned him down. Bright, sparky Merryn with her artistic talent and business sense. What could he offer her? A cabin at the bottom of his parents' garden out on the Helston Road. He wasn't surprised that she'd taken a shine to Matt; he seemed like a nice enough guy. Still, with the weather station wrecked he probably wouldn't be hanging around for long anyway. Then perhaps Merryn would notice him; the thought comforted him. He sighed and glanced around at the devastation. The fog was so thick he couldn't even see the church steeple now.

'Good morning, Rowan.' Reverend Kate appeared out of the gloom.

'Hi Rev, much damage?'

'Just water damage and the electrics are out. That church has stood the test of time, particularly in that position on the headland. I can't imagine much could wipe it out now.' She was holding a tatty notebook.

'Your diary escaped the damage then?'

She paused and glanced down. 'Oh this, yes. It was in the loft, just trying to move the dry stuff up high to stop it getting damp from everything else. I seem to have found all kinds of things. You haven't seen Elwood Curnow this morning, have you?'

'Err, no, but I know he's about – he was on the local news apparently spouting stuff about rituals and curses and stuff.' Rowan raised his eyebrows.

'Oh dear, I think I'll pop up to his place and check he's OK.'

Elwood had fallen asleep on the sofa and the trill of his phone alerted him to the fact that it was working again. He heaved himself to his feet and went to answer it.

'Elwood, it's Trevina. Are you alright?'

'Err, yeah, yeah, I'm fine. The storm was pretty bad though, have you heard?'

'Well, that's what I'm ringing about. The High Priest wants to meet with you.'

Elwood swelled with pride. Recognition at last.

'Can you meet him at the Seven Sisters tomorrow at noon?'

'Tomorrow? Yes, I'll be there.' Just as Elwood put down the receiver he heard knocking at the front door. He went into the front room and peered through the curtains. Reverend Kate was standing on the doorstep. Elwood shuddered. What on earth was she doing here? Didn't she know that he would have nothing to do with that evil? He quickly replaced the curtain and slumped onto the sofa and waited for her to leave.

'Mr Curnow,' she called.

What on earth did she want?

'I just want to talk to you. I've found something at the church.'

Elwood didn't move. He wasn't going to fall for that. He sat motionless for a few minutes more. Then tentatively peered out of the window just in time to see her departing back.

He waited a little to be sure she had gone then set off to see Johnny. As he approached the harbour he saw Reverend Kate coming out of the surf shop. He hung back a little until he was certain she was well on her way back to St. Petroc's. Then he approached the shop.

'What was she doing here?'

'Who? Reverend Kate? You spying on me?' said Johnny grinning.

Elwood looked at him dumbfounded. 'No, of course not!'

'Just kidding, Elwood, keep your hair on. Actually, she was in asking about you.'

'About me? That interfering so called do-gooder.'

'Eh, they're not all bad, Elwood, you know. She's just looking out for you.' He patted Elwood's shoulder. 'We all are.'

'Never again will I get mixed up with them.'

'She just wondered how you were after the storm. She said she wanted to talk to you.'

'She came 'round my 'ouse just now. I didn't answer though,' he said proudly.

'Well, perhaps you should next time. Anyway, what can I do for you?'

'Could you give me a lift up to the Seven Sisters tomorrow for noon?'

'What are you doing up there?'

Elwood drew himself to his full height. 'I've been summoned.'

'Summoned?'

'The High Priest wants to see me.'

'Really? Why?'

'It's the storm.' Elwood beamed with pride.

'The storm? You mean what you said on the telly, your curse or whatever it was?'

'That's right. 'Ere do you think that's why Reverend Kate wants to see me?' Elwood's eyes widened with the suggestion.

'What was this curse, you're on about? I would keep it quiet if I were you. There are some really unhappy fishermen in Porth Taran. If they thought you deliberately caused this storm they'll come looking for you.'

Elwood scowled. 'They all believe in Sea Witches, don't they?'

'Some of them still do.'

'Well, then I just brought things to the witches' attention, it was their anger that did this.'

'Anger at what, Elwood?'

'Bunjil coming here interfering.'

'Interfering? Elwood, I can't see that he has done anything except take a shine to our Merryn, and let's face it, who can blame him?'

Elwood glared at him then shrugged.

'Alright, I'll take you up there.'

'Where?' Elwood was lost in thought.

'To the Seven Sisters. Pick you up at eleven fifteen, OK?'

'Oh, yeah, proper job.'

A little dazed he turned and absent-mindedly walked out of the shop. Still thinking about Rev Kate, he began to climb the hill towards home. Was that why she wanted to talk to him? Because she knew about his powers? At last, even she was coming round. Everyone knows that the earth's energies are greater than God's. She said she'd found something at the church. The hex had been whisked off by the wind, perhaps that was it. By rights he should have buried it but now there was no need for its power to grow in the belly of the earth. The sea witches had been angered and the job had been done.

Matt stood outside the visitors' centre with a reporter. The floor where the weather station had been was pretty much flattened. He fought off a feeling of desolation. Just one night, and his life was turned upside down. He reminded himself that everything is temporary. This is not his home, and everyone is safe.

The reporter began to speak into her microphone. 'Last night Porth Taran was battered by a freak wave during the severest storm in twenty years. Over a hundred homes have been left without power and a thick sea mist has been hampering the clean-up operation.

'I am standing outside the Weather Centre, here in Porth Taran, which as you can see, has lost its top floor.

I have here with me, Matt Bunda, a doctoral student in meteorology all the way from Australia. He claims to have forecast the event and shared the information with Culdrose Weather Centre, but his prognosis fell on deaf ears.

'Matt, thank you for joining us today. So, tell me about the events that led to your forecast.'

'Aw, I'd just like to say that I'm a new kid on the block and um, I'm not sure I made a definite forecast. An 'err I didn't predict the wave that engulfed the village, but I called Culdrose to tell them that I believed there was a threat of tornadoes, so I'm afraid I got it wrong.'

'In layman's terms can you explain to us the abnormal conditions that led to your prediction?'

'In a nutshell, the steep rise in temperature in such a short period of time is grounds alone to set off tornadoes, though the wave would more commonly be a result of seismic activity. To my knowledge the British Geological survey has recorded no earthquakes in or near this area.'

'So, a mystery wave?'

'Yep, that's about the size of it. Science has its place but there is still a lot to learn and even in this day and age, we cannot explain everything.'

'So, do you think we should believe what Elwood Curnow of Porth Taran is saying about his ritual?' The presenter was laughing.

'Ah, Mr Curnow. We all have our own beliefs and whichever framework we choose is up to us, I wouldn't like to comment on his theory.'

'Thank you, Matt Bunda. Joanna Trump, outside Porth Taran weather station.'

Matt watched as the reporter and camera man drove away. He stood looking at the Lugger lodged on the roof of the supermarket.

Jack appeared by his side.

'Jeez, I'm sorry about your boat, mate.'

Jack shrugged. 'It's a goner, I'm afraid.'

'What will you do?'

'Insurance should pay up. I might be able to sell bits of it off, but I reckon that's the end of the road for the Helford Maid.'

The men stood in silence.

'We'll need to get your stuff, too.'

'Yeah, my passport and everything was in there,' Matt sighed. 'You seen Merryn?'

'She's at the gallery, trying to clean up.'

'I'll go and see if I can help her. Give me a shout if you need a hand.'

He sighed and stepped towards the gallery. He could see Merryn inside poring over a mosaic.

'Jeez! What a mess!'

She looked up startled. 'What do you want?'

Matt hesitated. 'To see that you're OK. That was some storm!'

'Yes it was, but as you can see, I am just fine.' She glared at him and disappeared into the kitchen.

'Merryn, what's that on your head? You've hurt yourself.'

She didn't answer.

He stepped inside. 'Can I give you a hand clearing this lot up?'

Merryn's head shot out from the kitchen. 'I don't need any help.'

'You're upset. Let me explain.'

'No need. You've checked on me and you can see that I am fine. Now, just go.' She darted back into the kitchen. Her head was pounding. Moisture welled in her eyes. She shut them tight to force the tears back down. She stayed in the kitchen clutching the edge of the sink, willing him to disappear. There was silence then she heard the plastic over the doorway rustle and she let out her breath and the tears began to fall freely.

TWELVE

The sea mist had turned from an opaque filter to a dense white shroud.

At the gallery, the electricity was restored and Merryn was making cups of tea for the glaziers. Uncle Jack was installing a new front door. Merryn lined up the cups on a tray. Her head was still sore and her eyes hurt from lack of sleep. A tear escaped down her cheek. She rubbed her eyes and took a deep breath. The gallery was a pitiful sight. The floor was squelching underfoot, she would need to get rid of the carpet. She felt a hand on her shoulder.

'Don't worry, Merry, we'll have this place shipshape by the end of the week,' said Jack. 'We have seen worse, my darlin'. We have to do what we did last time and just pick ourselves up and clean up.'

'Of course, we will.' Merryn wiped her tears and forced a smile. She poured tea into the cups and carried the tray out to the glaziers. They were sitting on their tool boxes in front of the newly installed window, silhouetted against the eerie glow of the muddy golden mist outside.

'It's something awful out there,' said one of the glaziers, picking up a mug and handing it to his mate.

'Yeah it's like the end of the world is nigh or summat. Never seen anything like it.

'Nor me. Well, not for years. Have you been on to the insurers for your boat yet, Jack?'

'Yeah, it'll all be sorted. The photo of it on the supermarket roof has hit every front page in the country. It's not like they can dispute it. It's those poor buggers that hadn't taken out insurance that I feel for. I don't know why they think they can get away with it. Cutting corners never pays in the long run. I told them at the Fisherman's Mission, at the meeting last month. Aah what can you do? You can lead a horse to water ...'

'Merryn Jewell?' A lady wearing a green apron appeared in the doorway with a huge bouquet of flowers.

'That's me.'

The florist handed her the bouquet. 'Should cheer things up!'

Merryn opened the card and read, *Firebuds! Meet me by the beach steps tomorrow at 12 – PLEASE! M x*

'Flowers, eh? You've got an admirer there, Merryn.' Jack's eyes were twinkling with curiosity.

Merryn blushed and made a face and took the bouquet to the kitchen.

What was Matt thinking? Didn't he get it? The betrayal stung her deep to her core. To imagine that this could be repaired was absurd, and that sending flowers was appropriate only compounded in her mind who Matt Bunda was. A breeze picked up and slammed the kitchen window to.

The glaziers helped Jack to heave the boulders and the sodden carpet out of the gallery door and on to the pavement. The men packed up their tools and moved on to the next shop front. At last, she was left in peace.

Merryn began to feel calmer. The gallery was looking a lot better. She mopped the last of the sludge from the floor and made some fresh coffee.

She stared at the flowers lying on the side in the kitchen. There was no denying that they were beautiful. She reluctantly began to unpack them from their cellophane. The flame red blooms lay vibrant against the stainless steel draining board. Some of the buds were ready to burst open from their deep green stems in triumphant celebration of birth. Firebuds. Matt had called them firebuds. Had she mentioned them to him? She thought hard, she couldn't remember. Or perhaps he'd seen them? Only Rowan had caught a glimpse of the mosaic, just before the party, as far as she knew. She took the note that came with the bouquet. *Firebuds!* All one word. The fragrance of the flowers began to fill the gallery. Firebuds to restore. Overpowering the smell of damp silt and even the stench of rotting seaweed from the harbour that was beginning to linger at the windows. Firebuds fighting destruction. She couldn't ignore them anymore. She began to trim them and arrange them in a vase, carefully cut to stand at varying heights, as if they were blooming directly on her mosaic tree of life.

She took Matt's note again. She ran her fingers over the letters. Had she overreacted? Perhaps she should hear him out. She glanced up at the window and out at the harbour, the mist was lifting and warm sunshine was beginning to filter through.

Johnny's van was winding its way up the moor to the Seven Sisters. Grass tussocks marked the centre of the narrow lane and the van brushed the ragged robin and ferns that lined the hedges.

With the chaos of the storm the nurse hadn't been able to make it to Elwood's to change his dressing, so he had wrapped his hands in torn up tea towels and secured them with plasters, leaving his fingers free. He'd managed a shower as best he could with his hands taped into plastic bags. He had carefully polished his pentacle and hung it round his neck.

'So, who is this guy you're meeting?'

'The High Priest. He leads the druids in this area.'

'What's his name?'

'Just 'The High Priest'.' Elwood shrugged and looked out of the window.

'What? You don't know who he is?'

Elwood didn't answer.

'Well, what does he look like?'

Elwood glared at him.

'OK, so why does he want to meet you?'

'I expect he would like to congratulate me.' Elwood paused, his eyes lighting up. 'On my hex.'

'Do you do them often?'

'Oh no, the hex must be treated proper, it is a responsibility having such powers and they must be used,' he cocked his head on one side. 'Sparingly.'

'So, the last time, was it you know, when ...?'

Elwood looked at him blankly.

'When Cribben ...' Johnny hesitated. 'You know.'

Elwood darted a look of alarm and yelled, 'Careful! You almost scraped the van on this side!'

Johnny was miles away from the Cornish hedge. He knew better than to press him. As they drove west, the trees became sparser, the few that survived the Atlantic winds were bent and twisted hawthorns which barely reached above the stone hedges. At last they reached a track off to the left and Johnny pulled up it and parked the van in a passing place by a stile.

'Stay here. The High Priest doesn't like an audience of ... well non-believers.'

Johnny sighed. 'Alright, but I hope it doesn't take a month of Sundays.'

Elwood got out of the van and from a carrier bag he took out a carefully pressed and folded light grey robe. He took off his trench coat and pulled the robe over his head. He put up the hood and took his staff from behind the seats and hooked it over the crook of his arm. He nodded solemnly at Johnny and stiffly climbed over the stile and into the field on the other side.

Beyond him, Johnny could see the stones glowing in the sunshine. They were pointing at odd angles where their foundations had been swollen and eroded by centuries of battering rain and dry summers. There was no one else in the field. Johnny watched as Elwood's robed figure approached the circle. He made a long, deep, sweeping bow to what appeared to be an empty space. As he stepped inside the circle, a figure appeared within it from the right. Also clothed in a robe, but dark blue and with a larger hood drawn up over his head and pulled down low enough to obscure his features entirely. He was not particularly tall, nor particularly small, he was neither broad nor slight. Johnny tried to identify him, running through all the people he knew but he couldn't.

Merryn flicked the light switch and the gallery was illuminated. The electricity was back. The concrete floor of the gallery would remain a deep damp charcoal grey for some time. The paint on the walls was bubbling and lifting in places. Merryn was thankful that that was all she had to contend with. When she thought of the visitors' centre losing the weather station, she realised how lucky she had been. In the harbour there were fewer lorries and most of the debris had been cleared, bar the larger items. Jack's boat was still lodged on the supermarket roof awaiting specialist demolition experts. The supermarket had been declared unsafe and hadn't been able to open. Perhaps the pubs could open again now the electricity was restored. The ice cream kiosk had been carried off in the wave. It would be some time before Porth Taran could return to business as usual. The storm had scared off the holiday makers and Porth Taran had fallen very quiet.

She looked at her watch. Ten o'clock; she had two hours. She set about wiping down the chimes and hanging them in front of the open kitchen window to dry off. She binned the postcards and the stock of paper bags, ruined by the wet. She wiped out the drawer of the till and cleaned the residue of fine silt that still clung to the grain of the countertop and skirting boards.

Then she turned her attentions to the mosaic. She gathered up the loose mosaic pieces that had been flung all around the gallery. She rinsed them under the tap then laid them out on a cloth. She began to reglue them, almost definitely not in their original positions. She allowed her fingers to lead. Naturally finding their places between the leaves.

Midday was approaching so Merryn turned the sign on the door over to *Closed*, stepped out onto the pavement and locked the gallery behind her. It was the last week of the school holidays and normally the busiest of the year, but the harbour was very quiet.

She walked up the road and passed the church. Reverend Kate was lifting boxes out to the boot of her car.

'Good morning. Need a hand?'

'Hi Merryn, how's your head?'

'It's on the mend, thank you.' Merryn stepped over to grab a box.

'Oh no you don't. I'm pretty sure you should be resting my girl. But thank you, I can manage. How's the gallery?'

'The broken windows were the worst of the damage but they're already fixed. I've had to bin the carpet but I was pretty lucky, really. How about the church?'

'It's not too bad in here, stone is resilient stuff. It just needs to dry out. I don't think there will be much damage – well other than all these documents. I'm taking them home to dry them off in my conservatory. Anyway, you off for a walk?'

'Yes, I thought I would check out the beach.'

'That's it, blow the cobwebs away.' Rev Kate waved at her and disappeared through the door of St. Petroc's.

Merryn turned the corner and there was Matt leaning against the railings at the top of the steps. Her stomach skipped. She was immediately angry with herself. She must not allow her heart to rule her.

His face was drawn though he managed to force out a smile. He raised his arm and waved awkwardly. 'You came.'

'Yes, I did.' She looked at him as blankly as she could manage, desperately trying to quell the conflict of emotions rising deep inside her. 'But I almost didn't.'

'Let's go down and find a place to sit and talk.' He gestured for her to go down the steps before him.

At the bottom, Merryn turned towards the café. The peat shelf had been completely uncovered of sand by the flood waters, she sat down on it, her arms folded and legs crossed.

Matt sat a little way away from her.

Merryn fixed her gaze on the horizon and waited for him to speak.

'I want to explain,' he said.

Merryn glanced up at him. His face was plaintive.

'I'm not sure how much you saw. I am guessing you didn't see everything.'

'There's more?' Merryn's face was heating up.

'There is more. That's why I had to talk to you.' He took a breath. 'You saw Bea kiss me, didn't you?'

Merryn nodded, fighting back tears.

'Well, that is exactly what happened, Bea kissed me.'

Merryn fixed her eyes back on the horizon and held her expression taut.

'I didn't kiss her. I didn't want to kiss her. If you hadn't taken off like that you would have known.'

Merryn still didn't speak.

'I stopped her, Merryn. I pulled away. I didn't want to kiss her.'

'And you didn't want to slow dance with her either?' Sarcasm flooded her tone.

'You really were watching?' Matt's eyes were teasing her. 'And you're upset because,' he paused, 'I should have done that with you?' He looked at her cheekily, the corners of his mouth ever so slightly turned up.

Merryn was aghast. She stood up angrily and turned to start walking away.

'Merryn, I'm sorry. I didn't mean...' He stood up and caught her hand.

Merryn swung round and cast an angry glare at him.

'Please, Merryn. I, I ...'

Merryn's eyes flashed with ire. She turned and marched back up the beach, up the steps and down the harbour road to the gallery. She went inside, slamming the front door, leaving the sign turned to closed and fled to the back kitchen, out of sight from passers-by. She leant over the sink, clutched the taps and wept.

Who did he think he was? To lead her on like that, suck her in, then turn his attentions to someone else. And now, he thinks it's funny? Merryn jolted as an almighty crack of lightning fired overhead. She looked out of the back window at the little courtyard but all was still. Then another reverberated across the village. Rain in huge drops began to fall, blotting the paving slabs, faster and faster. The courtyard quickly filled with an inch of water and began to seep under the back door. She grabbed a pile of tea towels and rolled them up against the bottom of the door. She breathed deeply and tried to quell her tears. Then she sank to the floor in desperation and held her head in her hands. Pain and humiliation swept her. She shouldn't have gone, she should have trusted her instinct. How could she have allowed someone to envelope her soul so deeply? And someone she had known for such a short time?

She took a long deep breath and closed her eyes. She focussed on breathing slow and evenly. Outside, the rain began to ease. The drops fell more sparsely and with less force.

Elwood and the High Priest walked slowly towards the centre of the circle, their paces synchronised. They stopped a couple of feet from one another.

'Elwood Curnow.'

Elwood bowed again.

The High Priest made a gesture to dismiss the reverence. 'I saw you on television yesterday.'

Elwood couldn't see his face but his tone was alarmingly solemn. 'Yes.'

'Do you believe in the eightfold wheel of the year?'

'Err, yes. O' course. You know I do.'

'And do you believe that the only energy to venerate is that of the earth?'

'Yes, I do.' Elwood was becoming indignant.

'And do you believe that our old religion is sacred?'

'Yes.'

'And that man is a mere mortal on this earth who can only follow and celebrate what has always been?'

'Have I done wrong, sir?'

The High Priest paused at length and Elwood began to fiddle with the torn-up tea towels around his hands.

'Our grove operates quietly and inconspicuously and that is the way we would like it to stay.'

Elwood nodded.

'Do you not see, that it is not you who has brought this wave to our shores?'

'But ...'

'It is not you that has such great powers to cause this devastation.'

Elwood bowed his head.

'Trevina tells me you fear that an evil force has arrived in Porth Taran?'

'I do, sir.'

'And you believe this evil force is Bunjil; the God of Creation of Dreamtime belief?'

Elwood nodded.

'Do you believe that creation is evil?'

Elwood shook his head. 'No.'

'So, tell me, how can the God of Creation, the force that creates, the force that brings into being, be evil?'

Elwood lowered his head. He glanced at the torn-up tea towels around his hands. 'But my hands, they were burned!'

The High Priest breathed in sharply, shook his head and tutted. 'Elwood Curnow, we are mortals, insignificant in the universe's landscape. We are here for but a short time and in that time we can only strive to contribute in a small way.'

Elwood nodded. Of course, he agreed with that. He knew that.

'There are superior beings who walk with us during our time on earth. It is of course, important that we are aware. That we can differentiate between those that should be kept at a distance and those that should be protected. If you threaten creation you will be punished.'

'But, I was protecting Ambis. For the sake of Porth Taran.'

'Do you not see? Ambis has entered her twenty-first year, she is coming of age. She has begun to approach her zenith. To discover and explore all that is available to her. The age when youth releases itself from parental shackles, from the limitations of apprenticeship. It is a fragile time and without a good teacher she may stumble and fall.'

Elwood listened hard trying to fathom the point he was making.

'I know you believe in fate.'

Elwood nodded. He did, and he believed himself to be part of Ambis's fate and intended to fulfil his promise to watch over her.

'You say that Bunjil is walking amongst us in Porth Taran?'

'He is, sir.' Elwood drew himself up tall.

'Could it be that Bunjil is part of her fate?'

Elwood cocked his head on one side. It was the thing that he was most worried about.

'You cannot change the will of the gods, but you can help.'

'I can?'

'Ambis needs only protection from herself. All of us reach an age when we must unfetter and fly on our own wings. Life is a series of obstacles to negotiate successfully. Obstacles are cunning for they are shape shifters. They can appear tantalising or inviting and draw us closer. They can be invisible and appear with no announcement, ambushing us when we are least prepared. They can shroud opportunities with a mantel of warning that turns us away from them, diverting our course and lengthening our path to achieving our potential. We cannot change fate but we can influence the shape of our trajectory be it beneficial or detrimental. This is your role.'

Elwood nodded solemnly.

'Of those that are left abandoned to puzzle through on their own some will fall down the crevasses, or between the cracks. We are not all blessed with a wiser older counsel who can identify the barriers, the pitfalls or the cliff edges. A guide who can understand our place in the world and deliver this information subtly and in a palatable manner. This is the gift that you have to give to Ambis and to Bunjil. For Ambis only needs protection from herself. Help her, show her, but Elwood Curnow, you must be careful not to anger her, for she knows not the powers that she wields.'

'Anger Ambis? I have no intention of doing such a thing.'

'Ambis and Bunjil together make a formidable force. Anger them and it will be your downfall and that of Porth Taran's.'

Elwood raised his head and met the High Priest's eyes, which were now visible beneath the hood.

'Do you solemnly swear to meddle no more in the ridding of Bunjil?'

'Sir.' Elwood's voice dropped.

'You must swear.'

'I solemnly swear to no longer meddle in the ridding of Bunjil.'

'Do you accept to serve as Ambis's guide? To help her understand her potential?'

Elwood flung his shoulders back and puffed out his chest. 'I do, sir.' He thought for a moment. 'But how should I do this?'

'You must get close to both of them.'

The thought of getting close to Bunjil filled Elwood with terror and his expression betrayed it.

'You are afraid?'

'His power is strong.'

'You must overcome your fear and join with Bunjil. Help him complete his mission.'

'His mission?'

'All will become clear in good time. And you, Elwood Curnow, will contribute to its success.'

Elwood thought quickly. Being allocated a role by the High Priest himself was an honour indeed and on a mission for the God of Creation; there was surely no one so blessed as that. Not even those hooded figures that kept their faces shrouded and their heads haughty at the festivals. The ones who didn't speak but muttered under their breaths. He, Elwood, would be an earth god's assistant. He met the High Priest's eyes once more, then bowed and backed away reverently.

Merryn was regaining her composure. She stood up and splashed water over her face from the kitchen tap. She could hear someone hammering on the front door. She stayed where she was. No customers today. The hammering continued. She waited. Then she heard her name. She peeped around the edge of the kitchen cabinets to the shop front. Matt was outside. His face was worried.

'Merryn!' 'Please.' 'I'm sorry.'

Merryn hung back. How convenient. He was sorry now, was he?

'I didn't realise,' he called.

Didn't realise what?

'Please, can we talk?'

Merryn didn't move a muscle.

'I promise you, nothing happened with Bea. You are the only one for me.'

Merryn's eyes widened.

'I knew it, the first time I met you.'

Merryn remembered that morning, when he had dropped by the shop so early. She remembered his flashing smile and his easy manner. Then she remembered Bea and the look on her face when she saw Matt. That look that she had seen time and time again. Bea, when she sets her sights on someone, is unstoppable. She would trample her grandmother for a handsome man. Merryn stepped gingerly out from the kitchen.

Matt was sitting on the pavement cross legged, his forehead leaning on the glass pane of the door. Sensing movement inside, he sat up.

'Merryn, I'm sorry. I'm sorry I teased you. I didn't mean anything by it. I didn't want to hurt you. Please believe me, it was a stupid way to behave. I was nervous. You're important to me. Please, let me in.'

Merryn's eyes met his. She searched his expression for mockery but found none. She edged towards the door and unlocked it.

Matt pushed it open. 'I wanted … I want,' he corrected himself. 'I want to kiss you.'

Merryn stared, immoveable.

'I have always wanted to kiss you.' His gaze was solemn, unshakeable. 'I just need to know …' he was clenching and unclenching his fists by his side. 'I need to know if you want to kiss me.' He flicked his eyes downwards, as if preparing for rejection.

Merryn could feel his angst. She took a step towards him. There was no teasing, nor dishonesty, it was clear.

'Please.' He took her hand and held it up to his mouth and kissed it. Then he put his hands on her waist and pulled her into him. He kissed her firmly but gently. She sank into his embrace allowing the warmth of his mouth on hers to envelop her. She slipped her arms around his neck and pulled him closer to her, kissing him back.

Outside, the clouds had parted allowing the sun's rays to shine down unfiltered, flooding the shop window. They stood holding each other in silence for a moment. Then Matt pulled away.

'I promise, I will never ever tease you like that again. I hadn't realised how you felt.'

Merryn glanced up at him nervously, frowning.

'I didn't realise how you felt about me. I didn't realise that your feelings were the same as mine. It all happened so quickly. Merryn Jewell, I love you.'

At last, she spoke, 'I have one word to say to you.'

Matt frowned, 'Am I in trouble again?'

She looked back at him. 'As I said, just one word.'

Matt waited.

'Firebuds.' She searched his face.

'Ah, those.' He smiled.

'How did you know?'

'It's good to have secrets,' he said and kissed her again.

The little shop was heating up in the warmth of the sun.

'Come on, I need some air,' said Merryn.

THIRTEEN

Johnny and Elwood were driving back towards Porth Taran.

'You're very quiet,' said Johnny.

'What? Oh yeah, a lot to think about.'

'So, was he pleased?'

'Who?'

'The High Priest, you know, with your hex?'

'Oh that. Yeah.' Elwood didn't look at Johnny.

'If your powers are that good, I might need a love potion off you!' Johnny chuckled.

Elwood was gazing out of the window and didn't reply.

Johnny peered at him, he didn't look cross, just distant. He gave up and they drove on in silence.

Johnny dropped Elwood at his front door and watched him stumble up the steps. He was really beginning to look old. His back had started to hunch. It was a shame he was so ridiculed in the village. For all his rantings and mumblings, Elwood Curnow was a good man. A little inappropriate at times; it's never good to be too open in a small community. He watched as he fumbled for his keys and then disappeared inside. Johnny put the van into gear and headed back to the surf shop.

Elwood sank onto the sofa in his sitting room and put his head in his hands. He felt drained and daunted and didn't know where to start. The High Priest had said he must get close to Bunjil and Ambis. He was already close to Ambis but now, he must court he who he had believed to be his arch enemy. First, he must ingratiate himself with Bunjil, for he had, so far, only tried to do him harm. Shame swept over him and he had an overwhelming urge to cry. He glanced up at the stern photograph of his mother on the sideboard. She hadn't been in the habit of smiling, except at the vicar. He remembered her grief when he died out there on the moors. She'd shut herself in her bedroom and only emerged for church each Sunday. It was curious, for when his father had passed away, there had been no histrionics, no sadness. Just a list of tasks to get done. She had simply picked herself up and organised the funeral as if she was doing the weekly shop. Sure, there'd been a good turnout at the church for him. Mainly his drinking pals. The wake at The Ship afterwards turned out to be quite a party. Bas Curnow was well liked in Porth Taran though he'd drunk pretty much everything he earned. But Elwood's mother had stayed for just one drink and then returned home to hang out the washing just like any other day. Yes, he was a waster but he meant well and perhaps in later life, if the drink hadn't killed him he could have been Elwood's guide, Elwood's older wiser counsel. He often wished his father had lived longer. Had he fallen through the cracks? Elwood quelled a tear and set his mind to the task in hand. First, he must talk to Bunjil. He shuddered, for his powers, he knew, were immeasurable.

Merryn and Matt were sitting on the top of a granite boulder at the bottom of the beach steps. Merryn was leaning comfortably into his chest, his arm draped around her shoulders. The sun was still high in the sky though it would begin to dip again before long, for autumn was not far away.

Merryn sighed, 'You were right about the storm then?'

'Aw no. There was no tornado. It was the wave that caused the most trouble. It's odd...' He paused and then shook his head.

'What's odd?' She kissed his free arm.

'Well, it's just,' He scrunched his brow, 'A wave of that size would have to be caused by a quake.'

'An earthquake? In Cornwall?'

'You sound surprised.'

'We don't get earthquakes, those are for Italy and America. Not the British Isles.'

'Well, it may surprise you to know that there is a quake every single week in the UK, they're only small and you wouldn't always notice them – but they are monitored and recorded.'

'But this wouldn't have been a small one?'

'No. It could have been a meteotsunami, which can happen when there's a sudden change in barometric pressure.'

'Maybe there was a quake.'

Matt shook his head. 'I checked on the internet up at Beatrice's.'

Merryn scowled.

'Don't do that. You ruin your beautiful face when you screw it up.'

Merryn pursed her lips.

'Beatrice is a good friend of yours, right?'

'She was.' Merryn pouted.

'She still is, Merryn. Nothing happened between us. You saw what happened to the boat and I couldn't find you. I slept on her parents' sofa. Anyway, Beatrice said that you've never been interested in having a boyfriend, and that wasn't for a lack of offers. I didn't think you were interested.'

'Oh, did she? And what else did Beatrice say?' she said indignantly.

He covered her lips with his and stroked the skin under her tee shirt, pushing her gently to the edge of the boulder until she slid down onto the sand. He fell after her and kissed her rolling over and over until they had to stop to gasp for air. He brushed sand from her face and her hair.

They lay on their backs side by side on the warm sand and gazed up at the sky.

'If you just stare up at the sky you could be in any country,' said Matt.

'Mmm, we could be anywhere in the world.'

'You know in Australia, parents in Aboriginal communities teach their children to astral travel.'

'Astral travel?'

'Yeah, bit mad, but you know you kind of trance and imagine yourself leaving your body.'

Merryn stared at him.

'And when you get good at it, suddenly you make it ...' he hesitated, 'Well, it happens. And you end up ...'

'Looking down at yourself,' she whispered.

'Yes.' He looked at her quizzically and cocked one of his dark eyebrows high on his brown forehead.

Merryn peeped at him sideways and grinned.

'You've done it?'

Merryn nodded.

Matt sat up abruptly. 'You have?'

Merryn just smiled.

'Now I'm blown away! There aren't many people who even know about it. Well, not outside Aboriginal groups.'

'Well, I didn't know it had a name.'

'Subliminal dreaming, astral travel, astral projection, out of body experience; the names are endless.' He gazed at her. 'So, when did you start?'

'When I was small. At primary school, mucking about in the playground with Rowan and Beatrice.'

'Rowan and Bea do it too?'

'I don't know if they do it now. It's not really the kind of thing you talk about when you grow up. It was Rowan that introduced me to it. I seem to remember he learned it from Elwood.'

'Aha, Elwood, not as mad as all that.'

'Well,' she looked doubtful. 'If you say so.'

'It takes quite some concentration and practice to actually pull it off.'

Merryn shrugged.

'Where do you go when you do it?'

'All over the place. The Scottish islands, Florida, South America. Once I even went to the Sahara. But mostly to the moors.'

'The moors?'

'Yeah, you know, to weather watch. The weather's amazing up there and I don't have a car so it's easier to do it like that. I mean you can't really feel it like you were in it, but you can see it. The weather in Porth Taran is always the same, well until the other night. I like to see the snow, the wind and the searing heat of the desert.'

'Another weather watcher.'

'You do that too?'

'Sure, it's why I studied meteorology.'

'Where do you go?'

'So far, mainly in Australia, you know it's good for checking the surf before setting out.'

'Did you come to Porth Taran to have a look before you arrived?'

'I might have.' He grinned mischievously. 'I sometimes use it to check on Granddad back in Palm. That's the great thing about it, you can keep an eye on everyone, everywhere. They can't see you, of course and you can't talk to them, but there's telephones for that.'

'I hadn't thought of that.'

'Telephones not made it down to these parts yet then?'

'Shut up, stupid.' She shoved him in the belly.

'Hadn't thought of what then?'

'Going away and keeping an eye on everyone.'

'You must have tried it.'

She shook her head.

'When you went away you never did it?'

'I never went away.'

'You never went away?'

Merryn cast her eyes into her lap and blushed.

'I didn't mean to ... I'm sorry, I'm just surprised. Did you never have an opportunity?'

'Well, all my family are here in Cornwall. I don't know anyone up country and anyway I couldn't leave them.'

'You couldn't leave your family? Not even for a trip?'

Merryn looked away out into the distance.

'So, if I invited you out to Australia with me, you wouldn't come?' He poked her playfully and grinned, hoping to lighten her mood.

'You haven't invited me.'

'No, I haven't but then I don't even have a roof over my head, at the moment.'

'Where did you stay last night?'

'Carrie put me up but I could tell I was in the way. She seems to have hundreds of nippers.'

'Ah yes, I expect three in that tiny house would seem like hundreds! Poor Carrie, she gets so worn down by it all. How about I see if Mum has space at Little Rosewarne? We had a bit of an exodus after the storm.'

'You and me under the same roof? Do you think that's wise Miss Jewell?' He raised an eyebrow.

'Your behaviour will obviously have to be impeccable.'

'My behaviour is always impeccable. Look!' He kissed her long and slow.

Merryn pulled back. 'Right, Mr Bunda, the impeccable kisser, let's go and see about this room, shall we?'

Rowan was leaning against the surf shop door as he watched Matt and Merryn walk along the harbour road hand in hand. They were laughing and smiling. He'd never seen her so happy. She was usually just sort of even, unflappable, enveloped in a calm wisdom. But now, she was bright and bubbly, and oozing joy and enthusiasm. He couldn't help wondering what it was that Matt had that he didn't. He was sure he was fitter than Matt, though he had to admit he did look like he was in good shape and he was taller. He sighed and went back inside to wax a board; he wasn't in the mood to be pleasant and pass the time of day with the love birds. Anyhow, the surf was supposed to pick up in the morning and he wanted to be ready.

At Little Rosewarne, Merryn showed Matt to an empty room.

'Here this one is ready.'

'Where's yours?' He twinkled.

'Right at the top – up those stairs.' Merryn gestured to a small wooden door off the landing. 'Our living quarters are behind that. Mine's next to Mum and Spike's.'

'Ah, ok, I see. Well-guarded then.'

'What are you talking about?'

'You'll just have to come down to me.'

'And why would I do that?'

'Why wouldn't you? How could you resist this pert, tanned slab of muscle?' He tensed his arms and torso playfully.

'Merryn!' Demelza was calling from downstairs. 'Supper's ready.'

'Saved by the bell!' Merryn giggled. 'Come on, time to eat.'

Matt followed Merryn down the stairs to the dining room. The French windows were flung open and Demelza had laid the table out on the terrace.

'Welcome to Little Rosewarne, Matt,' said Demelza carrying a hot casserole between two tea-towelled hands.

'Thank you for having me, Mrs Jewell.'

'Demelza, please.' She put the casserole down, flung the tea towels over her shoulder. She pulled a ladle from her apron pocket and laid it on the table next to the casserole.

'Mum, you know Matt was saying that a wave like that should've been caused by an earthquake.'

'They said that about the last big wave too.'

'Really?' Matt was listening properly now.

'I didn't know that,' said Merryn.

'I'd forgotten actually. It was long before you were born. Your dad and Jack were away at a conference. It didn't do as much damage as last night, but I remember that's what they said on the news. They said waves like that were usually caused by a tremor of some kind but none was recorded.'

'Can you remember what year that was?'

'Ooh, I'd have to think. I'll ask Jack, he'll remember. Or you could go down to the church, I think they keep the weather annals down there. I don't think they record them anymore but I'm sure someone was doing it back then.'

'Mrs Jewell, err, Demelza, had there been waves like this before that?'

'Well, not exactly waves, but the previous few years up until Merryn was born were quite bad. There was a run of awful storms and rough seas. Just the luck of the draw I reckon. There's nothing you can count on when it comes to the weather. Jack'll tell you, being a fisherman and all, he's always got a close eye on it. But the church annals will be your best bet. Oh Merryn, I meant to say, Beatrice called round this afternoon. She said you shut up the gallery early?'

Merryn glanced at Matt. 'What did she want?'

'Well, she just wanted to see you, I think. She was quite concerned about your head and the damage to the gallery.'

Merryn pulled a face.

Matt kicked her under the table.

'Oh right, I'll catch up with her soon I expect.'

The sun was sinking in a still sky. Matt held Merryn's hand tightly as they sat on the terrace looking out over the hills towards Penzance. They sat in silence until the sea glittered in the moonlight and the land had purpled to indigo. There was a clattering behind them as Demelza and Spike set the tables inside for breakfast. He looked at her and smiled.

'You really are very beautiful, you know.'

Merryn laughed nervously. 'Don't be daft, I'm just ... well, normal.' She could feel a blush coming on and she cursed herself.

'This is the point where you're supposed to say something similar back to me.'

Merryn turned towards him and took both his hands in hers. 'Matt Bunda, you,' she paused, 'Are very beautiful.'

He laughed and kissed her.

Demelza popped her head out of the French windows. 'Spike and I are off to the Ship for a snifter. Apparently, they've got the water back on. You two be alright?'

'Yeah, course. Have fun, Mum.'

They sat back for a moment, ever so slightly touching, and listened to the sounds of Porth Taran which was quieter than usual, with the exodus of most of the tourists. A blackbird was launching into its evening chorus.

The sound of a car driving towards Helston became fainter in the distance and then was gone.

'It must have been hard for your mum when your Dad passed away.'

'It was hard for everyone. Except for me, of course, because I wasn't born yet.'

'It's an odd thing, well odd to others. To us, of course, these facts, however huge to others, are ordinary to us. I don't even know my father's name.'

'Did you never ask your mum?'

Matt shook his head. 'I don't want to rake up old hurt, I guess.'

'What happened to him?'

'He just left; I think.'

'Did you never find out where he was?'

'No, all I know is that he was a white man in every sense of the word.' Matt's face

became pained.

Merryn frowned.

'I'm sorry, I didn't mean that the way it sounded. I don't have anything against non-aboriginals, I can't, I'm half and half. It's just that white Australians have given us aboriginals a hell of a time, and yeah we're now in the modern world and tribes are more protected than they used to be, but as I said before, prejudice remains.' He sighed. 'Anyway, that's enough of that. So, was your dad like your Uncle Jack?'

Merryn shook her head. 'No, not at all. He was a little wild if the truth be known. He was a good man and loved mum deeply, but he liked to live on the edge. Uncle Jack is more measured, more solid. They ran the businesses together, Dad did the fishing and Uncle Jack did the paperwork and the farming.'

'Have you got a photograph of him?'

'Up in my room, would you like to see?'

'Your room? Absolutely!' His eyes lit up theatrically.

Merryn swatted him round the head with a napkin. 'The photograph I meant. Now, you stay there!' she said bossily.

Matt stretched on the back of his chair basking in the warm evening. He could almost have been in Australia if it wasn't for the stone buildings all around. Merryn Jewell was quite something and he knew just how lucky he was to have met her.

'Here you go.' Merryn reappeared and passed him a framed photograph.

'Struth, you look like him.' A young man laughed from behind the glass. His eyes held the same sparkle as Merryn's though his hair was curly and dark with tell-tale streaks of copper of Merryn's colour. A string of floats was slung across his shoulder. 'Well, if he could see you now, he would be proud.'

Merryn looked away as a tear fought to appear in the corner of her eye.

Matt reached out to her, pulling her towards him.

Merryn laid her head on his shoulder. She closed her eyes and basked in his touch as he stroked her back gently. He kissed her behind her ear and she shivered. She opened her eyes and looked up at his face.

He smiled at her and then began to kiss her. At first gently, then hungrily. She kissed him back enjoying the touch of his tongue on hers, the feel of his breath on her face. She slipped her hand underneath his tee-shirt and felt his warm smooth skin.

And then, very quietly, in almost a whisper he said, 'I think I should help you put the photograph back in its rightful place, don't you?'

Merryn smiled and disentangled herself from his embrace. Standing up she took his hand and pulled him from his chair. She led him inside and up the stairs to his room.

'Not your room?' whispered Matt.

Merryn shook her head and put two fingers to his lips.

Matt kissed them. Then he took her hand and placed it on his waist under his tee-shirt. He put his hand under her blouse and teasingly stroked her skin.

Merryn could feel a warmth welling up inside her. She looked up at this beautiful, kind, handsome man and smiled.

'You OK?' he whispered.

'I'm OK,' Merryn said softly smiling. Through the window she could see the moon rising in the fading light. An owl was screeching somewhere nearby in anticipation of imminent darkness.

FOURTEEN

Matt and Merryn strolled down towards the harbour. The sun shone warm in Porth Taran and Merryn had never felt so at peace with Matt's strong grip in hers. The feeling that swept her was like no other; she didn't feel tense, or excited, there was just a simple rightness about it.

The surf shop was still closed up; it was too early for Uncle Johnny or Rowan. Elwood was sitting on a pile of wooden planks that had been gathered by the salvage team. He was watching a crane arriving in the car park to remove Jack's boat from the supermarket roof. He stiffened as he watched Bunjil, walking hand in hand with Ambis. It would take some effort to assuage his fears. He stood up as they approached and forced a smile.

'Elwood? Are you alright?' asked Merryn, wary of another outburst.

'Ambis, Bunjil. Good morning!' And he took a low sweeping bow, swinging his arms wrapped in tea towels, which only just escaped snagging on the pavement.

'G'day Elwood.'

'I am at your service.'

Matt and Merryn looked at each other astonished.

'Thank you, Elwood, that's very kind.' Merryn cocked an eyebrow at Matt. 'Well, we'd better be getting on.' She unlocked the door of the gallery and as soon as they were inside, she dissolved into a fit of giggles. 'What on earth was all that about?'

'I have no idea. But I prefer that to his wailing!'

Elwood returned to his seat on the debris and watched as Ambis and Bunjil embraced within. He glanced up at the weather station, the roof was tarpaulined against the elements. It could be months before it was repaired. Would Bunjil be able to complete his work? Could it mean that he would have to leave? Panic swept through him. The High Priest said that Bunjil was part of Ambis's fate. If he left it would be diverting the path. He must make enquiries, this would be his first task. Panic was replaced by relief. This was his starting point. First he must get home for the nurse's visit. He was hoping to rid himself of the bandages once and for all; his hands certainly felt better. He heaved himself from the planks of wood and fallen lampposts and set off up the road towards home.

Merryn kissed Matt before he went off to inspect the damage at the weather station. She watched him as he went out of the door and strode along the quay to the visitors' centre. She smiled to herself. She glanced over to the pile of wooden planks, but Elwood was gone. It's funny how things had a way of working themselves out, maybe there would be no more nonsense from him and she, Merryn Jewell, at last, had found her soulmate. She looked out across the harbour. The boats that had survived the wave had been hosed down of the silt that had coated them after the storm and now they gleamed in the bright sunshine. There was not even a hint of the murky mist of the morning before. She turned to her workbench and began to roll back the film.

The leaves were nicely fixed in place. The firebuds and stamens held fast. Now for the branches to be glimpsed between the leaves and the firebuds. Good strong branches, to embrace, to envelop, to nurture and protect all beneath her canopy. She rummaged through the crockery for just the right shade of dark brown, then she fell on a large amber plate. The branches in amber would make them stand out, make them glow, as if they were alight like warm safe arms. Peeping from beneath the rich green foliage, the obscured skeleton that held life suspended. She took her cutter and began to snap out small uneven rectangles and triangles to fit together over the sketched lines.

Carrie was sweeping water out of the visitors' centre. River silt and fine sand coated the linoleum. Upstairs, builders were banging away making the roof structure safe.

Matt put the phone down and sighed.

Carrie looked up from her sweeping. 'Everything OK?'

'Aw, yeah. I suppose. I'm just a bit worried what will happen if I can't carry on my research.'

'Oh Matt, I hadn't thought about that. What could happen?'

'They might suspend my funding. If they do, I guess I'll have to go home.'

'To Australia?'

Matt nodded dejectedly.

'They won't do that will they?'

'I have to send in a record of my activity to the University each month which they then transmit to Immigration. If I can't do that, I guess I have to leave.'

'So, you need to find a way to continue your research without the weather station?'

'That's about the size of it.' Matt sighed.

'Would a laptop help?'

'A laptop?'

'I dug out the old laptop, I used to use here when we first opened. You can borrow it while we're all messed up like this, if you like.'

'Thanks, Carrie, that'd be great.' He paused. 'You know, I'll find a way, these things always work themselves out. Listen, I have an idea. I'm just gonna nip over and see Rev Kate, I'll be back later to give you a hand.'

Reverend Kate was unloading yet more boxes from the boot of her car. She looked up as Matt approached.

'G'day.'

'Hello.' Rev Kate straightened up, rubbing her back.

'We haven't met, I'm Matt Bunda from the weather station.'

'How do you do? And yes, I know who you are,' she said, smiling. 'It's a small community. What can I do for you?'

'I wondered, could we have a chat about something?'

'Yes, of course. Here, could you grab one of these?'

Matt took a box from the boot. 'Moving house?'

Reverend Kate laughed. 'That storm soaked everything on the ground floor of the church. I took a load of the documents home and dried them in my conservatory, I'm just bringing them back. If you don't mind helping me unload this lot, then we can have a coffee and I'm all yours.'

As Matt carried the boxes into the vestry at the side of the altar he couldn't help but gaze up at the huge ceiling.

'It's impressive isn't it? Hammer beam they call that structure,' said Rev Kate.

Matt nodded. 'We don't have anything like this at home.'

'I suppose Australia's not quite old enough.'

'I think I'd be religious if we had churches like this.'

'Ah, does that mean I can't expect you in here on Sundays?'

'Well, I wouldn't mind seeing a church service, I don't think I ever have.'

'Not even a wedding?'

'None of my friends have jumped the broomstick yet and these days in Australia they're mostly civil ceremonies, and you can have them pretty much wherever you want. And no, I'm not...' he paused, 'Of the persuasion.'

'You don't have to be, you know. I'd be delighted to welcome you here.'

'Thanks, I'll bear that in mind.'

'Anyway, come on, I think you've deserved a drink.' She disappeared through a doorway at the back of the vestry.

Matt heard the kettle click on.

'So what can I do for you Matt?' she yelled over the sound of the hissing kettle.

'It was about the church weather records.'

'The church weather records?'

'Yeah, I heard that a lady about twenty years ago was recording Porth Taran's weather.'

Rev Kate cocked her head on one side. 'Ah now, I think that might clear up a bit of a mystery.' Her head popped out through the doorway. 'Come through, we can chat in here.'

Matt walked into a large kitchen. The surfaces were in old-fashioned Formica and a large dark wood table stood in the middle.

'A mystery, you say?'

'Well, with the ground floor flooding in that storm I've been forced to sort through boxes that have been sat in cupboards for decades. I've been rather lazy you see!' she laughed. 'I've had to unpack them all and lay them out to dry. Do you know, I've been here almost fifteen years and I'm still learning things about this community?'

'Really? Like what?'

'Sorry, I was forgetting myself for a moment, of course my parishioners' private business is confidential, forgive me. Please, sit down? Tea or coffee?'

'Coffee for me, please.'

She set the mugs on the table and pulled out a chair on the opposite side loaded high with ancient documents, scrawled with a heavy black ink, smudged in places. She began to unpile them on to the table until she came to a small black notebook.

'I found this.' She held the notebook up for him to see. 'I was wondering what it was. Inside, it appears to be some sort of journal.' She opened up the first page. 'There are dates written all down this left-hand column, the pressure, rainfall and wind speed is recorded here in the middle. The next one seems to be a commentary on farming activity and then this final column is very strange.' She handed the notebook to Matt. 'Can you see that last column is filled with rather odd lines and squiggles?'

'Do you know who wrote this?'

'I'm afraid not. It was before my time. But it does look like a record of the weather.'

Matt leafed through the pages. 'It seems to start in June 1986 and finish in December of the same year. Is that usual for a church to keep such records?'

'No, not usual at all. But Porth Taran is an unusual place.'

'Did you find any others?'

'No, that's the only one so far.'

'And you've no idea who wrote them?'

Rev Kate shook her head. 'I'm afraid not. But I expect someone here knows. It wouldn't be too difficult to find out if you ask around.'

Elwood was strolling back down to the harbour with his hands at last free from their bindings. The nurse had carefully replaced the bulky dressing with a finer gauze releasing his fingers and allowing him to wear gloves to protect them. He wandered past the gallery but could only see Ambis inside, working away at her bench. He waited a little to see if Bunjil might appear from the kitchen at the back, but she was clearly alone. He wandered on a little further to the visitors' centre.

Carrie was busy cleaning the windows and had propped the doors open to dry off the floors. 'Alright Elwood?'

'I expect you'll be off work for a bit.'

'Me, Elwood? Off work? Never. It's already a lot drier. As soon as the electrics have had the all clear it'll be business as usual.'

'Not for the weather station, though eh?'

Carrie stopped a moment and rubbed her brow with her rubber gloved hand. 'Not for a bit I suppose. Matt's trying to find out what he'll do.'

'Is he here?'

'He's nipped over to the church for something. Pop back later if you want to see him, I expect he won't be long. Shall I tell him you called by?'

'No, No. It doesn't matter.'

'Are you feeling alright? You've gone pale.'

Elwood leant on the doorframe to steady himself. 'No, I'm fine. Tired I expect. Best be off.'

Carrie watched as he staggered across the road and leant on the harbour wall catching his breath. She shook her head. He was a strange one, that Elwood Curnow. She sighed and cleaned off her wiper blade with a tea towel.

Merryn was sanding down the edges of the rough amber chunks of china, smoothing their jagged edges to form triangles. Three sides, for love, life, and death. For death, she pondered, is as much a part of life as life itself.

Her father was taken from her before she had drawn breath. His death had been as big a part of her existence as he would have been, had he lived. There had been nothing to grieve and little to remember. Her mother rarely spoke of him, save for marking the day he disappeared. Each January she would gather up camellia blooms from the tree at Tregarron that he had planted with his mother as a boy and take them down to the beach and throw them one by one into the sea. When Merryn was small she would go with her but now Demelza went alone. If he was mentioned in conversation she would sigh and open her eyes wide as if fighting emerging tears. Merryn couldn't bear to cause her any more pain by asking questions. Uncle Jack, Spike and Uncle Johnny had given her all the fathering she had needed. But now, perhaps Johnny was right, and that it was time she found out more.

She glanced up at the harbour, Elwood was perched on the harbour wall. His staff was leaning against the rough stone and his necklaces glinted in the sunlight. The thought of consulting Elwood on something so private galled her.

She shook her head and sighed. She absentmindedly started to sharpen the corners of the triangles with a file. These pieces must be fashioned to interlock perfectly to form strong, sturdy branches to support all who found life within.

Elwood continued to stare at the church door. Why would Bunjil be going into the house of God? Did he not know the danger that would lie in there? This is what the High Priest meant when he said that Bunjil and Ambis needed protecting. Not only did he need to make sure that Bunjil stayed in Porth Taran by Ambis's side, but that he was not distracted from his task by the taunting powers of the Church. He knew he should go in there after him. It had been over half a century since he had stepped inside St Petroc's. The thought of it made his skin turn icy. He drew a breath sharply and let it out slowly, his eyes closed.

As he opened his eyes, Bunjil appeared at the doorway restoring Elwood's composure. Bunjil began to walk down the harbour road towards him. He heaved himself from the wall.

'Bunjil.'

'Elwood, we meet again.'

Elwood smiled weakly.

Matt continued on to the gallery.

Matt pushed open the door of the gallery.

'What have you got there?' said Merryn, wiping a film of amber ceramic grime from her cheek.

'Do you remember what your mum said about the weather records?'

'Yes.'

'I went to see Rev Kate. She found this when she was clearing up after the storm. It looks like part of those records. It's dated 1986, before you, or I were born.' Matt's eyes were sparkling with excitement.

'Let me see.' She took the notebook from him and flicked through the pages. 'It's a funny thing for a church to be keeping records of.'

'Yeah, I know. Reverend Kate didn't know why and nor did she know who wrote them. There must be others. I'm going to ask around to find out who wrote them.'

'I expect mum knows. Or definitely Jack, if not.'

'Yeah, it shouldn't be too difficult.'

Merryn was peering closely at the last page of the notebook. 'It looks like there are some initials here at the bottom. Hang on, let me see, it's tiny.' She held the page up to the light. 'I think it says D. C.'

'D.C.?'

'Who do we know with those initials?' Merryn thought hard. 'Dave, Daniel …'

'Didn't your mum say it was a woman?'

'Yes, I think she did. Well, it can't be Demelza, Anyway, that would have to say D.T. if that was the case and if it was later, DJ.'

'Anybody there?' Uncle Jack was standing in the doorway.

'Uncle Jack, sorry, I didn't hear you.'

'I can see that.' He nodded at Matt. 'Matt.'

'Mr Jewell.'

'I'm just filling in the account of the storm to the insurers, what time do you reckon that wave hit the other night?'

'Well, it was properly dark. Hang on, I think the church bells rang just before. It must have been about eleven, 'said Matt.

'What's that you've got there?' asked Jack, looking at the black notebook.

'This? It's part of the weather records for Porth Taran.'

'The weather records? I'd forgotten about those.'

'You know about them?'

'Now, they were part of a project to help out the farmers. I was on the committee for it. It didn't really do much good.'

'What were they for?'

'It was years back. We had a really bad run of weather in Porth Taran. Lasted about fifteen years. Crops kept getting washed out or dried out. It was a period of extremes. We nearly lost the farm.'

'The weather records were to try and understand what was happening?' asked Matt.

'Yeah, well we couldn't get any help from the MAFF.'

Matt frowned.

'That was the Ministry of Agriculture, Fisheries and Food back then. We thought that if we recorded it then we could prove to the MAFF what was going on and get them to help. Anyhow, it didn't work. Because our weather problems were only here and only affected the agriculture very locally. Anyway, it all calmed down eventually and we're all right now. I guess it was just bad luck and luck changes.'

'When did it calm down exactly?'

'Well after that big storm. The day our Merryn was born. Apart from the other night we've had no problems at all.'

'Hmm. It could be a pattern.'

'Well, I hope it's not going to repeat itself, I mean I've got polytunnels now for the strawberries, but they would struggle in the very high winds we used to get back then and the broc'li don't like the wet, they rot.'

'Broc'li?'

'That's what we call cauliflower in these 'ere parts,' laughed Merryn in a strong Cornish accent.

'The forecast, at the moment is set fair for a few days, so I would say it'll be dry enough.'

'Well, I hope so, Matt. I hope so.' He sighed. 'Right, let me just lean on here and fill in the time of the storm, I'll need to get this off quick. They'll take ages to reimburse me I expect.' Jack bent over the form and scribbled in the space. 'I'll be off to the post office with this. Have fun with your weather, Matt.' Jack left the gallery and turned up towards the shops.

'Right, weatherman, I need to get on, so you'd better take your notebook somewhere else,' said Merryn to Matt.

'Getting under your feet, am I?'

She smiled up at him teasingly, 'And possibly my skin.'

'Do you think your mum will mind if I work in the dining room at Little Rosewarne?'

'Ask her, there's hardly anyone in the B & B, I shouldn't expect it's busy now.'

'See you later, gorgeous.' He kissed her gently on the lips and trailed his hands around her shoulders making her shiver.

FIFTEEN

Matt opened the laptop in the dining room at Little Rosewarne. He laid the notebook out next it. He tried to wipe the dust from its cover but some of it was ingrained. A little mould had stained the pages around the edges. He opened it to the first page. It was headed simply 'Porth Taran June 1986' and underlined in thick black ink. Each page was neatly scored into four columns, in pencil. The last one, with the squiggles, was narrower than the others. There weren't markings on every line. He looked at them for a long time, but couldn't see a pattern. The handwriting was neat and a little curly. The first comment box was filled with the words 'drought' and the following twelve with ditto marks. The weather data was enough to continue his research. He would just need the committee to corroborate their accuracy.

He began to build a spreadsheet to log the data, but he knew one notebook would not be enough. He needed records from a good period of time for it to hold sway. If he could get hold of the other notebooks it would maybe keep him going until the weather station was back in business.

Merryn's fingers worked quickly, tessellating the tiny amber triangles to form the branches, slotting them carefully, so they peeped from beneath the foliage and the firebuds, gluing them as she went.

She looked out of the window. The last of the dumper trucks had pulled out of the harbour. The debris had been cleared, and the Lugger craned off the supermarket roof. Apart from Elwood still sitting on the wall there wasn't a soul out. It was almost eerie to see Porth Taran so inert, just the gentle flow and ebb of the seawater stirred in the harbour.

It was five o'clock when Merryn locked up the gallery and set off for home.

Elwood jumped down heavily from the wall as she passed. 'Ambis.'

'Elwood, you made me jump.'

He bowed low and then stood just staring at her as if he was thinking of something to say.

'Is there something I can do for you?'

'No, no. Of course not.'

'Then I'll be on my way.'

'Well, yes, err actually there is.'

Merryn waited with a stern expression.

'Can you tell me? Will Bunjil be staying?'

'Staying? What do you mean?'

'Well, with the weather station destroyed he doesn't have anywhere to work, to carry out his research.'

Merryn stared at him. How stupid could she have been? She had been so taken up in the romance and joy of it all she hadn't been thinking straight. She hadn't even asked him about it.

'I don't know Elwood. I expect you will need to ask him. Why do you want to know?'

'Oh, just interested. You know, concerned for him.'

'Really? Well in that case you can start calling him by his actual name, Matt!' She snapped. She turned on her heel and stomped up the road, angrily. The nerve of the man, always meddling where he wasn't wanted. The man was mad. Her stomach was swooping, the suggestion was unthinkable. How could she ask him about what he saw on the day her father disappeared? What would be the point? He'd clearly begun to lose his faculties.

Elwood cowered against the wall, he could see he had annoyed her. The High Priest had warned him not to make her angry. A sharp breeze blew across the little port and Elwood pulled his jacket tighter around him. How could he get close to them if they rejected him? He was so lost in his thoughts that he didn't notice Reverend Kate coming down the road towards him.

'Mr. Curnow! I've been wanting to talk to you.'

Elwood gasped. Not her. He picked up his staff and turned to make his escape. His foot caught in a mooring ring, set in the quay, and he fell hard on the pavement. He landed heavily on his shoulder, wailing in pain.

'Mr Curnow! Are you alright?'

'Get away! Get away, Get away from me.' Elwood's cries were muffled by the concrete.

'Help!' Reverend Kate called out and looked around the deserted port.

Hearing cries as she reached the head of the harbour, Merryn turned around. She could see Elwood lying on the ground and Rev Kate leaning over him. Carrie was running towards them. Reluctantly she turned back.

'What happened?'

'He tripped over that ring in the quay,' said Rev Kate.

'Don't move. Tell me where it hurts,' said Merryn.

'Shoulder,' he wailed.

Reverend Kate leaned over him. She reached towards his right shoulder. 'This one?'

'Not her!' he shrieked.

Reverend Kate jumped back.

Merryn shot Kate a sympathetic look. 'Elwood, it's OK, it's me, Merryn. Which shoulder is it?'

'My left one,' he whimpered.

'Can you move the fingers in your left hand?'

He wiggled his fingers, then he rolled himself onto his right side. 'I'm alright. Here, help me up.'

Merryn took his right elbow and helped him up to sitting.

'Call Johnny.'

'Johnny?' said Merryn.

'He'll look after me.'

'Mr Curnow let me fetch my car and I'll take you to the hospital to get checked out.'

'I 'ent going in no car with the likes of you, thank you.'

'Elwood! Don't be rude.'

'Rude?! Nothing comes even near to rude, not with that lot.' He suddenly scrambled to his knees and stood up leaning on his staff.

'Elwood, careful!' exclaimed Merryn.

But Elwood was off as fast as he could go pushing himself along with his staff and holding his left arm as still as he could. The three women stood in consternation and watched him as he went.

'I'll pop in on Uncle Johnny on the way, he'll check up on him. Kate, I am so sorry he was rude to you.'

'Oh don't worry, it's not personal. It's what I represent.'

Matt was halfway through the notebook, when Demelza wandered into the dining room.

'How's it going?'

'Yeah, it's going well. I really need to get hold of the others though.'

'Can I have a look?'

'Help yourself.'

Demelza picked up the notebook and flicked through it.

'Can you really not remember who recorded these?'

Demelza didn't answer straight away. 'It was all such a long time ago,' she sighed. She continued to flick through. 'There was a lady, but she moved out of the village. When was it?' She thought for a bit. 'She moved just before Merryn was born.'

'Do you know how long these records were taken for?'

Demelza shook her head. 'It was a long time, I think. Did Reverend Kate not know who kept them?'

Matt shook his head. 'Before her time. This is the first she's known about them.' He took the notebook from Demelza. 'Look at these.' He pointed to the final column. 'These strange markings. What do you think those mean?'

Demelza peered at them. 'It looks like shorthand.'

'Shorthand?'

'We all did it at school, well the girls did.'

'Can you read it?'

Demelza shook her head. 'It's all too long ago now. I wonder, maybe Carrie'll be able to help you. I seem to remember she was really good at it.' Demelza took the notebook back from Matt and carried on flicking through it and then stopped on a page. She frowned.

'You alright?'

'Yes, it's just, stupid really. This notebook covers the time when Piran and I were courting.'

'Really?'

Demelza turned back to the first page. '1986. I was eighteen and Piran was twenty-one. It was a long hot summer. The worst drought I ever remember.'

'Can I see?'

Demelza gave him the notebook. The rainfall column showed zero after zero.

'That was certainly a dry summer, and hot. The temperatures here show 30, 33 and as high as 36 here. That's Australian weather.'

'Aah, it was a lovely time.' She sighed. 'Right, that's enough daydreaming, I must get on.'

Reverend Kate sat in her kitchen sipping coffee. She could see she would need to ask advice from the bishop. How could she approach a reluctant parishioner? If he didn't want to be approached, should she insist? She couldn't imagine the suffering the man must have gone through and still be going through every day. And what would approaching him achieve? Would it do any good? She couldn't take away his pain. She pulled at her dog collar which was catching on her neck. She pulled it off and slung it on the table.

There it was, her identity, a small piece of plastic casting a shadow over the worn wood. This table must have been in this kitchen since the time the church was built, a monument to the Victorians. Only they would have attempted to build such an edifice in the face of the Atlantic Ocean, battered day after day, but still standing as proof of their industrial prowess. Standing tall against the stormy waves that licked its steeple.

Kate pushed the collar round the table absent-mindedly and tried to imagine what the first parishioners might have been like. The vicar would have been a much more authoritarian figure in the community back then. Though she suspected her predecessor had held similar sway.

She'd expected it to be difficult for them when a woman took over. The congregation had dwindled initially. It was Elwood's mother who had snubbed her the most. She had made it perfectly clear that, in her opinion, this was an unsuitable job for a woman and an unsuitable appointment for Porth Taran. She'd continued to attend the Sunday Service, standing right at the front like a beacon for stalwart belief, through thick and thin. She remembered that at various points during her delivery of the sermon, Mrs Curnow would purse her lips and draw in her breath, as if she had been the witness to a shocking faux pas in a community of unerring religious conviction. With a mother like that, it was understandable why Elwood had become who he was. She flicked the collar away from her and drained her mug of lukewarm coffee.

The sun was beginning to sink behind Beacon Crag. Merryn and Matt were bathed in the embers of its glowing rays as they sat in companionable silence at the terrace table in the back garden of Little Rosewarne. The air was heavy with the fragrance of rosemary, released in the heat of the sun, from Demelza's hedges that surrounded the terrace.

'I saw Elwood today,' said Merryn.

'You see him every day as far as I can tell.'

'Well, yes, I do.' She rolled her eyes. 'He asked me if you were staying.'

'Ah, word gets round fast.'

'What do you mean?' The blood drained from Merryn's face. 'Are you leaving?'

'No, my darling, I am not leaving. Well I hope I'm not.'

Merryn's stomach started to swoop again. 'Please explain.' She worked hard to sound less panicked than she felt.

'I need to change my research project to be able to stay. You see with the weather station wrecked and the instruments destroyed I can't continue to log the weather. If I can get hold of the other notebooks and gather a data set to report on, I might be able to switch the time period I focus on. Or if the centre is fixed quickly, then I might use the notebook data as a comparison to the new data. I have to send a report on my activity every quarter to justify my staying here to the University and also to immigration.'

'You didn't say anything.'

'You've got enough on your plate, with the gallery flooded and all that.'

Merryn looked at him searchingly.

'I promise you, I am not leaving and if I was, you would be the first to know.' He held her hand tightly and kissed her. 'Merryn Jewell, I will stay with you as long as you will have me.'

She smiled and rested her head on his shoulder. 'You know, I was thinking about Elwood. I can't work it out.'

'Work what out?'

'He's obviously not quite all there. What with his mumbo jumbo and his drinking and all…' She paused and took a sip of coffee. 'But Uncle Johnny says that he saw something the day my dad…' She swallowed, 'You know, the day he disappeared.'

'And you haven't asked him?'

Merryn shook her head.

'Do you want to know?'

'I, I don't know.' She looked out into the distance. 'Well, yes, I think I do want to know, now.'

'Did you never, ever wonder before?'

'Of course, I did, but it's just, you know, it hurts.'

Matt took her hand. 'So, why now?'

'Well, I've never had to tell anyone about it before. Everyone here, just kind of knows. They don't ask me anything and I've never had to explain before. And I suppose you coming…'

'Hey, listen, you don't have to explain anything to me. And I'm really sorry if my asking questions has raked all this stuff up for you. I will stop immediately.'

'No, I'm glad it has been raked up. It's high time I found out more about my dad and who I am. It's just, Uncle Johnny thinks I should talk to Elwood. I don't know that I can trust him to tell me the truth and not embellish it in some way.'

'Uncle Johnny trusts him?'

'Well that's a funny thing too. Uncle Johnny has always been devoted to helping Elwood and he's hardly his type. I mean, all his friends are cool surfer types and then there's Elwood.'

'I don't think Johnny would suggest you spoke to him if he had any doubts, you know.'

'Hmm, maybe you're right.'

'There was an inquest, right?'

'Yes, there was.'

'Did Elwood testify?'

'I don't know.'

'There must be a report somewhere, I expect your mum has a copy.'

Merryn shook her head. 'I can't ask her. I don't want to upset her. Anyway, if there was something, I'm sure I would know about it.'

'I wouldn't bank on it, Merryn. If I were you, I would see if you can get hold of the report and depending what you find, then talk to Elwood. I'll come with you, if you like.' He paused. 'I'm sorry I'm railroading you; you must do what you're comfortable with, but whatever that is, I will help you.'

'You are just the nicest boy.' She leant across and kissed him warmly. 'You know, for some reason, Elwood is absolutely terrified of Reverend Kate.'

'Really? What makes you say that?'

'Today, he fell over on the quay and she ran to help him. He yelled, sort of like in panic. He really hurt himself so maybe it was that. I had to calm him down and help him to his feet. As soon as he was up he rushed off. Well, sort of hobbled. He wouldn't let Rev Kate anywhere near him.'

'He's a funny old thing, Elwood. But, you know, there's something caring about him. I mean, the way he's outside your gallery everyday waiting for you. I've watched him. He doesn't leave until he knows you're there.'

'Oh, that. That's just a bit odd. He's done it since I opened the gallery.'

'It's certainly a bit strange, but I don't think it's negative. I think he really does care.'

'Oh, Matt Bunda, I swear there isn't a bad bone in your body, you are the kindest,' she kissed him, 'Nicest,' she kissed him again, 'Loveliest,'

Matt dodged the kiss. 'Oi!'

'What?'

'Handsomest?' This time he kissed her.

Reverend Kate put down the phone to the bishop. She could understand his concern. Whilst it would be appalling publicity for the church, she knew it would be wrong to hush it up. Not that that is what he'd requested. But he was right, it had to be handled carefully. At the moment, that was immaterial; if she couldn't talk to Elwood then it had no chance of ever getting to that point. And even if she did, the chances were that Elwood wouldn't want to take it any further. What good would it do? His life must have been dogged by the events of those few years and coloured his outlook forever. It wasn't surprising he'd rejected the church and embraced paganism. But she knew she had to try to right some of the wrong. She took a piece of paper and began to write. If Elwood wouldn't talk to her, all she could do was write to him.

The sun was lowering in the sky and there was an autumnal nip in the air that made her do up her cardigan. Winter wouldn't be long. All the lights along the harbour were flickering on, their glare reflecting gold off the purpling water. The Ship Inn looked quiet this evening, the majority of the visitors had flown away to their lives in the cities, to escape the devastation of Porth Taran. The residents were settling down to a quiet evening after the summer rush.

Elwood was sitting on the sofa nursing his shoulder, it ached like heck. He was longing to massage it, but he couldn't reach it with his other arm, and anyway the burns were still too painful for prolonged pressure. He would get the nurse to look at it when she came to change his dressing. The television droned at him from the corner of the room. If it hadn't been for that supposed do-gooder Reverend Kate, he would never have tripped. Why did the Church always think it knew best? They only believed in one book; a book written so long ago about a people that were so different from modern society it was almost irrelevant. They should take a long look at themselves.

He believed in the Earth. The Earth was still here and as long as it was here, there would always be life.

There was a knock at the door that made Elwood jump. He heaved himself from the sofa, wincing at the pain in his shoulder. He looked through the letterbox but couldn't see anyone.

He yelled, 'Who's there?'

There was no answer.

Probably kids he thought to himself. He yelled again, but still no answer. He unlocked the door and peeped outside, there was no one to be seen. He stepped out and went to the side to check the gate, kids were always hiding there. There was no one. As he turned to go back to the front door, he found Reverend Kate on the doorstep between him and his escape route. She was holding her hands up as if in surrender.

'Mr Curnow, please. I just want to talk to you. I'm not trying to convert you. I respect your beliefs. That's not why I'm here.'

Elwood began to panic. She was barring the way to his home. The side gate was locked from the inside so he couldn't slip round the back, through the garden.

'Please, don't be afraid. I know what happened.'

Elwood looked at her frowning.

'If you don't want to talk about it, I shall respect that, but I just wanted to let you know that I've found Reverend Cribben's diaries.'

Elwood didn't move a muscle as his brain absorbed what she was saying.

'I know what he did.'

Elwood went cold, he thought he was going to faint. He began to sway. He leant against the wall of the house.

'Mr Curnow are you alright?'

He felt beaten, he couldn't fight anymore he just wanted it all to go away. He nodded. 'I'm alright,' he whispered. Tears came fast and uncontrollably down his cheeks.

Reverend Kate took his good arm and he let her. His fight was gone. She shepherded him into the house and sat him on the sofa. He sank into the cushions and closed his eyes. He could hear Reverend Kate moving around in the kitchen, but he just didn't care anymore.

SIXTEEN

Elwood awoke to birdsong, the cheerfulness of it mocking his heavy mood. His eyes fell on the familiar blank woodchip wallpapered ceiling, but something was different, he could sense it. He started to heave himself onto his elbow, but his shoulder stabbed with pain. As the pain subsided, he noticed a comforting smell of laundry powder. He was lying in crisp, clean bedding, that wasn't his. He rolled carefully on to the opposite shoulder and tentatively pushed himself to sitting. The bedroom door creaked open and Johnny walked in carrying a steaming cup of tea,

'You're awake!' he said brightly.

'What are you doing here?'

'Well, it would appear that you've pulled, Elwood!'

Elwood frowned; he was in no mood for humour.

Johnny spotted it immediately and calmed his tone. 'Here, I've brought you a cuppa.' He set the mug on the bedside table.

'What did she say to you?'

'Who, Reverend Kate? I'm surprised you let her in.'

Elwood shook his head. 'I didn't let her in, Johnny. God shop, they're all the same. Blinkin' do-gooders, think

159

they're holier than thou. But what do they know? The untouchables, that's what they think they are.'

'Rev Kate is a good sort you know, Elwood. She's modern. Not old school like old Cribben.'

Elwood shuddered at his name. 'Where is she? She still here?' Fear swept his eyes.

'It's OK, she's gone. She called me late last night. Said she didn't think you should be alone.'

'What did she say to you?' His tone was panicked.

'She just said you'd had a shock and that you didn't want to talk about it.'

Elwood worked hard to keep his expression even. 'Did she now?' He thought for a moment. 'The only shock I got was her at my door.' His voice was stronger and louder now. He could pull this off.

'What did she want?'

'God knows.' He managed a snigger, 'But I don't. She was rabbiting on about something she'd found in the church. Nothing to do with me, they're all mad.'

'She obviously felt it was important enough for you to need looking after. She even came back last night with these clean bedclothes and while you slept on the sofa, she spring-cleaned your room and changed the bedding before she'd let me bring you up to bed. Don't you remember any of it?'

Elwood shook his head. What on earth had happened to him? He was going to have to pull himself together if he were to escape this unscathed. 'Must have had a bit too much to drink,' he mumbled.

Johnny looked puzzled. He hadn't been in the pub last night and there were no empty bottles or cans downstairs, and he, unusually, didn't smell of alcohol. 'Right, well it's nearly eleven and Reverend Kate is sending round her cleaner to blitz your downstairs.'

'What's she doing that for?' Elwood was outraged.

'Come on Elwood, she's alright, Rev Kate. She just wants to help.'

There was a knock on the front door.

'That'll be her now, I'll go and let her in.'

Elwood opened his mouth to argue.

'And you, you drink your tea and let other people get on with knowing what's best for you.'

Before Elwood could remonstrate Johnny was halfway down the stairs.

Matt was taking a breather from the weather records and went to find Reverend Kate. Carrie was opening the windows of the visitors' centre.

'Morning Carrie. Any drier in there yet?'

'I wish, I've got dehumidifiers arriving today. It just seems to have soaked into all the concrete. I can't even get the biros to work properly it's so damp. Where are you off to?'

'The church. I was going to catch Rev Kate about something.'

'What's that you've got there?'

Matt held up the notebook. 'It's the weather records from the eighties.'

'Let's have a look.' Carrie opened it at the title page. 'Porth Taran Weather Records. I remember these being taken. It was that blonde lady, she was on the committee.'

'You know who wrote these? Do you know her name?'

'Hang on, let me think. Her husband was a farmer.'

Matt said nothing, willing Carrie to remember.

'Neighbouring Tregarron.'

'Tregarron?'

'That's the Jewells' farm, up over Beacon Crag way. Jack's farm, now. Methleigh Farm, she lived at. Now let me think, what was their name?'

Matt held his breath and waited.

'Constantine. Yes, that was it. He died, Kendrick, so sad.'

'The initials in the notebook are D.C. so that would fit. Can you remember her first name?'

'What was it? Yes, Di Constantine. Funny I haven't seen her in years. I didn't really know her. Just knew of her. I remember her taking these though. My mum was on the committee too and she used to come back ranting about Di, about how she was so full of her own importance all the time.' Carrie flicked her eyes skywards. 'Typical village committee stuff.'

Merryn sat at her worktable gazing out at the cool autumn morning. There was not a movement in the halyards and the seasonal smell of wood smoke was just beginning to tinge the air. She pulled the drape off her mosaic. The branch pieces had dried in place. She traced a line with her finger along the branches, where they ran beneath the foliage, holding the backdrop.

Next, would be the trunk. Smooth or ridged? Wide or spindly? Dark or light? She glanced up at the trees on the headland, their trunks wide and almost black with the sun behind them. This was an old tree, an ancient story of life, death and love. The trunk must show its wisdom and its scars. A gnarled channel of water vessels that carried sustenance from the roots to the canopy. Armoured against the elements, protecting their cargo to ensure the continuation of life.

She settled on a broad strong trunk to hold the canopy fast. Not as dark as the trees on the headland, for darkness on the tree of life was not good. She would choose a hazel or a more vibrant chestnut, a hue naturally set between the colours of the roots and the branches. The roots, dark and vital, channelling to the trunk immovable and protective, then the branches, flexible and dancing distributing their booty to the leaves and blossoms. Smooth would be idealistic and naïve. A good life is rich but wise, light-hearted but realistic. Textured to form the armour to protect the flow of life within. She carefully retraced the silhouette of the trunk in pencil and then set about fixing the pieces in place.

'Di Constantine?' Merryn looked up at Matt and shook her head. 'I've never heard that name before.'

'Apparently her husband ran the farm next to Tregarron.'

'That place is a tenant farm, well at least it is now. It's owned by a large holding company. I know that because Uncle Jack is always moaning about them.'

Demelza appeared at the kitchen door carrying a dish of lasagne.

'Mum, have you heard of Di Constantine?'

Demelza looked up sharply. 'Supper's ready, move that lot out the way would you Matt?'

Matt slid the notebook and his laptop to the end of the table.

'Mum?'

Demelza put down the hot dish and wiped her brow with one end of the oven glove. 'Erm, Di Constantine? I've heard of her. Lord knows what happened to her. Why?'

'Matt was asking. Apparently, it was her who made those weather records.'

'Oh, could well be. She moved away from here years ago. Matt, love, could you go out to the garage and tell Spike supper's ready?'

'Sure.' Matt got up and left the dining room.

Merryn looked at her mum. 'Mum. I think I want to know.'

'Want to know what, love?'

'Everything. I want to know what it was like back then.'

'Back when?'

'You know, when you were with dad, and what it was like in Porth Taran back then. No one seems to talk about it.'

'Don't we? I suppose it's just not very interesting my darling.'

'I want to know what happened to him.'

'To your dad?'

Merryn nodded, fighting back a tear. 'I'm sorry to bring this up but I think I do need to know.'

'Of course, you do. Let's get supper out the way and then we can talk properly.'

Matt and Spike came in from the garage, chatting about motorbikes.

'Young Matt 'ere, 'as been telling me about rounding up cattle on a motorbike in Australia. Now that's something I would have liked to do.'

'Rounding up cattle? Spike, I think you might be having a midlife crisis! Was washing up for me all these years not enough?' Demelza laughed.

'Ah, Demelza, washing up for you has been the be all and end all as far as I'm concerned.' He kissed her hand across the table. 'But, a man needs a bit of excitement every now and then.'

Matt looked out of the window and could see fog rolling in across the village like bonfire smoke. 'But, instead of excitement it looks like we're in for another pea-souper.'

Demelza glanced at Merryn. 'Are you alright, love?'

'What?' Merryn looked up to see everyone looking at her.

'You've gone quiet,' said Spike.

'Just tired, I think.' As she said it, a fatigue set on Merryn like a lead weight. 'I think I shall head off to bed after supper.' They finished their meal watching the fog thickening in the street.

'Right, that's me done. I'm off over to Tregarron to see Jack, we've run out of taties,' said Spike.

'Do you mind if I hitch a ride?' asked Matt.

'Sure, the more the merrier.'

'You going to see Jack, Matt?' asked Demelza.

'Yeah, I want to ask him about that Di woman.'

Demelza's eyes flashed, then she looked down into her plate.

'Is there something wrong?'

'No, no of course not. You go ahead.'

'Demelza love, are you alright?' asked Spike stroking her shoulder. 'Looks like our girls are a bit under the weather tonight, eh Matt?'

'I expect I'm just tired too. It's the time of year. Now you go careful in that fog!'

Left alone, Demelza and Merryn set about clearing the plates into the kitchen. With the table cleared and the pans washed up they sat back down at the table

'Now my darling, what would you like to know?'

'I want to know what happened to my dad.'

'I'm afraid nobody knows for sure. That's really the hardest bit. One day he was there, and then he wasn't.'

'Was there an inquest?'

'Yes, of course.'

'Did you go?'

'Yes, I did. It was almost the hardest day of my life. Except that day, you know the day he didn't come back.' Demelza took a sharp breath in. 'The day his boat disappeared. I can remember almost every second of it.'

Merryn took her mother's hand in hers. 'What did the inquest rule?'

'They couldn't find his body, so it was an open verdict.'

'So, there is a chance that he is still alive?'

'Oh love, your father is dead, I know he is. I knew it the minute it happened.' Demelza moved her chair closer to Merryn's and put her arms around her. 'Listen, I realise that we haven't had this conversation before, and that's my fault. I have missed your dad every single day since. Be safe in the knowledge that he loves you.'

Merryn looked at her mother, puzzled.

'I mean, he would have loved you. In fact, he already loved you. He was so, so, delighted when I told him over the radio that you were on the way.'

'So, he knew about me?'

'He did. I had a radio with me so that I could get in touch with him even when he was at sea. We didn't have mobile phones back then but with the fishing radios we were lucky. We would speak to each other two or three times a day. Now, I'm glad I did tell him then or his boat would have disappeared, and he would never have known.' Demelza caught a stray lock of hair that was hanging over Merryn's eyes and lifted it and tucked it behind her daughter's ear. She stroked Merryn's cheek. 'You look so much like him.'

Merryn squeezed her mother's hand.

'Perhaps now is the right time for you to read the inquest report. It's a transcript. You can read exactly what happened. I have it upstairs.'

Merryn looked at Demelza and hesitated. Now, she didn't know if she wanted to read it.

'There's no rush, but it's there if you want it.'

Merryn nodded.

Spike's Land Rover headed west out of Porth Taran. The fog was getting thicker.

'I can't fathom it,' muttered Matt.

'What's that mate?'

'This mist. I checked the temperature on my phone before we left, and it hasn't gone up. There were no thermals due to come in when I checked my computer earlier.'

'Ah, the weather, eh? Y'know Cornwall is like nowhere else. Take it from me, I've been here for years. If you don't like the weather, wait five minutes.'

'Well, yeah, in the rest of Cornwall, but here in Porth Taran it's well known for being uncharacteristically stable. That's why I'm here, to work out why.'

'I guess it's possible that it's changing, they say things go in cycles, don't they? I mean they've been saying for years that the ice cap is melting at a rate of knots and just the other night they said that the warming had slowed down and that all these scientists are talking poppycock. But then you're the expert.'

'Mmm, well, we shall see I guess.'

'You been out to Tregarron yet?'

'No, this is the first time.' Matt looked out at the fog. 'Hey, do you think there was a problem with asking about that woman who took the weather records?'

'No idea, mate. Don't you worry, Demelza's got a lot of worry on her plate at the moment, she's not quite herself.'

'Really? Why's that then?'

'It's since the storm. She lost a bit of money when the guests left early and quite a few cancelled for the following week. The bank holiday weekend is usually the biggest takings weekend of the summer and with the storm the village has become a ghost town. I've never seen anything like it. Well, not since that storm twenty years ago anyway.'

'You were here then?'

'Oh yeah, I was a bus boy and waiter at Demelza's caff'. That's how we met.'

'So, you were here when Merryn was born?'

'Yeah, I was even present. I held Melza's hand. On a table in the cafe with floodwaters lapping at our feet. Our Merryn, she don't do nothing by halves that one!' He let out a snort of laughter.

'Did you know her father?'

'Nah, not really. I knew who he was, he didn't talk to the likes of me. I didn't start working for Melza until just before Merryn was born. Poor girl, she was trying to run that cafe single-handedly and preggers. Lucky for me though, I got the job and well, as you can see the rest is history.' He went quiet as he negotiated the narrow lane.

'Look after Merryn, mate. These Jewell women are strong minded and all that, but they need support, though they'd never admit to it.'

'I don't think I could do anything else, Spike. I've fallen for her.'

Spike glanced sideways at Matt and smiled. 'And she for you, mate. And she for you. It's written all over her face. You're the first, don't break her heart.'

Spike slowed the Land Rover at a pair of stone gateposts overgrown with ivy. He swung it off the road and up the rough drive.

'Struth, I wasn't expecting anything quite this grand.'

'Ah, the Jewells were a wealthy family once. But this is all that's left. Now, Jack works his fingers to the bone to keep it all going.'

As they bumped and bounced over the potholes, the dark granite edifice loomed through the mist. Mottled with lichens clinging to its walls, it gave an allure of abandonment. They pulled up behind Jack's pickup truck by the front door. Dogs barked from the depths of the house. Spike swung the weighty knocker against the heavy wooden door.

From within they could hear Jack calling, 'Quiet!' The door creaked open and Jack appeared. 'Awright, Spike. Oh, hello young Matt, come in, come in.'

'Just popped over for some taties, Jack,' said Spike.

'Time for a tipple first?'

The two men winked at each other and chortled.

'Don't mind if we do,' said Spike. 'Matt?'

'For sure, count me in!'

Spike and Matt took off their shoes and padded in their socks across the threadbare rug through a hall lined with yellowing black and white photographs of children, and tractors and people of a bygone era. At the back of the house was a large kitchen with a flagstone floor. Two Springer Spaniels ran to greet them as they entered.

'Bed!' roared Jack, and the two dogs cowered and reluctantly returned to their cushions by a large range. Jack reached up to a tall Cornish dresser and pulled open its glazed doors. He took down a decanter of amber liquid and splashed it into three crystal tumblers. 'There, get that down your necks!'

Spike grinned at Jack and then his eyes met Matt's. He raised his eyebrows and gestured excitedly as he raised the glass to his lips. 'This is the gear.' He tipped the glass up and downed it in one swallow.

'Brandy, right?' asked Matt.

'Well, kinda,' replied Jack.

Both men were grinning like schoolboys. Jack picked up the decanter again.

'Could you grab those taties before we get stuck in, Jack?' said Spike.

'Sure.' Jack splashed a bigger serving into the bottom of each glass this time. 'I'll go and fetch them. Matt, come with me I want to show you something.'

The older men smiled and winked at each other.

Jack led him out of the front door, across the drive to a door in a side wing of the house. He stopped just outside. 'Now, what I'm about to show you stays between these walls, you understand me?'

Matt nodded solemnly. 'Scout's honour.'

Jack turned the handle and pushed the door open. He stepped inside, Matt followed him. There was a sweet smell that seemed to hang in the fabric of the rough stone walls. In the centre of the room was a huge copper receptacle with a horizontal pipe leading into a barrel.

Jack went over to it and tapped the tank affectionately. 'What do you reckon?'

'What is it?'

'This, young Matt, is a piece of history. This, my boy, is a still. Mead brandy has been distilled at Tregarron since the seventeenth century.'

'Wow, mead! This really is old England.'

'Watch what you say, this is old Kernow and well behind The Tamar, thank you!'

'Well, it packs quite a punch.'

Jack chuckled proudly. He went to the back of the room and opened a wooden door. He disappeared down a flight of stone steps then reappeared carrying a large sack of potatoes and set them on the floor next to the still.

'Listen Jack, I wanted to ask you…'

'Fire away, young Matt.'

'You know Methleigh Farm?'

'Of course, they're our neighbours.'

'Well, I'm looking for the lady who took those weather records, I showed you. I've heard she was from that farm.'

Jack turned to polish the still.

Matt went on, 'You see, there must be others and I need them to continue my work. With the weather station destroyed, I have to find another way to collect data or I may have to suspend my project and go home.'

Jack looked up and frowned at him, then shook his head. 'Methleigh is a franchise farm these days. Like so many farms, corporations buy them up and install teams of people to run them. Not like the good old days.'

'I'm looking for the people who used to live there. Was it the Constantines?'

'The Constantines? They're long gone.'

'Do you know where they've gone?'

Jack shrugged. 'Can't say I do.' He bent down and picked up the potatoes. 'Mustn't forget these,' he said.

Merryn opened her eyes and located herself for a moment. It was still dark outside. She wondered what time it was. She peered out of the window, the fog had thinned a little. The streetlights cast an orange filter over the village. She glanced at the clock on the wall. It was only ten. She can't have been asleep for more than an hour. She rubbed her eyes.

At the bottom of the bed was the folder. She picked it up. On the cover, in her mother's careful hand was written simply 'Piran'. She traced the letters slowly with her finger and let out a deep breath. Her fingers reached for the flap, and then pulled back. Not yet, it wasn't time. She got up and went over to the basin and splashed water on her face.

Her mind wandered to Matt. What would her father have thought of him? Would he have been proud or protective? Her mother had said nothing of her new relationship, she just treated Matt as a friend who was staying in a spare room. He seemed to fit in so terribly well with everyone. Even Elwood appeared to have accepted him at last, not that it mattered what Elwood thought. The only thing she could be sure of was the feeling that stirred within her when he came close. His face held a comfort and familiarity that she had never known before. She dried her face with the towel, pressing it comfortingly over her face and breathing in the scent of laundry powder. She folded the towel, enjoying its softness, and laid it on the end of her bed and went down the stairs.

Matt was in the sitting room with Spike. The television was on but both men were slouched and sleeping, there was a faint stench of mead in the air. Merryn knew that smell only too well. In the middle of the sitting room carpet was a large sack of potatoes. Well, at least, they'd remembered what they went over there for. She decided not to wake them though she knew they'd feel rough in the morning if they slept in the sitting room all night. She padded to the kitchen and fetched herself a large glass of water and went back to bed.

SEVENTEEN

Matt and Merryn were sitting at the breakfast table at Little Rosewarne.

'You never told me the Jewells were landed gentry,' said Matt, pouring coffee into a mug.

'Landed gentry? Where did you get that idea from?'

'I went over to Jack's place last night, remember.'

'Oh, Tregarron isn't a country estate, it's a working farm. Well it is now. I guess back in the day it might have been quite grand.'

'Judging by the gateposts I'd say it used to be something pretty special.'

'It's definitely special. Well, it is to me, my father and Jack grew up there. The Jewells do have land, but Jack works hard on the farm with the potatoes, broc'li, strawberries and cabbages, but wealthy they are not!'

'And mead brandy.'

Merryn put a finger to her lips. 'You mustn't breathe a word!'

'Oh, I know, Jack has sworn me to secrecy.'

'Did you ask about that woman? You know, the one who kept those records.'

'Yes, I did but Jack said they'd moved on. I think I might have hit a dead end. Anyway, gorgeous, I'd better get off. People to see.'

She watched his departing back. Matt Bunda, the surprise that blew in on the wind. She smiled to herself and drained her mug. She climbed the stairs to fetch a jumper from her room. As she went into her bedroom, the folder on the end of her bed caught her eye. She hesitated. She knew she couldn't put it off any longer.

Matt sat on the wall outside St Petroc's looking out over the harbour, the village, and the moors beyond. It was so far removed from the scenery he was used to. Even the sea had a whole different character here. At home, it was nearly always a blanket of undulating crystals as it reflected off the reef beneath it. The shallows in the mangroves were as clear as glass and laced with rays darting from their hiding places in the sand. But here, in Porth Taran, it could change in a moment from a deep piercing azure to a dark heaving animal that threatened the rocky coast with its lurching talons, ready to crumble any cliff or scoop up any who dared to approach its periphery.

He jumped off the wall and went to find Carrie. As he approached the visitors' centre, he noticed that Merryn hadn't put out the boards on the pavement yet to show the gallery was open. She wasn't quite herself at the moment, tired probably. He went closer and peered through the window, but all was dark inside, she wasn't there. Perhaps she'd gone back to bed.

He went on to the visitors' centre.

Carrie was sitting behind the counter, smiling. 'We have internet! I've no idea how we used to survive without it, you know.'

'Ah the good old days? When you used those red telephone boxes, you Poms are so proud of?'

Carrie laughed. 'And listened to vinyl records and knew how to lick stamps. – But you won't remember the

Neolithic times, young Matt! Hey, have you got any further with finding the weather records lady?'

Matt shook his head.

'You were right. She did live at Methleigh. But they've gone now. Jack didn't know where.'

'Ah, that's a shame.'

'Can I use your laptop a minute?'

'Sure.'

Matt darted behind the counter and started tapping on the keyboard. There was no listing for a Mrs D. Constantine on the white pages. He tried an open search – nothing. He sighed. 'There's no mention of her on the net.'

'You could try Elwood.'

'Thanks Carrie, you're a doll.' He blew her a kiss playfully and tore out the door. As he passed the gallery, there was still no sign of Merryn. He'd head straight back to Little Rosewarne after Elwood's to check she was OK.

Elwood was sitting on his doorstep behind the now fading agapanthus. His expression was solemn, contemplative.

'Elwood!' Matt yelled as he approached.

Elwood frowned and then shot to his feet. 'Bunjil! You want me?' he said, incredulous.

Matt stopped to catch his breath. 'I think you may be able to help me. I'm looking for a lady who used to live at Methleigh farm. A Mrs Di Constantine.'

'Dywana? I haven't 'eard 'er name in years. She left the village...ooh way back before you would have been born.'

'Do you know where she went?'

Elwood scratched his head. 'I'm not sure I do. I helped her move, but I can't remember.'

'Elwood, please. You're my only hope now.'

Elwood thought hard. 'Ooh now. I think she may have gone out the back of Penzance, Badgers Cross way.'

'Badgers Cross?'

'Near there. Hang on. Yeah, that was it. Chysauster, just next to the ancient village.' His eyes lit up. 'There's a farm there, split into houses it was. It was a long time ago, mind. She's probably moved on by now.'

'Can you remember the name of the farm?'

Elwood rubbed the uneven whiskers on his chin. 'Chy summat, I think.' He paused and screwed up his face. 'Chy Bowjy! Yes, that was it.'

'Thanks Elwood, you're a mate.' Matt turned and started down the steps to the pavement.

Elwood beamed, turning over *you're a mate* in his head. 'What do you want with her anyway?' he yelled after him, but Matt had already turned the corner up the hill.

Reverend Kate stood on the doorstep of St Petroc's looking out over the harbour. She could see the whole village from there. She could see Elwood's fading agapanthus outside his front door and even a little beyond. She could see Matt turning the corner up towards the Bed and Breakfast. He was a breath of fresh air in Porth Taran, that boy; so 'to the point' and uncomplicated. He was also a very lucky man to have caught Merryn Jewell's attentions. She smiled to herself. Perhaps in her younger days she might have attracted attention from young men like Matt, but now in her twilight years she'd settle for a peaceful existence of routine and basic comfort. The faint trill of the phone ringing in the vestry interrupted her thoughts and she went to answer it.

Matt knocked on Merryn's bedroom door but there was no answer. He pushed the door open a little and found the room empty. The air smelt of her perfume. He stood for a moment and breathed in the fragrance. Maybe she'd gone the back way to the gallery. He must have missed her when he was chatting to Elwood. He would pop in on his way to the bus stop.

Just as he turned to leave the room, he noticed a large green folder on her bed. On it, in marker was written 'Piran'. He leant towards it and flicked the flap back. It was the inquest paperwork. She must have talked to Demelza. He sat on the bed and leafed through it. He skim read the report at the front. Jack had reported on the safety guidelines for lobster fishing, and had confirmed that all was up to date and in order. The last person to speak to him was Demelza. She had spoken to him on the radio. Behind it was the transcription. He flicked through to Elwood's witness statement. He'd described the exact spot that he had been sitting, near a place called Rinsey, when Piran arrived by boat to set his pots. He reported watching him answering a call on his radio and then described the formation of a whirlpool and the boat being sucked under the waves.

The whirlpool would have had to be massive and very powerful to suck a whole boat under. Matt frowned and closed the folder. That was pretty unlikely. He closed the door carefully and went downstairs.

Demelza was in the dining room, ironing sheets and listening to the radio. 'Alright, Matt?'

'G'day Demelza.'

'You must be feeling pretty lost without the weather station?'

'Aw, no. I've still got stuff to be getting on with. He hesitated to mention Di Constantine again. I thought I'd head out to a place called Chysauster later, Elwood was telling me about it.'

'The ancient village?'

'Yeah, figured I may as well do some sightseeing before winter hits big time.'

'That's a tricky place to get to. How will you get there?'

'Bus, I guess.'

'You'll need a map too. Have a look in the bookshelves in the guest sitting room, there's an Ordnance

Survey in there. I doubt the bus goes right past it though, you'll have to walk a bit.'

'That's OK, it'll do me good. Especially with all your cooking.' He blew out his stomach and rubbed it.

'I don't think you will ever be fat, Matt!'

Matt laughed.

'Merryn at the gallery?'

'Yeah, I guess so. She's not in her room.'

Reverend Kate replaced the receiver. Sadness swept over her, but at least she knew that whatever came of this, there was nothing she could have done differently if she was to remain true to herself and to God. She walked to the front door and gazed once more across the village. Porth Taran's reputation for its weather, its beaches and its fishing was on borrowed time.

Matt was striding past the end of Elwood's road with the map tucked in his jacket pocket when Elwood ambushed him.

'Bunjil!'

'Jeez, Elwood. You frightened me.'

'You goin'?'

'Where, mate?'

'Badgers Cross?'

'Yeah, thought I'd take a look.'

'I'm comin' with you.'

'Aw Elwood, I think there'll be a bit of walking, not sure you're up to that.'

'I know the shortcuts, let me be your guide.'

Matt looked him up and down. It was true, it would be handy to have someone to show him the way, but Elwood was getting on.

'I'm fine walking. And I've got my staff, my hands are almost healed. Look!' He held his palms out. 'Let me show you the way. Please. The Penzance bus will be here in just a few minutes, we don't want to miss it.'

'Alright, you're on. Come on, let's go.'

They set off together, down to the bus stop in the harbour.

Elwood walked beside him, barely believing that he had found a way to be useful. He had at last found the quest the High Priest had talked of. He felt taller somehow, and he straightened his back, and holding his head high, he walked down the harbour road with Bunjil, the God of Creation.

They didn't have to wait long before the bus loomed from the top of the hill. Matt paid his fare and Elwood flashed his bus pass. Matt climbed excitedly to the top deck. Elwood struggled to keep up with him and arrived on the top deck puffing and blowing, a sweat breaking out on his brow.

'This has to be one of the best things Blighty offers. Double-decker buses are it, in my book,' said Matt.

They sat right at the front. Matt lurched nervously as they approached overhanging branches that then magically missed the bus's windows. As they neared Penzance, they passed St Michael's Mount. The sea around it was as smooth as glass. A couple of rowing boats were making their way from the shore to the mount, for it was high tide and the causeway was underwater. They disembarked at Penzance bus station and twenty minutes later they were climbing on another, destined for St Ives.

'We'll need to stay down here this time. The stop we need isn't so far,' said Elwood.

The bus crawled up the hill behind the town and followed the winding road up high onto the moors. At last, Elwood pressed the button to request the next stop. The bus came to a halt at a crossroads with a scattering of houses huddled round it.

Elwood had recharged his batteries and jumped off the bus almost youthfully. 'Now, there's a shortcut over the fields or we can go the long way round, down the road. What do you think?'

'The shortcut sounds good to me.'

Elwood nodded and set off at quite a pace towards a gate to a field.

Matt watched as he jumped up against the top rail and swung his legs over and landed heavily on the other side.

He turned red faced towards Matt and grinned. 'Not so old now!'

'I'm impressed.'

Elwood winced internally, cursing himself, he had forgotten about his shoulder. He straightened himself and set off across the grass more tentatively.

Then Matt vaulted the gate after him.

In the distance there was a collection of farm buildings.

Elwood pointed. 'That's where we're going.'

'What do you know about Dywana Constantine?'

'I used to do work for her years ago. In the garden and that. When she was at the farm. She's a very clever lady. She's interested in the weather too. She had all these instruments and stuff in her study, and a telescope too. Back then, we had terrible weather and she used to watch it all the time and write things down in books. I don't know much more, except ...' Elwood stopped and caught his breath.

'Elwood?'

'There was trouble.'

'What kind of trouble?'

Elwood's eyes twinkled with excitement. 'To be honest I'm not exactly sure but it was something to do with her husband. People said all kinds of stuff. Nasty stuff about her. But Dywana, she's special, a really nice maid, you know?'

Not far off the headland, a small patch of water gurgled and spun. Merryn watched it intently. The more she stared at it the bigger it became. There must be a shoal of fish just there, for all around the sea was smooth. A chill breeze blew across her, she could feel it on her skin but inside she was burning hot. Overhead, gulls wheeled hopefully for a loot of fish. So, this was the spot her father was last seen. If Elwood told the court the truth, this is where he'd watched him setting his pots that last time.

Merryn stood up slowly. She tied her skirt up high around her legs, like shorts. Her bare legs, though goose pimpled, were oblivious to the cold wind. She walked to the edge of the cliff. The water was spinning faster and had grown into a whirlpool. Within it, creamy surf began to dance and splutter. As the froth rose to the surface, the wind carried it off in tiny foaming clouds. To her left she could see a ledge and beneath it a route down to the water's edge. She sat down on the edge of the crumbling earth and slid herself a couple of feet down on to a granite outcrop.

Demelza carefully folded the last of the sheets and added it to the neat stack on the dining table. She heard the bell on the front door go and someone step into the lobby. She wasn't expecting any guests.

Rowan appeared at the dining room door.

'Ah, Rowan. Nice to see you!'

'Hi Demelza. It's good to see you too. I was wondering if Merryn was about.'

'Demelza looked at her watch. 'She'll be at the gallery at this time. She never stops working, that one.'

'Oh, the gallery was all closed up, I guessed she'd pulled a sickie and stayed at home.'

'No, she's not here. Maybe she's closed up for lunch or something.'

'Yeah, maybe.'

'I'll tell her you popped by though.'

'Thanks. I'll catch you later.'

As Rowan went back out through the door, Demelza glanced at her watch again. One o'clock. Merryn usually put up a 'gone to lunch' notice if she closed in the middle of the day. She picked up the pile of sheets and took them up to the airing cupboard on the landing. She knocked on Merryn's door just in case. There was no answer. She popped her head round. On the bed, was the folder she'd given her. She must have read it. Demelza cursed herself, she should have gone through it with her, what was she thinking just leaving it there? She knew that report almost by heart. She remembered her fear and grief as she heard those words for the first time in that court room. Since then she'd reread them so many times that they had become ordinary, they'd become part of her. Remembering her fear now made her angry with herself. What must Merryn be feeling right now, reading those words for the first time?

She went downstairs to the phone. First, she tried the gallery but there was no answer. Then she called the surf shop.

'Johnny? Hi, it's Melza…Fine thanks, I was just wondering, have you seen Merryn? …Ah ok, no it's nothing to worry about… No, I'm sure she's fine, she must have just gone off somewhere. I'll catch her later.'

Johnny said the gallery hadn't opened up at all. Unless she was working out the back and had just left the closed sign up. She would normally tell her if she was doing something different. Anyway, her little girl had become a grown woman, it wasn't for her to keep tabs on her.

EIGHTEEN

Matt and Elwood approached the back of the farm buildings.

'I don't think we should be leaping over the back fence as an opener. Going in the front way would be more polite.'

'It's alright, we'll go through the ancient village, then we can arrive by the footpath.' Elwood pointed to a network of wide low stone, grass topped walls that ran in circles.

'Wow, that really is an ancient village. How old is it?'

'I think some of it goes back to the Iron Age. The newest parts date back to the time of the Romans.'

'The Romans? Jeez, that is quite something.'

Elwood shrugged. 'It's the old country here. Not like your new-fangled Australia.'

'I guess so. But you know my people have inhabited Australia since men walked the earth. Nothing new there.'

Elwood picked up the pace and seemed even lighter on his feet. Matt sped up to keep up with him. As they approached the first wall, Elwood put his foot in a crevice in the face of it and levered himself up to stand on the top without even using his staff for support.

'Look at you go!'

'Ah, I know these walls like the back of my hand, my mum used to bring us here for picnics when we were kids.' Elwood dropped down into the remains of a roundhouse, and walked confidently through the maze of wall-lined paths, until they reached a barbed wire fence on the other side, enclosing a field. He put a foot on the lower wire and carefully held the top one aloft for Matt to get through, Matt then did the same for him.

At the far end of the field were a couple of Shetland ponies munching on grass. They briefly looked up at the two men then returned to their meal. Matt followed Elwood to the opposite side of the field, to a stile, and a footpath beyond. A little further along was a greenhouse. Elwood was just carrying his staff now and was walking lithely.

As they approached the glass structure, they saw the figure of a woman bent over a vegetable patch. As they got closer, she straightened and spotted them.

She strode over to the doorway of the greenhouse and took up a shotgun that was leaning just inside it and pointed it at them.

'Who goes there? Get off my land!'

'Mrs Constantine,' said Elwood, alarmed.

'The footpath ends there, you know. You are trespassing.'

'Mrs Constantine, it's me, Elwood.'

She lowered the shotgun a few centimetres while she studied his features then lifted it again. 'This is private land and you're not welcome.'

'Mrs Constantine,' Elwood repeated. 'Do you not recognise me? It's Elwood Curnow. I used to do your garden at Methleigh Farm.'

'Methleigh? What do you know about Methleigh?'

'I've not come to make trouble. I was just your gardener.'

Dywana continued to stare at Elwood. She was a tall woman, in her early fifties, with long blonde hair that had been scooped up into a bun, loose strands were dancing around her face in the wind. Her features were kindly and didn't sit well with such an aggressive demeanour.

Elwood faltered. 'I have someone here who wants to meet you.'

Dywana Constantine lowered the barrel once more. She spoke slowly, 'Elwood Curnow? From Porth Taran?'

'That's right.'

'Yes, yes. I remember you. You redid our stone walling, I think. Well, I don't have any work for you now.' The aggression returned to her face.

'I'm retired now, Mrs Constantine, I'm not looking for work. I helped you move in here, too. I wasn't sure if you were still here.'

At last she put the shotgun down, broke it open and made it safe, she let it hang over the crook of her arm. 'What do you mean by walking over my fields like this? I'm not on my own you know, there are people in those houses there.'

Matt stepped forward. 'Mrs Constantine, we're not here to do you any harm. My name is Matt Bunda, I'm a student and I'm hoping to talk to you about the weather records you made twenty years ago.'

'My weather records?' She looked him up and down. 'You're antipodean?'

'I am, I'm Australian.'

'And you're a student you say?' Her eyes began to soften and her stance relaxed.

'That's right and I've come to study the weather in Porth Taran, at the weather station.'

'It's started again hasn't it?'

'What's started?'

'What do you want to know?'

A chill breeze was brewing from the south and Matt shivered. 'It's quite nippy out here, could we go somewhere to talk?'

She stared back at them sternly. 'Alright, we can go in the kitchen. Just help me with these would you?' She gestured to the greenhouse. On the floor were wooden crates packed with earth. 'I need to move these into the garage. It's chicory, they need to be in the dark.'

The men picked up a crate each and followed her past the chicken coop and down to a collection of granite-built garages. Dywana swung up one of the doors.

'They need to go along this wall, here.'

They each put their crates down.

'Chicory?' said Elwood. 'Don't think I've ever had that.'

'Makes a good winter salad come the New Year. I don't hold with all that eating snow peas from Zimbabwe and winter strawberries. It's mucking about with nature. There's too much of that these days. I like to eat with the seasons, but if you want variety it means hard work.'

Matt and Elwood did three more trips with the crates. As they worked, the wind freshened. Dywana swung the garage door to and looked out over the hills.

'The mist is supposed to come in again tonight, but it won't with all this wind.'

'Which direction is that?' asked Matt. 'I've got disorientated.'

'That's the south coast. Porth Taran is over there.' She pointed in the direction of a patch of grey cloud that seemed to be turning darker. 'On a sunny day that is a splash of turquoise. If you walk up to the top of the ridge by the ancient village you can see both coasts, you know. I think that's why the ancient village was built there; they could see for miles all around. It's the best place for weather watching. You can see it coming. And there's something coming now,' she said frowning.

Merryn stood at the water's edge. The waves were crashing onto the rocks and soaking her feet and legs. The spray flew up and coated her hair with salt. The whirlpool was the size of a small swimming pool now. At Merryn's feet lay an empty water bottle, washed up on the shoreline. She picked it up and hurled it towards the centre of the eddy. The gulls swooped at it, as it flew through the air, hoping it was food. Frightened by the force of the water they wheeled away screaming. The circles became neater, more defined. As the bottle hit the water, it bobbed a little, and then was suddenly sucked beneath the surface, as if a hand had come from below and snatched it. She watched to see if it would reappear but there was nothing. The circles continued to spin. She wondered what would happen if she were to step into the water.

Elwood and Matt followed Dywana through a gate and up a steep granite path flanked by a deep stone clad gully that carried a leat from somewhere at the top of the hill by the ancient village down to the driveway.

'You get a lot of rain up here?' asked Matt.

'We get a lot of rain in Cornwall. Here we have to contain the runoff from the fields. You see the soil isn't what it used to be, it doesn't hold the water so well, and if that leat wasn't there it would run right through the house.'

She opened the front door and they were greeted by a Springer Spaniel that ran around their legs, sniffing and waggling the cropped stump of his tail.

'Jasper, bed!'

The spaniel immediately sunk low and slunk off to a tartan blanket neatly folded in a corner of the porch.

Matt and Elwood followed Dywana into a spotless kitchen. There was a large beech table in the middle, and the room smelt of lilies. She flicked the kettle on and arranged three mugs on the side.

'So, Elwood, what must it be? About twenty years I'd say. I remember now, you did help me move in here.'

'That's right, Mrs Constantine. It was just before Christmas.'

'Ah, yes. Christmas.' Her face saddened a little. 'We used to have marvellous Christmases at Methleigh with Kendrick. He loved Christmas, I loved Christmas.' She smiled to herself then her face darkened, and she sighed. 'Sugar?'

'Not for me, thanks, Mrs Constantine,' said Matt.

Elwood shook his head.

'So, Mr Bunda, you are from Australia.'

'Please, call me Matt.'

'And everyone calls me Di. So, what brings you to these parts?'

'Well, Porth Taran has quite a reputation in the meteorological world but no one has ever really got to the bottom of its microclimate.'

'Ah, I see. And you think you're going to crack it, where hundreds have failed?'

'Aw, I don't know about that but I'll give it my best shot and get a PhD into the bargain. The thing is, I'd only been here a couple of weeks, then that storm hit and the weather station has been destroyed. It has kind of put a halt on my work.'

'And what's your diagnosis?'

'That's what I'm trying to find out. It had all the elements of a seismic wave, but no quake was recorded. Or it could have been a meteotsunami, though it is a bit farfetched; they're so rare and so far, unheard of in these parts. Well apart from one around twenty-five years ago, someone told me, the other day. Though I'm yet to check that one.'

Dywana snorted. 'Well good luck with that.' She dropped teabags into a teapot and poured over boiling water.

'So which university are you studying with? Plymouth?'

'Townsville in Queensland.'

187

'That's a long way to come for a project.'

'Yeah, I was lucky they let me and lucky to get the funding too. Actually, that's why I'm here.'

Dywana looked up in alarm. 'I don't have any money if that's what you're after.'

'No, no!' Matt held his hands up in defence. 'That's not it, honest.'

Dywana relaxed again but continued to look at him suspiciously.

Matt pulled out his wallet and fished out his student card. 'Here look, and the dates are current.'

She studied the card in silence, nodded her head and handed it back to him. She poured out the tea. 'Here,' she passed them their steaming mugs. 'Let me show you something.'

She picked up her mug and led them out of the kitchen, down a corridor and up a flight of wooden stairs. At the top, she turned through a door into a bedroom. In one corner was a metal spiral staircase flooded with light. Dywana began to climb and they followed.

At the top they found themselves standing in what appeared to be a turret, its walls lined with curved bookshelves. A ladder, fitted with tiny wheels, leant against a runner set into the top shelf and at one end the bookshelf was broken by a small staircase leading up to a glass domed mezzanine.

'Mrs Constantine! This is handsome. This wasn't here when you moved in.'

Dywana beamed. 'This is my pride and joy. Indulgent? Yes. But when Kendrick was killed his insurance paid out well. I don't have any children, so I treated myself.'

'Struth!' said Matt gazing up through the dome to the clouds scudding by. His eyes fell on the shelves around him and he began to scan the spines. 'You've got yourself a full meteorological library. You're better equipped than the uni back home!'

'Not just meteorology, there's astronomy, astrology and Celtic mythology in there. They're subjects that are all linked you know. I've been collecting them since I was a teenager.' Dywana glowed with pride.

'This is really impressive,' said Matt.

'Thank you. It's rare that I bring anyone up here, not sure most people would be interested. But you haven't seen it all yet. She gestured to the central staircase. Only one person at a time though, it's not too large up there. Matt?' She gestured for him to climb the stairs.

Inside the glass dome was the largest collection of antique meteorological instruments he thought he'd ever seen. A large telescope set on a wheeled tripod stood to one side.

'Well, blow me! This is incredible. Elwood, you've got to see this.' Matt gazed out through the observatory windows. 'You can see three coasts from here!'

In the Porth Taran direction Matt could see a black cloud hovering over the sea. 'It's still brewing over there. Come on Elwood, it's your turn.' He went back down the stairs and made way for Elwood.

'Now, Mr Bunda, Matt. What was it you wanted to talk to me about?'

'Well, now that I've seen this, a lot more than I thought. You clearly have quite a knowledge of meteorology, I had no idea.' Matt rummaged in his jacket pocket and pulled out the notebook. 'I wanted to ask you, I believe you used to keep weather records for Porth Taran?'

'Lord, I'd forgotten about those!' She took the notebook from Matt and smoothed the cover while she reconnected with the memory. She opened the first page and smiled. 'Ah, another life. Kendrick was alive then you know.'

'Kendrick, was your husband?'

Dywana nodded. 'That's right. He's been dead twenty-one years this year.'

'You must miss him.'

'Every day.' She closed her eyes for a moment. 'More than anyone will ever know. The pain gets easier with time. You just sort of learn to live with it I suppose. But I can only be thankful that I met him. I think there are a lot that don't meet their soul mate.' She flicked through the pages wistfully. 'So, tell me, what's your project exactly?'

'Microclimates. I want to show what factors create the microclimate that Porth Taran enjoys.'

'Ah, yes. The eternal question that not a single researcher has managed to answer. The search for the Holy Grail. How can I help?'

'I've heard that you took the weather records for quite a few years.'

'That's right.' She nodded. 'Now let me see. Between 1983 and 1989.'

'Well this one covers just the second half of 1986. There must be quite a few more?'

'Yes, indeed. It was a lot of work.'

'The thing is I have only managed to locate this one.'

'And you'd like to get hold of the others?'

'I would, very much.'

Dywana looked pensively at Matt. 'Very much?'

Matt nodded. 'Do you have them?'

'I'd have to have a look. What would you do with them?'

'I will transcribe them and make a full picture of the weather in Porth Taran for those six years and see if I can piece together a pattern. If the weather station is functional again before my time is up then I can compare that data with these records.'

'What do you think that will show?'

'At the very least it might show if the microclimate has been a permanent fixture, linked to the geography and morphology of the peninsula or if there are evolving factors in climate change.'

'I see.'

Elwood climbed back down from the observatory.

In silence, Dywana descended to the ground floor and the men followed her into the kitchen.

Dywana put the notebook on the kitchen table. Elwood and Matt sat down. Dywana rummaged in the larder and brought out a loaf of saffron cake.

Elwood's eyes lit up. 'It's an age since I've had a piece of saffron cake.'

She put a pile of small plates on the table, and a large pat of butter. She carefully cut three slices of cake and passed the plates around. She settled herself at the table with the notebook open in front of her.

'So, you would like to know if I have the other notebooks? Then you want to write up the data and use it in your research?'

'Yep, that's about the size of it.'

'So, I am guessing you would need to reference the notebooks?'

'Yes, I would.'

'Surely you could get access to Culdrose's weather records? You don't actually need mine?'

Matt shook his head. 'Culdrose only measures the weather in certain spots and Porth Taran isn't one of them. My project is specifically based on Porth Taran's weather systems.'

'And if you can't get hold of the notebooks?'

'Then I will have to return to Australia and find a new project.'

'But if you stay, you think you can understand Porth Taran's weather?'

'That is my aim.'

Dywana pursed her lips. 'Well, I will think about it and in the meantime, I shall have a look for them. How can I contact you?'

'I'll give you my mobile number.' Matt rummaged in his pocket and took out a pen and a scrap of paper and wrote it down. 'My signal is terrible here, but I'm staying at Little Rosewarne if you need to find me.'

'Little Rosewarne?' Dywana's faced flashed with alarm.

'That's right, the B&B. Do you know it?'

'Yes, yes of course. It's up the top of Porth Taran, I've driven past it once or twice. I have heard it has a good reputation.'

'Yeah, it's a nice place.'

Matt finished his saffron cake and drained his tea. He stood up and pushed the chair under the table.

'Thank you for the tea and cake. I hope we can speak again soon. Elwood?'

Elwood stood up obediently and the men left.

Dywana closed the door behind them and sat down heavily at the table. She looked around but he'd taken the notebook with him. Jasper curled up on her feet, his warmth was comforting. Dredging up the past was hard. She'd got used to controlling her memories and had learned to keep only the happy ones bubbling at the surface, ready to bring out on a regular basis, rotating them for variety. The sudden jogging of the memories that she had managed to keep deeply buried in the bottom of her soul had jolted her. Her isolation had been her tool to keep on an even keel and this was proof that it really was the only way. Without others it was easier to just carry on. Feed her chickens, dig her garden. Fill time until there was no time left. Dywana stared out of the window at the moors, the clouds were racing across the sky. She sighed and stood up to clear away the plates. She was pretty sure that the notebooks were in the loft. She would need to decide if she would give them to him. A nice young man, full of the promise and ambition of youth. Perhaps she would go up there later and look them out.

NINETEEN

Elwood and Matt stood on the stone paved path, outside Chy Bowjy.

Matt patted his pocket; the notebook was safely stowed within. Dywana was clearly an intelligent woman. She carried an inherent air of kindness and warmth. There was something in her demeanour, her expression that seemed familiar, but he couldn't quite put his finger on it. He'd watched her eyes swoop between sadness and joy as if she didn't know which she was feeling. As if she was carrying a sad darkness that she was refusing to let get the better of her. Poor woman, living all these years alone up on the moor.

The leat gushed through the stone clad channel at their feet. The men began to walk back to the stile and across the field. Elwood again noticed the luxurious absence of pain in his joints. They climbed back through the fence to the edge of the ancient village.

Johnny wandered down to the harbour. Merryn's phone had remained unanswered. He could tell Demelza was worried, her cheeriness hadn't fooled him. He knew his sister like no other. Elwood wasn't in his usual place, but then it was late, and he'd probably already gone to collect his pasty. The gallery's blinds were drawn and the 'closed' sign was showing through the glass-paned door. If she had gone to Truro for the day she would have mentioned it to someone. Perhaps Matt knew. He went along to the visitors' centre and found Carrie emptying the dehumidifiers of water.

'You seen Merryn today, Carrie?'

'No. Actually, I was going to pop in on her in a bit.'

'Well, I would save yourself the trouble; she's not there.'

'Oh?'

'It's a bit odd. Have you seen Matt?'

'Yes, he's gone off to visit the ancient village at Chysauster. Perhaps they've gone together?'

'Yeah, maybe. Odd she didn't tell anyone though.'

'Ah, they're in love, Johnny.'

'In love? Do you think?'

'Absolutely. That Matt adores her, you can see it in his eyes when he looks at her.'

'Not sure about our Merryn though. She's a hard one to catch I reckon.'

'Do I detect a bit of fatherly jealousy?' Carrie giggled.

'What me? No, just looking out for her.' Johnny shivered. 'Corr, it's turned mighty cold, all of a sudden. Looks like we'll be getting the heating on early this year.'

'I noticed that. Mind you a bit of heating wouldn't do any harm with all the wet in here.'

Elwood looked at his watch. 'We've got an hour before the next bus.' The wind was whipping up and clouds swirled overhead. 'We'd better take shelter in the ancient village a while and then head down to the bus.'

Matt was deep in thought, he nodded absent-mindedly and followed Elwood along the grassy lanes of the skeletal village.

Elwood stepped through the walled footprint of a roundhouse doorway and sank to the floor, crossing his legs and leant against the grassy wall.

Matt caught a glimpse of how this curious man must have been in his youth.

Elwood rummaged in his pocket and produced a packet of cigarettes. He offered one to Matt.

Matt shook his head. 'I didn't know you smoked, Elwood?'

'Only on special occasions,' he replied, grinning.

Matt shrugged and leant back. He watched the smoke from Elwood's cigarette curl up to the tops of the walls and then be snatched away by the wind.

Elwood closed his eyes. Here he was, Elwood Curnow sitting in his favourite place on earth with the God of Creation. This place where, as a child, he would put his palms gently on the stones to feel their years. His mother would sit in the exact same spot where he was now, her skirts voluminous around her ample belly. Next to her a basket with a tea towel carefully laid over to protect its cargo. Sometimes Karenza from next door and her mother would come with them. While their mothers chatted and buttered bread and sliced cheese, he and Karenza would run around the tops of the walls, chasing each other, or playing hide and seek, or sometimes they just lay on their backs right on the grassy tops and stared up at the clouds. Losing themselves in the swirls and eddies that passed overhead.

Then, once, his mother had invited Rev Cribben to join them. That was the last time Elwood had been up there.

Matt suddenly stood up. 'How long to the bus?'

Elwood opened his eyes and tried to focus on his watch, but Matt grabbed his wrist to look.

'Forty minutes. It's too long. Come on.' Matt disappeared through the roundhouse doorway.

'What you doin'?' said Elwood, scrambling to his feet.

'It's Merryn, she's in trouble.' Matt called behind him.

'What kind of trouble?' yelled Elwood, after him. As he emerged from the roundhouse, he could see Matt's head above the walls of the village. He was heading back towards the farmhouse.

Elwood sped after him. By the time he caught up with him, Matt was at the door of the farmhouse and was knocking on it.

Dywana opened it.

'Mrs Constantine, there is an emergency, can I use your phone? I don't have a signal on my mobile.'

'An emergency?'

Matt thought quickly. 'Look, over there. That patch of cloud, I have to get there.' To the south, the patch of grey cloud they had seen earlier had darkened to an ominous rich purple.

'That's Rinsey. The phone is over there next to the microwave.'

Matt rushed past her.

Dywana looked at Elwood, her eyebrows raised.

Elwood shrugged and said nothing. He waited by the leat and watched the water trickling over the stone paved channel while Matt spoke on the phone.

Matt replaced the receiver, thanked Dywana and went outside to join Elwood.

'Wozzon?' asked Elwood, confused.

'Johnny's coming to get us.'

'Why?'

'Merryn's in trouble. We have to get to her.'

'Where is she?' Now Elwood was very confused.

'She's climbing down the cliffs.'

'Which cliffs? What's she doing that for? How do you know?'

But Matt was already setting off down the drive to the gateway and the road beyond. 'We'll start walking and get a head start,' he called behind him.

Elwood only just caught his words on the wind as he tried to keep in step with him. As they got further away from the farmhouse, Elwood's knees and ankles started to hurt. He was struggling to catch his breath and had no choice but to slow down. It wasn't long before Matt disappeared completely from view. Elwood gave in to the pain and began to hobble. He was almost at the main road, when Johnny's van rounded the bend ahead, with Matt already in the front seat. Matt flung open the door and grabbed Elwood's outstretched hand and hauled him in.

'Where is she, Matt?' Johnny sounded desperate.

'The cliffs.'

'Which cliffs?'

'There's a tin mine, I think it might be Rinsey.' Matt closed his eyes. 'There's a small beach at the bottom, it's a pebble cove. The pebbles are wet.'

'So, there's no beach at high tide.' Johnny thought fast. 'It could be Rinsey.... What would she be doing at Rinsey? She never even goes for a walk on her own, our Merryn. Are you sure?'

Matt looked out of the window ignoring him and Johnny drove on in silence.

'Hang on, Elwood. Wasn't it down by Rinsey that you said you'd seen Piran setting his pots for the last time?' asked Johnny.

'That's right, but Ambis wasn't born. She won't know that will she?'

Matt looked at Johnny. 'Demelza gave her the folder.'

'What folder?'

'The record of the inquest. Elwood's statement's in it.'

'She asked me about it the other day, at that party. I told her to speak to her mum and to speak to you, Elwood.'

Elwood shook his head. 'Ambis never speaks to me, Johnny. I haven't said a word.'

Johnny pulled the van off the main road and followed a winding lane towards the coast for a couple of miles. The moors were turning a deep dusky pink with the heather beginning to bloom. The closer they got to the coast the fewer trees dotted the vista and those that did leant at right angles in the Atlantic breeze. Beyond, the sea was dark grey, reflecting the sky. Flashes of white tipped the choppy waters. Johnny pulled up by an engine house and they clambered out.

'This is it,' said Matt. He charged ahead, almost leaping the boulders as he went. 'We need to find the path down.'

'Watch it mate, you'll come a cropper jumping like that,' Johnny yelled after him, but Matt was gone.

'I'll stay up here,' shouted Elwood into the strengthening wind, but his words were carried away.

Gulls were wheeling overhead and diving downwards towards the surface of the sea and out of sight behind the rocky incline.

Matt leapt from ledge to ledge following the path. As it curved round, it revealed a stony cove below. A small promontory jutted into the sea and on the tip of it stood Merryn. Matt called out to her, but she couldn't hear him in the raging wind.

She was standing with her arms out by her sides, her head tilted back with the wind blowing her mane of red hair behind her and her face held to the breeze.

As Matt got closer, he could see that just in front of her, a couple of feet from the tip of the promontory the water swirled and eddied. It was whirling round and round in an almost perfect circle.

Gulls were screaming and circling, one dived towards the water but swooped sharply skyward again a little way above the water.

Matt called her again, but the sound was whipped away from his mouth. He leapt the last drop in one jump and landed heavily on the shingle beneath.

As he straightened, he saw Merryn lower her arms and gently swing them back as if she was about to take off. Then she bent her knees.

Matt bellowed with all his might as Merryn jumped into the very centre of the whirlpool. He ran to the spot where she had stood and jumped in after her. As he resurfaced the water had stopped swirling. He couldn't see her. The wind had dropped and a strange silence, bar the lapping of the waves, prevailed. He spun around in the water, but there was no sign of her.

'Matt, over there!' shouted Johnny. 'By the side of the spit.'

Matt paddled sideways, looking all around him frantically. Clinging to the rocks on the side of the promontory was Merryn. The tide was rising fast and there would soon be no cove.

'Merryn!' he called.

She looked round at him. Her complexion was wan, but her eyes sparkled curiously.

Matt reached the rocks Merryn was clinging to, and clambered on to the promontory. Grabbing her by the wrist, he lifted her out of the water and held her to him. She was sodden and shaking. Her teeth were chattering.

'Merry!' yelled Johnny as he arrived behind Matt. 'Have you gone mad?'

Merryn looked up at her uncle, but she didn't speak.

'Here, I'll take her.'

Matt reluctantly relinquished his grip and let her uncle take her in his arms.

Matt shook himself off, he was shivering violently now too. The wind had dropped but the cold was penetrating.

Johnny carried Merryn slowly up the stony path, carefully watching his footholds to be sure he didn't drop her. Matt followed. At the top of the cliff, Elwood stood with his staff. His long hair spread across his shoulders with the sun streaming around his silhouette like a shaman.

Johnny reached the top of the cliff and carried Merryn to the van. He bundled her into the front seat between him and Matt.

'I saw him,' whispered Merryn faintly.

'You saw who, my darling?' asked Johnny gently.

Merryn looked up at him and simply smiled. Then she leant against his shoulder, closed her eyes and seemed to fall instantly asleep.

Johnny drove back to Porth Taran, as smoothly as he could manage so as not to wake her.

As soon as Matt had signal again, he called Demelza ahead of their arrival and she greeted them on the doorstep with a warm blanket to wrap Merryn in. Johnny carried her up to her room and Demelza changed her wet clothes for a clean nightdress and tucked her up in bed with a hot cup of sweet tea.

Matt changed out of his wet clothes and came downstairs clean and warm again. Demelza was in the kitchen making tea.

'How is she?' Matt asked.

'Asleep, thankfully.' Demelza switched on the kettle and pulled out a couple of mugs. 'What on earth happened out there, Matt?'

'I…, I don't know.'

Demelza looked at him sternly.

He shrugged his shoulders. 'I honestly don't know, Demelza. She didn't speak to me.' He hadn't understood what had happened himself, how could he tell anyone else?

'You didn't know she was going there?'

'I hadn't seen her since breakfast.'

'So how did you know where she was?'

'I just had a feeling, that's all.'

'You just had a feeling?' Demelza was fighting irritation.

Johnny walked into the kitchen. 'I've taken Elwood home. Matt, you alright?'

'Yeah, I've warmed up now, thanks.'

Demelza was still staring at Matt. 'I don't understand. Where were you when you had this feeling?'

'I was over at Chysauster, at the ancient village with Elwood.'

'It's a strange business, this. What's got into her?' said Demelza.

'There is one thing. She said that she saw someone,' said Johnny.

'She saw someone? Where?'

'It sounded like she saw them in the sea.'

'In the sea?'

'Well, yes, but there was no one there. Was there, Matt?'

Matt shook his head.

Demelza sighed, then turned around and began to wipe the work surfaces vigorously.

Johnny pointed at the cups of steaming tea. 'One of these for me?'

Demelza nodded. 'I'm worried about her, Johnny. She's not been right since that storm.'

TWENTY

Matt woke feeling more tired than when he went to bed. A film of fine drizzle coated the windowpane. He lay still replaying the events of the day before in his head. Merryn had jumped in the sea in the exact place where Piran had disappeared. Where Elwood had said he'd last seen him setting his lobster pots. In the panic, he couldn't remember seeing any narrow channels nor converging currents, though there must have been some, to cause a whirlpool like that. He would need to go back and check it out. The only other cause for a whirlpool could be the shape of the seabed. He looked at his watch. He'd go and have a look at low tide.

He got up, pulled on a pair of jeans and a sweatshirt, and went upstairs to listen at Merryn's door – there was no sound. He carefully opened the door. She was sleeping deeply. He could see the gentle rise and fall of her chest as she breathed. Her face was peaceful, and her brow was free from frowning. He leant over and kissed her forehead. She stirred, murmured, then shuffled and turned over. Her copper hair was spread over the pillow like draped silk and his heart filled with love. He would make this right. He had to.

He quietly went back down to his room to grab his trainers and then tiptoed downstairs to the dining room. The tables were clear and there was no sign of Demelza or Spike. Matt stepped out of the front door into the drizzle. He needed a lift to Rinsey.

The surf shop wasn't open yet, he would wait for Johnny. He sat on the wall outside the church and looked out to sea.

A whirlpool was a phenomenon caused by fast flowing currents in narrow bodies of water, or by the relief of the seabed. That cove definitely wasn't narrow. When he had jumped in, the whirlpool had ceased its spinning, almost instantly. Nothing could stop a whirlpool that suddenly. He shivered in the freshness of the morning, the drizzle was beginning to soak through his sweatshirt. The sea lay silent and glassy, as the drops melted into its surface soundlessly. Gulls swooped and skimmed the water, scanning the depths for shoals of fish. Not a breath of wind jingled the lanyards.

'Awright, mate? Bit wet out here.'

Matt spun around.

Rowan was standing on the pavement smiling at him awkwardly.

'How are you goin'?' replied Matt.

'I just wanted to say, like ...' Rowan shuffled and put his hands in the pockets of his hoodie and then took them out again. 'I just wanted to say, thanks.' He said the last word decisively and broke into a smile as if he was triumphant for having found the right thing to say.

'What for, mate?'

'For savin' 'er, Merryn, I mean. Johnny told me what you did. Jumping in and that. I can't imagine what would have happened if you hadn't ...' His face fell with the imagined horror.

'Ah yeah. No sweat. You would have done the same.'

Rowan nodded. 'Yeah, I reckon.' He looked at the pavement and shuffled again. 'So, I'll be seein' ya.'

'Yeah, no worries mate.' Matt watched as he swaggered back along the harbour towards the surf shop. Then called after him.

'Rowan, mate.'

Rowan turned back. 'Yeah.'

'Could you give me a lift somewhere?'

'Where do you want to go, bud?'

'To Rinsey.'

Rowan glanced at the surf shop and at the time on his phone.

'It won't take long, I promise. It would help Merryn, if you could.'

'Johnny's expecting me to open up.' He glanced up and down the deserted harbour road. 'What the hell, it's dead as a doornail here, as long as it doesn't take long. Come on, Johnny left the van out the back.'

Matt jumped in beside Rowan and they headed west out of Port Taran. The drizzle began to retreat, and shards of turquoise sea illuminated by the emerging sun flashed from beyond the rocky cliffs, as they drove by. The van twisted and turned along the steep narrow lanes. The heather was turning, and its russet pelt vied with the dark feathery emerald of the bracken sprouting in the rocky hedges. As they neared the coast, a breeze blew up from the cliffs and through the van's open window.

'Jeez, it's beautiful here.'

Rowan looked at Matt sideways. 'Yeah, I suppose it is.'

They reached the entrance to the lane that led down to the engine house. Rowan pulled the van off the main road, its wheels rumbled over the tussocks of grass in the centre of the lane, as it turned. The stone of the engine house glow pale grey in the warm sunlight, unlike its bleak allure of the day before.

'Low tide is in half an hour,' said Matt. 'So, we should be able to see almost all of the beach right now.'

The men got out of the van and clambered down the rocky path at a slower pace this time. Matt was surprised at just how deep and far apart the boulder steps were. It was a wonder he hadn't tripped and fallen to the cove below. It couldn't have looked more different; the sea was a pale brilliant blue, magnifying the rocks and swathes of seaweed beneath. There was barely a ripple on the surface of the water. They reached the glistening shingle, still damp from the departing water.

'So, what are you looking for?'

'There was a whirlpool. Did Johnny say?'

'A whirlpool? That's mad.'

'Yeah, I know. Well, I'm not familiar with the coast here but I have to say that I have never seen anything like it.'

'Me neither and I've surfed these waters all my life. How can that be?'

'Well, a whirlpool is caused when rushing water is forced round an obstacle either on the surface, like tall rocks that jut out, or a river estuary that has waters flowing out to sea and the tide coming back is forcing itself on it and making it spin. Or even a sink hole in the seabed that sucks the water down. But look, the bed here just slopes gently. It doesn't look as if there would even be a rip off this cove.'

'Oh yeah mate, over there to the left that's where the rip runs usually.'

Matt looked over to the edge of the cove. Tall rocks jutted out of the seabed. 'Yeah, I see it but that wouldn't cause a whirlpool over here. The seabed is completely flat and pretty much smooth save for those rocks scattered around. Matt scratched his head and frowned. 'I just don't get it.'

Merryn was sitting up in bed and staring at the square of blue sky framed by her window. The house was silent, it must be late. She ached all over. She felt calm but dazed. She couldn't remember going to bed. Mum must have put her in her pyjamas. She gently swung her legs over the side of the bed and sunk her feet into the carpet. Her eyes fell on the photograph of her father and she smiled.

Her stomach was growling with hunger, so she dressed and went downstairs to look for some breakfast. Demelza and Spike were out, and she was glad; she knew there would be questions later and she needed some space. She poured some cereal and milk into a bowl and ate slowly. Her belly full, she stepped out of the front door and walked down the hill towards the harbour. The village was quiet and the sun was shining warmly on damp pavements. A light breeze fluttered over the little port and danced in the ambering leaves of the trees on the headland. It felt like a year since she had last walked into the gallery, though it had been no more than a day.

She unlocked the gallery and stepped inside. She uncovered the mosaic and ran her fingers over the wide, shiny trunk now dried and fixed firmly in place. She looked at the leaves that formed the canopy. Emerald, olive and myrtle and some so dark they were almost black. It was missing new growth, on the tips of its branches. Her fingers led her to some glass in chartreuse, lime and mint. She chose chartreuse and carefully fashioned it into a tiny leaf with her nippers. She held it up to the light to see it sparkle and glimmer in the thin autumn sunshine that began to radiate through the window. The same glimmer that had shone from deep within the sea.

The light of Piran, the love of Piran. The myth, the quasi memory that had shaped and gilded every part of her life as much by its existence as by its absence. The light was all around her now, that she knew. She fashioned another with her nippers and held it up to the light. The bell on the door jangled and Merryn leapt for her old curtain to cover the mosaic.

'Hey beautiful.' Matt grinned. 'How are you feeling?'

'I'm feeling really good, thank you. I slept like a baby.'

'Yes, I could hear you,' he said teasingly.

'Very funny!' she said clipping his ear with a tea towel.

'I've managed to find the lady who took the weather records.'

'Oh Matt, that's wonderful! Who is she?'

'Her name is Dywana Constantine, she lives up on the moors on the way to St. Ives.'

'Does this mean you can stay?'

'I hope so. She's going to look for the notebooks and if she finds them, I'm all yours!' He winked. 'If you'll have me?'

'Ah well, I'll have to see,' she joked.

'I didn't expect you to be working today. Not after yesterday.'

'Why? I'm feeling on top of the world.'

'You were nearly at the bottom of it, yesterday. You gave us all quite a fright.'

'A fright? Really?'

'Well, yeah. You hurled yourself into a pretty rough sea.'

'I just went for a swim. That's all. It was quite a surprise to see you there and with Johnny and Elwood. What were you doing there?'

Matt stared at her. 'We ...' He stopped. There wasn't a hint of recognition of the danger she had been in, in her tone. 'We just went for a walk.'

'At Rinsey?'

'Yeah, quite a coincidence. So, you just thought you'd go for a dip?'

'Well, it was such a beautiful day and the sea was glassy and clear, I just love this time of year. It just, sort of, beckoned me in.' She smiled.

'Fully clothed?'

'I didn't have my swimming togs with me. I did take off my shoes.'

'Ah Merryn Jewell, I'm not sure I will ever fathom you out.'

'Nothing to fathom, dear Matt. Just a swim, that's all.'

'So, you don't remember the whirlpool?'

'Whirlpool?'

'Yes, a whirlpool. I watched you dive right into the middle of it. You're lucky to be alive.'

She frowned and looked away from him and began to pull out tubs of broken crockery from beneath the workbench.

Matt could see he shouldn't insist and changed tack. 'Have you seen your mum yet?'

'She'd gone out when I got up.'

'Well, I'm glad you're OK.' He kissed her, but he could tell she wasn't fully present.

He stepped out of the shop and with his shoulders rounded began to climb the port road towards the guest house. The sun shone brightly overhead. Matt took off his jacket as he climbed the hill. An Indian summer was what they all needed. It was clear that Merryn couldn't remember anything. She'd gone under, the whirlpool had dragged her below and she said she had just gone for a gentle swim. Matt stopped halfway up the hill to catch his breath and looked out over the port. There was not a single ripple in the surface of the harbour water and the tide was beginning to seep up the shingle towards the port head. All was still. He continued up the hill to Little Rosewarne.

He sat on the edge of his bed. A whirlpool with no cause, Merryn with no memory of what happened, Matt was baffled. Dywana's notebook lay on the dressing table. He got up and picked it up. He opened it and looked at Di Constantine's feathery hand swirling across the pages. He really needed the others. He glanced at his phone but there was no message from her. First, he knew he must talk to Elwood about the whirlpool yesterday and the whirlpool the day Piran disappeared.

There was no answer when Matt knocked on Elwood's door. He went around to the side gate and pushed it open. 'Elwood?'

Only the seagulls screaming overhead answered him.

He gingerly walked up the path at the side of the house, wary of taking him by surprise.

At the back of the house was an awning, slung between the eaves and supported by poles fixed in the ground. Beneath it, sat Elwood sheltering from the sun. His arms were bare, revealing tattoos that obscured his skin almost completely. His eyes were closed. About a foot away from him perched a raven, pecking at a pile of grain.

Matt hung back. He could see Elwood's lips were moving very slightly and listening hard he could just detect a low rhythmic hum. The raven every now and then looked up at Elwood, tilting his head from side to side in cadence with his humming.

Matt decided that this wasn't a good time and turned to leave. His foot knocked an empty beer can that toppled over and rolled down the path and came to a stop as it reached the lawn. The raven flew off and Elwood's eyes flashed open in alarm.

'Who's there?'

Matt hesitated.

'Bunjil? Is that you?'

Matt stopped. How did he know?

'Bunjil, come.' Elwood called again, louder this time. 'Come and sit by me. I knew you would come.'

Matt turned back and stepped out from the path and onto the lawn. 'Elwood, I'm sorry. I was…'

'Come, come and sit. I was expecting you. I think you have some questions for me?'

Matt approached the awning.

Elwood painfully heaved himself from the floor and sat on a makeshift bench of two railway sleepers piled on top of each other. Next to him, on the lawn, was a six-pack of lager. He gestured for Matt to sit down next to him. 'What troubles you?'

'I wanted to talk to you about yesterday.'

'Ah, yes, yesterday.'

Matt sat down cross legged on the grass. 'The whirlpool.'

Elwood reached for a can of beer, tugged on the ring pull and passed it to Matt. 'I think the sun's over the yardarm, don't you?'

Matt took the can from him. 'Tell me about whirlpools around here.'

Elwood took another can and opened it for himself. 'Ah whirlpools. Well, they don't happen very often round this side of the peninsula. But over on the north coast at Hayle, you wanna be careful round there, that I can tell you.'

'But, this was at Rinsey.'

'Yeah well, that's right it was at Rinsey.'

'You've seen one there before, haven't you?'

Elwood looked at him a moment and took a sip of beer from the can he was holding.

'Who told you that?'

'The inquest report.'

Elwood eyed him solemnly. 'Yesterday, was the second time only, that I have seen a whirlpool at Rinsey.'

'Is it a well-known phenomenon at Rinsey?'

'No, not at Rinsey.'

'I went down there today.'

'You did?'

'I wanted to see what could be causing them?'

'And?'

'I found nothing. The seabed is smooth. There are no narrow channels. The only rip is way out and off to the side. It couldn't have contributed.'

Elwood took another sip of beer. He looked up and fixed Matt's gaze. 'You already have the answers, Bunjil.'

Matt frowned.

'If you search deep enough, you will see that you already know.'

'I already know what?' Matt could see this was going to be a waste of time.

'You just need to bring yourself to accept. Accepting is believing. Aah, so many don't,' he said, shaking his head. 'But you? You should take your understanding further and believe and accept.'

'Why me?'

'Because of who you are.'

Matt tossed his head back and laughed. 'What, Bunjil?'

Elwood stared at him immovable.

'Elwood, I am not Bunjil, the aboriginal god of creation. I am Matt Bunda of Townsville, born in Palm Island.'

'You mock.'

'Bunjil is a mythical character of aboriginal dreamtime.'

'And you know that because you were taught it by your people. Your people believe yet you refuse? Do you not respect the beliefs of your people?'

'It's not that simple, Elwood. Of course, I respect them and it's part of me and my heritage.' He thought of his Palm Island playmates, Balun and Jarra, who would act out dreamtime stories every playtime at school. They would talk of the fantastical creatures and the spooky symbolism. They would lie on Main Beach and close their eyes and astral travel to foreign lands. He shook himself. 'But it has no place in the modern world. Not in this world.'

'No place? But don't you see this is exactly its place. That culture didn't evolve for no reason, it applies to all of us, to this earth and the supernature of our universe.'

Matt snorted and shook his head.

'They taught you about personification of the gods, right?'

'What you mean the coming of gods in human form?'

'That's exactly what I mean.'

'Na, I don't remember a single story of that, well apart from the good book, the Bible.'

Elwood's face darkened. 'You don't want to listen to that nonsense!' he said angrily. 'This is the real stuff. It's the stuff that affects us every day, the here and now. The weather and the seasons.'

'What are you saying? You think I am Bunjil, the god of creation come in human form to save the universe?'

'That is exactly why you're here. To be more precise, to save Ambis and to help her save Porth Taran.'

'OK, so tell me what is it that we are supposed to save everyone from?'

'The weather, of course.'

'Elwood, I am a meteorologist, I study the weather and if I can, I predict it as accurately as I can, I do not make the weather.'

'At last we're getting somewhere.'

'I don't follow.'

'You don't make the weather, but as you say you predict it.'

'Well, of course I do and sometimes I get it wrong like every weatherman in the world.'

'Yesterday the weather turned bad right over Rinsey Head and where was Ambis?'

Matt stared at him.

Elwood went on, 'The night of the party you knew there was a storm coming. You called Culdrose.'

'There was nothing supernatural about it, the data showed it and anyway I thought you said it was your hex that made it happen. You need to get your story straight.' Matt was getting annoyed.

'So, you don't believe my hex caused the storm?'

'Of course not.'

'And the giant wave? No seismic activity nor even a spring tide, you said it yourself. So, what caused it?'

'It must have been a meteotsunami. It's the only thing left.'

'And how did you know that Ambis was in trouble yesterday?'

Matt didn't reply.

'You felt it didn't you? When we were up at the ancient village.'

'It was a lucky guess.'

'Perhaps you need time. You sense things before they happen, and you can see things when they happen, a very long way away. When you first came to Porth Taran, I could feel your energy. I could feel your force and it scared me. I thought you would harm us and Ambis. Yesterday, I saw first-hand what you can do. You have the spirits and you use them for the good of others.'

'My people all believe they can see things before they happen, Elwood. In Palm Island if a Frigate bird wheels overhead, they say there will be a storm.'

'And was there?'

'The frigate bird will fly high when bad weather is on the way, the fish will gather into larger shoals before heading out to deeper waters to shelter from the storm. The birds are ready to catch them. So, yes, often when the frigate flies high there is a low coming in but it's not magic, it's nature. I'm a meteorologist, I use instruments and science not some greater power, Elwood. Stories are all they are. Stories that fuel an ancient and admirable culture for which I have every respect. But I can assure you I am no god.'

'But Culdrose didn't forecast that storm, with all their new-fangled equipment. But you did.' Elwood stared at him intently. 'Someone somewhere has told you this before.'

Matt sat down again. 'So, let's say I am special, that I have some magical gift, what then?'

Elwood smiled with satisfaction. 'Why are you asking me when you led us there?'

Matt went quiet. The image of Elwood standing up on the cliff silhouetted by the sun holding his staff and his hair blown all around. 'What did you see from the top of the cliff?'

'This isn't the time. You would do well to go back and see Dywana Constantine. See if she has found the notebooks. They will tell you.' Elwood put down his beer, slipped off the sleepers and down to the lawn and crossed his legs. He closed his eyes and began to hum.

Matt could see it was no good pushing him. He got up silently and left Elwood to his humming.

Johnny was sitting in a deck chair at the front of the surf shop drinking coffee and soaking up the afternoon sun. The West Briton lay open on his knees. He turned the pages, skim reading the headlines: *Helston School to become an academy, Man killed falling from a cliff edge, Approval to build on the edge of Camborne granted.*

Merryn could have fallen from that cliff or even drowned. What on earth did she think she was doing, jumping in the sea like that? Demelza was right, things had changed with her. And if he was to be honest, as much as he liked him, it was when that Matt arrived. Maybe there was some truth in Elwood's fear of him. Besides, he'd been right before.

He took a sip of coffee and turned to the notices. There, on the next page, at the top, was a notice headed Devon and Cornwall Police. Johnny gulped, his skin went cold and sweat began to bead on his forehead. He closed the paper as his stomach churned and his head began to spin. What was Reverend Kate up to? His panic quickly turned to anger. Everyone said a woman taking over St Petroc's would cause a problem in Porth Taran and now, twenty years on, they were right.

He got up and strode angrily towards the church, he would give her a piece of his mind. He was halfway along the harbour road when he realised there were two police cars parked outside. He stopped, turned back and walked back to the shop. He sat down heavily in the deck chair. He drained his coffee mug and stared at the newspaper folded on the concrete.

TWENTY-ONE

Merryn was up early. She felt her energy replenished and she couldn't lie around in bed any longer. She wanted to be up and get on with the new life she had found. There was no sound from Matt's room when she passed it, so she slipped downstairs, grabbed a hunk of hevva cake from the kitchen, wrapped it in a napkin and set off for the gallery.

The sun was shining, casting penetrating warmth over the harbour. It was too early for Elwood. She unlocked the gallery door and went inside. She opened a window to allow a warm summer breeze to circulate, it jangled the wind chimes gently. She smiled as she looked around her. The gallery was restored and so was her family. And then there was Matt; she felt blessed. She put the kettle on to make some coffee and unwrapped the hevva cake and set it on a small plate on her workbench.

Today would be a sky day. She pulled a tray from underneath her workbench. On it, were panes of glass in an array of blues. Smooth and clear, blue glass and shimmer. Merryn gazed out of the window at the sun beating down on the pearly white decks and cabins of the boats in the harbour. The water glowed azure as if it was the height of August. Not a single cloud hung over Porth Taran. She took a sheet of opaque blue glass and set it in her cutter. As she drew the arm down the pane, the clean strips clinked onto the worktop. She took each strip carefully and with her wheeled cutter she split them into triangles, turning them to offset their grain against each other. The varying sizes of triangles tessellated perfectly, yet irregularly, just the way happiness and calm appeared and reappeared apparently arbitrarily. Angular, and jagged, like crystals reflecting the light in every direction, darting this way and that, in time with the changing skies. Laid out on the board, they glimmered frivolously, mocking the solid unreflecting trunk and branches. Clouds and air and breeze, swirling free in the atmosphere and below, anchored by the roots in shingle, the trunk, the framework of branches to hold life. Constant and dense, unfailing and immoveable, the arms outstretched adorned with the burgeoning leaves, some round, some jagged, some perfectly circular and here and there nestled amongst them, a firebud. Balanced like a jewel, a tight pearled red flame poised upward into the leaves.

Merryn glanced over the harbour, to the cliff above The Ship Inn. The trees were already beginning to turn there. Her tree carried all four seasons at the same time; ambered leaves and fresh green leaves, the flowers of spring and dark branches of winter.

At Little Rosewarne, Matt stirred. Elwood's words had swirled through his head as he'd fallen asleep. He'd dreamt of his grandfather and the elders, of the rainbow serpent, the platypus and the emu that adorned the pub walls in vibrant dots and strong outlines. Behind them the beach glowing in the sunlight, edged with a palm forest and in the distance, mangroves that stretched along the coastline as far as the eye could see. He could see the children playing on the sand, sitting crouched in circles. They were chattering excitedly and pointing to the sky. He remembered when he was one of them, guessing the weather to come, imitating the elders' sooth sayings and visions.

Then the visions had come to him, premonitions of storms and cyclones. When they came to pass, even as a small boy, his reasonable mind knew that there was a plausible explanation. Palm Island was prone to cyclones, there was nothing unusual in that. Then he sensed that there would be an outbreak of sickness amongst the villagers. A few days later, a large number of islanders fell to a stomach bug. Scientists came to the island to test the water. For weeks after, a tanker brought freshwater to be stored in vast containers along the main street.

At first it was like magic; he could see into the future. It was like he was in his own fantasy story, he was the boy with superpowers. Then one day, he was playing with his friends near the pub. A group of elders were sitting outside the pub drinking beer and laughing together. Jarra Bob was amongst them. He was telling a detailed and animated story to the others who were listening intently and laughing heartily at certain points. Matt had studied him, as he sat there, gesticulating and storytelling. In that moment, he had known Jarra Bob was going to die. He wasn't particularly old, nor was he sick. Matt didn't know why he'd thought of it. He kept it to himself.

Then just three days later, he was gone. Jarra Bob had died at his kitchen table of a brain haemorrhage. Matt became frightened. As he grew older the premonitions came thicker and faster. He saw riots coming on the island, houses burning, children in danger. Palm Island was no longer a desert island idyll on the Great Barrier Reef but an enclave ravaged by discontent and unrest. Drinking increased amongst the inhabitants and with it the fighting. He had seen all of it before it happened. His uneasiness grew. He began to fear his own thoughts. He became afraid that if he thought something then it would actually happen.

Then, one morning, when he was ten years old, his mother announced that they were leaving Palm Island to go and live in Townsville. She wanted to go where there were jobs, and no arguments among the elders, where pay day didn't result in binge drinking across the island and the inevitable violence that ensued. Townsville could offer her boy a 'proper education'. He could remember his mother standing in the kitchen, her hands on her hips, telling him proudly that he was going places, that he was going to be somebody.

She seemed so happy, so proud. And all he could feel was terror. The fear of abandoning all he had ever known. He'd heard of Townsville, sure. That was the airport that served Palm. That was where people went when they needed to see a lawyer or deal with important papers. As he absorbed the news, he slowly began to feel relieved. Then his relief turned to elation, for he realised he hadn't predicted this. He hadn't foreseen that they would leave Palm and their shabby prefab house with two bedrooms and the yard with the guava tree, and Naji, his grandfather.

In Townsville, he began to live like a white Australian boy. He wore a uniform to go to school and hung out in cafés with his new friends after school. He learnt to surf and he started to hang out with girls. The premonitions stopped abruptly when they left the island. They stopped dead. He decided that they had been a product of his imagination, influenced by the power of suggestion of his fellow islanders. He'd never had one again.

So now, why would they be coming back? There was no one around him who could influence him with aboriginal dreamtime culture. That familiar feeling of falling seized him; his stomach was flipping, and his head was swimming. Was it starting again? And this time with no explanation. He lay back down on the pillow and closed his eyes in an attempt to anchor his emotions.

Had he seen Merryn in danger or had he put her in danger by thinking it? Maybe he was no good for Merryn. He'd asked her all those questions about her father, stirring up things that weren't any of his business. He thought of her standing there in the wind, her damp skirt clinging to her brown legs. Her auburn hair blown around her like an aura. Her arms outstretched ready to dive. What right did he have to encourage her to read the inquest report? Self-loathing added to his angst. Merryn Jewell was special. She was not just the loveliest girl he'd ever met. Sure, she was beautiful and shapely and intelligent and kind, but there was something in her that he could see in himself. Something that he understood. He had felt it that very first morning that he'd walked into her shop. He couldn't label it, but he'd felt it, there was no mistake. Now, the weather station was destroyed, and he stood to lose his funding; perhaps this was fate. Perhaps he should just leave. Just go back to Townsville and write this off as a bad experience. He buried his face in his pillow and fought back tears.

As he always did when he was low, he conjured his grandfather in his mind. He remembered the last time he saw him. He was sitting outside his house in Palm. It was just before he flew to England. Naji was sitting in a deck chair, painting a giant turtle shell that rested on his lap. His brush working quickly and easily, filling the blue green shell with brightly coloured dots. Every now and then he would lick the tip of the brush leaving orange or blue paint staining his lips. He was a man of few words. He would greet Matt in silence, nodding to him then continuing what he was doing. Matt knew better than to interrupt. Instead he would sit next to him, feeling his presence, as his grandfather was feeling his. And then, when he was ready, he would speak carefully and slowly.

'So, they tell me you're going to be a scientist, Wungarra?'

'I am, grandfather.'

'Then now we must call you Garadyigan.' He'd looked up at him and smiled showing his blackened teeth. 'You will serve the white people well in London, with your wisdom and your vision.'

For his grandfather, only London existed in England and Matt knew there was little point in trying to explain.

'Don't forget who you are and where you came from. If you need me, I will be here, waiting for you. Now go, Garadyigan and be well.'

Matt closed his eyes again and pictured his grandfather, sat in his faded deckchair with the Bundaberg rum logo and the slogan 'There's a fight in every bottle, mate' emblazoned just above his shoulders. A feeling of homesickness rose in the pit of his stomach. He consciously and purposefully relaxed his muscles one by one. His arms and legs, his feet, then his shoulders. His neck, his jaw, and his tongue. He breathed deeply and slowly. He fixed his gaze on his grandfather's face and counted down. Five, four, three, two, one. Matt opened his eyes. Naji was wearing his favourite pair of denim shorts, faded and frayed at the hem. The skin on his legs was wrinkled and hung off his bones like sagging cloth. A stained baseball cap shaded his face from the sun. He wasn't painting a turtle shell this time. He was sipping tea. Next to him was a lady in the Fosters deck chair that Matt usually sat in. She was younger than his grandfather, she had a kind face. His grandfather was smiling at her. Good for him, thought Matt. What would he say to Matt now? He remembered the time he had predicted the storm that had flattened the pub and the police station,

He'd looked at him, filled with pride and said, 'You are fulfilling your purpose. You have inherited the gift.'

Matt shook himself and rubbed his eyes. Merryn had been in trouble, what would have happened if they hadn't got to her in time? His grandfather would say the same again. He would say that he was here for a reason and that the reasons weren't always clear.

Elwood loomed in his mind.

He brought himself quickly back and looked around him at the Victorian mouldings and the sash windows of Little Rosewarne.

Johnny pulled up outside Elwood's house. The paper lay folded on the passenger seat next to him. He hesitated before getting out.

Elwood's front door opened, and the old man appeared on the doorstep and waved at him.

Johnny picked up the paper, put it under his arm and got out. 'Alright, Elwood.'

'Beer?'

Johnny looked at his watch. 'Oh, go on then!'

Elwood took a couple of cans from the fridge and gave one to Johnny. 'How's tricks?'

'Elwood,' Johnny pursed his lips.

'Yes, mate. What's up?'

'Remember Rev Cribben?'

Elwood's eyes flashed with alarm. 'What about him?'

Johnny opened the paper and passed it to him.

Elwood rummaged in the kitchen drawer for his glasses and perched them on the end of his nose.

POLICE APPEAL FOR ATTENDEES OF ST PETROC'S SUNDAY SCHOOL, PORTH TARAN, WEST CORNWALL, BETWEEN 1955 AND 1985

Devon and Cornwall Police has launched an appeal for attendees of the Sunday school, Porth Taran, between 1955 and 1985 to come forward. The Force is working closely with St Petroc's and the Diocese to investigate serious allegations. Assistant Chief

Constable Conrad Johns said: "I would like to reassure the public and anyone yet to come forward that we are investigating these allegations with the utmost sensitivity."

Anyone with information or requiring confidential help and support in relation to this inquiry can contact Devon and Cornwall Police on 101 or call the 24-hour helpline on 0800 462 9783

Elwood's eyes widened and his jaw fell. His knees buckled, and he dropped the paper.

Johnny caught him under the arms before he collapsed on the floor.

'How dare she? What's the point?' he exclaimed in a whisper. Was it not enough that they had survived Reverend Cribben? Was it not enough that his deeds had been avenged? What use is it that it becomes public knowledge, the punishment has already been dealt. A dead man cannot be prosecuted. He leant against Johnny for a moment while his heart raced and his head spun. The implications, the potential for public humiliation was intense and worse than the original deed.

Johnny held him, searching for the right words, but they didn't come.

Tears coursed down Elwood's whiskery face. His mind cast back to the last time he'd cried. He was a child, weeping in the very same kitchen. He let go of Johnny and began to pace up and down, wringing his hands and sobbing louder and louder.

As his wailing increased Johnny took him firmly by the hand and led him to the sofa and sat him down.

Gradually, he calmed. He was slumped, his head in his hands and closed his eyes.

Outside the window, the raven was pecking on the pane and hopping to and fro agitatedly.

Johnny sat with him until his breathing was even. At last, he was taking long deep breaths,

He looked at Johnny and said, 'Do not speak of this again. You must never speak of this, do you understand?' His tone was shrill. Then he closed his eyes again.

Johnny stayed for a little longer. When he was satisfied that Elwood had recovered his composure, he got up and left, leaving the newspaper behind on the table. Elwood was right. What good would it do?

Matt got off the bus and leapt the gate into the field that flanked the ancient village. The slate roof of Dywana's farmhouse was just visible above the remains of the roundhouses. He crossed the field and sprung onto the top of a grassy wall and leapt from wall to wall until he reached the path to Chy Bowjy. The leat outside the front door was just a trickle. He knocked on the door.

Di opened the door. Her face broke into a smile. 'Matt, how lovely to see you!' Jasper ran out and started to sniff around his feet.

'G'day, Mrs Constantine, er Di.'

'Please, come in.' She stepped aside, kicking the dog out of the way. A comforting aroma of lilies wafted around the kitchen.

Matt sat down at the pine table and took the notebook from his pocket.

Dywana flicked on the kettle and sat down opposite him. 'Now, I expect you're wondering if I've found those notebooks.'

'Yes, I am. I don't mean to be pushy, but I am keen to get started.'

'Come and see.' She led him into her sitting room. The wood burner was alight, and the dancing flames filled the room with warmth. On the hearth lay a dozen or more notebooks. Just like the one in Matt's pocket.

'You found them!'

'I did. They were a bit musty from the loft, so I'm taking the damp off in front of the fire. Here, look, I've arranged them in date order. You see here is where there is a gap. Do you have it?'

Matt put his notebook in the space.

'Now the set is complete, and you can start your work.'

'Di, that is great news. Can I take them with me today?'

Di shook her head. 'The notebooks must stay here.'

'Oh?'

'The notebooks are my property and the one you had was missing for a very long time. They belong here with me. If you want to consult them then you are welcome, but you must do it here.'

'If that is what you want?'

Dywana nodded. 'That is how it must be.'

'Can I know why?'

'They are a memory. An important memory to me. That's all.'

Matt nodded. 'Yeah, I get that.' 'Can I come back tomorrow?'

'Of course.'

'I'll bring my laptop, but do you mind if I take photos of the first few pages so I can get started tonight?'

'Be my guest.'

Matt drained the rest of his tea and turned to leave. 'Before I go, I meant to ask.'

'Ask away.'

'That final column, the one with the markings in. What do they mean?'

'The final column?'

'Yes, see here.' He opened a notebook. 'Right at the end there. There are some marks, it's like some sort of code.'

'Ah, those! Hmm, I'm not sure I can remember.'

'Really?'

'It was a long time ago, Matt. Perhaps my memory will be jogged. Anyway, I'd better be getting on. I'll see you tomorrow.'

'Sure thing. See you tomorrow.'

TWENTY-TWO

Demelza was changing the beds at Little Rosewarne. Merryn took the end of the sheet and they spread it across the bed together.

'Do you remember, Mum, when I used to help you make the beds when I was little?'

'I do, my darling. You were my little soldier.'

Merryn smiled. 'I used to have pillow fights with Spike.'

'Yes, you did,' said Demelza waving a finger in mock admonishment. 'And I remember when that pillow exploded all over the room and the pair of you looked like snowmen! It took me weeks to get all the feathers up with the vacuum.'

They laughed as they tucked in the corners.

'Do you ever wonder...?'

'Wonder what, my darling?'

'Do you ever wonder what life would have been like?'

Demelza stood up straight and put her arms round Merryn. 'If your Dad was here?'

Merryn nodded, fighting back a tear.

'Of course, I do. I wonder every day.'

'How would you feel if he was to walk into this room now?'

'Now you're being silly.'

'Well obviously he won't, but what would you feel?'

'Oh Merryn, I can't see what good this is doing but I would probably faint, then when I came round, I would be ecstatically happy, and then …'

'Yes?'

'I would be very, very angry and ask him where the hell he'd been for twenty years!'

Both the women laughed.

'You know he's still here, don't you?' said Merryn.

'Of course, he is, I talk to him all the time. Sometimes he answers.' Demelza's voice trailed off and she pushed an unruly lock of hair behind her ear.

'I talk to him too.'

Demelza gave her daughter a hug. 'I'm glad. He was a good man, Piran Jewell.'

Between them they shook out the duvet and threw it over Matt's bed.

'Mum, when you talk to him, do you see him too?'

Demelza looked at her daughter. 'Well, sometimes I suppose.'

'I don't mean in your head; I mean actually see him in front of you.'

'Merryn, are you alright? What do you mean?'

'Please, Mum. Just tell me. Do you see him?'

'I go to the beach and talk to him and sometimes.' She hesitated. 'It's like I can see him, looking up at me from beneath the waves. It sounds ridiculous. Ah, it can be easy to conjure what we want to see and hear. It's comforting.' She looked at Merryn. 'Why are you asking all this?'

'I saw him. And I talked to him.'

'What do you mean, you talked to him?' Alarm swept Demelza's face.

'Yesterday, when I went for a swim. He was there.'

'Come and sit next to me.' Demelza took her daughter's hand and pulled her to sit on the bed. 'Tell me what happened, my lovely.'

'I read the folder and I wanted to see the place he was last seen.'

'So, you went down to Rinsey?'

'Yes. At first, I just sat on the cliff and looked at the waves and tried to feel. You know feel him, and imagine he was still there, setting his lobster pots.'

Demelza nodded. 'I have done the same thing myself.'

'Have you?'

'Yes, of course. I don't have a grave to visit, so I go to Rinsey.'

'I didn't know. But when you scatter the camellia petals you do that here in Porth Taran?'

'That's because here is our home, it's where we were happy together. Now, tell me what happened.'

'Well, I was staring at the sea. Then I could hear this voice. A man's voice.'

'What did the voice say?'

'I, I don't know. It was odd. I could hear the voice; it was deep. It carried a smile.'

Demelza breathed in sharply. 'That's Piran,' she whispered.

'I couldn't hear words, but I just sort of knew it was him. Then I looked for him. There was a shadow beneath the surface. I couldn't see him very well at first. He kind of became bigger and bigger and then I could see his face properly and it was his face; just like in the photograph, the one on my dressing table. He held out a hand for me to take it. Then, he said clearly, "Come with me. I will keep you safe. Come with me." At first, I didn't really understand. I stared at the waves and his face shining through from beneath them. It was hypnotising and then I felt a force deep within me, urging me forwards. I wanted to go to him. To be near that voice, to be with him, with my father, the father I'd never met but had always known.'

Demelza closed her eyes to suppress the tears that were welling uncontrollably to the surface.

'Then, he opened his arms to embrace me and the force became stronger than ever and I …'

'You jumped in?'

Merryn nodded, tears began to stream down her face. 'As soon as I was in the water with him, he swam a little away from me, beckoning me to follow. Then, suddenly the water became very still, and I rose to the surface and then Matt was there.'

Demelza's stomach swooped at the thought of the danger her daughter had been in. Suddenly she was overwhelmed with anger. How could Piran do this to them? How could he do this to their little girl? Was it not enough that he had left her alone? Now, he wanted to take Merryn too? She closed her eyes.

'Mum.' Merryn said gently, 'Mum, are you alright?'

Demelza opened her eyes again, unable to stop the tears. 'Yes, of course my love. I'm just frightened for you. Weren't you scared?' she said in a small voice.

'That was the strange thing. It felt so right. It felt right that I should join him.'

'Join him? Do you mean join him under the waves?'

'It was like that was where I should be.'

'If you had, then I would have lost you.' Demelza could hold the tears back no more. 'I should never have given you that folder.'

'Mum, I'm a grown woman. I needed to know what happened. And now I do, well I know as much as anyone else. Why do you think it happened? What happened to Dad?'

'My darling, I don't know, and we won't ever know.'

'Am I losing my mind? Do you think I'm mad?'

'You had just read the inquest report and it would have been traumatic. As I said before, our minds conjure what we would like to see. I am just so sorry that I didn't read it with you.'

'No, Mum. There is more to this. I know it. I can feel it. It's like he is calling me. He needs me.'

'Merryn, your dad is gone. Piran is gone. This is just your mind playing to your dreams.'

'Mum, listen to me. What if it was true? What if he was really still here in spirit?'

'Merry, my darling, perhaps his spirit is still here but if his spirit is putting you in danger then we have to find a way to protect you.'

Downstairs the front door slammed.

Demelza took a tissue from her pocket and wiped her daughter's face. 'Let's talk about this some more. In the meantime, on no account are you to go to Rinsey. Do you hear?'

Merryn nodded reluctantly.

'Now, I'm glad you told me, and I don't want you to worry. You will see, it will pass. Come on, I think the boys are home.'

Johnny and Matt were standing in the kitchen dripping wet.

'What on earth happened to you two?'

'We just got caught in one hell of a downpour. See, you didn't predict that one, did you?' Johnny punched Matt on the shoulder.

Matt frowned.

'I was just kidding mate,' said Johnny.

'Huh, yeah, yeah I know.'

Jack Jewell stood in the rain looking out over the English Channel. The weather had turned cool and he'd donned his oilskin and a sou'wester to fend off the sharp sea breeze that swirled from the East. At his feet, the dogs cowered, leaning against his legs, willing him to return back to the warmth of the farmhouse. The posy he'd left the day before hadn't wilted; the cooler damp air had kept the flowers fresh. He decided to leave them and just added today's bunch alongside. He leant over and placed them carefully in the lea of the wind.

He came here whatever the weather, just like the old days when Ginny would be there, waiting to meet him. In spring, he would bring bluebells, then valerian in early summer and poppies. In the winter, he gathered bunches of heather and gorse. Then, she didn't come any more. Still, every day he came and every day he wondered what had gone wrong. At first, he thought she must be ill and would come the next day.

When she didn't, he'd popped by her house in Porth Taran but there was no one there. A 'For Sale' sign stood in the front garden. He'd peered through the windows; the rooms were empty of furniture. There were no longer any curtains hanging in Ginny's bedroom at the front of the house. He couldn't ask anyone, for no one knew about him and Ginny. Except for Demelza. Demelza was her friend, she must have known, but Jack Jewell was too private a man to ask. If she had gone and not told him, then that was her choice, she must have had her reasons. It still hurt even now, twenty-five years on. The pain had lessened, of course, but he knew it would linger forever.

He glanced down at the wildflowers lying at the foot of the wall, their petals dancing in the breeze as it fluttered over them. He pictured her standing waiting for him, leaning against the wall. Her long blonde hair blowing wildly in the sea breeze. Her eyes meeting his and lighting up. Her laughter tinkling like falling crystals. She was taller than the other girls, almost as tall as Jack. She would sit on the wall and stretch her long slim legs out in front of her, as they talked.

When she had gone away, he had mourned. He had always hoped there would be some sign from her, a card, or a phone call. He knew he would never meet another like Ginny. Instead he came here, to think about her, hoping she was well. Then he would turn back and take the path back to Tregarron.

After supper, Matt and Merryn lay on Matt's bed. He told her about Dywana and the notebooks and showed her the photos he'd taken of the first few pages.

Merryn pored over them. She tapped on the screen to enlarge the picture. 'What's this, here?' She was pointing to the final column.

'I'm not sure. They look like some kind of weird annotations.'

'Didn't you ask her?'

'I did ask her, but she couldn't remember.'

'She couldn't remember?'

'No, she said she would try to.'

'That's a bit odd. I mean, I'm not very old but I can't imagine ever forgetting a thing like that. Can you?'

Matt shrugged. 'I'll ask her again tomorrow.'

'I'd like to meet her, she sounds interesting; living all the way out there on her own.'

'Why don't you come with me?'

'That's a good idea, I'll ask Mum if we can borrow the car. At least this means you can definitely stay.'

'Well, almost definitely. I have to resubmit my project plan and as long as it's approved back home then I'm good to go.'

'By the way, did you go and see Elwood yesterday?'

'Why?' asked Matt.

'Rowan said he thought he saw you up there.'

'This village, you can't move a muscle without everyone knowing.'

'Yeah, well, that's Porth Taran. So, did you?'

'Well, yes. Yes, I did.'

'Why?'

'I needed to ask him something.'

'Ask him what?'

'About the beach at Rinsey.'

'What about it?'

'About whirlpools.'

'You're not still on about that, are you?'

'Well, yeah. Whirlpools are not a common phenomenon and places where they exist, they usually recur. I wanted to ask him, if it does.'

'You read the report too?'

'Yes, sorry. It was on your bed and when you'd gone out before me, I found it. I was curious, I just wanted to have a look.'

'That's OK. I would have shared it with you anyway. What did Elwood say?'

'He said that whirlpools don't usually happen there.'

Merryn frowned. 'But it did on the day Dad disappeared and it did the other day when I went for a swim?'

'Yeah. It's odd. You see I went to check the beach and the form of the land doesn't show any possible cause of a whirlpool.'

'Curious. I might go and see Elwood myself.'

'I thought you said he was a crackpot.'

'He is a crackpot. But even crackpots know some things.'

TWENTY-THREE

Matt and Merryn pulled up the drive of Chy Bowjy and got out of the car. Matt knocked on the door of Di's farmhouse.

Jasper came flying out and almost knocked them both over. He jumped up at Merryn, covering her in muddy paw prints.

'Jasper!' shrieked Dywana. 'I am so sorry, I didn't realise you weren't alone. Jasper isn't normally this badly behaved. And look at the mess he's made. Please come in, I will get you cleaned up.'

'Oh, it doesn't matter, they're only jeans,' said Merryn.

'I insist, I couldn't forgive myself. Please come in.'

Merryn and Matt followed her into the kitchen. Dywana fussed around with a cloth and a clothes brush scrubbing at the muddy patches on Merryn's jeans.

'I hope you don't mind. I was talking about you last night and Merryn wanted to meet you.'

'Merryn! Now that's a very Cornish name.' Di beamed at her. Then she stared.

'Is everything alright, Di? I thought you wouldn't mind.'

Dywana didn't answer. She took both Merryn's hands in hers and looked her up and down.

Merryn stiffened and looked nervously at Matt.

At last Dywana spoke, 'It's you, isn't it?'

'I, I'm sorry, I don't understand.'

'No, I don't expect you do.' Di was smiling widely now. 'You, are Merryn Jewell.'

'Well, yes, I am. Do we know each other?'

'No, and that is the saddest bit about this.'

Matt and Merryn exchanged confused glances.

'I hoped that this day would come. Merryn Jewell, I am your Aunt Dywana.'

'Dywana?' said Merryn, racking her memory for the name.

'Everyone calls me Di.'

Merryn remained blank.

'You've never even heard of me?'

Merryn shook her head.

'We have only met once but you were a very tiny baby.'

Merryn's frown deepened. 'My aunt? I don't have any aunts.'

A visible wave of sadness swept Dywana's face. 'They didn't even tell you about me?'

'Who?'

'Your family haven't told you about me.' Dywana said it slowly like a statement that shouldn't be uttered.

'Are you my mum's sister?'

Dywana shook her head. 'Piran and Jack were my brothers.'

Merryn gasped. She studied her face. She could see a likeness to Uncle Jack, and her eyes were of the same piercing blue as her father's in the photograph. 'You are my aunt,' said Merryn slowly. The room began to swim, and she wobbled on her feet.

Matt took her elbow to steady her.

'You'd better sit down and actually, so should I. We've both had a shock. Matt, dear, can you make some sweet tea? You know where the kettle is.' Dywana pulled up a chair next to Merryn.

'You are my father's sister and I don't know about you?' Merryn was aghast.

Dywana shook her head sorrowfully.

'You know my mum?'

'I used to, but I haven't seen her for years.'

'So why do I not even recognise you. Do you ever come to Porth Taran?'

Di shook her head. 'No there's no reason to. I'm nearer the shops in Penzance here.'

'And it was you who took the weather records?'

'That's right, I did.'

'But Matt, you asked Uncle Jack, didn't you?'

'I did.' He raised his eyebrows in puzzlement.

'Don't blame him, Merryn. Things… happened. A long time ago. You will need to understand before you jump to conclusions. Now, let me look at you.' Dywana took her arm and stood back from her as if to admire her. 'My very own niece. My only niece.'

'And you are my only aunt!'

The women laughed.

'You have your father's laugh,' said Dywana.

'Do I?'

Dywana nodded not taking her eyes off her. 'Ah I do miss him, even after all these years. You know I think about him all the time.'

'So, do I,' whispered Merryn. 'And you have his eyes.'

Di picked up the teapot and looked at her reflection in it. 'Our father's eyes.' She said softly and sighed. 'Only Jack and I left now. And you, of course. The only grandchild. And how your grandfather would have loved you. He was a redhead, just like you.'

'But why don't I know about you and why do you never visit?'

'I think that will be for another time, but right now I am delighted to know you, Merryn Jewell. My niece!' And she laughed again. 'You're very like him you know. I could see it as soon as I laid eyes on you. Your father was my closest friend when we were children.'

'It must have been difficult for you when he ...'

'It was very hard for everyone. Not least your mother. She was expecting you and had the café to run. But she's obviously done a good job, as I can see that you are a very lovely young lady.' Di stood up, 'It's got rather warm in here, let me just open a window.' She stood up and pushed the window above the kitchen sink open. 'The sky has cleared. After all that weather today and we had a frost up here this morning, we're further from the sea, you see. Now, Matt, have you made that tea?'

Matt poured boiling water from the kettle into the teapot and swirled it round and set it on the table in front of Dywana.

'I'll pour you a cup and then I expect you would like to make a start on the notebooks? Take it upstairs to the observatory. You'll have plenty of light there. Don't let us hold you up, my niece and I have plenty of catching up to do.' Dywana beamed.

Matt took his tea and climbed the spiral staircase up to the observatory. He laid his laptop on the desk. He settled himself in the captain's chair and looked out over the moors and the sea in the distance. He opened the first notebook. Temperature, humidity, pressure, rainfall, wind speed.

Why hadn't Elwood told him that Dywana was Piran's sister? He would have to have words with him when he saw him next. He began to enter the data into his spreadsheet. An entry caught his eye. The pressure recorded was unusually low, the wind speed recorded as hurricane force and the precipitation higher than anything he had seen on past weather records for Porth Taran. In the last column there were more incomprehensible markings. In fact, on every entry where the weather had changed, or it was an unusually long stretch of rain, or sun, or drought, there were markings in the final column.

In an hour Matt managed to log almost half the first notebook's data on his laptop. He got up to stretch his legs and went downstairs.

Merryn and Di were in the kitchen, a basket of freshly laid eggs sat on the kitchen table between them.

'Here, I'll mark up these egg boxes with the names of my customers and if you don't mind can you put the eggs in?'

'Sure,' replied Merryn. 'Matt, will you be alright getting the bus? I'm going to have to get off and open up the gallery.'

'Gallery?' asked Dywana.

'Yes, I have the gallery in the harbour, Rainbow Mosaics. Do you know it?'

'Oh, yes, yes, I do. That's yours, is it? I've never been in. May I?'

'Of course, you may. Come whenever you like.'

'I will! When I can pluck up the courage. You will come back to see me though, won't you?'

Merryn smiled at Dywana and gave her a warm hug. 'Of course, I will. I am so, so pleased to have found you.'

'Merryn, before you go.'

Merryn turned back.

'Go easy on your mother, it's not her fault.'

Merryn nodded and glanced at Matt.

Merryn set off in Demelza's car. As she turned down the opposite side of the moor towards Penzance, St Michael's Mount came into view.

Why had they never mentioned her? Why has no one in the village ever mentioned her? She suddenly felt as if she had been deeply betrayed. Her mother had hidden a

whole member of the family from her. How could that be?
A tear ran down her cheek. She needed a little time before
she confronted Demelza with this. She parked in the yard
at the side of Little Rosewarne and quietly opened the
front door. The house was empty and Merryn was
thankful. She went straight to the private sitting room and
opened the sideboard. At the bottom was a box of
photographs. She pulled it out. As a child she would spend
rainy days poring through the photos of people she didn't
know, while her mum worked. She knew the photos of her
father and of Uncle Jack but couldn't remember ever
seeing a photo of a girl with them.

The wind began to whistle in the window frames
and clouds soon mottled the sky.

She took the box over to the sofa and settled
herself. One by one she took out the photographs. The
first was of Piran in the cricket team, there was Jack
standing at the back with Piran in the front holding a
cricket ball with his wicket keeper's gloves on. Then
another of Jack and Piran coiling up lobster pots when
they were in their twenties. There were photos of her
grandparents and of dogs, long since dead. There were
group photos of farm workers at the end of harvest but
nowhere was there a photo of a little girl. She went
through the whole box until it was empty.

Right at the bottom wedged underneath the
cardboard flap that formed the box she could see another
photo. It was in colour. She carefully slid it out and held it
up. It was a photo of her mum in her wedding gown with
her bridesmaids and maid of honour. At Demelza's feet
were two little girls of five or six years old wearing
miniature versions of the same dress as the maid of
honour. She glanced back at the maid of honour, she was a
slender young woman with blonde hair, all piled up high
on her head and loose ringlets framing her face. She was
holding a bouquet and smiling at the camera. She was
stunningly beautiful. Her eyes were unmistakeable.

Dywana had been Demelza's maid of honour. So, it was true. Here was her father's sister, her aunt. Kept secret from her, all her life.

The sky was much darker now and the rain was hammering against the windowpane.

Merryn carefully replaced the other photos in the box and put the box back in the bottom of the sideboard. She sat on the sofa and stared at the photo, her mind racing.

She'd been so lost in her thoughts she hadn't heard the front door. Demelza came into the sitting room.

'Hello Merry. What are you up to?'

Merryn looked up startled.

Demelza smiled at her. 'What have you got there? Let's have a look.' She leant over. 'Oh, you found that old photo?'

'I did,' said Merryn solemnly.

'Whatever is the matter?'

'This person, here.' Merryn pointed at Dywana. 'Who is she?'

Demelza hesitated. 'Why? You look upset.'

'I'm upset because I just met her, and I didn't know she existed.'

'Oh Merry. You met Dywana?' She sat down on the sofa next to her.

Merryn began to cry. 'I have met her. I didn't know who she was and then she told me she was my aunt. Why didn't I know about her?'

Demelza took Merryn's hand in both of hers and began to rub it soothingly. 'I wanted to tell you. I really did.'

'It was she who took the weather records. You knew that.'

'Yes, I did know that.' Demelza looked at her feet.

'So, why? You had an opportunity to tell me when Matt was asking about her. He even asked Jack and you

both pretended to know nothing or to not remember. How can you not remember a sister?'

'Merry, I know. You're right. I'm not proud of it. Jack and I took the decision a long time ago not to include Dywana in our lives.'

'How can you exclude a member of the family like that?' Merryn was outraged.

'Something happened and it tore our family apart.'

'What happened?'

'There was a disagreement.'

'About what?'

'It was about Piran. About your dad.'

'What about?'

'Dywana said some things, things that were really hurtful. Your dad had not long been gone and it was horrible to hear them.'

'What things?'

'It's all such a long time ago, now. I don't want to repeat them and anyway it's all water under the bridge. Perhaps it's time.'

'Time for what?' Merryn wiped the tears from her face and looked at her mother earnestly.

'Perhaps it's time we made our peace.'

TWENTY-FOUR

Merryn had lain awake most of the night. There was not a sound in Little Rosewarne. She pulled herself to sitting. She got up and padded to the window. Outside everything was still. A frost had cast its spiky fingers across Porth Taran and the moon, low over the rooftops, lit up the pavements making them glow white.

Merryn looked at her watch; it was seven o'clock. Matt would still be fast asleep. She pulled on some jeans, a tee shirt, and a thick jumper. She tied her hair into a chignon and secured it with a pencil. She slipped quietly down the stairs, grabbing her coat from the hall stand on the way. She heated herself a coffee in the microwave and poured it into a thermos mug and took Demelza's car keys from the dish in the hall. As quietly as she could, she opened the front door, pulling it to, so that it only made the slightest audible click. As she stepped on to the icy pavement, she felt the pull more keenly than ever. She went around to the side of the house to Demelza's car and got inside.

She started the engine and waited a little for the car to warm. The windows were coated in a fine filigree pattern of ice. She couldn't ever remember a frost quite as severe as this. She clutched the coffee in both hands to keep them warm and watched as the intricate patterns on the glass began to melt and drizzle down the windscreen. As soon as the ice had melted enough for her to be able to see out, she pulled out of the yard and drove up the harbour road.

School children dressed inadequately for the season were walking to the bus stop, hunched and shivering. Over by the Ship Inn someone had lit an incinerator and fishermen were gathered round it, rubbing their hands together.

She swung round the harbour and headed out of Porth Taran towards the west. The trees along the road glistened icily in the dawn light, palm trees in front gardens looked incongruous in their winter mantles.

Traffic was building on the main road. She pulled off left towards Rinsey, slowing to be sure her wing mirrors didn't snag the walled hedges on each side. At last she reached the engine house and parked up next to the chimney. She climbed out and did up her coat against the chill wind that was blowing off the Atlantic.

The water was smooth and shone platinum reflecting the awakening sky. Only on the shore was the surface disturbed as it lapped on the beach like undulating silk. She looked down at the grassy steps cut into the cliff. Warmed by the sea, the lower part of the cliff was free of frost. She took a deep breath and began to descend to the cove, carefully watching each step lest she stumble in the half light. As she got closer to the shore, her heart began to flutter.

The spit stretched out dark and grey into the lapping crystalline waters. The tide was going out. She stepped onto the spit and made her way to its tip. She lowered herself on to the cold granite and sat cross-legged and stared into the calm lapping waters beneath.

She closed her eyes and brought the image of her father into her mind. His piercing blue eyes and his flashing white smile. At first there was no sound other than the gulls calling as they wheeled overhead. Then she heard it.

'Merryn, my darlin', you've come. I've been waiting.'

'Waiting for me?' she answered in a whisper. She opened her eyes. Just under the surface of the water, Piran's face smiled up at hers.

'Yes of course, for you. For my little girl.'

Merryn couldn't speak.

'What's wrong my darlin'? Is it Dywana?'

Merryn was startled. 'You know about that?'

'I know everything my darlin' for I have been watchin' over you since the day you were born. Always here, always watching.'

'They didn't tell me about her.'

'Dywana is misunderstood. She sees things that others are scared of, so they reject her. I have done it too. I didn't want to believe but now I know it all to be true. She is a good person but headstrong. It's the Jewell way.' He let out a long hearty laugh. 'You must forgive them, they only want to protect you.'

'Protect me from what?'

'From yourself, sweet Merry. Dywana knows. Go and ask her. She will explain it better than me. She always explained everything better than me.'

'Piran.' She hesitated. 'Dad. What happened? What happened to you that day?'

'It was the will of the gods. It was the right thing, I promise you. You must trust me. But you, my darling, you must not go the same way. You are different.'

'I don't understand.'

'You will.' His voice began to fade out. 'I promise, you will.' Then his face began to sink lower in the water. As his voice faded, she heard him cry 'Dywana, talk to her. Help them listen to Dywana.'

Merryn stood up to get a better view but he was gone. Only the gulls squealed into the wind. She stood and stared out over the ocean, desperately searching the spot where her father had been, but there were only empty waves, reflecting the sky. She climbed back up the cliff to the road and to the car.

As she drove, the clouds drew in. The sky turned a shade of dark green and a wave of hailstones rained like bullets onto the road. The wheels juddered as they crunched over the balls of ice. The hail came down faster, she could feel the steering was loose and the tyres were slipping as if on thick gravel. She reached the main road to St. Ives, driving gingerly. Further up, towards Penzance, she could see that cars had pulled over onto the side of the road with their headlights on, waiting for the hail to pass. She pulled up and looked skyward. The heavens were darker than ever and the visibility was getting poorer by the minute. She couldn't wait. She slowly pulled out into the middle of the road to clear the stationary cars. At least Badger's Cross wasn't too far. She drove slowly, compensating with the steering wheel when the wheels swung in the wrong direction. Merryn forged on until she reached the lane to Dywana's. The surface of Chy Bowjy's drive was so thick with hail that the tyres on the car couldn't grip and the car kept slipping backwards. Merryn gave up and reversed and parked on the side of the lane. She got out and trudged up the drive through the unrelenting hailstorm and banged on Dywana's front door. The door swung open.

'Merryn! You're frozen and soaked!' Dywana bundled her through the door and sat her down next to the range. Merryn's teeth were chattering and she couldn't speak.

She undid Merryn's wet jacket and draped a blanket around her shoulders.

'What have you been doing? I'll get the kettle on.'

Merryn sat and stared absently. Gradually her teeth stopped chattering and the shivering subsided. Di put a steaming mug of tea in front of her.

'Put your hands round that and you'll soon warm up.' Di sat down next to her, putting her arm around her. 'What on earth were you doing out in that hailstorm? I swear I've never seen anything like it before. It looks like we're in for a pummelling this autumn.'

Merryn took the photo from the back pocket of her jeans and put it on the table.

Dywana picked it up. 'Ah, that day! How young we were! Such happy times. It was so hot; I remember I had a tan line across my bodice line from posing for photographs in the sun.'

'Why didn't they tell me?' whispered Merryn.

'Oh, my darling, it wasn't about you. We fell out. Grown-ups do. Families do. Over things that happened before you were born.'

'What things?'

Dywana hesitated. 'Did you talk to your mum?'

Merryn nodded.

'What did she say?'

'She said the same thing. She said there was a disagreement and she and Uncle Jack decided it was better to keep you out of their lives.'

Sadness swept Dywana's face.

'But Mum said that perhaps it was time to make peace.'

'She did?' Dywana brightened.

Merryn nodded and took a sip of tea.

'Please, tell me what happened.'

'Oh, my love, the past is the past. It is our past, not yours. You are here now and for that I am blessed.' Dywana rubbed Merryn's arm.

'Dywana, do you believe that you can talk to the dead?'

'Talk to the dead?'

'Do you believe that sometimes peoples' spirits are left behind after they die?'

'Some people do, I think. Though, I have not experienced it. Have you?'

Merryn nodded. 'I talk to my dad.'

'To Piran?'

'Yes, to Piran. And he talks back. I have seen him and it's why I have come.'

'I see.'

'Once or twice, I have been down to Rinsey, to where his boat disappeared. If I close my eyes and call him, he appears. This morning I went there again, and he appeared. He already knew that I had found you.'

'He did?'

'I asked him why you had been kept a secret and he said that it was to protect me. To protect me from myself.' She looked up at Dywana searchingly.

Dywana frowned.

'He told me to come and see you. He said that you knew. You know what he was talking about, don't you?'

'I'm not sure I do, my love. It's a lot to take in. Finding you again. Hearing about all of this. I wonder...'

'What do you wonder? Dywana, please.'

'I need some time.' She stroked her niece's forehead. 'I promise, I am not hiding anything from you, I just need a little time to think.'

Merryn sighed and took a sip of tea.

'Listen you get out of those wet clothes and I'll pop them in the dryer. You can change in the spare bedroom. There's a dressing gown on the back of the door.'

An hour later, Merryn was back in her dry clothes, finishing up a plate of bacon and eggs. 'Thank you for breakfast. I need to get back. Please, think about what I said, I really need to understand.'

Dywana nodded and gave her a hug.

Merryn drove straight to Little Rosewarne, parked the car round the side and replaced the car keys in the dish in the hall. She didn't check if Demelza or Spike were home, she didn't feel like explaining herself, she went straight off to the gallery.

There was no sign of Elwood. It was later than usual; he may have been and gone. As she unlocked the door she glanced through the front window. The shop walls reflected the sky and everything within was cloaked in grey. Her mosaic lay uncovered on the workbench, almost complete save for the sun, the giver of life, the warmth and comfort. She couldn't be in there. She needed the open. She turned around and locked the door again and put the keys in her pocket and headed for the beach. Today was not a day for working, and not a day for the sun.

Porth Taran was deserted. The weather had seen off the last of the holiday makers and the temperatures had driven everyone else to their firesides. Merryn revelled in the stinging cold on her cheeks and kept walking until she reached the headland at the other end of the beach, she felt as cold inside as out.

At this end of the beach there were huge boulders the size of small buildings. Their surfaces covered in smooth indentations from the relentless stroking of the sea. Limpets and mussels clung to them. At the base of some, were deep clear pools left by the retreating tide. They harboured tiny sea urchins and by-the-wind sailors, their cobalt shells floating like rafts on the surface, each bearing a cellophane sail.

She needed to keep moving, she turned and marched back concentrating on her steps, the sand giving way beneath her feet as she went. She walked faster and faster, she was sweating, and her breath was heavy. As she reached the steps up to the harbour road, the wind began to strengthen. She wanted to keep walking, but her body needed to stop. Merryn knew where she must go. Her body, damp from sweat, began to shiver in the gusts of the icy wind that stabbed her as she walked up the hill.

She banged on Elwood's door. There was no answer. She pushed open the letterbox, she could hear music inside. A gentle solitary flute was playing deep within.

'Elwood,' she called. 'It's me.'

The flute stopped, then there was silence.

'Elwood, it's me,' she yelled a little louder this time. Then hesitating, she called out, 'It's Ambis.' She heard a bang as if something had fallen to the floor. Then footsteps. She stood up straight and heard the chain unhook and the bolts slide back.

Elwood opened the door. 'You've come!'

'Err, yes. I suppose I have. Can I come in?'

'Of course, what is mine is yours, Ambisagrus. I am honoured to receive you in my humble home.' He bowed deeply and gestured for her to go through to the back of the house.

In the back room, the curtains were drawn and it was cloaked in darkness, save for a single candle. There was a lingering smell of burning herbs.

'Please, sit down.'

Merryn chose a seat at the far end of the sofa.

Elwood took up the single armchair opposite her. He looked into her eyes. 'You are troubled.'

Merryn swallowed. 'I need to know.'

Elwood didn't speak or move.

'I need to know, what happened that day. The day my father disappeared. I need to know what you saw.'

Elwood breathed in deeply and nodded. 'You have a right to know but I could not tell you until you had asked, but now you are here.' He sat up straight, puffed out his chest and folded his hands in his lap. 'I was walking out at Rinsey Head, I used to go there every day back then. I would sit on the same tussock of grass high up on the headland and stare out at the sea. It was your father's favourite spot to set his pots. Sheltered between the headlands but exposed enough for the sun to warm the waters and bring the lobsters out, you see. It was the middle of the morning, I think. I was watching him, throwing the pots slowly off the back of the boat in the little bay. Then, he stopped suddenly and spoke on his radio. He let out a yell, you know, of joy and did a little jump. The sea suddenly got up, you know, there was a current, it began to swirl around the boat. He put down the radio and the boat began to spin, slowly at first. Then it got faster and faster. Round and round, the pots spilled off the back as it went. Then the circles got larger around the edges and tighter around the boat until suddenly the boat was sucked right under. Pots, Piran and all. As soon as he had disappeared, the surface was smooth again, not a bubble or a ripple. And nothing there. I couldn't believe my eyes.'

'What did you do?'

'I got up and ran, as fast as I could back to the village. I found Jack and told him. He didn't believe me, but he took a launch out to look for him all the same. I went with him. But there was nothing there, just as I'd told him. The coastguard was called. They searched for him for two days and found nothing. There was no wreckage, no pots, nothing.'

Merryn stared at the little man in his armchair.

'You saw him, didn't you?' he asked. 'That day Bunjil rescued you from the sea. It was the same spot. He was calling you.'

Merryn nodded. 'How did you know?'

'The same spot, the same whirlpool. Did he call you there?'

'I don't know, I just felt compelled to go. I can't describe it. When I got there, he called to me and appeared. He held his hand out to me.'

'And you went to take it?'

'Yes, I did. He spoke to me. He said, "You will be safe here, safe with me."'

Elwood frowned. 'He wanted you to join him?'

'Yes, and I wanted to go. But when Matt jumped in the water, he disappeared. I was so close.'

'We almost lost you.'

'What do you mean?'

'He was calling you to join him beneath the waves and if you had gone, you would not have been able to come back.'

'Why would he want that?'

'All fathers want their children to be near, don't they?'

'I suppose, but you say I wouldn't have been safe? Did he want to harm me?' Alarm was welling up in her.

Elwood shook his head. 'Your father could be a selfish man sometimes. It would have harmed your mortal self, but you, Ambisagrus, are just like him. You will live forever.'

'What do you mean, just like him? Who is Ambisagrus? Why do you call me that?'

'Ambisagrus, you are the daughter of Taranis, the god of thunder. That's why you're here. You want answers.'

Merryn looked puzzled. 'I don't know.' Suddenly, she wanted to cry. She closed her eyes and breathed deeply.

'No one has told you?'

'Told me what?'

'Ambis, you have taken over from Piran. You are now the guardian of the weather.'

'What does that mean?'

'You, like your father can control the weather.'

'What do you mean, control the weather?'

'Have you not noticed that the wind is up?'

'Yes, of course I have.'

'It's getting stronger.'

Merryn stared at him incredulous.

'The more upset you get, the worse the weather turns.'

Merryn didn't move, her frown deepened. She fixed her gaze on a stain on the carpet to anchor her mind.

Elwood got up and pulled back the curtain. A raven was hopping on the terrace at the window. He was pecking at the floor and cocking his head on one side as if he was trying to peer into the house. The trees in the garden were swaying in the wind.

'Look. Do you see that wind?'

Merryn looked up. 'It's been like that off and on all day.'

'And how have you been feeling?'

'Elwood, are you honestly trying to say that the weather reflects my mood?'

'Think back, Ambis. Remember the day of the party. It was hot, really hot.'

Merryn remembered her excitement at going to the party with Matt and the preparations. She remembered getting ready and looking forward to it.

'This weather, now. It's autumn. It's normal autumn weather.'

'It is. You're right. Did we have normal autumn weather last year? Or the year before that? And what about that wave on the night of the party?'

'You think, I am responsible for that?' Anger was welling up in her. 'This is ridiculous!' She got up to leave.

'Ambis, listen to me. Listen, please sit down.'

Something in Merryn made her stop. She needed to hear more. She sat down on the sofa.

'Ridiculous, yes. But ridiculous doesn't mean it can't be true.'

Then she cleared her throat and swallowed. 'Elwood, if everything I think and feel is translated into the weather going on around me and around the people I love, then I have a huge burden to carry. And not just for the people I know, but for the whole village, the farmers, and the businesses. Everyone!' The tears began to fall in an unrestricted torrent. 'Perhaps I should have taken my father's hand. Was that what he was trying to protect me from?' Suddenly she wanted to be alone, back in her bedroom at Little Rosewarne. She wanted to be where nothing had changed. Her heart was swooping and lurching. A dustbin in Elwood's back garden was suddenly picked up by the wind and slammed against the fence. Merryn screamed. 'Was that me?'

'Ambis, calm yourself. There is a way.'

She opened her mouth to remonstrate.

He held a finger to his lips and shushed her. He leant forwards and pressed the play button on his music system. The solitary flute echoed out of its speakers.

'Now sit up straight and close your eyes. That's it. Focus on your breathing, deep even breaths. In and out. Now relax your shoulders... And your arms, ... your hands, ... and fingers.'

As he spoke Elwood's voice slowed and took on a syrupy richness that she had never heard from him before.

'Relax your hips, and your legs... your feet and now stretch your toes. Relax. Listen to the music, hear the flute as it blows your troubles away. Breathe in and then out, slowly. Long deep breaths. When a thought comes just bat it away. Focus on your breathing, that's it. Slowly now, in... and ... out.' Elwood's eyes were closed now too.

They sat there for a few minutes without talking, just the solitary flute playing its tune.

Then Elwood took a deep breath and opened his eyes. 'In... and ... out,' he whispered. 'In... and out. I am going to count down from five and when I have finished, and you feel ready, open your eyes slowly. Five..., four ..., three ..., two ..., one...'

Merryn opened one eye and then the other.

'Now stretch,' said Elwood.

Merryn did as she was told.

'Look outside now.'

Merryn looked. The wind had dropped, and the clouds had decelerated.

'You see, you must separate your mind from your heart. Only then can you have true control.' Elwood smiled at Merryn's astonishment.

'Is it really me that has done that?'

Elwood nodded.

'And I have calmed it too?'

'Of course. For you have given your heart a long-awaited break.'

Merryn shook her head. 'I can't feel like this all the time What if I get angry or sad when bad things happen? This is purgatory. I would have no freedom to feel…, to feel anything at all.'

'Practise what I have taught you every day and you will master it.'

Merryn was still shaking her head.

'Heed what I tell you and all will be well with you, and with Porth Taran.'

'Is that what my father meant, when he said that he was in the right place for everyone? Perhaps that is the right place for me, too.'

'You think that is better for Demelza, and for Jack, and for Johnny?'

Merryn began to weep again. 'It seems I will have to hurt someone, if my feelings make the weather. If I love, I risk getting hurt. If I hurt, I will hurt those around me.

'You want to renounce your love?'

'I cannot love. It is not my right. Is that why my father called me?'

'Ambis can love, but Ambis can only love a higher being, a being whose very powers are as strong as hers. Whose powers can calm hers, can make the sad happy and the turbulent peaceful. Ambis can love Bunjil.'

'Bunjil?'

Elwood nodded.

TWENTY-FIVE

Demelza opened her eyes. Spike's place next to her was empty. She looked at her watch, it was nine-thirty. He must have gone to the Cash-and-Carry without her.

She felt dizzy and her body was weak. She had lain awake thinking about Merryn, and Dywana, and Jack, their faces swirling in her head. Merryn in tears, Dywana angry, yet helpless, and Jack, wearing the frown that took ten years to fade.

Then, suddenly she realised that Piran hadn't been there. He was always there in the background, always. Sometimes he'd speak to her. He'd tell her what he thought about what she was doing, or what she was worrying about. Although he was gone, she'd always felt him near, since that first night when Merryn was born.

He sat in the chair next to her at the hospital, cradling their baby daughter. Merryn had wrapped her tiny hand around his finger, as she'd slept in his arms.

She remembered her bereavement counsellor telling her that she mustn't be frightened. He'd said that visual hallucinations were common for people who had lost someone, that it marked the beginning of her healing, and the end of the loneliness that she'd felt between Piran's disappearance and Merryn's birth.

She hadn't been scared. She'd felt an overwhelming sense of relief, for Piran had not left her. But last night, he was gone. She had not conjured him. Was she subconsciously keeping him from Dywana's theories? Or was her two decades of grieving, finally coming to an end?

She heaved herself from her bed and went downstairs to make coffee. She caught her reflection in the kettle, she looked old and drawn. Seeing Merryn so unsettled was breaking her soul.

She poured boiling water over the coffee grounds in the cafetiere.

Perhaps what Merryn was experiencing was grief. Seeing Piran, talking to him, hearing his voice. Was she mourning the passing of a father she had never known? Meeting Matt and talking about him could have set her on a journey, a journey of acceptance.

Dear sweet Merryn, so much like her father; the same colouring, the same sparkle. Yet so different. She was not fiery, nor impulsive like Piran. Until now, she had always been so happy in her skin. Even through her teenage years she had not waivered, or struggled.

They'd always been close, she and Merryn. The look in her eye, when she'd found the photo of Dywana, shot through her like a spear to her heart. Demelza knew it was a well-deserved spear. Losing Merryn would be even worse than losing Piran. A tear rolled down her cheek.

How could she have been so stupid? She knew what she must do.

She poured the coffee into a mug and knocked it back, scalding her throat. She went upstairs, splashed water on her face, brushed her hair and pulled on some clothes.

She checked herself in the mirror. What she had done, what she had agreed to, had felt right at the time. Now, she struggled to believe that she had supported such a wrong. A wrong that had hurt her own child. She went downstairs and took the car keys from the dish in the hall.

The peninsula was shrouded in grey. As she drove west, towards Penzance, the bitterness that she had felt all those years before rose up in her gut like bile. Had she felt outdone in her grief? Dywana had lost her husband and her brother, perhaps she had the right. Resentment and guilt jousted in her head, each fighting for supremacy. She knew she must allow the battle to run its course.

She came to the turning for Marazion and swung off the main road. The terraced cottages that clung to the meandering main street, were dark grey with mizzle. She pushed on through the village to the other side, to the Mount. She parked up by the beach.

Demelza glanced up at the little ferry that ran between the shore and the mount. It was poised on the beach waiting for the causeway to be covered over by the sea again before it could make its way back across with supplies. Every day the same, just the time and the weather conditions changed. Some days the weather was too bad even to go that short distance and the island would remain isolated from the mainland. Dywana, was so near, up there at Chysauster, yet like this little ferry she was isolated from her mainland. Excluded. Not for one day, or one tide turning but for nineteen years. Dywana had been her friend, her ally, and she had walked away from her.

Just as she thought that guilt had its hands on the trophy she remembered the allegations. She could hear Dywana's voice, shaking with anger and grief. She remembered Jack's outrage. Then she remembered her own fear and the nagging doubt that gnawed at her core, that somehow Dywana might be close to the truth.

Demelza wiped away her tears and restarted the engine. She would not allow this family to be subjected to any more tragedy. She pulled out of the car park and headed towards Penzance and the St. Ives Road.

The mizzle hung seemingly motionless in the air as she pulled up the drive of Chy Bowjy. She drew to a halt, put on the handbrake and got out of the car. She looked around her. It reminded her a little of Tregarron, though it was tidier. The stones that paved the front path were clean and free of moss. Pots outside the front door spilled scarlet trailing geraniums that contrasted against the granite stone wall of the farmhouse. Demelza could hear chickens clucking in the distance. All was trimmed, and newly painted and tidied. At least that much hadn't changed with Dywana, she had always kept a neat household.

Demelza noticed a movement in the curtains in one of the front windows. She took a deep breath and went up to the front door and knocked. A dog barked excitedly from within. Demelza stood back a little and waited.

The door opened slowly. Dywana was holding a springer spaniel back by its collar.

'Demelza,' said Dywana.

'Dywana.'

Their eyes met, each trying to gauge the other's reaction.

'It's been a long time,' said Dywana.

'It has, it's been too long.'

'Please, come in.'

At the visitors' centre, Matt was manning the desk while Carrie nipped out for pasties. He was looking through the assessor's report of the damage to the weather station. It didn't look like it would be up and running any time soon. Matt sighed. He flicked open his phone and looked at the photos he had taken of the first notebook. He glanced at the final column and the strange annotations.

Carrie came through the centre doors clutching a couple of paper bags and a loaf of bread. 'Here you go.' She passed him a pasty.

'Jeez, thanks Carrie. What took you so long? I was proper hungry.'

'Boys your age are always hungry.' Carrie sat down behind the desk and laid out her pasty on its wrapping. 'I meant to ask; did you ever find Di Constantine?'

'Yeah, yeah, I did.'

'Where is she nowadays?'

'She's over at Badgers Cross, do you know it?'

'Oh, it's nice over there. Bit lost though. Was she helpful?'

'Actually, yes. She's found all the other notebooks, so I'm all set. I can carry on my work even if the weather station is out of action.'

'Oh, Matt, that's great news.'

'Yeah, it is. Shame no one told me she was Merryn's aunt.' Matt eyed her accusingly.

'Ah, that.'

'Yes, that. What's the story?'

'Ah, Matt, stuff went on and there was a falling out, that's all. It's really not my place to say.'

'It was quite a shock for poor Merryn.'

Carrie's eyes widened. 'Merryn met her?'

'She wanted to come with me.'

'But how did she know who she was?'

'Dywana recognised her. Not many families round here, got those eyes.'

'No. No, I suppose not.'

'Listen, Carrie, since you neglected to tell me that important bit of information, perhaps you can help me with something else.'

'I can try.'

'Can you look at this? Look at the last column.' Matt passed his phone to her.

'Oh, that looks like shorthand to me.'

'Shorthand?'

'Yeah back in the day, all the girls learnt it at school. Di would have done it too.'

'And... did you do it?'

'Well, yes, yes I did. And Demelza. All the girls did.'

'So, can you tell me what it says?'

'Ooh, now. It's all a long time ago. Let me see.' She screwed up her eyes. 'Well, it's definitely Pitman's shorthand. This shape here, I think the consonant sounds are P-R-N.'

'What about after that?'

Carrie shook her head. 'I could work out the consonant sounds but the vowels aren't marked. They never are once you get good at it. Without the vowels or having written it myself, the words would just be a guess. You'll need to ask her.'

'I don't suppose you've got a book on Pitman's shorthand, do you?'

'Not anymore I'm afraid, sorry. You could try the library; it should still be open.'

'Yeah. Yeah, I will. Thanks Carrie.'

Demelza and Dywana sat at the kitchen table.

'You've got a nice house, Di.'

'Thank you, I like it. It's just missing a bit of life, you know?'

'Yes, I can imagine it's a bit lonely up here.'

'Oh, I've got used to that over the years.'

Demelza closed her eyes and took a deep breath in. 'I am partly to blame for that. I'm not proud of myself.'

'Demelza, it was a difficult time for everyone, and my reaction was unhelpful.'

Demelza stared into her mug of tea.

'I am truly sorry for all the things I said about Piran' said Dywana.

'Why did you say them?'

'Because, I wasn't in a good place.' Dywana clasped her hands together on the table.

'Was that the only reason?'

'What do you mean?'

'Merryn. She came to see you.'

'She did.' Dywana smiled. 'What a truly wonderful young woman she has become. She is a credit to you, Melza.'

'Thank you. She has grown up beautifully, but she is young and impressionable, still.'

'Ah, I see. You are worried that I will put strange notions into her head?'

'Yes, I suppose I am.'

'I can assure you, I have no such intention. But …I fear the notions that you believe I am responsible for, may have a life of their own.'

'Why do you say that?' said Demelza in alarm.

'She came to see me again. She said,' Dywana took a moment to plan her words. 'She said she'd spoken to Piran. She said that he had told her that she needed protecting from herself and that I knew why.'

'Oh, Di. It's starting again. History is repeating itself.'

Dywana put her hand over Demelza's. 'It doesn't have to; we can stop this.'

'How can this be happening again if no one has sown the seed in her mind? Her vision of her father in the sea telling her cannot be real. It just can't. Someone else must have told her something.'

Di shook her head. 'Maybe but I promise you, Melza, it wasn't me.'

Demelza looked at her long and hard and she knew she was telling the truth. 'So, what did you tell her?'

'I told her that I need time to think.'

'We do need time to think. I know my daughter well enough to know that she won't let go of this. She will be back looking for answers.'

'She won't find any from me. I simply don't have any answers. What on earth can I say to her?'

'Di, do you think that she could be grieving?'

'Grieving? For Piran?'

'Yes. Everything she is saying is what I felt when I lost him. Did you go through it when Kendrick was killed?'

Dywana thought for a moment. 'You mean, actually seeing him?'

Demelza nodded.

'You actually saw Piran?'

'I did.'

Dywana frowned. 'I did talk to Kendrick and imagined him listening, and how I thought he might answer. But I'm pretty certain I didn't actually see him. I suppose everyone is different.'

'You know, Di, I think that must be it. Her visions of Piran can't be real. They have come from her own mind. She only recently started asking questions about him and that will have brought it all into her mind. It's her imagination running wild, that's all.'

'Why did she start asking questions all of a sudden?'

'Merry has grown up. She's got her own little business and even a boyfriend, now. He's the first one. Since she met this Matt...'

'He's a nice lad, that Matt.'

'Yes, he is. But since she's met him, she's been asking questions about how Piran disappeared and obviously I've told her. I thought it was time she knew. I gave her the inquest report. You know, with the transcription.'

'She read Elwood's statement?'

Demelza nodded.

'It's Elwood that's done this.'

Demelza shook her head. 'Merryn doesn't talk to Elwood she just thinks he's the local crackpot.'

Dywana rolled her eyes, 'Well, there is some truth in that but there is more to Elwood than people realise.'

'It's just,' Demelza took a sip of tea. 'It's just I get the feeling that she really is speaking to him. I know it's ridiculous, but she repeated their conversations to me, and his words actually sound like his. She couldn't possibly have known how he talked.'

'Melza, Piran talked like all of us. Jack talks like him.'

'Well, what can we do to help her?'

'If Merryn is who you say she is, then we must tell her what we know. Just the facts.'

'Everything?'

'If we don't it will come out. It is better that she hears it from you, from both of us. No more secrets.'

'What about Jack?'

Dywana breathed in sharply. 'There was another big storm in Porth Taran a couple of weeks ago, wasn't there?'

'Yes.'

'The last one before that was the day Merryn was born, wasn't it?'

'Coincidences. That's all they are, coincidences.'

Dywana was pushing a paperclip around the table absentmindedly. 'What if they aren't, Melza? What if Elwood has been right all these years?'

'Dywana, stop! We can tell her the facts, but only the facts. The rest will be up to her.'

'I agree and she can make her own mind up. We can tell her that I had been left out of the family because I was going through a hard time which led me to say upsetting things about her father.'

'And you're prepared to do that?'

'Yes, of course, I am. Anyway, it's the truth. Isn't it?'

Demelza squeezed Dywana's hand gratefully.

'Melza, I am so, so happy to see you and really thrilled to know Merryn. Now, I would like my family back and I will do anything for that. Trust me.'

Matt was sitting on his bed. He'd spent the whole day studying the Pitman's 2000 handbook that the librarian had dug from the archives. Carrie was right, that shape was indeed P-R. Then after, D-ST-N-T and K-W-T. Nearly every entry began with P-R. He scratched his head. He wouldn't be able to decipher these without Dywana's help.

He heard footsteps on the stairs above him. He peered out of his door, as Merryn descended.

'What are you doing here in the day? I saw you didn't open up today.'

'I didn't sleep very well, so I came home for a rest. What have you got there?'

Matt showed her the shorthand.

'Hmm, P. R.,' Merryn pondered.

'I can't work it out.'

She took it from him and peered closer. 'I can't fathom it.' She shook her head. 'Only Dywana can tell you.'

Matt sighed.

'I went to see Elwood today,' said Merryn.

'Oh no, don't go listening to that nonsense.'

'How do you know about it?'

'I told you, I went to see him about the whirlpool, and he came up with a load of mumbo jumbo about some of us predicting the weather and others controlling it and …'

'He meant you, didn't he? You predict the weather and … I control it.'

'Yeah but it's rubbish.'

'Just from Elwood, yeah, it is all rubbish. But it's not is it? My dad said it too. This is what dad said I needed to be protected from. Elwood showed me. He showed me that I was causing the weather and how to calm it.'

'Merryn, that man is putting ideas into your head that are just not possible. You cannot believe there is a link between you, your father and the weather.'

'I do not believe; I now know it to be true.'

'I will show you, sweet Merryn. It is not true. We will go and see Dywana, we will ask her straight out. You will see. We will iron this out.' Matt took her hand and stroked it soothingly.

TWENTY-SIX

Merryn tossed and turned and dreamt heavily. She dreamt of her father, beckoning her into the sea. Of her mother standing next to him in the centre of a whirlpool, both of them calling her in. She dreamt of Demelza and Piran, hand in hand up at the ancient village. A bridal bouquet in Demelza's hands. Spike and Dywana throwing petals on them like confetti and Elwood in a cassock with a prayer book.

She awoke with a start. The walls of her bedroom at Little Rosewarne were just as they were, her sanctuary, ordinary and unchanged. Her face was wet with tears. She wiped them away with the back of her hand.

It was still dark outside. She lay still until light began to show at the edges of her bedroom curtains. She got up and looked out of the window. There was no frost, the streets gleamed grey with the polished coating of mizzle that clung to the stone and tarmac of Porth Taran. Desolation swept her.

She pulled on some clothes, brushed her hair, and slipped downstairs. All was quiet in the Bed & Breakfast. She stood in the hall and looked about her. Demelza's coat was on the coat rack, her shoes on the floor underneath.

266

Merryn brushed the cloth and smelt her mother's perfume. She breathed deeply and slipped out of the front door and into the street.

The rain was falling in a fine mist, the kind that soaks you unawares. She didn't care. She walked down the harbour road, past Elwood's road, past the supermarket. She reached the gallery and looked inside as if it belonged to someone else. Another person's life. Not hers. For this was not her life. She was no longer Merryn Jewell. She was Ambisagrus, daughter of Taranis. Daughter of Piran, lying beneath the waters, calling her. Ambis, whose mere emotions could harm the people she loved, in the place that was home. The responsibility weighed on her heavily. A life of restriction and moderation was too much to bear. It would be safer and better for everyone. She didn't think of her mother, or Uncle Johnny, of Spike or Uncle Jack. The hardest of all was Matt. She would not let him carry this.

She kept on walking until she reached the beach. The tide was high. She climbed down the cliff path to the peat shelf, the grey waves were lapping at it gently. She sat down cross legged, the water washing over her knees. She closed her eyes and thought of him. She conjured his smile, head of curly hair flecked with copper. She breathed deeply and focussed on his face.

Elwood awoke abruptly. He pushed himself up to sitting. Drizzle coated the windowpane. He stumbled from his bed and looked outside. All was grey in Porth Taran. Ambis was sad. He shook his head. His heart lurched as he thought of her, weeping in his sitting room the day before. Poor, sweet Ambis. He looked out over the harbour. A cloud of seagulls was circling over the beach. He sensed that something wasn't right. He got up and pulled on his clothes. He took his staff from the hall and stepped out of the front door. This time he didn't worry about his route, no time. He strode boldly down the harbour road and past the church. Adrenaline was shielding him from the pain in his joints. He reached the cliff top and looked down.

There at the bottom of the steps just beneath the wheeling gulls was Ambis. She was standing on the peat shelf, her arms held out to her sides, in the shape of a cross. He looked down at the water, but he couldn't see well enough through the misty rain. He began to make his way down the steps. He kept his eyes focussed on each stride, lest he trip and fall. As he neared the sea, he could see the surface of the water was troubled just in front of her. He picked up his pace keeping his gaze fixed on Ambis. Just as he reached the bottom step, she bent her knees.

Elwood didn't even think. He launched himself, pushing off with his staff and hurled himself forwards at Ambis. He grabbed her around the waist and pulled her to the ground. She screamed as she fell under his weight.

'Nooo...' she howled like an animal in slaughter.

Elwood held her tight, lest she try and get up, and hurl herself in the waves, once more. While he hung on to her, he kept an eye on the bubbling water, but he saw no one. He called out, 'Leave her alone, Piran. She is not ready.'

Only the gulls answered.

'It is not her time,' he yelled. 'Do you hear me?'

The bubbling subsided and the surface became smooth.

'Ambis, you are safe. I have got you.'

'I needed to go,' wailed Ambis. She started to sob. 'I wanted to swim with him, it's where I should be.'

'Under the waves with Piran? Never to return to us?' His pitch was high with desperation.

He could feel her body go limp.

He released his grip on her. 'Are you hurt?'

Merryn rolled over and buried her face in the peat shelf and sobbed.

Elwood sat next to her quietly until she calmed enough to hear him. 'Ambis, we love you. We can't lose you. Porth Taran can't lose you. Bunjil can't lose you.'

Eventually Merryn turned over and looked up at Elwood, her face covered in dark peat sand. 'Elwood, I cannot stay. I am putting the people of Porth Taran in danger.'

'Ambis, that is not the way. There are better ways. We will find them.'

'He said he had been watching me, all these years. All those years, the weather was calm and stable. But look at me now, I am not calm and the weather has turned. I caused that storm that flooded Porth Taran. I put Uncle Jack's boat on the supermarket roof.'

'Ambis, no one was hurt. You didn't hurt anyone.'

'Not this time. But what about next time, and the time after that?'

'Come on, let's get you home. We will find a way.'

Elwood took Ambis's arm and led her back up the steps to the clifftop. They walked slowly up the harbour road and up the hill to Little Rosewarne.

Elwood banged on the door.

'Did you forget your keys?' said Demelza as she opened the door. 'Oh. Elwood, what are you doing here?'

'Hello Demelza. Can I come in?'

'Err yes. Yes, I suppose so. Merry, are you alright?'

'I think we need to talk,' said Elwood.

'You're both soaked. Merry, my darling, what's wrong? I didn't even know you were up.'

Merryn's face crumpled and she turned and fled up to her room.

'Elwood, what on earth has happened?' asked Demelza.

'I think we need to sit down.'

Elwood followed her down the hall and into the dining room. He sat down at the table.

When they were both settled, Elwood began. 'It's happened again. I sensed it. I went down to the beach and found her. She was about to jump in the sea again.'

Demelza frowned. 'Poor Merry.'

'We need to talk to Mrs Constantine. She's the only person that can help us.'

'Elwood, I won't have you filling her head with all your mumbo jumbo. Can you not see the upset all this is causing?'

'Demelza, this is real. This isn't just some myth, you know that really. You can see for yourself, your daughter is in danger and we have to do something.'

'Mrs Constantine can help. She was close to Piran, she can help her. She can find a way for her to move on from this. I can show her how to control her feelings but she needs to let Piran go. She needs to understand what happened and leave it behind. She needs to say goodbye to him and not to us.'

Demelza looked at Elwood in his damp raincoat, his tattoos distorted by the wrinkles that crept over his skin in the past few years. Elwood Curnow, the village crackpot, the drunkard at the end of the bar, the druid that everyone laughed at.

Jack stepped out of the front door of Tregarron and pulled his sou'wester down low. The damp was penetrating and he could feel his bones aching just as they did every year as winter approached.

The dogs rushed out of the door after him, sniffing the ground and picking up the scent of foxes and rabbits. Jack strode off to check the perimeter boundary. He wondered if Ginny was feeling aches and pains, now that she was older. He wondered what she looked like now. Perhaps she'd let herself go. He could only imagine her beautiful, with that tall, willowy frame that she moved so gracefully. Perhaps her hair was grey now, or maybe she dyed it. Was it short or long? Perhaps he wouldn't recognise her.

As he walked the pain in his joints eased with the movement. He breathed in the damp fresh air, savouring the sweet and sour smell of the fields mingled with the sea. He glanced at the wall where he'd left his posy. He could see it there, just where he had left it two days before. He took another look; there was something different. There was the posy, but it wasn't the same. He picked up his stride and approached. This wasn't the posy he had left. He picked it up. This one was bigger, it had buttercups and clover, a tall cow parsley flower, and all around it sprigs of heather bound together with a long marram grass.

Dywana, Demelza and Merryn, were gathered around the kitchen table at Chy Bowjy.

Dywana spoke first. 'Merryn, we want to help you.'

Merryn cast her eyes downwards and didn't speak.

'Merry, we love you. All we want, have always wanted is the best for you,' said Demelza.

Merryn looked up, her eyes flashing with anger. 'And the best for me is to keep secrets, is it?'

Outside the mizzle turned to rain. It started to batter the windows.

Demelza and Dywana exchanged glances.

'You're right, there have been secrets,' said Dywana. 'Rightly or wrongly, they were made with the best of intentions. Your mum and Jack, they love you, they didn't want to hurt you. They thought they were keeping you safe.'

'Safe from what? Safe from who?'

There was a knock at the door.

Dywana opened it.

Matt and Elwood were on the doorstep.

'Elwood told me what happened. Is Merryn alright?' Matt looked worried.

'I'm not sure this is a good time.' Dywana glanced round at Merryn and Demelza.

'Please,' said Merryn. Let them in. I want Matt to hear this.'

Matt and Elwood sat down at the table.

'First of all, tell us about the notebooks, the notes in the end column.' Merryn glanced at Matt. He produced a notebook and opened it, setting it on the table for all to see.

'Here, it says *P-R*, and again here.' Matt turned the pages.'

Dywana glanced at Demelza.

'Dywana, I need to know,' said Merryn.

Demelza picked up the notebook to look closer. 'Di, please tell us what this is.'

'This isn't fact. I promised. I promised you I would stick to facts,' said Dywana.

'Just tell us, please, said Demelza.

Dywana looked up at Merryn. 'There's something you need to understand. There's those in Porth Taran who think I'm not right in the head. It's why I live out here. It's why you and I have not met, and it's why I have been isolated from my family.'

Demelza's face saddened.

'Melza, please don't blame yourself. It is not your fault. It is mine, entirely. Now, I will start at the beginning.

'My brother, your father, was my best friend. We did everything together.' A shadow of sadness cast across her eyes. 'As a child he was the naughtiest in school, but ...' She raised a finger. 'But, the most charming. Later when he grew into a young man, he was the life and soul of every party. He liked a drink that was for sure. But he was moody. He could flip from being sunny and jovial to flying into a rage over something small. He was impulsive, you know. It comes with being a sensitive soul.'

Demelza nodded.

'I loved him more than anything in the world, well except Kendrick of course. We were very close, I understood him. He wasn't a bad person, not by a long chalk. But he questioned everything and pushed boundaries, out of curiosity, you know. It was almost a matter of principle. It was a wonder he didn't get kicked out of school. Saved probably by the fact that our dad was a governor.' She let out a snort of laughter.

'He got brought home a couple of times by the police, for speeding, or being drunk and disorderly. Nothing too out of the ordinary. But this is the thing, and you need to listen to this with an open mind.

'These notebooks, they weren't simply to record the extreme weather events we suffered in Porth Taran. Well, that was what the parish had asked for, but I wanted to record what my brother was doing during those weather episodes. I began to notice that when he became anxious, or cross about something, the weather always turned. When he was happy and contented, the sun came out.' She glanced around the table.

'I know, it sounds preposterous. It did to me too and that's why I started to note down in this end column a record of my brother's movements to see if they were linked. As I continued to record, I could see clearly that the weather reflected almost exactly, to the minute, how he was feeling.'

Elwood was nodding his head triumphantly.

'You see, I married Kendrick Constantine. He was the son of the neighbouring farmer at Methleigh. Their farm bordered Tregarron. Our father died just after we got married, and I moved onto the Constantine farm. Jack and Piran took over the running of Tregarron.

'Our two farms shared the same water supply from a borehole at Methleigh. In 1986 a drought hit Porth Taran. That was the year, your mum and Piran met. Wasn't it Demelza?'

Demelza nodded.

'The drought lasted on and off for nearly two years. There was barely enough water for one farm, let alone two. Kendrick's farm was dairy, and water for the cows was a priority. It had to be. Kendrick's father decided that he couldn't afford to share the water with Tregarron anymore and without telling them, he went out and diverted the pipes that supplied their water cannons.'

Dywana shook her head.

'It was a terrible business and it put me right in the middle,' continued Dywana. 'Kendrick was furious with his father and could see my family's crops failing almost straight away. My brothers were so angry with me. They couldn't understand how I had let this happen. But, you see, neither I nor Kendrick could get his father to see sense. There was nothing we could do. My brothers stopped talking to me.' Dywana swallowed hard. 'It nearly broke my heart.'

'Then one particularly warm morning, Kendrick couldn't bear it any longer. He strode out to the field and began to dig at the junction of the pipes where his father had diverted the supply. He'd brought a new irrigation pipe with him so that he could reinstate the supply to Tregarron. Piran was out in the fields inspecting the sorry state of the dry soil. He saw Kendrick working on the pipes and flew into a rage. He started walking over to him to have it out with him. Kendrick could see him coming and knew there would be an argument. He wanted to get the pipe installed quickly before it rained. He wanted to be sure that the water would be captured and contained. He couldn't risk wasting any. He worked as fast as he could.

'There was a clap of thunder. I remember it so well; I was feeding the chickens and they all jumped. It flashed and banged at the same time; it was right overhead. Then there was another thunderclap. Kendrick was holding a length of metal pipe just as the lightning hit.' A tear ran down her face. 'By the time Piran reached him he was unconscious. He radioed through to the farm and got them to call an ambulance.' Her voice trailed to a squeak. She took a sip of tea and coughed. 'They were too late,' she croaked. 'Kendrick had gone into cardiac arrest and by the time the ambulance got there, he was dead.'

No one spoke. A tear rolled down Dywana's face. Demelza rubbed Dywana's back comfortingly.

Dywana continued, in a small voice, 'I had only been married four years when I lost my Kendrick. I was devastated. I had seen the link between the weather and Piran and I knew.' She glanced up nervously at Demelza.

'I thought I knew. I thought my brother, Piran, had caused Kendrick's death. And the worst of it, was that Piran believed that Kendrick was up to no good with those pipes. He didn't understand that Kendrick was trying to restore the farm's water supply. So bitter had that feud become that he could only imagine foul play.'

'When Piran disappeared at sea, in, what Elwood reported to be, a whirlpool it just compounded my suspicions. You see, it was the day that your mum called him on the radio to say that she was expecting you.'

Demelza was weeping now. 'If only I had waited 'til he got home.'

'And I wish that I had kept quiet. If I hadn't said all those things we could have supported each other all these years. Me, you, Spike and Jack.'

There was a long silence as everyone took it in.

Then Merryn spoke,

'So, like Elwood, you believe that Piran could influence the weather?'

'I did believe it then.'

'And you don't believe it now?'

'It's just not possible.'

'But what about the notebooks? What does P-R mean?' asked Merryn.

'Piro. Piro was my nickname for Piran,' said Dywana. 'And the rest, they're all coincidences. I may have enhanced some of those records too. I don't know, I can't really remember.'

'But Mum, you said you wished you'd waited for Dad to get home before you told him I was on the way?'

Demelza nodded. 'I did.'

'So, you believe that had an effect on what happened?'

'No, my darling not on the whirlpool, if there was one.' She glanced sideways at Elwood, who made a face. 'But I do believe that perhaps your dad wasn't concentrating very hard and that's why he went overboard.'

'But his boat disappeared!' Merryn exclaimed.

'It's very easy to read all kinds of things into it. I mean, how can that be? People can't affect the weather – we all know that.'

'Yes, and people can't see or talk to the dead, but I can.'

'Do you remember when we talked about this, the other day?' said Demelza. 'I've been doing some thinking and I remember when, just after you were born, your Dad seemed to materialize in front of my eyes and we would talk.'

'You see! You experienced it too!' Merryn's eyes widened.

Demelza shook her head. 'Merry, it's common for bereaved people to get such visions. It's not real. My counsellor told me that it was a sign of grieving.'

'But how can I be grieving?'

'Merryn, my love,' Demelza leant over and took Merryn's hand. 'We need to find a way for you to close this chapter.'

'Dad said I needed to be protected from myself. That's what he meant wasn't it? I have inherited this curse from him. Elwood said so. He calls me Ambis. Ambis is descended from the god Taranis, the Cornish god of thunder. I need someone to help me. I cannot go through the rest of my life terrified of how I am feeling from one minute to the next in case I do harm.' Her voice was shrill.

Elwood piped up. 'There is a way.'

Dywana turned to Elwood. 'There is? Let's hear it.'

'Whether you believe that individuals can affect the weather or that some people can speak to the dead, for Ambis's sake we need to find an answer to both.'

'OK. What do you propose?'

'The first, is that Ambis needs to learn to control her emotions and that way, at the very least she can keep herself calm. I can help her with that. We already tried it didn't we?'

Merryn looked at him sideways. 'Yes, I suppose so.'

'And the second?'

'She needs to say goodbye to Piran. She needs to say goodbye to him symbolically in a way that will allow her to move on from this. To allow both her, and her father to be released. So that Piran does not appear to her anymore.'

Matt raised his eyebrows.

'Oh Piran! You are still causing trouble, even though you are gone,' said Dywana.

'But that's it, Mrs Constantine. He's not gone, he's still here with us. We need to find a way for him to pass on and for Ambis to be free of all of this.'

'Elwood, it is quite clear that none of this is real,' said Demelza.

'Mum, please. It is real to me. I can see it and I need it to stop. I will try anything to stop this. Belief or no belief, I have to do this. Elwood what do you propose?'

'First, we are going to practise the meditation I taught you. We will practise and practise until you can call on it at a moment's notice, when you need it most. It will be a lot of hard work, but you'll see, it will pay off. And then, we need to speak to the High Priest. He will help us. Soon we will be marking Samhain. It is the festival of the dead, it is when the veil between this life and the next is at its thinnest and we can communicate with those that have passed on. It is also the time that we can communicate with the gods. We must ask them to free you both and you can say goodbye to your father.'

Matt and Demelza exchanged glances.

'There must be a reason that Piran has been kept in the interworld, under the sea. For he should have passed on by now.' Elwood paused. 'On the night of Samhain, we must go to the Seven Sisters and assemble the Grove and the High Priest. We must show your courage and your strength to those who have passed on. We must ask them for help. Show them that you can separate your mind from your heart and say goodbye to your father and to Taranis forever.'

'Say goodbye forever,' muttered Merryn.

Elwood shook his head. 'Not forever, you must let him go for now. Let him go in peace, safe in the knowledge that one day you will join him, but not until your natural life is spent.'

Merryn could feel tears pushing at the corner of her eyes. She swallowed and took a deep breath. 'I will do it. This is what I want. There is nothing to lose.'

Dywana stood up.

'There's something I need to fetch. Hang on.' She disappeared up to the observatory.

In the library, Dywana, racked her brains for the title of the book. She ran her fingers along the spines and tried to picture it. Blue, she thought. The Mythology of Cornwall, that was it. She climbed the ladder to reach the Ms. There it was, a little dog-eared. It had been years since she'd bought it in a second-hand bookshop. She took it down and blew dust off it. She carried it downstairs to the kitchen and handed it to Matt.

'Here, you look up Taranis and read it to us while I make more tea.' Dywana turned to the kettle.

Matt opened the book and looked up Taranis in the index. 'Here we are.' He began to read.

'Taranis, the God of Thunder. 'In Celtic mythology Taranis was the god of thunder. He was worshipped across Gaul, Gallaecia and Ireland and, of course, in Cornwall. In the epic poem, Pharsalia, the Roman poet Lucan mentioned Taranis as a god to whom human sacrifices were made.'

Elwood looked up in alarm.

Matt took a breath. 'This is ridiculous. What good is this going to do?'

'Read on,' said Dywana sternly.

'He was often depicted as a bearded deity with a wheel on one hand and a thunderbolt in the other. The wheel was a chariot wheel with six or eight spokes,'

'The eightfold wheel!' said Elwood excitedly.

Matt continued, 'It is thought to refer to a sun-cult practised in the Bronze age. The wheel representing the sun. Taranis is thought to be the equivalent of Jupiter in Roman mythology. A strong character with much power over his subjects. He had many children and it is said that some of these children were sent to roam the earth, to live amongst the mortals. It was believed that these children were charged with a mission to prove their strength. Saddled with the mortal baggage of emotions they were to learn to master them. If they failed, they would be relegated to the interworld beneath the waves where it is said they terrorised ships and caused earthquakes that sent damaging waves across the land.'

'Sea witches!' said Elwood.

'I can't read any more of this, it's just a load of nonsense.'

'Matt, please, read on.'

Matt pursed his lips and sighed. 'His most prominent child was Ambisagrus, meaning 'about strength'. Ambisagrus was primarily a god of the continental Celts but was also important in Cornish mythology, a weather deity who controlled the rain, wind, hail, and fog. It is believed by pagans that Porth Taran on the south coast of West Cornwall is the Jerusalem of Taranis.' Matt looked up. 'Is that true? Did you know that?'

Dywana shook her head. 'I had never heard that before. Elwood?'

Elwood shook his head. 'But it fits. Everything there fits!'

Merryn shook herself, trying to take it all in.

'Merry, it's a story. Just a story.'

'Mum, I think this is my story and I need it to have a happy ending. Elwood, let's start my training tomorrow and who can get in touch with the High Priest?'

'I'll call Finn,' said Dywana.

'Finn McGann?' exclaimed Matt.

Elwood's eyes widened.

'Yes, Finn is the High Priest,' said Dywana.

TWENTY-SEVEN

The clocks had changed and the air was thick with the smell of wood smoke. Merryn's meditation practice was progressing. Some days she could feel it helping her to be calm. Some days she couldn't concentrate and a cold wind got up. Working helped and today,

Merryn was at the gallery. She glued the final piece of the root structure in place. She stood back to admire the network of sinuous, wiry rhizomes. The foundations of a story that can only be built near the end. The beginning, discernible only when the tale is near completion. The vessels of revelation, the underpinning of the series of events, that would soon reach their culmination. But first, the sun.

Merryn and Demelza had kept the plan for the ritual very quiet. It was only this morning in bed that Demelza had decided to share it with Spike.

'What does Jack say about all this?'

Demelza looked at him and said nothing.

'He doesn't know does he?'

Demelza turned over and sunk her head into the pillow.

'You have to let him know.'

'In good time, Spike. In good time. There's no point upsetting him at the moment. And Merryn needs it all to be calm. Have you not noticed how much better she's been since she's been learning to meditate with Elwood?'

'Yes, well, that part's good obviously but it's the Dywana part and the mumbo jumbo part.'

'Look, I will not step in the way of my daughter's healing and Dywana, she is family. We shouldn't have shut her out like that, and I for one, am glad to have her back.' She touched Spike's arm. 'You won't say anything will you?' She kissed him. 'Please, for me.'

'As long as you don't expect me to be part of this circus. I will feign ignorance. I am not sure Jack would be too pleased with me if I kept this from him.'

'I won't drop you in it. I promise. Anyway, Merryn doesn't know I've told you, so let's leave it like that.'

'It's not my place to get mixed up in Jewell family business.'

Just two days until Samhain. The weather had, for the most part, been calm, and for that she was thankful. But this morning she could feel a tension rising inside her with the impending ritual. Mizzle was coating the windowpanes of Little Rosewarne and a chill breeze was beginning to blow. Merryn felt helpless. Ambisagrus, the god of the continental Celts, a weather deity who controlled the rain, wind, hail, and fog, but today she was failing. Desolation enveloped her. For some reason, she couldn't even bring herself to try. She lay beside Matt listening to the gentle rise and fall of his chest as he slept.

Sensing her awake, he stirred.

She put her hand on his back and kissed his shoulder.

He opened his eyes, winked at her and whispered, 'G'day.'

Merryn smiled, soaking up his good humour gratefully, she put her arms around him and lay her head on his chest, her body wrapping perfectly around his. The rain on the windows took on a gentle rhythm as they hit the panes.

'What's up?' asked Matt.

'What if it doesn't work?'

'It's already working, darlin'.'

'Sometimes, I can't focus. I try and shut everything out and just hear Elwood's voice. It's odd, when it works it's like magic. I focus and detach myself and everything stops. The wind drops, the clouds slow. But what if I can't do it, you know on the night?' She got up and looked in the mirror. Her hair was dark and lank. Her face was pale and drawn, and bags hung beneath her eyes like beacons of anxiety.

Matt lay still, thinking. 'How does he try and get you to concentrate?'

'He tells me to relax each of my muscles in turn. Then he gets me to breathe evenly and take longer and longer breaths and to bat away any thoughts that come to me, but sometimes I can't control it and my mind wanders and I lose it. With all this going on I just can't seem to do it.'

'You know, Merryn that sounds like how I astral travel.'

'Is it?'

'Yes. How do you do it?'

'I'm not sure, I just do it.'

'Think about it.'

'Well, I think about a place I want to go, or a person I want to see. I close my eyes and I think about them until I'm there.'

'Let's try it together.'

'Can we do it together?'

'I've no idea, let's try. Come on, come back to bed.'

'Where shall we go?' Merryn got back into bed and lay beside him.

'Where would you like to go, who would you like to see?'

'I want to see the weather up on the moors.'

Matt took her hand and held it tightly. 'Close your eyes, sweet Merryn.'

Merryn closed them and thought of the heather and bracken stretching to the rocky north coast. The gorse bushes scattered randomly. The engine house towers jutting into the dawn. Then, suddenly, she was there. It wasn't raining. Gulls were screaming in the half light, wheeling over the sea. She looked around her, but she couldn't see Matt. She could still feel his hand in hers, but he wasn't there. She pushed on to the coast. The sea was messy and splashing on the rocks but it wasn't rough. Then, she could hear shouting in the distance. She turned around and went towards the sound but it didn't get any nearer. She stopped and tried to discern which direction it was coming from. She couldn't hear what they were saying, it was just a distant echo.

Then Matt was gone. She couldn't sense him anymore and his grip was no longer in hers. She jolted and opened her eyes. Her bedroom at Little Rosewarne reappeared before her. Matt was standing at the window.

'Look! Look my love. Outside.'

Merryn looked out over Porth Taran. The rain had cleared and the clouds had moved into the distance. Sun was bathing the landscape once more.

'We did it! We have found a way. It was there all the time. All you have to do is astral travel.'

'But were you with me? I couldn't see you.'

'I couldn't see you either, but I was there.'

'What did you see?'

'I saw the gulls and the dawn and I felt you there with me. You can do this. We can do this. Everything is going to be OK.'

Jack Jewell sat at his kitchen table. In the middle, in a pint glass filled with water, was the posy, the marram grass binding intact. He looked at it closely, whose fingers had tied those grasses around it? No one knew about the posy ritual, did they?

Outside, the drizzle was clearing. He looked at his watch. He would go into Porth Taran. He could pick up some chicken feed, have a look around. The dogs were scrabbling and whimpering at the front door. He'd take them for a walk on the headland afterwards.

Jack drove into Porth Taran along Methleigh Bottom. Porth Taran was busy. There were quite a few people going about their business. He pulled into the car park by the supermarket and got out. He looked around him but nothing. He walked around to the farmers' feed store and bought a sack of chicken feed. He carried it back to his car and stowed it in the boot. The morning drizzle had departed and the sun was warming the streets. He could see Johnny sat on his deck chair outside the surf shop, so he decided to head over.

'Mornin' Johnny.'

'Hiya Jack. How's it going?'

'Yeah, alright thanks. Just popped in for some chook pellets.'

'Yeah? Do you want a coffee?'

'Ah no, you're alright. I'm not stopping long. Any news?'

'How d'ya mean?'

'Oh, you know, just haven't seen you for a while.'

'Oh right, yeah. You know me, Jack, nothing changes. Still happy, still here. How about you?'

'Yeah, I'm alright. There's a lot of cars outside the church isn't there?'

'Yeah, I noticed that. Not sure what Rev Kate's up to.'

'Actually, I will take you up on that coffee, if I may?'

'Oh right. Yep sure.' Johnny looked confused. 'I'll get you one.' He disappeared inside.

Jack unfolded another deck chair that was leaning against the shop front and set it next to Johnny's. He sat down and looked out across the harbour. Clouds were floating slowly across the sky, intermittently casting shade. Johnny reappeared with a couple of mugs and sat next to him.

'Well, Jack, this is a surprise. I can't say we've had a chat like this in a long time.'

'No, I was thinking that so I thought now's a good time.'

'Right.'

''ere, did you notice who went into the church?'

'Er no, no I didn't. I wasn't looking if I'm honest.'

'Right.'

'Were you looking for someone?'

'What, me? No, no of course not. You know, just wondered.'

'Right.' Johnny looked at him quizzically and the men fell silent.

Jack's gaze fixed on the church. A young man emerged. He squinted through the sunlight trying to get a good look. He was tall and blonde. Jack didn't know him. He must be a visitor or a newcomer. Jack returned his attention to his coffee. 'A lot of upcountryites moving down again, I see.'

'Who you talking about?'

'Ah no one. Just saw a lad come out of the church there.'

Johnny glanced over. 'There's been a steady stream of people in and out of there all morning. Maybe Rev Kate's doing a roaring trade in weddings!'

Jack laughed then his expression turned serious. 'Or, maybe,'

Johnny looked up at him.

'Maybe it's that business that was in the paper. Y'know, about Rev Cribben. I always knew he was a wrong un.'

'I guess it's possible. Well, who knows eh? Steer well clear I reckon. Right, I'd better be getting on.'

'Yeah course.' Jack swilled back the last of his coffee. 'I think I'll just take a stroll down the beach – it's turning out to be a lovely day.'

'Proper job. Catch you later.'

Jack walked along the harbour towards St Petroc's and the beach. As he reached the church he could see the young man he'd spied sitting in a car outside, obviously waiting for someone. He walked on and reached the top of the steps to the beach. He stood there for a minute. There were some people enjoying the morning sun, and some dog walkers. The sea was smooth, just the odd cloud drifted across the sky casting a little shade here and there as they went. He looked out west, towards Tregarron, and could see the headland drenched in sunlight.

He turned and began to walk back up to the supermarket car park. As he passed the church the car with the young man in it was pulling away. In the drivers' seat was a woman, perhaps the lad's mother. She was wearing dark glasses and her hair was white blonde, cut shortish. Maybe it was that Rev Cribben thing. That lady would have been the right age. He carried on walking. The car overtook him and drove slowly out of the harbour road and on to Main Street and was gone.

TWENTY-EIGHT

Dywana stood at her front door looking out over the moors. The leat at her feet was still high but the sky had cleared; it was a good sign. Finn McGann had stayed into the small hours and he was tired. Elwood was on his way and Matt and Merryn had gone for a walk. Rosemary hung in bunches from the ceiling beams, their smell imbibing the whole house. All was ready. There was a sense of celebration, of joy. She could feel the warmth of it welling up inside her, chasing her exhaustion away.

Just a few weeks before she had been Dywana Constantine, the sad widow living alone on the moor who tried not to focus on the past and busy herself with mundane daily tasks until sundown. And now, she was an Aunt, a sister-in-law and a loved member of the family she had once thought lost. Soon perhaps she could again be a sister. Laugh with her brother. Share old stories of their parents, of events long past, of things only a sibling could know. She sighed.

Jack Jewell searched around the fields, it was harder to find flowers in October. Only gorse and heather was truly in flower. Instead, he would have to take blooms from the

288

flower bed at the front of the farmhouse. Sedums, and pansies, and autumn crocuses, perhaps some of the tall grasses not yet mown. The flowers in the pint glass had long since faded. No new posy had appeared at the bottom of the wall and he could feel his disappointment overwhelming him more and more each day.

For years he had walked down to that wall, and placed his bunch of wild flowers, and stood and looked out to sea, and thought about her. Each day it had made him feel better. But now, since the day he had found those flowers in the place of his own, his pilgrimage to the wall on the cliff had become more urgent and more soul destroying. He lay awake at night wondering. He searched the streets for a glimpse. He'd been down to the Fishermen's mission, but otherwise he had tried to distract himself on the farm. There was always plenty to do. Walls needed patching and the peas had been sown. The cabbage harvest would soon come around. He'd booked the pickers and then he'd be busy. Perhaps then he'd forget.

He looked at his watch. He would have to set off for the Seven Sisters in an hour. He wasn't happy when Merryn had told him about the ritual, or about Dywana. He had thought of her, these past years, of course he had. But what was done was done. He couldn't see why it had to be dragged up again. He sighed and turned back towards Tregarron.

Elwood got off the bus to St Ives and began to walk along the road to Dywana's. He'd decided not to cross the fields to save his energy for the day ahead.

Samhain is the time to strip everything back to bare to hasten the rotting of flesh to allow new growth, to communicate with the departed and to lay them to rest. A time to tend the grieving and celebrate the future. A time to resolve conflicts past, the final battle, the settling of scores.

Overhead, the raven flew in his wake and he smiled. He always found him, however he travelled. It had been a long time since he had celebrated Samhain and not without reason. But this one was more important than all the others. This would be his last one. He had reached his destiny, his zenith. He must focus on the euphoria and banish the fear.

Dywana and Demelza were in the kitchen tying up the last few bundles of rosemary with twine and hanging them from the beams. The smell filled the house. The ironing board was set up in the corner and a number of white robes hung on hangers off the kitchen cupboards.

'Finn is out in the orchard cutting the mistletoe. He will set off in a minute. We will meet him there at four.'

Elwood nodded. He didn't trust his voice.

'You load the van with the brush I gathered this morning and as soon as Matt and Merryn are ready we can set off.'

Matt and Merryn were in the ancient village of Chysauster. Merryn needed to feel the weather, to see it. She stood on the top of a roundhouse wall and felt the wind in her hair. She looked out over the hedgerows and the trees bent over against the Atlantic wind, the clumps of fading ragged robin that clung to the earth clad walls. She watched as the seagulls wheeled overhead, buzzards hovered over the fields, clouds hung threateningly in the grey sky ready to release their ammunition.

On the day she was born, the village had almost been destroyed. It was her responsibility to protect these people from her own influence. She thought of Piran, smiling out from the photograph on her dressing table. Those eyes that were hers, that were Dywana's. He had called her to that place, and called her into the waters. It was but for Matt and Elwood that she would have taken his hand and sunk beneath those waves. What right did she have to cause her family more suffering? Her mother's life had already been blighted by too much sadness. Tonight, she would do this for her mother, for herself and for Porth Taran. She must say goodbye to her father. If she failed in this then she belonged beneath the waves with Piran Jewell, together for eternity. A lump grew in her throat and she fought back tears.

'Darlin'. You OK?'

Merryn opened her eyes. She looked at Matt; his expression was solemn. 'I'm OK.' And she was. She felt calm, and in control. She had Matt by her side. He was a good man. His face was wracked with worry for her, and for that she was sorry. Not once had he refused to help her. She knew he wasn't comfortable with the ceremony and that he was going against his better judgement and all for her. She would get through this. She would get through this, because of him. He had listened to her every fear, thought and concern. He had offered advice and wiped her tears. And when she'd asked, he'd made love to her, kindly and generously and with all his love. Elwood was right, he could offer her eternal happiness, of that she was now sure. Merryn took his hand and kissed him.

'What was that for?'

'That, Matt, is for being you. Thank you for being you.' She jumped down off the wall, pulling him with her. 'Now, come on. Let's do this.'

'You're sure?'

'I'm sure.'

They reached Dywana's front door and had to jump over the leat, which had risen and was so high it was gushing and spilling its load over the paving, and running down the drive in a torrent.

Inside, Dywana handed them each a white robe. 'Put these on over the top of your clothes. It will be cold up there on the moor tonight.' She gave them each a bundle of rosemary. 'This is to throw on the fire just before the unweaving of the circle.'

They both took their bundles from her silently.

'It is time. Merryn you come with me and Demelza in the van, and Elwood, you go with Matt in the land rover. Finn and Trevina have gone ahead.'

They set off for the Seven Sisters in convoy. The sky was grey but calm. Merryn, Demelza and Dywana didn't speak as they drove up over the moors. They glimpsed the north coast as they drove over the crest of West Cornwall and then down again along the winding roads.

At last, they turned down the grassy track that led to the stones. There were already cars parked up. A tall figure in a black robe approached the van and suddenly Merryn was swept with fear.

Dywana touched her arm. 'Don't worry, it's just Finn, you know him, remember.'

They got out of the van.

Finn was standing waiting patiently for her.

Merryn eyed him nervously. She couldn't see his face for his hood was pulled low, and although she had already met him, he was different.

He bowed low and made a curious gesture with his hand, then turned towards the stile that led into the field.

A minute later, Elwood was by her side dressed in his white robe. He looked younger, cleaner, healthier, standing there his face enveloped in angelic white. He smiled at her and then said quietly, 'Remember what I told you, your mind and your heart, keep them apart.'

Merryn nodded and took a deep breath.

Elwood stretched his hand towards her face. He stroked it. 'Farewell, sweet Ambis. After today, all will be well.'

More and more cars drove up the lane and parked on the grassy verges. Their passengers got out clothed in white robes just like Merryn's. Only Finn wore black. A crowd began to form which then funnelled over the stile and poured into the field.

Dywana took Merryn's hand. 'Come, my child. The sun will be setting soon, and we must be ready.'

Merryn turned to her mother. Demelza kissed her on the forehead. 'Remember, I love you. Now go.'

Dywana led her over the stile to join the others. Nineteen stones were set in a circle with one just off centre leaning at a precarious angle. An altar was set up near it and in front of it was a bonfire of brushwood bedecked with baskets of tomatoes, cauliflowers, French beans, apples and pears. The white robed newcomers filed towards the altar adding their contributions of fruit and vegetables. Then they turned to their fellow grove members and shook their hands.

As Dywana and Merryn approached, the circle, The High Priest handed Merryn a wreath of mistletoe. Merryn glanced at Dywana who gestured to put it on her head. Merryn did as she was told. Then the priest led her to the spot where she was to stand in the circle.

The members each came to Merryn and shook her hand in turn. They smiled at her, and chatted animatedly amongst themselves. There was an air of celebration and Merryn began to feel that this was a happy occasion, and started to relax.

As the congregation took their places around the edge of the circle, Dywana took Merryn's hand and the hand of a lady with long flowing blonde hair, who was standing on the other side of her. Matt stood to Merryn's right and did the same. Elwood was next to him, and then Demelza. The rest of the circle followed suit and the circle was complete. On the ground were pairs of large sticks, evenly spaced around the circle, a pair for each participant. The High Priest began to walk around the inside edge of the circle, greeting each person in turn and bowing his head reverently. Then he came to Merryn.

'Feel the breath, feel the energy. Pull the energy from the golden cord that reaches from the centre of the earth through your body and up to the sky. Feel it springing and tensing.' He stayed there a while until Merryn felt herself calm and focussed.

Then he pulled a sword from beneath his robe. He kissed the blade of the sword and then held it high above his head.

The group began to tap their sticks together, rhythmically in time with each other.

Dywana picked up hers and Merryn did the same. At first it sounded deadened in the vastness of the moor and as the beats synchronised, they became sharper and seemed to echo, bouncing off the stones. Merryn concentrated on the beat and tried to empty her mind. She focussed her gaze on the altar.

Then the High Priest lowered the sword and held it in front of his face in salute, pointed it outwards from his belly and paced once more around the circle. He chanted as he went. 'Come, ring of energy.'

The grove repeated each phrase, their words echoing across the landscape.

'To mark the boundary of our world..., and the realm of our ancestors..., our protection, our guardian. Hold us within, contain our energy. Here and now we cleanse and consecrate.'

Merryn let the words wash over her.

The High Priest sprinkled sea salt around the circle, as he paced. When at last he'd reached his starting point in front of Merryn, he nodded to her, turned on his heel and walked to the centre and faced east.

He called out in a high-pitched dramatic call, 'Air, we call you to help us breathe, to fuel our minds and inflate our imagination.' Then he walked to the North. 'Earth, we call you to form our foundation, our homes and our chattels, to give us our grounding.' Then he paced westwards. 'Water, we call to you to fill our rivers and seas, to quench our thirst and calm our emotions.' And finally, he walked to the south. 'Fire, we call you to warm us, to light our energy and activate change.' He turned and walked to the stone in the centre, he lit a torch set in the earth near the central stone. The circle fell silent as the members lowered their sticks and held them by their sides.

The High Priest faced the sun as it sank towards the horizon. His figure silhouetted in the orange glow. The circle waited and watched. Just as the edge of the sun touched the horizon, the High Priest planted the blade of the sword into the turf theatrically and raised his arms above his head.

'Spirits we call you. Black spirits and red, white spirits and grey. Come ye, come ye as ye may. Lord Taranis we call you, this day. Come into our circle and help our Lady Ambisagrus, for she is troubled. We call on you to release her from her responsibility to you, to Porth Taran and to all those that have gone before her. Grant her permission to lead her mortal life. In return, when her natural life has passed, she will be returned to you for all eternity. We beg you to hear our plea. She has proved her worth and has paid her penance. We call on you to release this daughter of yours.'

Silence fell upon the field. Only the rushing of a faint breeze coming from the coast could be heard. The circle stood quietly waiting.

Merryn began to tense. It was a waste of time. Nothing was going to happen. She closed her eyes and conjured Piran before her.

A murmur rose amongst the circle and she opened her eyes. A dark purple cloud was moving into view. It slung itself across the setting sun and the field went dark. The cloud grew larger and began to hover over the circle. It hung lower and lower until it engulfed the circle. Dywana's hand slipped from hers and Merryn could no longer see her. Merryn was standing alone in a vacuum of purple mist.

Overhead, floating in the gloom, appeared Piran. Just a cameo of his face, moulded in the mist. He was smiling, just like he did in the photograph on her dressing table.

Merryn tried to reach out and touch him but she couldn't feel her limbs. She wanted to be with him, to touch him, to kiss him. Then suddenly, she found herself there, right next to him. Within arm's reach. She tried to touch him, but her arms were gone. There was nothing there but purple vapour.

Then there was another face. In the distance, behind her father, she could see the face of an old man, a vicar's collar at his throat. His skin hung thinly over his wizened skull. He was scowling and Merryn suddenly felt scared. She felt a touch. Someone was holding her hand. She looked down but couldn't see.

Piran spoke, 'Daughter of mine you are the most precious, my love, my heart.'

'I have watched over you all your life and you are strong. You have the courage of your mother, which has carried you through. For that you are to be released and the time has come for us to say goodbye.' His expression became pained. 'The gods will release you through love, but I will always be with you in your heart. Call me and I will come, but only then. Then he hovered low and the purple mist wrapped around her, as if hugging her. Merryn felt the heat of his embrace. She felt a warm touch on each cheek and then he said, 'Farewell, precious one.'

Tears began to course down Merryn's face, and her stomach lurched with yearning. She watched as the figure of Piran became smaller and floated up higher.

As Piran shrank, the face of the old man in the distance became larger. His expression was contorted and angry. He opened his mouth wide revealing jagged teeth. Then there was someone else. Matt was by her side. The skull suddenly dived downwards towards Merryn. She flinched, her stomach swooping. Matt lunged at the old man, but he darted around him and downwards to the circle. A desperate whimper echoed from the west. Merryn looked around but Piran had evaporated into the heavens. Then a bolt of lightning shot through the mist and down into the circle. Matt let out an agonising scream as the charge lit up the cloud illuminating his silhouette, then he fell, plummeting towards the earth. Merryn gasped as she watched him fall. She could hear her heart beating in her head. The crowd screamed and Merryn could feel herself falling, racing towards the circle after him. She hit the earth with a thud as the lightning struck the turf. She lay on the cold damp ground for a moment. She opened her eyes, the mist had cleared and Dywana was standing over her.

'Merry, Merryn,' she said in a panicked voice.

A commotion broke out at the side of the circle and Merryn could see a figure lying on the ground. She pushed herself up to sitting and cried out, 'Matt!'

The High priest yelled, 'We must reopen the circle!' And he began to bellow, 'By the air that is her breath, by the fire of her bright spirit, by the waters of her womb, by the earth that is her body, the circle is open but unbroken.' And the priest turned and lit the brushwood fire with the torch.

Merryn was on her feet and running over to the figure, lying motionless, face down in the damp grass. Tears were coursing down her cheek as she gently turned his body over just in time to see the life leaving Elwood's eyes. His white gown was shredded and burned in a perfect line from his forehead to his feet. Merryn sat back on her heels as a mixture of shock and relief took hold. Then Matt appeared next to her and held her close. She clung to him and let out convulsing sobs as a crowd gathered.

Dywana was loosening Elwood's clothing and began to pummel his chest in even bursts, counting in the breaks. She put her lips to Elwood's and tried to breathe life into his lungs, but none came.

After what seemed like an eternity, they could hear an ambulance screaming in the distance. It pulled up the grassy track. Two paramedics jumped out carrying a defibrillator. They leapt the stile and ran to Elwood's lifeless body. The crowd continued to watch murmuring hope under their breath.

The ambulance men sat back on their heels and shook their heads. They covered Elwood's face with his robe and carried him away on a stretcher.

TWENTY-NINE

At the crematorium, Merryn, Matt, Dywana and Johnny stood woodenly, in a line, waiting. The chapel's ceilings were high and vaulted, there was an altar and pews. Merryn and Johnny exchanged glances. This was not a place for Elwood. Merryn closed her eyes and willed the minutes to pass quickly. His values and beliefs transcended the conventionality of modern society, so ill- suited to the current world. Was he ahead of his time or behind it? Merryn wasn't sure. Three days of his remains in this place was a wrong that needed to be righted. At least he would be laid to rest at the Seven Sisters, up on the moors, up where he belonged, in the weather.

At last, the attendant appeared and handed the urn to Johnny. They nodded and turned and left the chapel in silence. They climbed into Johnny's van, Merryn holding the urn resting in her lap. Johnny started the engine and drove out of that awful place and headed for the A30. Elwood was on his way, on his final journey.

The lanes on the approach to the Seven Sisters were lined with cars and vans. It was as busy as the gathering at Samhain. Johnny parked up on a grassy bank some distance from the circle. As Merryn emerged from the van,

299

Finn McGann appeared in his black robes and took the urn from her. He held it carefully up high, then lowered it and kissed it. A subdued murmur hummed from the crowd gathering in the circle. Not all were wearing robes, some were dressed in winter clothes befitting of the moor in November. She could see Reverend Kate just climbing over the stile with Carrie not far behind her.

The gentle drizzle of that morning had given way to an even battleship grey that stretched without interruption all the way to Land's End. Merryn pulled on her robe. Sadness weighed on her, though inside she was at peace, she could feel it. That is what Elwood Curnow had done for her. She thought of how she'd shunned him and disregarded him for all those years when in the end he had been her saviour. He had helped her move forwards and see off her demons with the simple power of the mind. Elwood Curnow, his wisdom hidden from most, for all of his life. Elwood the crackpot, the madman, the alcoholic who draped himself at the end of the bar at The Ship Inn on most evenings. And now, he had become Elwood Curnow, the wise man, the soothsayer and above all the greatest Pagan Porth Taran had ever nurtured. The gathering before her, around those sacred stones, was evidence to his goodness, his insight, and his presence.

The High Priest moved to the centre of the stones with the urn held up high and lowered it to the ground and set it in front of his feet next to a flaming torch, an incense lantern and a silver ewer. The crowd melted into a circle around the stones, joined hands and fell quiet. The High Priest raised his arms up, his hands held open and turned towards the east and called,

'Let there be peace in the East, so let it be.'

In response, the crowd murmured, 'Let it be.'

He turned to the south. 'Let there be peace in the South, so let it be.

Again the crowd repeated, 'Let it be.'

Then, West and North.

'Let there be peace through all the Worlds. So let it be.'

'So let it be,' chanted the crowd.

The High Priest lowered his arms and clasped his hands in front of his chest.

'We gather in peace, soul to soul, within this sacred place and with clear intent, on this the 14th day of November, the waxing gibbous Moon, in the year 2010. We stand in the eye of the Sun and upon this hallowed Earth, so to witness the sacred Rite of Passing for Elwood Curnow. Together we come to honour him, who—in body– has left our company.

'Let us now weave our circle, that the spirits of those who are gathered here may be blended in one purpose, one voice and one sacred space.'

The holders of the circle stepped inwards rubbing shoulder to shoulder.

Finn picked up the incense lantern and the silver ewer and began his blessing, 'Let us now call to the Four Directions, to the four elements of creation that we may ask for their blessings at this time of change.' He walked slowly around the circle stopping at each of the cardinal directions to cast the incense and sprinkle water from the ewer.

A raven began to fly around the heads of the circle holders as the priest continued to chant.

'I call in peace to the ancestors of Elwood Curnow, those of the blood line that have lost this, their companion. Gathering together as the hidden company on this sacred day, joining those who have come to say farewell, guiding the soul of Elwood Curnow and honouring his life, know that you are welcome here in peace. It is in this spirit that we release his soul in this, his cherished place.' He picked up the urn and removed the lid. He held it high and as he began to sprinkle its contents into the air a November breeze picked up the dust of Elwood Curnow and whisked it into the atmosphere.'

The raven circled once more then flew to the west.

'Elwood Curnow, you are on your way, but your spirit will remain with us always.'

The High Priest bowed his head and the crowd followed suit. They remained silent for a minute then the Priest raised his head, lowered his hood. He waited for the murmurs to subside.

'Thank you for joining with us to bid adieu to our brother Elwood. You are all invited now, to Elwood's other favourite place, The Ship Inn in Porth Taran to share with this gathering, memories of our brother, expressing love and honour, friendship and kinship, in music and poetry, in prayer and acknowledgement, with thanks and as a blessing and farewell. Let each according to his or her own soul and sources of inspiration come forward and make their offering and of course, enjoy the Feast!'

A cheer went up and the circle began to disperse.

Jack Jewell heaved a sigh of relief. He disliked large groups, and outlandish rituals such as this were far outside his realms of acceptance. Only for his niece, would he agree to take part in such a thing. He glanced over at Dywana, his baby sister, standing so close, yet nineteen years lay between them. Today would be a difficult one. How would she react to him now? How would he react to her? He watched as she lowered her hood. She was a little fuller in the face, her hair was still blonde but now she held it up, strands of hair framed her face. Not so different to the lean, lanky teenager she had been, running barefoot around the farmhouse at Tregarron. Her skin, golden from the hours outside in the sun.

The crowd began to pour out of the field, over the stile. He hung back, to wait for a clear path to his car. He would leave Dywana to go on ahead. If he must acknowledge her, he did not want an audience. He stood on the damp edge of the field and watched the congregation as they took off their hooded robes and discarded their staffs in the boots of their cars. The lanes would be blocked for a good half hour with this many cars.

Merryn appeared by his side and kissed him warmly on the cheek. 'Thank you, Uncle Jack.'

Jack smiled at her. 'For you, Merry, anything.'

'Come on, let's get to The Ship. You can give me a lift.' She took his arm and led him to the back of the crowd waiting to climb over the stile. They didn't have to wait long. Jack climbed over first and as he stepped on to the other side, his foot slipped on the wet wood. He could feel himself falling but a hand grabbed him under the arm and held him upright. He looked up into the eyes of a young man.

'Easy does it,' said the young man.

'Thanks mate, I'm OK.'

'You're welcome.' The young man turned and followed the others down the lane.

Jack stood for a moment, a little stunned.

'You alright, Uncle Jack?'

'Yeah, yeah. I'm fine. Merry, do you know that young man who just helped me?'

'No, no. I don't think so. Why?'

Jack shook himself. 'Nah, it's nothing. I just thought he looked familiar, then most people do round here. Come on let's get off.'

They climbed into Jack's land rover and followed the column of traffic towards Penzance. As Jack drove, he couldn't get the young man's face out of his head. Where did he know him from? He pulled into Porth Taran, down past Methleigh Bottom, and drove round the harbour head to the car park. He got out of the car, and glanced towards the church. He remembered, that was the young man that was waiting in the car, that day.

Merryn got out of the land rover and they walked together to The Ship.

A car was pulling up outside just as they reached the steps up to the front door of the pub. The young man from the Seven Sisters got out.

Jack stopped him. 'I, er, I just wanted to thank you for helping me back there.'

'You're welcome!' He smiled and his eyes smiled too, dark grey blue with flecks of copper.

Jack hesitated again and couldn't help staring.

'Come on, Uncle Jack. They'll all be waiting for us,' said Merryn.

On the other side of the car, the driver got out and came to stand next to the young man. She was in her fifties, tall and her hair was cut into a neat blonde bob.

Jack let Merryn pull him away towards the pub.

'Jack?' said the blonde.

He turned round.

'It's you isn't it? Jack Jewell?'

Jack looked at her blankly.

'It's Ginny. Ginny Dewhurst.'

Jack gasped. 'Ginny!'

The young man looked at him questioningly.

'Jack, this is my son, Luke.'

Luke stretched out a hand. 'Pleased to meet you.'

Jack took it. 'Pleased to meet you too. Err, this is my niece, Merryn.'

'Hi,' said Merryn, staring at the young man. She pulled herself away. 'I'll leave you to it, catch you later.'

Inside the pub, Demelza, Spike, Dywana, Matt, Johnny and Finn McGann were sitting on the table specially reserved for them. The pub was heaving.

'Jack not with you?' asked Demelza.

'He's outside chatting to someone. A Ginny Dewhurst?'

'Ginny Dewhurst? You're kidding!' Demelza rushed outside to see her.

'Lord, Ginny Dewhurst, eh? That's a blast from the past,' said Dywana.

'Who is she, Di?' asked Merryn.

'Ginny Dewhurst was Jack's long lost love.'

Merryn raised her eyebrows, 'Really?'

Guitars were played, songs were sung and poems were read. Everyone and anyone made sure they were there at The Ship Inn to pay their respects to Elwood Curnow. Merryn was overwhelmed by just how many people had known him.

Eventually, Jack came inside with his long lost love and her son and they sat at a separate table talking excitedly until it was almost time to leave.

Merryn was struck by Luke. She caught his eye and for a moment, she thought she saw Piran. She had to stop herself from staring. She shook herself and downed the last of her cider. She needed some peace and quiet. She turned to Matt.

'I think I'm going to go over to the gallery to check on things.'

'Can I come?'

'Sure.'

'Merryn, before you go. I need to give you this.' Johnny pushed an envelope into her hands. 'Best read it today. Not sure what's in it.'

Merryn nodded.

Matt and Merryn walked slowly around the harbour, breathing in the sweet smell of wood smoke that drifted across the little port. In the distance, mist was rising as evening approached. They walked past the surf shop, closed up for the winter, now. The gallery stood in darkness; its blinds drawn. Further up the harbour road the scaffolding rose high on the visitors' centre. Work had started on the top floor.

As she started to unlock the door of the gallery, she sensed a presence behind her. She glanced round, but there was no one.

'You alright, darlin'?'

'Ah yeah, just thought someone was there.' She shrugged and went into the little shop. She went to the back kitchen and flung open the windows and switched on the kettle. She pulled back the old curtain that shrouded her mosaic and stared at the space where the sun would go.

She looked at the branches, at the roots and the jagged leaves to protect them from the harsh sun and the searing cold. She looked back at the journey that had started with those first few strokes of charcoal. Tears began to fall. Tears for the past few weeks, tears for Elwood, and tears for Piran. Matt held her.

'There is something I need to do.' She tore open the envelope and unfurled the letter inside.

Dearest Merryn,

I have known you all of your life. In reality, I knew you before your life began. You were always going to come to us and you will be with us, now, and for always, with the living and with those who have passed to the other side as I will have done if you are reading this.

I want you to know that what happened at Samhain was not your fault. I knew it would happen and I was ready. I have served my purpose, but I am only sorry that I am not with you to aid your recovery – for it will be a recovery. You will need to find yourself again and to adjust. You will have seen what I saw, up in the sky but you, you are now safe.

Ambis has returned to the heavens for now, I saw her go. But Merryn Jewell remains and must live and love, but this time, with all her might. Do not be scared, you may have the feeling that you still have a little power and this may be true but so do we all. Just be watchful lest Ambis returns. Humans are bodies of actors, of energy and electrical force fields. Not everything we experience can be explained.

Remember what I taught you. Separate your mind from your heart as often as you can to keep your spirit balanced and healthy.

And lastly you must love. We all have our destiny and Matt Bunda is yours. Follow that destiny and live a full and happy life until we meet on the other side. You have been, and will always be, everything to me.

Your loyal servant,

Elwood

Merryn glanced up at the harbour, and there, where Elwood's bench had been, was the raven hopping skittishly then stopping and staring at Merryn, its head cocked to one side. She smiled and looked back at her mosaic.

The strong solid roots that twisted and turned, holding the tree firm in the earth. The thick dark trunk to transport the water and nutrients to its branches and the spiky leaves, some golden, some green, armoured against the elements to soak up the sun's rays. The firebuds nestled amongst them. Some in full bloom, others tight ready to burst forth with new life and those that were fading and losing their petals. The sunlight glimmered off the blue glass that formed the sky, reflecting their light over the gallery walls.

Matt watched as she pulled out the box of china from under her workbench. She picked out shades of yellow, of ochre and lemon and arranged them with the darker colours in the centre. The light was getting brighter as it emanated from its core, to make the world gleam. She tipped some glue into a dish and pasted the bare board in the remaining space. She glued each piece starting from the outside in. There was just room for one more. She stood back and looked at Matt.

He reached for her hand and found a mosaic piece clutched between her fingers. He took it from her. 'May I?'

Merryn smiled and nodded.

Matt took the glue brush and coated the back of the piece and pressed it into place, in the centre of the sun.

ABOUT THE AUTHOR

Susan Louineau was born in Mumbai, India to a linguist father and a school teacher mother. She holds a first Class BA (Hons) in French and English Language from La Nouvelle Sorbonne and the Open University.

She's worked in bookshops, publishing and theatre, and was a freelance translator of French - English for many years. Having lived in Australia, France and West Cornwall, she has now returned to her hometown of Oxford. For inspiration, she draws on her experience of living, for most of her life, in small communities.

Printed in Great Britain
by Amazon

12076090R00182